# THE
# GOOD
# NEIGHBOR

## OTHER BOOKS BY JAY QUINN

*Back Where He Started* (BY ALYSON BOOKS)

*The Mentor: A Memoir of Friendship and Gay Identity*

*Metes and Bounds*

*Rebel Yell: Stories by Contemporary Southern Gay Authors* (editor)

*Rebel Yell 2: More Stories of Contemporary Southern Gay Men* (editor)

# THE
# GOOD
# NEIGHBOR

A NOVEL

*Jay Quinn*

alyson books
NEW YORK

© 2006 by Jay Quinn. All rights reserved.

Manufactured in the United States of America.

This trade paperback original is published by Alyson Books,
P.O. Box 1253, Old Chelsea Station, New York, New York 10113-1251.
Distribution in the United Kingdom by Turnaround Publisher Services Ltd.,
Unit 3, Olympia Trading Estate, Coburg Road, Wood Green,
London N22 6TZ England.

First edition: June 2006

06 07 08 09   10 9 8 7 6 5 4 3 2 1

ISBN 1-55583-933-9
ISBN-13 978-1-55583-933-8
Library of Congress Cataloging-in-Publication Data has been applied for.

Cover photograph by Vera Atchou © 2006 Jupiterimages Corporation
Book design by Victor Mingovits

# Dedication

As always, this book is dedicated to Jeffrey Auchter,
the author of love in my life.

# Acknowledgments

My editor, Joe Pittman, gifted me with his invaluable insight and considerable intelligence, making this a better novel, and me a better author. My publisher, Dale Cunningham, gifted me with her kind patience, inspiring enthusiasm, and profound loyalty. Along with them, I'd like to thank the team at Alyson Books, all of whom have worked with great skill, commitment, and creativity to bring this novel about.

I am especially grateful to my first readers, Susan Highsmith, Joe Riddick, and Jack Krough, whose opinions are well considered and always wise. I am thankful for the friendship, encouragement, and love of Harold and Mary Parks, Michael and Malinda Weiss, and the Auchter family; for the wisdom of Nathaniel Keller, M.D.; and for the constant companionship of Patsy and Hailey.

CHAPTER ONE

# St. Mark's Court at Venetian Vistas

A GREAT POET once wrote that good fences make good neighbors. Open gates can make the best of friends. But need often respects no boundary, even when lovers are drawn together harder than they come apart. For lovers, unlike good neighbors and best friends, love is sometimes never enough.

Rory Fallon had never really been to Venice. Back in college, he'd been in love with the idea of that city. He'd dreamed of spending time there, imagining himself washed in the unique light reflected off the broad waters of the sea and the narrower canals. His was a dream drawn from art history classes, colored by the paintings of Tiepolo and Caneletto. Rory would have fitted in there, back in the Renaissance and Baroque times, with his reddish-gold hair and lashes, and his cream skin highlighted with gold flecks of freckles across his nose and shoulders. He wouldn't have been out of place in one of the city's frescoes as a lithe angel or a grave doge's gilded favorite. But the real Venice remained far away as Rory walked his dog in another kind of favorable, early evening light, in another idea of Venice.

"Hold on, girl. We'll be home soon," Rory said to Bridget, his bullmastiff, as they rounded the corner off Grand Canal Drive onto St. Mark's Court, where Rory lived in one of Venetian Vistas' first houses. Rory had moved into the new neighborhood on the edge of the western Broward County suburbs when it was still recently claimed from the Everglades. The entire development was all flatland then; only the newly dynamited canals and lakes gave any interruption to the lunar landscape that would eventually become a lush gated community. There was no sign then of the promised luxury homes that sprang up within a year. Rory and Bridget had walked the recently paved streets when the houses going up around them looked bombed out and lonely as a view of Kabul, not the palazzos of Venice.

"Are you ready to see your daddy, then? Daddy Bruno?" Rory asked the dog, who glanced back at him and began to pull him along with greater determination. Rory sharply tugged her leash in response, and the heavy dog slackened her trot to a stately pace. Rory smiled as he looked around him. He could name the home models—the Raphael, da Vinci, Caneletto, Michelangelo, and Caravaggio—alternating on his street with predictable regularity. Nearly all the homes had SUVs and stray bikes and Big Wheels parked in front of their stately, blank facades. They presented little individual personality to anyone walking down the street, but this neighborhood didn't have many pedestrians. The homeowners came home, left their cars and bikes out front, and immediately went inside their trophy homes. Rory was living on this street as all its houses became finished and occupied, but he had never met more than a handful of his neighbors, certainly none that needed anything other than a nod or smile in the way of interaction.

Rory shook his head, bemused at the fact that he could not name a single neighbor. He allowed himself to be towed by the stout Bridget along the still blindingly white new sidewalks of Venetian Vistas, past the five variations of house styles, and he missed what had been the views of the waterways behind them until the houses had built up and filled in, lot by lot. Unlike the real Venice, its ersatz South Florida imitation hid the water behind its McMansions, all the better to view it from their large "family" rooms, with their screen-enclosed pool areas on their rear sides. It was a backward, inward-looking way to live, discouraging interaction with one's neighbors and community. Still, the large fantasy houses sold and sold dearly. It was a real financial achievement to be able to afford Venetian Vistas' design-enforced privacy.

Bridget stopped a drive away from the drive of the house next door to Rory's. Rory nearly walked past her, so absorbed he was in his own thoughts, cocooned by the familiarity and repetitiveness of his view. He looked up to see a man lift the hatch of a minivan and reach inside among the stacked boxes Rory saw through the car's windows. Bridget gave a low warning growl, and the man looked up at Rory and smiled.

Rory stopped, returned his smile, and bent slightly to rub the big dog's ears. "It's okay, girl. Be nice." Bridget looked up at him and gave him a reassuring panting grin. "C'mon Bridget," Rory encouraged her and deftly stepped into the street to put some space between them and the man standing at the back end of his car.

"She's a big girl," the man said easily as they neared him. "Does she bite?"

"No. She's a love pig. It's more likely she'd slobber you to death," Rory replied, giving the man a brief, friendly once-over. He was tall, taller than Rory by several inches, and had the look of an amenably aging basketball jock—all loose-limbed, long and easy. Dressed in cut-off gray sweatpants and an agreeably tight pink polo shirt, he had a high, round butt and no gut, but he did betray a certain slackening of what must have once been a lean, rangy younger man. Rory imagined him to be around forty, his own age, if not a bit older.

"Awww. Who's a big girl?" the man asked and turning from the back of his minivan, took two steps onto the sidewalk and squatted down with the back of his hand extended. "What kind of dog is she?" he asked, looking up for Rory's response.

Bridget, too, looked up at Rory, asking with her eyes for permission to approach the man and scent him. In response, Rory nodded at the dog and then said, "She's a bullmastiff. But she's an old girl, not mean at all."

The man nodded and allowed himself to be sniffed before he gently reached out his hands to rub the sides of Bridget's massive head. "How old is she?"

Rory watched as Bridget allowed herself to be rubbed and then unfurled her wide tongue and panted happily. "She's seven. Their life span is only about nine to ten years. Eleven at the outside."

The man gave Bridget another brief, vigorous rub behind the ears and stood extending his hand to Rory. "Name's Austin. Austin Harden. I just bought this house, tomorrow's moving day, but I'm getting enough stuff in to sleep here tonight."

Rory took his hand and shook it. "Rory. Rory Fallon. I'm next door at 5150. Nice to meet you."

Austin gave him a smile and gestured toward his house. "Your place is nice. Is it custom?"

"Excuse me?" Rory asked, confused.

"Is it a custom-built home? I mean, it doesn't look like any of the other models in the development," Austin elaborated.

"Oh! Okay . . . no, it's not custom. It was a very early floor plan. It was called a Tintoretto, but they changed the design into the Caneletto. They're similar. Actually, because the builder changed the plan into one they weren't going to offer after it was already built, we were able to buy it and move in right after the models were finished. We've been here since day one," Rory explained.

Austin laughed. "And we're the last one sold. You must know this was a model too," he said, gesturing over his shoulder at his new home behind him. "You must have gotten a real deal. I understand the values have gone up over a hundred grand since the first units were built."

Rory smiled. "Oh yeah, we got a very good deal, considering the developer wanted to unload it quick before people started asking for it. Still, it was kind of a hassle living here while the sales were going on. If I left the front door unlocked, I'd hear people come in and

start looking around. We finally had to put up a 'private home' sign."
Rory smiled. "I know you got a lot of upgrades by buying the model
of the da Vinci. Marble mosaic in the foyer, granite countertops,
cherry-finished cabinets, hardwood floors . . ."

"Yeah," Austin said with a wry smile, "they never let us forget
it when we were looking to buy the place. Still, it appraised out
so . . ."

"So you got a really nice-looking place," Rory finished.

"You've seen it?"

"Right. We came over to look at it a few times. Pure curiosity. It's
a great-looking home."

Austin grinned. "I can't quite believe it's ours."

"Ours?" Rory asked with calculated detachment.

"My wife, Meg, and my two boys, Noah and Josh," Austin
explained. "You said we?"

"My partner, Bruno, and I," Rory responded with a note of
challenge.

Austin gave him a brief once-over and quickly put on a studiedly
casual look. "Oh . . . you guys been together long?"

Rory had to fight to keep from sighing. It was the usual response
he got when he told neighbors he and Bruno lived there. As far as
he knew, he and Bruno were the only gay couple in all of Venetian
Vistas. Everyone wanted to know how long they'd been together, as
if the length of their partnership gave some insight into what kind
of neighbors they'd make and how long they intended to stay. He
covered by looking down for Bridget, who had sauntered to the end
of her leash toward home. "Off and on since college. We've really
lived together now for nearly seventeen years."

Austin gave him a polite nod. "Bruno . . ." he began as something
seemed to strike him, and he gazed down the street. Bridget started
to bark, and both Rory and Austin heard and saw a GMC Yukon pull
into Rory's drive with a fierce impatience, only to stop inches from

the garage door with an angry snarl of its emergency brake before its engine cut off.

"Speak of the devil," Rory said and gave Austin an amused smile. Both watched as Bruno got out of his car, slammed the door, and strode toward them with an open grin.

"Whazzup, girl?" Bruno growled at the dog, who responded by leaping at the end of her leash in a display of eager athleticism that belied her age and thick, bulky build. Rory let go of her leash and she hurled herself at Bruno. He knelt and absorbed the shock of her head butting his chest without any apparent effect.

Austin looked at Rory and lifted his eyebrows, impressed. From the looks of both of them, the dog and the man were well matched.

Rory cocked his head at Austin. "They're two Mack trucks," he said dryly. "They cancel each other out."

"Whazzup, guys?" Bruno said as he roughly shook the dog's head, stood, and, thrusting it aside, strode over. Undaunted, Bridget happily trotted along by his side.

"Hey," Rory said, and Austin noted a degree of coy affection that couldn't be concealed. "Bruno, this is our new next-door neighbor, Austin Harden."

Austin took two steps to meet Bruno's outstretched hand. It closed around it with enough force to let him know there was more behind it. Austin returned the pressure with a corresponding pressure. It was visceral communication that managed to say much. "Pleased to meet you."

"Sure thing," Bruno responded heartily. "Welcome to the neighborhood." That said, Austin watched as Bruno looked fondly and possessively at Rory. Bruno's free hand rose with a degree of swiftness that made Austin flinch as if the bigger man were going to cuff Rory on the back of his head. Instead, the hard hand grasped at the scruff of Rory's neck and shook him gently. The brief gesture brought Austin a flash of memory, and an earlier place to hold the couple before him.

"Long day, beast?" Rory asked.

"It's over now," Bruno responded, and turning to Austin he asked, "So, how about a beer?"

Austin glanced back at the boxes waiting in his minivan. It had been a long day. Meg was due in with the boys any minute, but a beer sounded wonderful. "What the hell. Sure . . . "

Bruno glanced at Rory significantly.

"Is Corona okay? Rory asked Austin. "I'm afraid it'll have to be no GDL,"

"No GDL?" Austin asked.

"No God Damn Lime," Bruno answered and smiled.

"Sure," Austin said to Bruno, taken aback by the man's proprietary forcefulness, even arrogance. "No problem," he said gently to Rory.

"I'll be right back." Rory said, and without a word he took Bruno's briefcase from his hand, picked up the leash and tugged Bridget's adoring attention from Bruno's side, then started for the house.

Austin watched as Bruno gave his partner a frankly appraising look as he walked away. He half expected him to swat the other man's ass before he returned his attention to him saying, "I'm sorry, I hate lime in my beer. I could have offered you a Coke or something as well. You're sure a beer is okay?"

"A cold beer sounds great, to tell you the truth." Without anything more said, Austin could tell how things went in his new next-door neighbor's house. Evidently, Bruno was used to getting what he wanted and only thought of what somebody else might have in mind after the fact—*well* after the fact.

"Did you do your closing today?" Bruno asked.

"Oh yeah." He gestured half turning to the house behind him. "Thirty years from today it'll be all mine."

Bruno laughed. "Are you moving in tonight?"

Austin jammed his hands in his sweatpants pockets and bounced a couple of times on the balls of his feet. "Yeah. Just sleeping bags though. The moving van will be here tomorrow. You know how it goes. You have to get out of one place before you can close on another."

"It's rough that way, but you gotta do what you gotta do, right?" Bruno responded. "Nice place you bought, though. By tomorrow night, you'll be living the life."

Austin grinned. "You got that right. It's a hell of a long way from where the wife and I started out."

Bruno nodded. "Where's the wife? We'd love to meet her."

"Oh, she's due with the kids any minute," Austin said uncomfortably. He was aware that the big man next to him on the sidewalk was sizing him up, not sexually especially, but assessing him in a way that was discomfiting nonetheless. He felt Bruno looking at him as if he was reading his relative status in the world, to see if he measured up to a standard of some sort. He wanted to change the subject and deflect the scrutiny. His earlier flash provided a way to gain the upper hand. "By any chance did you play lacrosse in college?"

The question barely registered with a flicker in Bruno's eyes. "As a matter of fact, I did."

Austin nodded. "Bruno the Beast, they called you. But your real name is Will . . . Will something?" Austin was pleased to detect a slight look in Bruno's eyes of being caught off balance before he regained his affable, albeit aggressive, assessment.

"Will Griffin. If you follow college lacrosse you're going back a long ways to put that together," Bruno responded off-handedly.

"Nearly twenty years," Austin said. He heard the front door of Bruno's house close and looked up to see Rory making his way toward them with one long-necked bottle of Corona in one hand and two knitted in the fingers of the other. "Eighteen to be exact," he said. "I know you guys."

Before Bruno could answer, Rory was offering Bruno the single beer before extending the beers between his fingers toward Austin. Bruno and Austin took their beers and Rory offered Austin a shy smile. "Know who?"

"Austin's got one on me. He says he knows us," Bruno said and took a long swig of his beer without his eyes leaving Austin's face.

Austin gestured his beer at Rory in thanks and said. "We went to the same school. I was Eddy Daniels' roommate one semester when you guys were in that cover band . . . Bad Halen . . . "

"No shit," Bruno exploded, and then wiped his mouth with the back of his hand. He laughed and punched Austin on the arm. "Well fuck me harder, I bet you're the only person within five hundred miles that ever heard of Bad Halen. Goddamn, Rory can you believe this?"

Rory smiled and rolling his eyes looked away.

Austin laughed, unexpectedly delighted at their response. "Bruno, you played bass, as I recall. And Rory, you sounded like a younger, better Sammy Hagar. I heard you play twice. Once in a club, and once when you did that weird thing at your senior show, Rory."

"Oh god. You came to that? I almost didn't graduate because of that," Rory responded.

Bruno laughed and drained his bottle of beer.

"Why?" Austin asked. "I mean, I thought it was brilliant, mixing the band's performance with your art work. Do you still paint?"

"It's a long story," Rory answered noncommittally. "No. I don't paint anymore. I'm an electrician."

Bruno loosened his tie and freed his thick neck from the top button of his shirt before continuing to undo two more of his buttons. Austin caught a glimpse of the dark hair at his throat, stark against the crisp whiteness of his shirt. "He's more than an electrician," he said, brooking no argument. "Rory is a commercial lighting designer."

Rory smiled and shrugged. Bruno responded by cuffing him lightly on the back of his head. "He's *soooo* modest" he said to Austin. "He's still an artist. He just paints with light now," he concluded proudly.

"What do you do, Bruno?" Austin said, already dreading the part where they would look at him in turn and demand he answer the same question.

Bruno's lips tightened into a half-feral smile. "I'm an investment analyst," he said simply and then mentioned the name of a firm that Austin recognized to be both sufficiently venerable and also as feral as Bruno's smile. Inwardly, Austin shuddered. He recognized now why he felt so naked under Bruno's earlier scrutiny. He would have hated to have seen Bruno come into his former job to assess its fitness for financial speculation. "And what about you, Austin? What do you do?" Bruno asked.

Austin welcomed the sound of an approaching vehicle that grew into the noise of Meg's Range Rover's tires on the stamped concrete beside them. He looked up to see her tired smile in greeting as she maneuvered into the drive. He noted the boys already tugging at their seatbelts in the backseat. "Medical equipment sales," he said as Rory and Bruno turned their attention to the car. He was relieved their attention had been diverted as his wife and kids spilled out.

"Well, I'm glad to see you've found some friends and a beer," Meg said breezily as she walked toward him. Quickly she pecked him on the cheek and then looked at him expectantly.

"Meg, these are our new next-door neighbors, Bruno Griffin and Rory  I'm sorry, I can't recall your last name," Austin said apologetically.

Rory stepped forward and offered Meg his hand. "It's Fallon. Rory Fallon."

Meg smiled reservedly and shook his hand as the boys came to stand politely beside their mother. Austin watched as Meg withdrew her hand from Rory's clasp and offered it daintily to Bruno. Something about the man made him want to punch him, Austin thought. Guys like him, big, dark guys, were used to intimidating other men and making women feel all dainty and pretty.

"Welcome home," Bruno said gravely to Meg.

"It is home now, isn't it?" she replied and widened her smile in return.

"These are our boys," Austin interrupted. "Noah and Josh." He was pleased to watch his sons manfully stretch out their little paws and shake hands solemnly with the two men.

"Ow, man! Don't crush my hand!" Bruno said to Josh, the youngest. Austin smiled grudgingly when the little boy laughed. He glanced around and was surprised to see Rory looking at him with an intuitive look on his face. Austin shied away from Rory's look and turned his attention to the genial conversation Bruno was starting with his wife and kids.

"So how old are you guys anyway?" Bruno said to the bigger boy who was trying very hard to appear blasé about the proceedings.

"I'm fourteen," Noah responded grudgingly, "Josh is six."

"You're going to be fourteen," Josh corrected his brother. "You're thirteen for two and a half more months."

Noah responded with a murderous look for his brother and a shrug before pretending to be fascinated with the house across the street.

"I was a surprise," Josh continued confidentially to Bruno. 'You know how it is."

Bruno laughed out loud, while Rory fought to keep an earnest look on his face, having seen Meg and Austin trade appalled glances.

"I can see you're full of surprises," Bruno replied with a wink for Meg.

"Yes, he is," Meg commented drily.

Bruno grinned, and it seemed as if the group dissolved around him but for Meg. Ignoring Rory and Austin, he asked her if the kids would be changing schools.

"No, they're at American Heritage," Meg said, giving Bruno the name of the county's most expensive secular private school, "so a mid-year move won't affect them. It just means a bit of a longer drive for us to get them to and from. But my office is in downtown Fort Lauderdale, so it's no difference, really, for me."

"So, you were in Plantation, then?" Bruno asked.

"Plantation Acres," Meg responded. "But it was an older home and we really wanted to move further west into something new."

"We hope to find some parents here who also have kids at American Heritage, so we can maybe get in a carpool," Austin offered. "You guys don't happen to know of anyone, do you?"

Bruno spared him a charming smile for his interruption and looked to Rory to answer him before continuing his conversation with Meg. "We have moved every couple of years to take advantage of the real estate boom since Hurricane Andrew," Bruno continued.

"Please forgive Bruno; he'd rather talk real estate than anything else," Rory said quietly.

Austin turned toward Rory gratefully and said, "He's really a personable guy, you're very lucky."

Rory rolled his eyes toward the street, where his look lingered, and he said, "Lucky to get a word in edgewise." Quickly, he cut his eyes back to Austin with a look that said he understood what he had read on Austin's face.

Austin nodded, but was unprepared for Rory's knowing glance.

"And to answer your question, we really don't know any other people in Venetian Vistas," Rory continued. "It's not exactly a very sociable place. People pretty much keep to themselves."

Austin gave Rory a slight smile and turned his attention back to his family and Bruno.

"We've been moving west, in jumps, for years," Bruno explained expansively. "My office is downtown as well, but as a short-term investment, trading up has made us money. All of our moves west couldn't have been more solid in terms of return."

"Well, this is the end of the line then," Rory interjected. "The next stop is Fort Myers."

Austin laughed. Bruno and Meg looked at Rory as if they didn't get the joke.

"I mean, hey . . . the Everglades is literally on the other side of Venetian Vistas," Rory said quietly.

"I suppose you're right," Meg said pleasantly.

"Tree-hugger," Bruno said, cutting Rory a cold look.

"Goddamn hippie!" Josh piped up in a weirdly affected voice. His parents stared at him in open-mouthed amazement.

"Josh! Where on earth did you hear that, young man?" Meg asked as she snatched at his arm.

"South Park," his older brother smirked. "He heard it from Cartman on South Park. Tree-hugger . . . hippie, get it?"

Bruno laughed out loud. Even Rory laughed. Josh looked at his mother and tried not to laugh, as his upper arm was still held tightly in her grasp. Meg shot a look at Austin that pleaded for reinforcement.

"You boys know better. I see some discipline ahead for you very shortly."

"His timing was perfect," Rory said.

"Please. We don't mean to interfere," Bruno pleaded. "But we watch South Park and we got the joke. Could you let it slide this time? We'd hate to see the little fella get punished on account of us."

Meg laughed weakly, but let go of Josh's arm. "Well . . ."

Austin just shook his head and looked at Rory. "Kids." Then, more authoritatively, "Boys, I think it's time you headed in and got washed up."

"I'm sorry I called you a goddamn hippie," Josh said looking at his feet and then toward his mother.

Austin groaned. Meg glared.

"It's okay, Josh. No problem," Rory smiled, fighting the urge to laugh.

The little boy gave Rory his father's grin before his mother turned him by the shoulders and gave him a gentle shove toward the front door. Noah fell in step behind his brother. When they were at their door, Meg turned to her husband. "They're not supposed to be watching South Park in the first place," she shot at Austin.

"I can't monitor them every minute when they're home, and God only knows what they hear at school," Austin shot back.

Rory and Bruno glanced at each other uncomfortably, having just learned from that exchange far more than they wanted to know. "They're just boys," Bruno offered. "I'm one of four brothers. Let me tell you, we had more ways of getting around our dad . . . "

"I know that's supposed to be encouraging," Meg interrupted, "but . . . "

"Meg, I'll talk to them about their language, okay? Still, you have to admit, it was kind of funny."

Meg glanced around the group of men. "I can see it's three to one on the testosterone scale. I rest my case."

"You must feel a little overwhelmed," Rory said evenly.

Meg laughed. "It's not always easy living in a men's barracks. Well, now I have my own bathroom and closet I can go hide out in. Thank god for this new house. If you boys will excuse me, I really want to get out of these heels."

"Good night, Meg. It's good to meet you," Bruno said.

Meg waved and headed toward the front door. Austin finished his now warm beer and gave the front door a glance, then turned toward Rory and Bruno with a wan smile. "I think that's my cue as well."

Rory smiled at him in return and Bruno offered, "If you need a place to hide or chill, just knock on the door, we're here for you, man."

Austin looked at Bruno and cocked an eyebrow. "I might just take you up on that."

Bruno gave a quick look up and down the street before finding Austin's eyes once more. "Um, I don't know if this interests you these days, but if you're the kind of guy that enjoys some *relaxation*, that's always available next door."

For a moment, Austin wasn't sure he wasn't being propositioned. Rory thought the confused look on his face was endearing. He interjected, "What Bruno's saying is, he still has a bong and he still has rolling papers."

Austin's face broke into a happy grin. "Oh man," he said. "I haven't visited with the crippies in a while."

Bruno snickered at Austin's knowing use of the slang term for excellent marijuana. "Crippies, chronic . . . whatever. All I'm saying is at my house, college days live on."

Austin looked at Rory. "You?"

Rory shook his head. "No, not for years. But my pothead boyfriend still gets high. If you see his car in the drive, feel free to come over."

Austin glanced anxiously at his house.

"All on the down low, of course. No need to get the missus' panties in a wad," Bruno added conspiratorially.

"Oh man," Austin sighed. "I'm going to like having you guys next door."

Rory gave him a long look through heavily lidded, sleepy eyes and smiled. Bruno caught Rory by the nape of his neck, laughed, and turned toward home. "See ya, Austin." Rory just lifted a hand and allowed himself to be steered toward their door.

### 5160 ST. MARK'S COURT

AUSTIN WATCHED AS the two made their way up their drive. "Yeah, later," he said and wondered at finding those two living next door to him, so far from home. Out of his line of sight, he heard their front door open and close. They didn't look as if they'd aged that much. Austin glanced down his long form and sucked in the slight swell he'd acquired in his midsection. It was as if the weight of the ensuing years since he'd first encountered Rory and Bruno had settled on him, and left them as curiously insular and comfortably coupled now as they had been then.

Austin thought how odd it was that he had ever crossed paths with them, even in college. Essentially it all boiled down to a few poorly timed flukes of circumstance. Austin had found himself without a place to live at the beginning of the second semester of his senior year in college. After some desperate searching, he found a place in a two-bedroom apartment with Eddy Daniels, a guy he knew from his business school classes. Eddy's old roommate had graduated in December and moved out, leaving him stuck with the full rent. Though Austin and Eddy knew each other only through their shared courses, Austin's moving in seemed like a good solution to both their housing problems.

Eddy was a pretty good roommate. He played drums in a popular cover band, and between studying, rehearsals, and weekend gigs he was hardly ever around. That gave Austin plenty of chances to spend long periods of time alone with Meg, studying, talking, and making love. That sweet semester was a prelude to the summer when they would marry, followed by their graduate and law school years as a married couple. They had already been as circumspect and narrow in their goals and range of acquaintances as they were now. Eddy was the only person they knew who was louche in any respect. It was through Eddy that Austin's path had crossed Rory and Bruno's.

Standing now in his driveway, he recalled one late Saturday night long ago letting himself into his apartment after a night out partying to find Rory standing alone in his kitchen, wet-haired and nude but for a towel around his waist, smoking a cigarette at his kitchen sink and staring out the window into the darkness outside.

"Uh, wow." Austin remembered saying. "Hello."

Rory flicked an ash into the kitchen sink, turned his head, and smiled. "You must be Eddy's roommate."

"Yeah. I am," Austin said guardedly. "Excuse me, but who the hell are you?"

Rory had made no move toward him. He'd only half turned away from the sink and leaned against its rim on his hip. "I'm in the band with Eddy. We're crashing here tonight. I hope it's okay with you."

Austin nodded. He'd seen Rory around campus. It was hard to miss him. He skateboarded to class in a blur of lean motion, his red gold hair, trimmed in a surfer's bowl cut, swinging as he cut in and out of the foot traffic on the campus's brick-paved walkways. He'd heard Rory was in a band, but Austin had never seen Eddy's band play. Van Halen wasn't his favorite group, and that's what Eddy's band mostly covered, quite faithfully he'd heard, belying the name Bad Halen. After putting all this together in his mind, he'd said, "Sure. No problem."

"We appreciate it," Rory had replied as he casually ground his cigarette out in the sink.

Austin was about to ask who else was staying when a dark form appeared from the doorway behind Rory. Bruno emerged into the light—also wet-haired, but naked—and reached for the nape of Rory's neck, taking hold of him there. Austin was distracted and embarrassed by the hefty swing of Bruno's limp dick. Quickly, he looked at Bruno's face and saw him lift his chin up by way of a greeting. Austin responded likewise. The two stared at each other in the dim light for a moment, warily assessing each other.

Bruno squeezed the back of Rory's neck hard enough to make him wince and tilt his head back in response. "Bruno, this is Eddy's roommate," Rory said.

Austin watched as Bruno relaxed his fingers on Rory's neck enough to gently massage it with a slow circular motion. He nodded at Austin gravely.

"Well, do you guys need anything?" Austin said awkwardly.

"No thanks," Bruno said. "We're fine. Thanks for letting us crash." With that, he steered Rory by the neck past him toward the living room.

Austin stared as Rory allowed himself to be directed toward the doorway. Looking back over his shoulder, Rory said goodnight as Bruno let go of his neck and half turned to follow him.

As Rory left the kitchen, Bruno continued to stare at Austin. Finally, he said somewhat threateningly, "Are sure you don't have a problem, man?"

Austin was honestly drunk and somewhat disconcerted by the obvious possessiveness and authority Bruno had asserted over Rory. He'd never been around anyone so blatantly gay on the one hand and so threatening on the other. It was almost as if Bruno thought he was trying to hit on Rory or something. Austin laughed nervously. "No way, man," he said holding up his hands palms out. "None of my business."

Bruno nodded and unexpectedly smiled. "Eddy said you were cool. We'll be out of here early. Nice to meet you."

Austin nodded and said, "I'll be passed out. Make yourself at home."

Bruno nodded, then loped through the door after Rory.

That encounter had left him unsettled back then. It was strong enough for him to recall undimmed after all the years between then and now. The memory added to the dislocation he felt coming home to a new house on a new street. Now, however, the thought of the two of them so obviously coupled wasn't as unsettling as it had been; he'd changed along with the world. There was room and experience in his mind to shrug off the reality of having a gay couple living next door. He had too much to deal with at present to give it any serious thought.

Austin's front door opened, interrupting his reverie, and he heard Noah yell, "Dad! Mom wants to know is pizza okay for dinner or do you want Chinese."

Austin smiled and patted his stomach. The Fallon-Griffins would probably be eating delicate greens and boneless chicken breasts, he figured. "Pizza! Extra cheese!" he yelled back.

"Where do we live now?" Noah shot back.

Austin turned and looked at the few remaining boxes in the back of the minivan. He looked back west before he called out, "Noah, how about giving me a hand right now? If you help, I can get the last of this stuff inside, and I'll call the pizza place myself."

Noah appeared quickly, trailed by Josh, who said "I want to help too."

"You're too little," Noah said dismissively.

Austin smiled. "I think there's something in here he can manage." He moved a large box and found two rolled sleeping bags he hadn't yet carried in. With a tug, he freed one, and the other followed, pulled forward by the force of its twin. Austin considered them a moment, and then decided Josh could handle both. "Put this one under your arm," he instructed the little fellow as he drew it from the back of the van.

"Dad, are those guys we met brothers?" Josh said as he took the sleeping bag and placed its bulk under his arm.

Noah snorted. "No, retard, they're gay."

"They are *not* lame," Josh retorted. "They're funny and nice."

Noah laughed. "No, stupid, they're gay, like, married."

Austin emerged from the back of the van holding the other sleeping bag and looked from one son to the other, amused.

"Nuh-uh, boys don't marry boys, do they, Dad?"

Austin looked at Noah and said, "You started it. Instead of being such a smart-ass, why don't *you* explain it to him." He was interested in how Noah would work his way out of this one.

Noah rolled his eyes and shot his father a dirty look.

"*I said*, you explain it to him, Noah. I'd really like to hear what you have to say," Austin demanded.

Noah shrugged and squatted down to his brother's eye level. "Look, man . . . it's like this, there are some guys who love other guys, and they live together, like Mom and Dad are *married*. It's no big deal, it's just the way they are . . . that's *gay*, got it?"

"But do they have kids?" Josh demanded. "Mom and Dad are married and they have us, and other kids have moms and dads."

Noah looked up his father for help. He received only a slight nod in return. Sighing as if he had to explain calculus to his six-year-old brother, he continued, "Josh, not all men and women who are married have kids, right?"

Josh nodded soberly.

"Well, you see? Gay guys who live together don't have kids, not like that. Okay? Jeez . . . "

"But . . . " Josh demanded.

"That's enough questions for now, Josh," Austin said, stepping in to rescue Noah. "Here, take this other sleeping bag and get them both upstairs, okay?"

Josh produced a mirror of his older brother's expressive shrug and accepted the second sleeping bag against his chest, cradling it in his free arm.

When he had turned and trudged up the drive to the front door, Austin turned to Noah and gave him a friendly shove. "Well, you handled that pretty well. You know he takes in everything you say. You have to help him understand things. I don't know if I could have done a better job with that."

"It's not easy when you have to leave out the sex part," Noah replied confidently.

"What do you know about the sex part?" Austin asked, again curious about what his oldest son had to say.

Noah rewarded his father with a rare, if arch, smile before pushing past him to retrieve the largest box remaining in the cargo area of the van.

"Can you handle it?" Austin asked when he staggered a bit getting it out of the hatch.

"No problem," Noah sighed with annoyance as he turned toward the front door.

Austin took out the last box and, balancing it on his upraised knee, managed to get the hatch door shut. Further ahead he heard Noah close the door after him, unconcerned that Austin was burdened by what he was carrying. Austin followed and allowed himself his own annoyed sigh before he sat the box down and opened his very expensive new front door.

## 5150 ST. MARK'S COURT

NO SOONER HAD Rory and Bruno stepped in their front door than Bruno's cell phone rang, and they separated, Bruno to his office and Rory to the kitchen to feed an obviously expectant Bridget. As he placed her bowl before her on the kitchen floor, Rory thought briefly about his new neighbors. His immediate impression registered them as little more than generic Venetian Vistites. Even their automobiles were clichés. What snagged his perception of them most was the fact that Austin had recognized him and Bruno after so many years. As he watched Bridget snarf and munch her kibble, he tried his best to place the man. Try as he might, he couldn't find a single hook of memory to hang Austin on. But then, that was not unusual.

Rory had difficulty marrying people to particular times or places. From the time he was born until he graduated from high school, he'd lived on marine bases from Camp Pendleton to Camp Lejuene. He could recall dun hills and blue seas of the Pacific and sand dunes and the gray-green ocean of the Carolina Atlantic. He could feel the sun on his shoulders from both. But as an only child left with his taciturn military father when his mother abandoned them when he was seven years old, he had long learned to discount people from his deepest and fondest memories of place and time.

When Austin spoke of college, and of the band he and Bruno had been a part of, Rory recalled the quiet "studio" Fridays in the art school building that smelled of linseed oil and gesso. As for the band, he thought of the scent of stale, spilled beer and quiet spaces painted entirely in black in the set-up times before a show, before the noise and swell of music and a crowd. Always a solitary child, shuffled as he was between schools and towns that looked much the same on the strip-malled streets that led off base, Rory had always been disconnected from the friendships so many other people seemed to thrive on.

His mother's abrupt departure was the first lesson in self-sufficiency. His father's military-style nurture and discipline was the other. He knew what *semper fi* meant long before he learned it was an abstraction that could be complicated by genuine love and connection. He never knew that in any lasting sense until he met Bruno. In many ways, Bruno's rough cupping of his neck was no more than a gentler extension of his father's similarly articulated affection. After being hauled around by a full-grown marine, Rory felt Bruno's possessive and rough-handed touch was a familiar expression of love both tender and comforting.

In his way, Rory had adored his father, even when he had gifted him at age twelve, without explanation or fanfare, with a stepmother barely eight years older than him. In many ways, Rory came to learn that men held little loyalty or regard for loyalty. It was a fact driven home to him when he was also gifted with two stepsisters in alarming succession following his father's marriage. Heavily pregnant and massively insecure, Rory's stepmother had made it well known that he had become suddenly irrelevant. And so, Rory's certainty of male betrayal and female conniving became cemented and his center of reference became himself.

There were other betrayals and connivances to come. They were the result of his tentative connections with what other people called "friends." As his father retreated into his new family, Rory grew to understand his own needs and desires advanced toward the boys who spoke laconically out of the corners of their mouths and swaggered with newly formed chests carried well forward. Their needs he divined quickly and met eagerly, only to find himself despised and discounted once those same boys found breasts blossoming all around them. Those boys found the feminine shape promised more in the long run when it came to emotional connections they could both tolerate and enjoy.

Bruised, Rory found himself to be his father's son. He took all this on the chin and sucked it up. He believed that was just the way things were. Then, when he was in college, he met a certain brawny swaggerer named Will Griffin, who'd earned the nickname Bruno for his darkness and fast fists, and he was amazed to find Bruno had been looking for Rory Fallon all of his life.

It was no wonder Rory had no recollection of Austin from college. Naturally inclined and reared to be self-reliant, if not self-absorbed, Rory met Bruno, and they were so besotted with each other that the world around them became irrelevant. By the mid-eighties, there had been enough exposure to the reality of gay people, their plight, and particularly their plague, to warrant a tenuous acceptance in Rory and Bruno's college world. Bruno's truculence and Rory's obliviousness made that world appear more accommodating than it probably was, but neither of them cared. For many years, through college and then graduate school for Bruno, they enjoyed a perfect mesh of neuroses and need. In many ways, it sustained them still, even through Bruno's little betrayals and Rory's subsequent strengthening of his own defenses.

Rory knew all this without the eloquence of self-examination. When Bridget finished her dinner and looked up expectantly for a cookie, Rory dismissed any thoughts spent trying to recall Austin from a past he associated more with the scent of oil paint, linseed oil, and Bruno's Right Guard than with a flock of collegial faces. He scooped up Bridget's steel dish, filled it with water, and went to the cookie jar for her treat. As he tossed the dog her treat, Bruno himself came into the great room dressed for running.

"I saw the doctor today," Bruno said as he made his way to the bar separating the kitchen from the family room. "I need you to get this filled for me tomorrow," he said laying a blue prescription slip on the bar.

Rory picked it up and read it. "Vytorin? What was your HDL this time?"

Bruno shook his head. "Got it down to 280, but that's still way too high. You'd think with the crap you've been feeding me and the five miles I've been doing a night that I'd have gotten it down a lot more."

Rory reached across the bar and put his hand on Bruno's thick wrist. "It's hereditary, Will. And face it, you and I both are middle-aged now."

Bruno glanced at Rory's hand on his wrist and then looked up to offer Rory a tired smile. "That's what the doctor said. This Vytorin crap should help with the cholesterol my body produces naturally. The rest is still diet and exercise. I swear, if my old man hadn't dropped dead with a heart attack at fifty-four, I'd say the hell with it."

"No fucking way," Rory said. "I want you around to torment me for a long time."

Bruno snorted. "It'll be a long time, too. Look at you. You have the metabolism of a twelve-year-old. I fucking hate you."

Rory laughed. "You'd really hate me if I told you how much weight I've lost since we've been on your heart diet."

"I don't want to know," Bruno grumbled. "What I want to know is what kind of cardboard and gravel shit we're eating tonight. I'm starved."

"Roast pork tenderloin with roasted vegetables," Rory announced. "No fat."

"I'd murder for some pork chops, rice, and gravy, and some of my mama's banana pudding. You know?"

"I know, baby," Rory said genuinely. "But go run now. When you get back that cardboard box and gravel crap will taste good."

"Whatever," Bruno said and walked toward the front door.

Rory sighed and placed Bridget's bowl on the floor. Noisily, she began lapping up the water, and Rory smiled. As far as he was concerned, the only faces worth remembering were those of his big dog on the floor and his big dog now trotting down the street before breaking into long strides that would eventually return him home. As far as he was concerned, the Harden family was pleasantly irrelevant as long as they stayed on their side of the property line and enjoyed their big da Vinci model home without making pests of themselves.

## CHAPTER TWO

# Later that night . . .

### 5150 ST. MARK'S COURT

BRUNO SHUT OFF the water in the shower and toweled himself energetically. Dry, he dropped the damp towel on the floor and stepped over to the vanity and rubbed his jaw. The mirror suggested he needn't shave until morning. His fingers concurred that he was only three hours past his five o'clock shadow. Though not necessarily a vain man, he did regularly assess himself nude in the bath's generous mirror. All considerations of his cholesterol aside, extra weight, even on his six-foot-four-inch frame, sent the wrong signal. It suggested a certain slackness, a lack of precision and care that invited speculation that he might, perhaps, be less careful in his actions elsewhere. Bruno made his living in a tough world, and he wasn't as far up in that world as he intended to be. With rigorous care, he closely monitored himself and his work so that neither would get in the way of the future he saw for himself.

In an eighteen-month lapse of time between leaving Rory and getting him back, he'd married briefly. She was mostly forgotten and, to some extent in hindsight, no more than an accessory at a time when a wife was more necessary to his career than one was now. She'd loved his body. Looking at his assets now, he tried to see himself through her eyes as he catalogued his looks from the thick neck, to the broad shoulders and firm chest, the long waist and longer legs, the bulky genitals still flushed and full from the heat of the shower. Bruno knew he had an enviable body fringed with what his ex-wife had irritatingly called John-John Kennedy chest chair.

Bruno snorted recalling that. He preferred to think that stupid s.o.b. had *his* chest hair, or would have still if he could tell up from down. Bruno could tell up from down. He never, he thought as he surveyed himself in the mirror, would have been arrogant enough to think he was so blessed that nothing could ever pull him in a downward spiral. Bruno cupped his balls in his hand and squeezed them gently. He knew, except for easily dismissing a certain few of a real man's natural prerogatives, the biggest balls in the world couldn't help you if you took it all for granted and thought it couldn't all be taken away from you. Bruno let go of himself and squared his shoulders. He had no intention of letting himself think he couldn't fall at work if he let go for one minute.

"Hey beast," Rory said from behind him.

"Hey yourself. What are you doing?" He replied to Rory's reflection in the mirror.

"I've just got in from taking Bridget for her bedtime walk." Rory folded his arms across his chest and leaned against the bathroom's door jamb. "When you get done admiring yourself, you want to sit outside with me for awhile? The moon's full and it's really nice out."

"Why don't you bring what's left of that bottle of Shiraz outside and wait for me? I could stand some downtime. I'm beat," Bruno said as he opened a vanity drawer in search of his antiperspirant.

Rory dropped his arms and walked into the bathroom. Stopping behind Bruno, he put his arms around his waist and leaned his forehead in the declivity that ran down his spine. Bruno popped the cap off his antiperspirant and, raising one arm, then the other, slathered the gel under each arm. Finished, he took one of Rory's hands and pulled him from behind to face him. Lifting Rory's chin with a firm grasp on his jaw, he said, "Miss me today?"

Rory allowed himself to be searched by Bruno's dark eyes. "Everyday. You work like a dog, Bruno."

Bruno bent to kiss him and then pulled Rory to his chest. "A man's gotta do what a man's gotta do."

Rory rubbed the side of his face in the high arcing branch of hair where it curved away under Bruno's right shoulder. "Yeah, I know." He pushed gently away, kissed the hollow of Bruno's throat and said, "But at least I get some time with you before we both fall asleep."

Bruno slapped Rory's ass and steered him toward the bathroom door. "Get the wine. I'll be out in a minute."

Rory left as Bruno reached for the clean pair of boxers that lay waiting for him on the vanity. He bent to step into them, noting his dick had firmed and lengthened in the course of close contact with his partner. It tented his boxers as he pulled them up and snapped the elastic around his waist. "Maybe," he thought, and almost called Rory back. Instead, he thought of his meeting at eight o'clock the following morning and sighed. Lovemaking would have to wait for Saturday morning and, if he played his cards right, all Sunday afternoon. He smoothed the dark, close-cropped hair on his head and leered purposefully in the mirror. The effect was halfhearted and tired.

Still a little buzzed from the couple of bong hits he'd had before dinner, he just wanted one more glass of wine and some cuddling on the pool deck under the full moon. The pot was the one indulgence he allowed himself, his one link to a time when he'd been a wild man and not a buttoned-down corporate animal. Even Rory had ceased to be an indulgence. With the corporate world suddenly tolerant, Rory was treated as an interesting eccentricity Bruno donned like a loud tie. Still, his eight o'clock was going to be grueling, and he needed to be honed and not dulled by the lingering languor a hot night riding

Rory would bring. Regretfully, he shifted his dick in his shorts and turned his thoughts toward the wine waiting for him. That would have to be enough tonight.

Bruno strode from the bathroom, through the master bedroom, and out the French doors by the pool to find Rory waiting for him on the wicker sofa and Bridget sprawled out on the pavers. With no small amount of elegance for such a big man, he sat down, slipped his arm around Rory's shoulders, and stretched his legs with a sigh. He rubbed the dog's side with his toes, enjoying the softness of her fur. Bridget reached over her shoulder and licked his toes.

"So, what do you think of having neighbors after all this time?" Rory asked as he handed him his wine glass.

Bruno looked up through the pool's screened roof and noted the lights on upstairs in the house next door. Shadows moved on the room's ceiling. From where he sat, that was all he could make out. He took a sip of his wine and allowed his hand to find its way inside the stretched-out collar of Rory's T-shirt. He brushed his fingertips lightly against Rory's smooth bare chest. "I think they'll be in for an eyeful the next time I decide to fuck you in the pool."

"Uh-huh," Rory responded and leaned his head against the encircling curve of Bruno's arm. "That's what I was thinking." Awkwardly, he took a sip of his own wine, and then said, "They seem like okay people."

"I hope they are. These damn houses are so close together, we're in for a nightmare if they turn out to be assholes," Bruno said.

"Or worse, if they are totally chatty and feel the need to carry on a conversation every time we both find ourselves out by our pools," Rory responded quietly.

"Well, put up a privacy fence if it looks like they are. Just call and get it done if they make you unhappy. Pay for it out of the house account."

Rory sighed gratefully in reply. "Are you cold just sitting out here in your drawers like this?"

Bruno shook his head no. "You're warm. I feel good, sitting just like this."

"I hate it, feeling like they can just look down at us sitting out here."

"Why?" Bruno asked. "Fuck 'em." With that, he planted a wine-tinged kiss on the side of Rory's head.

"Can you believe that littlest one calling me a goddamn hippie in that Cartman voice?" Rory snickered. "He sounded just like him."

Bruno laughed loudly. Then a bit lower he said, "Did you see the look on his mama's face? I thought I'd piss my pants trying not to laugh."

Rory stretched out his legs and held them six inches off the pavers for a count of ten. "God, I'm glad I don't have kids."

Bruno drained his wine glass and tickled as close to Rory's side as he could reach. "Aw c'mon. I wouldn't mind having a red-headed pretty boy like you running around the house spouting off like a kid on South Park."

Rory squirmed under his tickling fingers. "If he was yours, he wouldn't have my coloring. He'd be dark and tough as hell. My god, a fucking thug child."

"Hey!" Bruno said. "Watch it. What makes you think he'd be a thug?"

"You. The apple never falls too far from the tree. Look at Bridget." Rory said. "We've even got a thug-looking dog. Admit it; you're just a thug with an MBA. Can't you see a kid of ours? God, we'd spend our lives in juvie court."

"No," Bruno said wistfully, "he'd be all golden and talented like you. Sensitive and shit."

"Ya think?"

"Sure." Bruno took his arm out of Rory's shirt and stretched it across the back of the wicker sofa, opening his legs wide in relaxation. He put down his wine glass and readjusted himself in his shorts and sighed. "Is there any more of that wine?"

"A bit. Hand me your glass."

Bruno handed Rory his glass. He watched as Rory shifted and found the wine bottle in the shadow of an overhead beam that obscured the moonlight on the table by the sofa. Absently, Bruno said, "He's a nice-looking guy. You think his pecker is as big as he is? You can never tell with those basketball player guys. Their dicks always look small in proportion."

Rory emptied the bottle into his glass and handed it back to him. "I dunno. I didn't see any swing in his sweats, but he could have been wearing tighty-whities. He looks like the type to be all cooped in" Carefully, he sat the empty wine bottle back on the side table. "She's not a bad looking woman."

"Hmmm," Bruno responded as he took a sip of the wine.

"Hmmm? That's it?" Rory asked.

"Are you fishing, Rory?" Bruno responded quietly. He was well aware that there was always a part that remained deep in Rory that didn't trust him after he'd broken up with him years before to get married. It had laid minefields in their relationship that Bruno still had to negotiate after nearly twenty years.

"Not necessarily. I'm just saying . . . "

"She's very pretty. He's lucky to have her. But," Bruno lifted a hand to ward off any further questions, "did you hear her jump dead in his shit about the boys watching South Park? I bet she can be a real bitch."

"You got that too, right?" Rory said. "Did you hear him tell her he couldn't keep a constant eye on them? I'll give you four to one he's got the bulk of responsibility for those kids. Did she say what she did? I missed it."

Bruno snickered. "She's a lawyer. Just made partner."

"Oh my god." Rory gaped. "And he sells medical equipment? Well, there you are."

Bruno lifted his arms over his head, threw his head back and yawned. "I'm fucking glad I'm not straight. I couldn't put up with the bullshit."

"You and me both." Rory said and gave him a look in the dark. Bruno's face was silvered by the bright January moon overhead, exaggerating the dark circles under his eyes.

"Busy day tomorrow, Bruno?" he asked gently.

"Oh yeah. Presentation of findings at eight. I need to be at my desk at seven to go over the numbers one more time," Bruno replied tiredly.

"How does it look for them?"

Bruno grunted. "They're top-heavy. It's all chiefs and no Indians. They've got some sound thinking, but they've downsized to the point of freezing themselves and their productivity all out of proportion to their potential if they were staffed in the right places. They'd have done better by themselves if they cut upper management and left themselves some room to respond to market shifts with their production department." Bruno shook his head like a bull ridding himself of annoying flies. "Why are we talking about this? I don't even want to think about those fuckers right now. What were we talking about before?"

"Not being straight. Well, married and straight anyway."

Bruno reached to tickle Rory's side again and laughed as he shifted away. "I'm too old for all that hassle. God, I'm glad you're not a bitch."

Rory smiled. "C'mon beast. One of the great things about gay marriage is you have somebody who's only concerned with you. And, I say it's time for you to call it a night."

Bruno grinned. "One of the great things? Hell, I thought that was *the* great thing."

"What's *the* great thing?"

Bruno slipped an arm around Rory's waist and kissed the side of his head. "Just being looked after by you."

"A couple of glasses of wine and you get mushy. You know that, beast?"

Bruno only yawned hugely once more and nodded his head.

"What are the odds of that guy knowing us from college?"

Bruno grunted. "I can't place him, but hell, how many people were there at that school back then? Maybe sixteen, seventeen thousand? Besides, you and I are probably more recognizable because of me playing sports and us being in the band. The guy said he remembered me from the lacrosse team."

"Yeah," Rory agreed. "He did say he was Eddy's roommate and mentioned the band. But, I swear to god, I can't place him."

Bruno yawned and stood. "Why should you? We met a lot of people back in those days. Besides, you and I didn't leave much room for other people."

Rory laughed. "Yeah, that's true. We were pretty stuck together, still are."

"Like white on rice," Bruno said, and reaching out he pulled Rory up from his seat by the upper arm and steered him across the pool deck. Bridget got to her feet stiffly and padded ahead of them toward the bedroom door.

"Some guy we only met, like twice, back then, and now he shows up in fricking Broward County, Florida." Rory mused. He paused at the door to their bedroom to allow Bridget to go in before heading in after her.

"And moves in next door for god's sake," Bruno said tiredly as he passed into the bedroom.

"Well, if he barely knew us then, let's hope he's a good neighbor and keeps on barely knowing us now," Rory said as he closed the door and pulled his T-shirt over his head.

## 5160 ST. MARK'S COURT

AUSTIN LOOKED IN on the boys to make sure they were bedded down and the television was turned to a fairly innocuous channel. After Joshie had decided to spout off like Eric Cartman earlier that evening, Meg wouldn't be watching them to make sure they weren't wallowing in South Park, she'd be watching him to make sure he monitored the boys' viewing choices. Austin frankly didn't want the hassle of Meg's pointing out any laxity on his part in that regard.

Both boys were asleep in their sleeping bags on the floor of what would be their upstairs play area. He knelt and tucked the edge of Noah's sleeping bag around his shoulders against the chill of the air-conditioned night. In sleep, his breath was slightly sour, betraying his last glass of milk before bedtime. Austin wondered if he'd brushed his teeth, but decided it was pointless to speculate. He wouldn't wake him up to brush. That was the difference between him and Meg. She would have shaken the boy awake and steered him in his half sleep into the bathroom to brush. Meg had little tolerance for half measures.

Impulsively, Austin kissed his sleeping son's cheek and smiled. The whole South Park thing in the driveway that evening was funny, really. It was all he could do to be stern and not join in the boys' joke. It was also funny when Josh clocked Noah on claiming fourteen when he was still shy of that birthday by more than two months. His oldest son was now impatient to be grown, but sleeping as he was now, there was still more than a trace of the little boy he had been.

Tiredly Austin moved on to tuck in his brother. He patted Joshie's little rump, which he thought stuck out at an oddly obtuse angle to his shoulders inside the sleeping bag. He comforted himself with the notion that Josh had to be comfortable to be sleeping so soundly and then raised himself painfully off his knees. With a sigh, he flicked off the television, then the overhead lights, to leave his sleeping sons some peace to dream on their first night in their new house.

Austin made his way into the room that was to be his office. Before he'd brought the few things they'd sleep on tonight, he'd transported his desk, computer, printer, fax, and phone to the new house. Though the phone and the Internet service wouldn't be connected until tomorrow, he still quickly plugged in all the cables that allowed the various components to talk to each other. Satisfied, he stood by the window under his desk and switched everything on. He was rewarded with the computer operating system's welcome screen and then a picture of the boys and Meg on the beach that served as his screen's wallpaper. He felt reassured by the continuity of this image from his old home to this new house. Obviously, nothing had changed and everything had changed simultaneously.

Curiously warmed by the glow from the computer's screen, he looked out the second-floor window to the broad reach of the moonlight silvering the canal. It looked to be a vast distance to the line of lit houses on the opposite shore. Austin was pleased with his view. He told himself that was a good thing, considering the premium he'd paid for this house on the water. It was a costly view, but he had no doubt, as he worked from this desk day in and day out to pay for it, he'd be glad he sat and looked where he did.

Austin glanced down and was startled to find his neighbors and their huge dog sitting on their deck by their pool. He had no idea they would be so close under his gaze. He felt almost as if he was spying on them, but he didn't look away. He could see them linked, intimately relaxing side by side on their wicker sofa in moonlight bright as day. He watched as Bruno stood and eventually tugged Rory to his feet. The dog stood as well. Casually, they headed toward a set of French doors that offered a glimpse of the foot of a bed beyond.

Austin watched as the dog led the way in and they broke their touch only to pass through the door and into the pool of lamplight inside. Bruno wearily trudged in first, followed by Rory, who quietly closed the door behind them. Austin watched through the door's glass panes as Rory turned and stripped off his T-shirt and tossed it into the room before moving out of his line of sight.

He recalled in full then the memory that they'd sparked earlier standing out in front of his new home, and the discussion between Noah and Josh about their gay neighbors. Surprisingly, Noah had been sanguine about their relationship. To him, it was an accepted fact of life, two men living together. Times had certainly changed, but then Noah's attitude wasn't too far from what Eddy had said all those years ago when Austin had brought up the discomfiting encounter with Rory and Bruno. He had just laughed. "Man," he'd said. "Those two are like white on rice. You couldn't pry them off each other with a crowbar."

"Damn," Austin had replied. "Could they be more obvious? I mean it's no big deal to me, but you'd think they'd get the crap beat out of them."

"Bullshit," Eddy had snorted. "You saw Bruno; you want to piss him off?"

"I thought I had, the way he was acting. It was like he thought I was after Rory or something."

Eddy then had opened the refrigerator and threw him a beer. "Bruno's a big dumb pit bull when it comes to Rory and anybody giving them any grief about the gay thing. He's sneaky though. On the lacrosse team, some guy was giving him shit about being queer. He waited until he had a shot at the guy while they were at practice and goddamn near broke his jaw. The guy's parents almost brought him up on assault charges. It was pretty fucked up."

"But I couldn't care less," Austin had said. "What makes him think I was, damn, hitting on his boyfriend? No way."

Eddy had laughed again and opened a fresh beer himself. "Forget about it, man. Bruno's weird. It ain't got nothing to do with you. He's so up in his own head; he looks at himself in the mirror and figures if *he* can be queer, every other guy has half a notion to. He's an arrogant motherfucker, but he's a pretty good guy if he likes you as a friend."

"What about Rory? I mean, he seems like a regular sort of guy," Austin had said. "Seeing him around, I'd never figure him for a fag. How does he put up with Bruno jerking him around by the neck and shit? Damn, I'd have to kill Bruno if he treated me like that."

Eddy had just shrugged and said, "Look man, I'm not a great big authority on fags. I just know those two. All I got to say is, they're pretty great guys once you get to know them." Eddy took a long hit on his beer can. "Hell, they're just like everybody else." Then Eddy had said something that had struck Austin for nearly two decades as particularly wise. "Don't question the tie that binds, man. Don't question the tie that binds."

Eighteen years later, Austin looked from Rory and Bruno's darkened bedroom door out over the wide moonlit canal and sighed. *What, he* thought, *are the odds I'd end up with those two as next door neighbors?*

"All set up, sweetheart?" Meg asked from his office doorway, bringing him fully back from the past.

Jerked from his reverie, Austin looked down at his desk into the welcoming glow from his computer's screen. "Yep. Got it all fired up and working."

Meg walked from the doorway and came to stand behind him. Wrapping her arms around his waist she stood on tiptoe and kissed the side of his neck.

"Look out at the view, honey." Austin said, and taking one of her hands he pulled her to stand next to him. "The moon's full. Isn't it beautiful?"

Meg rarely allowed herself to be so pulled. She squeezed his hand and looked out the window. "Yes, it is. It's lovely from here." Austin felt her unclasp his hand and turn toward the side window. "My god! We can look right down to their pool deck. I can see everything on it."

"So?"

"Well . . . so . . . so what if they lounge out there and stuff?" Meg said worriedly.

"Isn't that what people do on their pool decks?" Austin asked as he placed his hand gently on the back of her neck and squeezed.

Abruptly, she shrugged off his touch. "So, what if they swim and lay around all lovey-dovey? I'm not so sure I like the idea of the boys having a full view of their lifestyle that way," Meg said as she turned to face him. "I had no idea we'd have *gay* next-door neighbors right under our noses."

Austin turned away from the window and leaned against the lip of his desk. "Come on, Meg. This isn't like you. Besides, I doubt very seriously if they are going to be fucking in their pool. Neither one of them seems to be really obvious. Besides, Rory said they've been living together for seventeen years. If that's the case . . . "

"If that's the case, what?" Meg said as she turned to face him.

Austin replied with a weak laugh. "Seventeen years. They're probably lucky to fuck once a month."

"And what's that supposed to mean?" Meg bristled.

Austin pushed himself away from the edge of his desk and held his hands up in mock surrender. "It was a joke, Meg. It didn't *mean* anything."

Meg turned away from the window and sighed tiredly. Edging past Austin, she leaned against his desk as he had. "I'm sorry, Austin. I'm just tired and a little sensitive about that subject."

Austin wanted to hug her. It would be so easy to reach across the small space between them and take her in his arms, or even just take her hand, but he was hurt from her earlier rebuff. Instead he only smiled ruefully. "It's okay, sweetheart. Give yourself a break."

Meg rewarded him with a smile and looked back over her shoulder through the window to the house next door. "Well, this is your office. I doubt very seriously if the boys will be in here taking in the view of our gay neighbors doing whatever the hell they probably do on their pool deck."

"They probably just sit and have a glass of wine. That's what they were doing five minutes ago. They probably won't . . . well, I don't think they'll be out there butt-fucking every day."

Meg stood and took his hand. "I know you're right. I'm sorry. I don't know why I'm being so tense."

Austin squeezed her hand gently and said, "You're not tense, you're just very, very alert. Are you ready for a cup of tea and bed?"

"A cup of tea sounds heavenly, but how?"

Austin smiled. "I know you like a cup of tea before bed. I packed a few tea bags, some Equal, and your favorite mug to bring here with the stuff for us to sleep on. I know how to take care of my honey after all this time."

"And how do you think you're going to get hot water? Did you bring a kettle too?" Meg teased.

Austin grinned. "Nope. Didn't need to. The morning kitchen in the master suite has one of those instant hot-water tap things. You've moved on up, girl. The Hardens have arrived in that dee-luxe apartment in the sky-y-y."

Meg giggled. "If I wasn't so tired . . . you're the greatest, Austin." Meg stood and leaned against him appreciatively as they stepped toward the door. "I'll just check on the boys and be right in."

Austin noted she didn't let go of his hand. For a moment, hope for a bit of private time together flared and threatened to kindle. "There's no need," he said soothingly. "They're asleep. I just tucked them in, turned off the television, and shut off the light. They're fine."

"Did they manage to brush their teeth?" Meg demanded.

Austin felt the fragile spark of promise die. He swallowed hard, and then lied. "I saw them do it myself."

Meg nodded and took off toward their master suite with Austin's hand still firmly in her grasp. He didn't let go, but did resist her urging long enough to switch off his desk lamp. He allowed himself to be pulled through the air-conditioned, near-dark coolness into their bedroom. He quietly half closed their door but left it open enough to hear any cries the boys might make in their sleep.

Meg found her overnight bag in a corner on the floor. She fished in it briefly and found an oversized T-shirt emblazoned with an image of Shamu from Seaworld. Glancing behind her, she noticed Austin standing there, watching her. She turned her back to him, pulled her polo shirt over her head, unhooked and removed her bra, and quickly pulled the T-shirt over her head before removing her jeans.

Austin turned away and walked to the area of the master bedroom that was outfitted with a small sink in a marble countertop. The alcove where it was situated came equipped with a diminutive microwave and refrigerator as well. Quietly, he put together Meg's cup of tea and left it to steep as he undressed to his jockey shorts.

Meg walked past him with her makeup kit into the palatial master bath. She selected a sink from the pair on the marble vanity top and methodically began removing her makeup. "Austin?"

He walked into the master bath and sat on the edge of the large soaking tub opposite the vanity. "What?"

"You said you knew those two next door from college, didn't you? I can't remember either one of them."

Austin scratched his shoulder absently and thought a moment. "There's really no reason why you should. Don't you remember my roommate that last semester when we were seniors?"

"Eddy?"

Austin responded to her inquiring look in the mirror. "Yeah, Eddy. Those two were in the band with him. I don't really *know* them, I just met them a couple of times. Once when I came home without you and they were crashing at the apartment."

Meg washed her face with a cloth and some soap she pulled from her makeup bag. Her eyes never left her own face as she lathered her cheeks, nose, and forehead with gentle circular motions. "When was the other time? Why wasn't I with you?"

"I don't know where you were the first time, but the second time I know you were back home doing wedding stuff. It was at the end of the semester. Rory had the band play at his senior show. He was an art major."

Meg rinsed her face precisely three times. Following the third, she patted it dry with another clean cloth and said, "Well that figures. What does he do now? Lay around the house and paint?"

Austin shrugged. "No, he said he's an electrician. Bruno says he's a commercial lighting *designer*."

Meg chuckled and searched in her bag thoughtfully before pulling out two small jars. She screwed the lid off one and touched the pad of her right little finger into the crème. "And what does Bruno do? He looked very buttoned down. He mentioned his office was downtown."

Austin stretched, then readjusted himself in his jockeys. "He's an investment analyst. My god, can you imagine that one snooping around your business like a bull in a china shop?"

"Please don't do that," Meg said as she rubbed the crème around the outside of her eyes.

"Don't do what?" Austin said defensively.

"Tug at your privates like that. It's vulgar. The boys are picking it up," she said as she looked at his reflection in the mirror.

Austin sighed. "The boys are probably tugging at themselves because their nuts are knotted up in their drawers. It's uncomfortable, you know."

"Well, that may be the case, but I don't like to look at it. Every guy I know does it. It's like all of you are afraid your balls are going to jump off and run away."

Austin snickered.

Meg reattached the lid to her first jar of crème, then picked up the larger of the two jars and unscrewed its lid, "You're no help. Can you believe what Joshie said to Rory? He called him a *goddamn hippie*. I don't care if they got the joke. I didn't think it was funny at all. We've really got to start monitoring their television better. I don't want them watching South Park, okay?"

Austin stood and started for the door, "Okay, whatever."

Meg rubbed the crème from the second jar over her forehead and cheeks. "Wait, hon . . . don't take off. You never finished telling me about the second time you met Rory and Bruno."

Austin looked at his wife's reflection in the mirror. Her face gleamed in the bright bank of lights over the mirror as if she'd been greased. Without her makeup, she looked oddly featureless, as if she had wiped away all the personality from her face. "There's not much to tell," he said. "I looked at his art while the band played, and afterward I went up and said hello. It was no big deal."

Meg turned from the mirror and smiled. "C'mon. Something about it must have stuck with you for you make the connection with those two faces after so many years."

Austin looked away from her blank face and stared up at the ornate crystal chandelier hanging from the bath's ceiling. "They were taking a break outside the gallery in the art building, you know where I'm talking about . . . that brick wall about three and a half feet high? They had their shirts off and were wearing these wings . . . "

"Wings?" Meg said incredulously.

"Yeah. It was part of the show. Bruno had on black feathered wings that were huge. Rory had a smaller pair—white ones—but now I remember he'd taken his off. Anyway, Bruno was sitting up on the wall and Rory was standing between his legs, leaning back against Bruno's chest." Austin looked down from the chandelier and found Meg's face. "Here's the weird part. Bruno had one arm around Rory's waist and was thumping his stomach like he was still playing bass.

It was like he was *playing* Rory."

"No wonder it stuck in your mind," Meg said and turned her attention back to the vanity where she meticulously began placing her various jars back into her makeup bag. "That sounds like an awfully intimate thing for them to be doing out in public."

Austin watched her, wondering why she didn't just leave her cleansing and night crème things out. They'd be living in the bathroom from now on. It was an unnecessary point. Meg liked everything to have a place and everything to be in its place. Offhandedly he said, "I bet those two have been together longer than you and I have."

Meg zippered her bag closed and turned toward him once more. "Still, they're *gay*. What kind of a life is that, no matter how much they're devoted to each other? No kids to love and raise. It's not natural; it just goes against the grain somehow. I mean, look at Bruno. What a waste. There are single women my age who are really missing out because those two are still *experimenting*, for godssakes."

"And what about Rory?"

Meg shrugged. "Oh, he's too pretty for my taste. But Bruno, oh my god. I guess Rory's lucky to have him."

"So you like Bruno, huh? Am I going to have to keep an eye on you two?" Austin teased.

Meg gave him a scornful look. "Not really. He's good-looking, but I run into his type every day. I work in an office full of guys just like him. Sharks in coats and ties and none of them with an ounce of respect for women. He's all macho bullshit as far as I'm concerned."

"He's the man of the house, that's for sure. Rory plays up to it. You should have seen him jump to bring us out some beers. All Bruno did was look at him. And the way Bruno pulls him around by the neck like he was five years old. Oh man . . . "

Meg giggled. "No question who's the pitcher and who's the catcher there."

Austin laughed. "Ya think?"

Meg nodded and cut him a long look. "Next time you see Rory, check his elbows for carpet burns."

Austin shrugged and held out his hand for her. "Never question the tie that binds, my dear. Never question the tie that binds."

# CHAPTER THREE

# Sundays go like this . . .

## ST. MARK'S COURT

TIIE GROCERIES SHIFTED and settled as Rory pulled up in his drive and shut off the Volvo's engine. Unlike Bruno, he didn't make the tires or the emergency brake of his station wagon squeal as he came to a full stop. Rory always thought Bruno had a wager with himself that he could actually touch the garage door as he stopped before he crashed into it. But then Bruno never had a car loaded with groceries. Rory pulled off his sunglasses, tucked them in his visor, punched the garage door opener clipped there, and got out of the car. He paused to stretch before he headed around the car to gather the groceries.

"Good morning, Rory," Austin said.

Rory looked up to see his neighbor of two weeks striding down the sidewalk toward him, dressed in a coat and tie. He looked handsome and boyish, and Rory smiled. "Good morning. What are you doing up and dressed so fine on a Sunday morning?"

Austin stuck his hands in his dress pants pockets. "We're on our way to church. That is, if Meg and the boys will ever get the hell out of the house and into the car. What are you doing just coming home at this time of morning?"

Rory gave him a smile as he opened the Volvo's back hatch and glanced at his grocery bags. The contents had spilled and rolled.

Looking back at Austin, he said, "Actually, I have you beat. I've already been to church and done some grocery shopping."

Austin whistled. "What church do you go to, that you've attended and gotten groceries by ten o'clock?"

Rory strolled the few feet of sidewalk to meet him and said, "I go to eight o'clock mass. There's an Italian market that opens early near my church, so I always swing by there and pick up some things to cook on Sunday."

Austin nodded. "And where's Bruno?"

Rory snorted, rolled his eyes and smiled. "Bruno goes to St. Mattress. It's about time I get in and wake him up. What church do you guys go to?"

Austin glanced over his shoulder to his front door, and then looked at his watch. "Oh we're Baptists." Noting the look of instinctive alarm on Rory's face, he quickly added, "But not fundamentalists. We belong to a very forward-thinking church. It's more of a sort of Baptist-lite kind of place. We're not intolerant, believe me."

Rory gave him a long look through his heavily-lidded eyes and, finally, an open smile. "It's none of my business, really. I'm not intolerant myself."

Austin thought that Rory always looked as if he just woke up, and just woke up from being thoroughly fucked. He couldn't decide if it was studied or completely natural, but there was an erotic undercurrent to it that made him a little uncomfortable. After a moment, he said heartily "Well, that's good to hear."

Rory nodded toward Austin's house. "Are you settling in? Feeling at home?"

Austin nodded, and taking his hands out of his pockets he opened his arms slightly. "I suppose so. I work from home, so I've had more of a chance to get acclimated. The boys seem as if they've always lived here. Meg has underestimated her commute, I think. The traffic on I-595 is a bitch at rush hour."

Rory took a half step toward Austin and said, "I thought I saw your minivan around a lot. You know, I work from home too. Are you often on the road?"

Unconsciously, Austin was aware of his step closer into his comfort zone. He was inclined to take a step back, but decided to stand his ground. "I'm only out when I have appointments. Some weeks it's hectic, but it's been slow lately. It's taken some getting used to, staying home so much."

Rory smoothed his longish bangs back from his forehead. Austin recalled his haircut from their college days. Rory's hair was cut much the same, only in a shorter version. It caught the sun, neither red nor gold but a kind of blond streaked lighter on top than the light chestnut underneath. "Why is that? Haven't you worked from home for awhile?" Rory asked.

Austin did take a step back from Rory then. "No. I . . . I've only had this job a few months. I was downsized from a company I worked for in Boca. It was a high-tech firm, and you know how all that went in the crapper. I was an assistant chief financial officer. I was unemployed for awhile before I found this sales job."

Rory opened his eyes and sought out Austin's. "That sucks. I'm sorry to hear it."

Austin felt no condescension in his voice. He shrugged. I'm doing the medical equipment sales thing while I'm looking around. I have a ton of resumes out there. It's just tough right now. It can't last forever."

Rory dropped his eyes, and when he lifted them again Austin found empathy, not pity. "Don't give up, Austin. It's all cycles. You just have to ride them out."

"I hear you, man," he said. "It just does something to you when you've been getting up and heading into an office every day of your whole adult life. I miss that, you know? Even the typical office bullshit." Austin straightened his spine and squared his shoulders and said, "But why am I bothering you with all this? My little red wagon to pull, you don't need to hear all this shit out of me."

Austin would have expected anyone else to mumble something appropriate, or to punch him in the arm and tell him to suck it up. Rory did an amazing thing; he cocked his head and said, "It must get awfully lonely beating your head against the wall trying to move CAT-scan machines or whatever. Don't put yourself in a cell, man. If the walls start closing in on you, give me a call, come have a beer. Don't forget I'm always trying to hustle clients and projects just like you are. I'm around if you . . . "

"Dad! Dad! Mom says you left the coffee pot on," Josh scolded from the front door.

"So tell her to turn it off and come on! We're going to be later than we already are!" Austin shouted back. As his son darted back into the house, he looked at Rory with mock panic and said, "I left the coffee pot on. I'm in big trouble."

Rory laughed. "Well, look . . . I've got to get my groceries in and see if Bruno's still snoring. Hang in there, buddy."

Austin found himself smiling in reply. "I'll do that."

Rory nodded. "Well. I've got groceries to get in."

Austin fiddled in his pocket and jiggled his car keys. "It's good to see you, Rory. To tell you the truth, I feel kind of marooned out here. You guys are the only people who've spoken to us since we moved in."

Rory's eyes darted toward Austin's crotch, following the sound of the keys' muffed jangle. "It's not the most welcoming place," he said as his eyes quickly found Austin's once more. "Most of our neighbors keep to themselves. But Bruno and I are just as bad."

Austin had noted Rory's furtive glance. He removed his keys from his pocket and jauntily tossed them in the air, catching them neatly before he said, "Don't you guys socialize with old friends?"

Rory let slip a small laugh that betrayed some feeling Austin couldn't identify. "Most of our friends are business-related. Bruno and I are so complete as a unit, we've never had many friends."

"Really?"

Rory nodded and looked toward his car. "I guess we're just jealous of our time with each other. Bruno's away a lot on business, and when he's home, we . . . well, we just don't seem to have a lot of time for other people."

In a way, Austin felt something akin to both wistfulness and jealousy for a time when he and Meg were just as closely knit. He said, "Then you must be lonely when he's away."

Rory laughed, this time more genuinely. "I'm pretty self-amusing." Then his face betrayed the need to explain himself. Rory's forehead crinkled with earnestness as he continued, "I know I must sound like an asshole. We're really not antisocial . . ."

"You're just two busy people." Austin finished for him. "No need to explain."

"That's not to say we wouldn't enjoy getting to know you guys," Rory added quickly. "We've just never had neighbors who seemed to want to know us better. We've spent years living in family-type neighborhoods. Bruno's kept us moving up the real estate ladder so we never have lived anywhere longer than a couple of years. And, you know, people with kids don't seem to have too much in common with two gay guys."

Austin gripped his keys in his fist. He suddenly understood a great deal. "I'd say they cheated themselves out of knowing you two."

Embarrassed, Rory looked away. "That's a very nice thing to say, Austin."

Austin glanced toward his front door. "No, it's not just nice. It's true. We don't socialize much ourselves. Between work and the boys' extracurricular activities, there's not much time for adult conversation. All of our friends only talk about kid stuff or work. It can become tedious."

Rory nodded.

"Look. Why don't we try to get together sometime, you and me and Bruno and Meg? We can talk about college days if nothing else. I'd like that."

Austin noted a blush rise over Rory's cornflakes-and-cream complexion. He nervously ran a hand through his bangs and smiled. "Sounds good."

Austin heard his front door open. Both he and Rory turned to see the boys spill from the doorway, followed by Meg. Dressed in their Sunday finest, they seemed vivid to Rory, almost as if their dress clothes were too tight to contain the fullness of the life that boiled beneath them.

"Good morning!" Meg exclaimed as she caught sight of Rory.

"Good morning, Meg," he replied. "You guys look great all dressed up on a Sunday morning."

"Thanks, Rory," she replied distractedly as she searched in her pocketbook. Finding her keys, she turned away to lock the front door.

The boys ignored their father and Rory as they flung open the passenger doors of their mother's Range Rover and climbed in.

"Take it easy, Austin," Rory said.

"You too, buddy," Austin replied with a smile.

Shyly, Rory returned his smile before he turned and strolled away, eagerly putting as much sidewalk as he could between Austin's front yard and his Volvo's open back hatch.

### 5150 ST. MARK'S COURT

BRUNO IDLY CLICKED through all the available channels on the plasma television screen mounted on the family room wall. Tucked into the corner of the sectional sofa with Rory lying between his legs and comfortably resting against his chest, he settled on one of the ongoing recaps of World War II on the History Channel. "TV sucks," he said to the top of Rory's head as he put the remote on the coffee table. Rory mumbled as he turned the page of the novel he had perched on his own chest.

"How's your book?" Bruno asked.

"I have never read a more pointless novel in my life," Rory responded, and he pushed his glasses up on the bridge of his nose.

"Bored?" Bruno asked and stretched.

Rory closed his book and reached around Bruno's angled leg to place it next to the remote. "Buzzed?" he asked Bruno.

"Mellow," Bruno responded, and gently reached with both hands to remove Rory's glasses, which found their way onto the coffee table as well. "I was thinking about going for a swim. Wanna join me?"

"Kinda cold. I bet the water's only about sixty-five degrees." Rory said as he rubbed his eyes.

"Ummm, I was thinking it might wake us up enough that I could spend a little time getting you warm again," Bruno said as he bent over to find Rory's face.

Rory laughed and stretched himself. "That sounds like a great way to end the weekend. Rory craned his neck to look up at Bruno's smirk as best he could. Chuckling, he placed his palms on Bruno's thighs and pushed himself up and scooted away. Standing, he glanced at Bruno's leering grin, then stepped to the set of French doors that opened from the family room onto the dark pool deck. The house next door was unlit except for a dim light from the second floor window that provided a direct view of their pool below. Turning to Bruno, he said, "We'll have to be quiet."

Bruno groaned and stood up. "It's ten-thirty. Don't you bet they've gone to bed by now?"

Rory stepped back into the family room and gave Bruno a sleepy-eyed smile. "I think it's worth the risk."

"You bet it is," Bruno said as he stripped off his T-shirt, followed with a no-nonsense, double-handed tug on his boxer shorts that left them puddled on the floor at his feet. Nonchalantly, he stepped out of them and walked to stand between Rory and the door. With both hands he grasped the hem of Rory's tight-ribbed wife-beater. "I want to see you naked, bitch," he said matter-of-factly as he yanked it upward.

Obediently, Rory raised his arms as Bruno peeled off his tank. He shivered at the roughness in Bruno's voice. After all this time, it still strummed the tight cord of desire in him, calling out all the resonance of a prolonged bass note that worked down his spine to reverberate between his legs. Bruno was already tugging at his boxers when Rory took a step back. "Is the bedroom door unlocked," he whispered huskily.

"Fuck, I don't know," Bruno said in frustration.

"Go ahead and get in," Rory said. "I'm just going to slip around and make sure we can get back to the bed, okay?"

"Whatever," Bruno replied gruffly. "Just hurry up." With that, he stepped through the family room door and broke into a heavy trot to the deep end of the pool. He dived in cleanly and swam underwater to the shallow end, where he stood and gasped at the chill of the water and the cool night laid over his wet shoulders.

Rory appeared and opened the bedroom door, hesitating for a moment, he looked out at Bruno. "Shuck 'em off, Rory," Bruno whispered harshly.

Rory glanced up at the light on upstairs next door, then ran his hands under the elastic sides of his boxers and let them fall.

He was already hard, Bruno noted with a grin. "C'mon, baby," he urged. "Dive in. It's not so bad once you get your breath back."

Rory stepped from the bedroom door and loped toward the deep end of the pool. He stood for a moment on the lip, hesitating against the bracing shock that was to come. Then he dived in. Opening his eyes underwater, he saw Bruno's blurry form sink under the water at the other end to wait for him. After three strong kicks propelling him forward, he was caught by Bruno's hands under his arms and lifted up and out of the water with a gasp that Bruno swallowed with a firm open-mouthed kiss.

Rory wrapped one arm around Bruno's shoulders as he reached behind Rory and caught him with one hand firmly under his ass. His hand roughly spread Rory's cheeks to allow a searching middle finger to find and tickle him intimately. Rory choked back a sound that Bruno thought sounded like a cross between laughter and a sob. Bruno felt his dick harden improbably in the cold water. Rory pushed him away and swam toward the deep end of the pool. Bruno ducked under the water and swam beneath him, grabbing for and finding Rory's dick.

With Bruno's hand tugging at him, Rory stood immediately. His heels grazed Bruno's side as he climbed for the surface as well. They stood still in chest-deep water, slowly circling each other. "C'mere," Bruno insisted.

When Rory stepped toward him, he reached up to place his hands on Bruno's shoulders. Bruno responded by tugging downward on his own dick with one hand and pulling his partner closer with the other. Bruno forced himself between Rory's legs, feeling the hard reach of the corded muscle that ran from the base of his scrotum toward his ass rubbing along the top of his dick. Rory tucked the tops of his feet behind Bruno's knees and opened his lips to gently bite the side of Bruno's neck. Slowly, the big man turned with Rory in his arms. Buoyed by the water that felt warmer every minute, Bruno turned them round and round, generating small waves that reached out from them, as steady and gentle as ripples on a pond.

"Hey," Rory whispered.

"Hey yourself," Bruno answered happily.

Rory stretched in Bruno's arms, bending his own back from his elbows and sighed.

"Feels good, doesn't it," Bruno said amiably.

"It's not as cold as I thought it'd be," Rory said glancing upward as he untangled himself from Bruno's legs and found his footing on the floor of the pool.

"Will you quit looking up there?" Bruno said irritably. "If they want to look, let 'em."

In answer, Rory took a deep breath and slid out of Bruno's arms to sink below him in the water. Bruno felt his dick become enclosed by the warmth of Rory's mouth and the gentle tug of his lips. It was all he could go not to reach below the water's surface to grab and hold Rory's head there, battering his face until he fought for breath. Instead, he opened his arms wide and swayed his fingers in the water in rhythm with Rory's ministrations below.

Finally, Rory pushed away to swim on his back underwater until he reached the steps of the pool. Once there, he sat on a step and lifted his head with something between a gasp and a giggle. Bruno responded by swimming toward him underwater. With his eyes opened to the sting of chlorine, he reached for Rory's waist and lifted his hips from the water. Raising him effortlessly, he brought his hips to his face and ran his tongue over the length of Rory's dick. Bruno felt his shudder and welcomed it. Letting go of Rory's hips, his hands found their way under his arms and urged him upward to sit on the pool's edge. Leaving Rory to sit in the chill, he sank back into the water and put his face in Rory's groin, teasing him until Rory grasped the sides of his head and shook him.

"Are you ready to go in now?" Bruno whispered.

"Uh huh. I'm cold." Rory replied.

"No you're not. You're a hot little fuck, aren't you?" Bruno said as he stood and took Rory's neck in his hands. Bruno's thumbs caressed the base of Rory's neck gently.

Rory shivered involuntarily as he looked at Bruno with the same measure of trust and vulnerability that had turned Bruno on for twenty-two years. That was how many years had passed since they'd first met as juniors in college. "You want me to fuck you, don't you?" Bruno had asked then as he asked now.

Rory looked down and away from him shyly, recalling the script that was etched indelibly on his brain, never old, never exhausted as a well of desire. He nodded shyly.

Bruno stood in the water and used his thumbs to lift Rory's chin to meet his eyes. "Tell me. Say it. Tell me you want me to fuck you."

"You want me to beg you, don't you?" Rory whispered huskily. "You're used to being begged, you cocky bastard."

"Oh, you'll beg me. I swear to god you'll beg me," Bruno whispered in return.

Rory laughed, and Bruno let go of him and slogged to the steps of the pool. Dripping, he rose to offer his hand to Rory.

Rory took his hand and Bruno pulled him to his feet. He looked deep into Rory's eyes and whispered, "It never gets old does it?"

Rory lifted his free hand and stroked the side of Bruno's face in reply. "It's been only you for all these years, Bruno. How could it have ever gotten old?"

Bruno turned his lips to the palm of Rory's hand. He kissed him there and said, "C'mon, let's go inside."

Rory hesitated as Bruno began to pull him toward the bedroom door. Bruno turned to look at him. "Please fuck me, Bruno," he whispered into the night as he picked up the thread of their most private dialogue.

Bruno grinned and pulled him through the bedroom door.

### 5160 ST. MARK'S COURT

AUSTIN HAD GIVEN up any pretense of working by the time he heard the first splash below his window. He was playing video poker on his computer. The boys were asleep, and Meg was moored in bed, banked by pillows and tied down with a scatter of files lying across the toile-covered comforter. Obliquely, she'd made it clear that she had work to do when he'd presented her with her nighttime mug of tea. Austin pretended he had work to do as well and returned to his office.

Curious and bored, he watched the pas de deux of his neighbors as they turned a dip into the pool into a performance Austin had to admit he envied. He could make out little of their entwined forms, but it was easy to tell the dark one from his lighter-complexioned partner. Idly, he found his hand in his lap and the weight on his dick turning from curiosity to confirming a need he'd subsumed for far too long. He stood painfully and made his way to the master bedroom.

Meg still sat up in bed, reading a file that had to have been as dull as the phone book. Awkwardly, he lay across the foot of the bed and propped himself up on an elbow.

"Meg?" he asked gently.

Meg raised her eyes blearily from her file and gave him a small smile. "What, sweetheart?"

"Is there any way you could forget about the files for a little while and let me love you a little bit?" he asked earnestly.

Meg allowed the file to drop to her lap. "I'm sorry, Austin. I'm neglecting you aren't I?"

He reached across the short space between them and lightly grasped her foot and massaged it as best he could through the comforter. "It's not that you're neglecting me. It's just that it's been a really long time," he said.

Meg sighed. It seemed to Austin that she braced herself, as if for an annoying conversation she couldn't avoid. Before she could reply, he said, "I don't mean to sound needy. I know that's certainly not an aphrodisiac. But I can't seem to find a way back to the intimacy we used to share," Austin said choosing his words carefully.

"What's brought this on, Austin?" Meg said tiredly.

Austin let go of her foot and sat up. "What do you mean? It's not the flu. I haven't just caught a bad case of horny," he replied.

"There's no need to get defensive. Why do you always get defensive?" Meg replied sharply.

He simply looked at her and shook his head. "What do I have to do to help you get in the mood? It used to just be so natural between us. Now, just negotiating sex feels like the Yalta Conference. Please don't turn this back at me, Meg. I'm not a litigator, you are. I can't out-maneuver you. Just help me understand."

Meg sighed and started gathering up the files scattered around her. "Just give me a minute. I need to brush my teeth."

"Forget it," Austin said and started for the bedroom door. "If it's just something else to be dealt with like an item on your 'to do' list, I don't need it."

"Wait, Austin . . . " Meg said sincerely.

He turned around and watched her lay back the coverlet and swing her legs off the side of the bed. That accomplished, she rubbed her eyes tiredly and then gave him a bleak smile. "You're right. You're not supposed to be an item on my 'to do' list. I apologize."

Austin remained standing and looking at her until she patted the bed next to her and reached for his hand. He stepped back to their bed, took her offered hand, and sat, waiting.

"Austin, it did used to be so effortless, you're right. But everything in my life right now seems like an effort. My job, my kids. You. I'm sorry; I just can't make enough time to keep all the plates spinning on the sticks."

"What can I do to make it easier on you, babe? Just tell me how to take some of the pressure off you and I will," Austin replied and squeezed her hand.

Meg gave a sharp, bitter laugh. "Can you just *be* me for a week? It has nothing to do with you. It's the expectations I put on myself."

"I was beginning to think it did have something to do with me. I keep looking at myself in the mirror and wondering if I'm fat, or if I stink, or if you're just tired of me."

Meg leaned across the small space dividing them and kissed him on the cheek. "You're none of those things, darling. I want to have sex with you; I just keep putting it aside. Please just give me a little time to find my feet with all this . . . " Meg lifted her hand and waved vaguely around her. "Since I've been made partner, the pressures on me are enormous. You have no idea how much I appreciate you taking off some of the pressure with the boys. Please don't think for one minute that I'm tired of you, or I don't find you attractive. It's just women are hard-wired differently. Men can think about sex if they're broke, or stressed or unemployed."

Austin let go of her hand and stared straight ahead.

"Oh! Oh darling! I didn't mean that . . . "

Austin stood and gave her a bleak smile. "Another sore spot, I guess. I'm going back to my pretend office to work at my pretend job."

"Oh Austin, c'mon," Meg cried. "I know you're trying."

"Leave it alone, Meg," Austin said quietly and walked toward the door.

"Austin!" Meg whispered emphatically, "Come back. I didn't mean . . . "

Austin closed the door and walked back to his office. He sat at his desk and put his head in his hands. Getting laid off had been a tremendous blow to his ego. Meg making partner was like getting kicked in the nuts after his big letdown. They both knew it was her salary that was paying the bulk of the bills and the mortgage on this ridiculous house. Deep inside, he knew things couldn't stay this bleak for him. He'd invested too much time and energy—hell, he was too *young*—to just be dealt out of the game at this point in his career.

Determined to let it go and stay positive, he glanced at his computer screen and started again to play the hand of video poker he'd been dealt before he decided to try and get lucky. Within three keystrokes he was out. He hit re-deal and watched his hand spread out on the screen. It just seemed too pointless. Bored and locked into a very personal loneliness, he looked out his window and down into his neighbor's pool enclosure. The area was empty.

Austin let himself wonder where they were in their lovemaking. He glanced toward their bedroom door and was surprised to see it standing wide open. In a pool of warm lamplight, he could see, quite clearly, that they were not finished. Rory lay on his back with his head and arms dropped off the foot of the bed. From his angle, Austin could see the jerks of his head responding to a thrust he could feel, but not see. His eyes followed from Rory's open-mouthed pleasure, across his bared throat to his chest. He could see his nipples stretched on his chest beyond the tightened curve of muscle along his ribs.

Austin felt himself get hard again. Guiltily, he glanced at the computer screen holding playing cards. Flashing graphics asked him to place a bet, draw, or fold. Austin stood and walked quietly to his office door. He drew it closed and softly turned the lock. Hurriedly, he searched the floor of his closet for the dirty T-shirt he'd used to dust off his computer components two weeks before. Finding it, he eased back to his desk chair, sat, and undid his pants. With the dirty T-shirt spread across his belly, he shifted slightly and pulled the elastic band of his jockey shorts under his nuts and spit on his palm.

From the edge of the doorway, he saw a dark, hairy arm move into view. Its muscles strained and he saw Rory's kneecap was pinioned by the arm from behind. Never slowing the rhythm of Rory's head, he saw Bruno's face move in profile to take Rory's nipple in his mouth.

Slowly, Austin began to jerk, all the while telling himself it was just this one time.

# CHAPTER FOUR

# Let's save the date

## 5150 ST. MARK'S COURT

BRUNO JERKED HIS fishing pole and stepped up the incline that ran from his backyard down to the canal. He reeled in the line, noting its slack weightlessness. No strike this time. He sighed, only slightly frustrated. The few bass there were in the long canal behind his house were wily. The more witless Oscars snagged his line more frequently, but they didn't impart the same sense of satisfaction the canny bass did when he managed to catch them. Happily, Bruno stretched in the hot Saturday morning sun. It shone down his broad, bare shoulders and chest, giving him a sheen of good health and well-being. Fishing was one of his forms of relaxing when he had a few minutes to spare on the weekend. With Rory off running errands, he caught a buzz and stepped out back to see if he could catch a fish or two.

Bruno checked the shiner lure once more and cast the line near a stand of water grasses growing in the short slope of the canal before it dropped sharply to a depth he didn't really want to think about. Blasted with dynamite out of the caprock by the developers, the canal was dredged to provide fill for the lots the houses of Venetian Vistas sat on. Bruno knew the canal was near thirty feet deep at its center. It took a great deal of fill to make new land out on the edges of the

Everglades. With the caprock broken and excavated, the ground wept fresh water into the gash and the broad deep ditch became a canal, shimmering under the strong Florida sun.

The fish liked to congregate in the grasses along the shore. The rich oxygen exchange along with the friendly insects made it a playground, nursery, and picnic for the bass and oscars that congregated there.

"You're not going to catch anything," a small voice advised.

Bruno looked round to see the new neighbors' children standing with their sneakered feet lodged into the open spaces of the knit in the chain-linked fence between the two properties. The elder of the two swung half-over the top while they younger managed to climb high enough to rest his arms across the top bar.

Bruno couldn't recall their names, but he could recall their mischievousness. "Hello, Stan. Hello, Kyle," he responded.

The boys rewarded him with cautious, but slightly condescending chuckles. "Stan and Kyle are South Park. We're not cartoons," The older one said and pitched himself over the fence into Bruno's backyard. He hesitated for a moment and gave his brother a jerk of the chin. Encouraged, the younger fellow managed to make his way to the top of the fence where he considered the ground awkwardly before jumping. Satisfied his brother was up and over, the bigger boy walked toward Bruno and said, "I'm Noah." Gesturing behind him, he said, "He's Josh, remember?"

Bruno nodded and looked out to where the thin filament of his cast line disappeared into the water. He gave the pole a slight twitch to flash the lure in the water. "My bad, you goddamn hippies."

The boys looked at each other and giggled at the familiar phrase from their favorite, forbidden cartoon. "You're not going to catch anything," Noah repeated more insistently this time. "My dad said there's no fish in this canal. There's no way for them to get in. Because fish don't just *happen*. They've got to come from somewhere."

"Yeah," Josh seconded.

Bruno nodded, eyes intent on his line. A healthy-sized oscar sniffed at the hook. With another wiggle of his pole, Bruno teased him. "That right?" Bruno replied.

"Yeah, *word*," Noah said smugly. "You're just wasting your time."

"Word," his brother echoed.

Bruno teased the line once more and the oscar struck. Bruno jerked his line and set the hook. Casually, he reeled in the dull fish, made bright by the flash of struggle in the morning light. Expertly, Bruno reached out to grasp the fish and squatted to let his pole rest on the ground. The boys gasped and crowded around him to take a look at the very fish whose existence they had so vigorously denied.

"Wow! What kind is it?" Noah asked excitedly.

Bruno grinned as he gently took the fish in hand and freed it from the hook. Extending it toward the boys for a better view, he said, "I don't see no fish. There ain't no fish in this canal."

"Aww man," Noah said. "C'mon. What kind of fish is it?"

"It's an oscar," Bruno replied.

"Can I touch it?" Josh asked eagerly.

The captured fish struggled in Bruno's grasp. "Hold out your hands," he said. "I'll let you throw him back." The little boy held out his hands. "Now, hold on, and take him back to the water and let him go." He placed the squirming fish into Josh's hands. "Be gentle," Bruno cautioned.

In a single fluid motion, the boy took the fish and fled to the water's edge. He squatted and placing his hands in the water, then released the grateful fish back into the canal. "Cool!" He said looking back to Bruno with lit eyes.

"Why didn't you keep him?" Noah asked, as he squatted next to Bruno.

"You could eat him," Josh said as he made his way the few short steps back to where they waited.

"No. The fun is in catching them," Bruno said gently. "Oscars aren't good to eat. It's better to let him go free so he can live a long time and make other fish, right?"

The boys looked at him dubiously. Bruno smiled and reached for his bait.

"Where did Oscar come from?" Josh piped up.

His brother gave him a condescending glare, "It's *an* oscar, stupid. His name isn't Oscar." Then he looked at Bruno, obviously interested, for the answer.

Bruno gave Josh a smile, sorry for the tone of his brother's correction. With many brothers, he had been corrected many times in the same way as he grew up. He baited his hook and stood. He searched the nearby banks for what he was looking for and pointed to a small flock of spoonbills poking along in the grass. Then, wordlessly, he pointed again at a good-sized, patient gray heron nearby.

"Fish don't come from birds," Noah said dismissively.

"Oh yes they do," Bruno said. "Why would I shit you? I swear, fish can come from birds."

"No way," Noah said to his big-eyed younger brother.

"Yes way," Bruno insisted. "Josh, you see the birds are standing in the grasses don't you?"

Josh nodded, as did his skeptical older brother.

"Well, fish lay their eggs in the shallow water around those stalks of grass," Bruno continued. "The eggs stick to the birds' legs in one place, like in the Everglades. When the birds fly to another body of water, the eggs tag along. When the birds land and stand in the water in the grasses at another place, the eggs wash off. That's why fish seem to appear out of nowhere in canals and lakes where there might not have been fish before."

"No shit," Noah said, happily incredulous.

"No shit," Josh echoed.

"No shit," Bruno affirmed. "And there's other ways. I once saw an osprey drop a ten-pound bass right out of the sky and into the canal."

The boys gave him a long sideways look.

"I swear," Bruno said. "Now, what if that was a mama bass?"

"More eggs, right?" Josh asked tentatively.

"That's right, big guy. More fish!" Bruno said triumphantly as he turned and skillfully cast his line near the shore once more.

"Boys!"

The brothers' heads turned toward a familiar reproachful voice. It was at once commanding and slightly panicked. Meg Harden strode out her pool enclosure's door and made her way into the backyard and down the fence toward the canal. "What are you doing bothering Mr. Griffin?"

"They're not bothering me, it's okay," Bruno said as he reeled in his line and, smiling, turned to face her.

She stepped to the fence and gave him a tentative smile in return. "Even so, how did you boys get into Mr. Griffin's backyard?"

"We climbed the fence, Mom." Noah answered as if it was the only obvious answer.

Meg rolled her eyes. "Well, climb it again and come back into your own yard. Now!"

The boys gave Bruno a look betraying both resentment at being ordered about and also an exasperated surrender to feminine demand. He nodded sympathetically. Taking his fishing pole, he followed behind them. As they made their way back over the fence, he said, "I'm afraid I distracted them, not the other way around." Giving her a rueful grin and stepping up to the fence, perhaps closer than necessary, he continued, "I caught an oscar and they had to see it. It's no big deal. You know guys and fishing."

Meg, flustered by his physical closeness, took a step backwards. She became aware of his sweaty physicality by scent and well-built mass. Aware of how she was responding viscerally, her practical experience with overweening males kicked in and she stepped back to the fence. She was a woman not easily intimidated, yet she was a woman still. She lowered her eyes and tucked a stray strand of hair behind her ear before taking in the long length of Bruno with an appraising eye. She had to admit, he was an impressive man, if a gay one, all the same.

"Don't worry about them jumping the fence," Bruno continued. "It's no big deal. I'm not a jerk about things like that."

Meg smiled. "I appreciate that. Still, good fences make good neighbors. Don't let the boys get on your nerves. Boys, why don't you go see what your father is doing."

Aww, Mom." Noah said and jerked back from her reaching hand.

Meg cut him off with a look. "Tell Mr. Griffin goodbye."

The boys said their obligatory goodbyes and walked off toward the pool's screen door. Meg watched until they were out of earshot, then more warily she continued, "You have to understand, these days, we have to be careful with the boys . . . with . . . well, you know. You can't trust everyone not to . . . take advantage."

A light of recognition flickered in his eyes. Rather than being taken aback, Bruno's smile took on a more set cast. "Let me assure you, you have nothing to be concerned about in that regard on this side of the fence. From either of us." He coolly appraised her, "I hope you understand that."

Meg, used to professionally putting people off guard and gauging their reactions when she did, nodded. Point proffered and taken. "Thanks. I think we understand each other completely."

Bruno straightened his shoulders and nodded. "I'm glad we have that bit of unpleasantness out of the way, then. It would be very difficult to live next to each other, or to step out into my backyard, if you thought your boys would be in any type of danger every time I did."

Now Meg was taken aback. Hoping to blunt her harsh inference, quickly she replied, "Oh! I didn't mean that at all." She noted Bruno looking at her skeptically. "Please forgive me if I gave you that impression, really."

He searched her face and noted her discomfort, then gave her a sincere look saying, "The world is a crazy place these days. I understand your concern. There is nothing to forgive."

Thoroughly uncomfortable now, Meg offered him an embarrassed half laugh in return.

"Rory and I were talking. We feel like we haven't had the opportunity to welcome you properly to the neighborhood, things have been so busy lately," Bruno said.

"It has been crazy," Meg replied. "We're still getting settled."

"Boy do I know that feeling," Bruno answered. "Rory and I have been playing the real estate game since we've been together. It seems like we've moved every two years or so. It's a bitch, moving and meeting new people. Would you and Austin like to come for dinner some time?"

Meg was disarmed once more. While she had reconciled herself to having gay neighbors, she had never entertained a notion of socializing with them. The idea was alien, but could hardly be dismissed, offered as it was so openly, so genuinely. "That would be really nice of you guys. I'm not sure when . . ."

"How about two weeks from tonight? Is that enough time to plan ahead?" Bruno asked earnestly.

Meg was charmed by his sincere invitation and insistence. On top of that, he had the look of an endearing little boy for all his size and imposingly sweaty appearance. Meg considered it briefly and smiled. "I don't see why not, if we wouldn't be putting you out."

Bruno gave her a grin, the tenseness in his shoulders disappeared, and he said, "No, it would be really great. It'll give us a chance to get to know each other. We're nice guys if you give us a chance."

Meg laughed. "I never doubted you were. It's a date then, two weeks from tonight. I won't even need a sitter, being out just next door."

Bruno raised his arm to wipe the sweat from his forehead with the back of his forearm, making his bicep and triceps bunch impressively. "Great! We'll see you then if not before. And look, um . . . " he gave Meg a searching look.

"Meg. It's Meg," she encouraged extending her hand.

Bruno wiped his hand on the side of his shorts and grasped her hand gently, "Sorry, Meg. Your name disappeared for a second there." He looked her in the eye, "Until then, if you guys need anything. Anything at all, well, we're right next door, okay?"

Meg met his eye, then looked away suddenly shy. "Thanks, Will."

He laughed and let go of her hand. He took a step back from the fence and stretched his arms, palms out, as if to say "you can see why," but saying, "Bruno. You can call me Bruno."

Meg laughed. Deciding it would be well within bounds, and certainly to her advantage, she offered, "I think that's an ugly name for such a handsome man."

In response, Bruno blushed under his already sun-reddened skin and stagily kicked his toe in the grass and ducked his head, as if embarrassed as a six-year-old. "Aw shucks, ma'am," he said and gave her a long once-over under his long lashes. He stared appreciatively until Meg felt herself flush as well. Laughing pleasantly, they both turned back to their morning.

Bruno fished for awhile longer, congratulating himself on defusing an awkward situation with Meg Harden. As far as he was concerned, the best way to deal with the problem of Meg's reservations with living next door to him and Rory was to give her a chance to get to know them. It was a great deal harder to be a bigot if you broke bread with the people you really didn't know. That was the way he'd learned it could be when he'd divorced his wife and gone back to Rory.

It was Bruno who'd made the decision to go straight. From the way he'd looked at it as he was finishing his MBA, it would be a great deal easier to get ahead if he had a proper wife. For two years, he'd actually lived with Rory and dated her on the side. Once it became time to look for a job, he'd cast off Rory and married the woman. Living with her, and with himself, proved a lot harder than he'd projected it would be. Then, too, there was the fact that he was in love with Rory and missed him with a need and appetite that wouldn't be denied. When the choice came down to Rory and possible discrimination at work, or no Rory and a successful life with a woman he neither loved nor could force himself to care about, he'd chosen Rory. From the first, he'd confronted the whispers head-on and presented Rory to his world as if there could be no discussion on the issue. He'd brazened it out all those years ago with no ill effect on his career. Bruno handled potential snickers from his neighbors through the years in the same way.

It was Bruno's way of doing things. Growing up in a houseful of competitive brothers, he got nothing he wanted, from his parent's attention to his choice piece of chicken on the supper table, without sheer balls and brawn. He'd long since stopped questioning the need to bully his way through things; it worked in life and at work. If the same tack was what it took to be at ease in his own back yard, so be it. Still, the conversation with Meg Harden took some of the sheen off the morning for him. He cast his line out repeatedly, but he was lost in his own thoughts, too much so to be very productive as a fisherman.

He stood in the sun, enjoying the heat and his own defiance of Meg's unreasonable judgment, until he heard Bridget barking from the pool enclosure. He reeled in his line and looked around. Sure enough, Bridget was standing at the sliding glass door, baying with impatience. Rory was home. Happily he dumped the dwindling remainder of his bait into the canal and trudged up the sloping backyard. Once inside the pool enclosure, he made his way to Bridget.

Setting his pole against the wall of the house by the kitchen, he let himself and the dog inside. The kitchen was empty, but the door to the garage was open. He stepped through to find Rory hauling in the last of the grocery bags. "Hey," he said, and his heart filled with a bright sense of happiness.

"Hey," Rory said and gave him a smile. As he struggled past, Bruno blocked him and stooped to kiss him, ignoring the open garage door.

"Damn, I'm glad you're home," Bruno said as he allowed Rory to pass and managed to pull Bridget away from her own happy greeting.

Rory laughed. I thought you'd both be getting hungry. I brought you some fresh bread and some deli stuff. Close the garage door, you're letting all the air-conditioning out."

Obediently, Bruno pressed the button and was rewarded with the growl of the heavy door as it slid back into place. Then he folded his arms across his chest and leaned against the kitchen doorjamb, watching Rory as he placed the groceries on the counter and began to unload the bags. Rory was economical in his movements, but lithe. He reminded Bruno of a large cat moving concisely between counter, cabinets, and pantry. Bruno enjoyed just looking at him.

Finally, Rory looked at him and raised his eyebrows. "What are you doing over there?"

Bruno grinned. "Watching you. I'm always amazed watching you move around doing stuff. You're like a dancer."

Rory snorted and moved to the refrigerator. Opening it, he said, "You must want a beer." He took one out, opened it, and sat it on the counter of the bar. "Come sit down, you'll be more comfortable while I dance."

Without a word, Bruno moved to the bar and took his seat. The cold beer did sound appetizing and he was thirsty. He watched Rory as he took a long pull at the bottle, wondering how people like Meg could get it so wrong. How could he want to touch her children, or any one's children for that matter, when he had this man in his kitchen? This man he could touch and hold and love? This man who touched and loved him back was what his life was really all about. Embarrassed by his own introspection, he let out a loud burp and grinned at Rory.

"Nice," Rory commented as he unpacked the last of the groceries into the refrigerator and pulled out a beer of his own. He opened it as he came to stand close to Bruno on the opposite side of the bar. "You look like you've got some sun. Did you fish the whole time I was gone?"

"Pretty much," Bruno said. Then, "I had a nice chat with Meg from next door."

Rory nodded and took a gulping drink from his beer. Sighing with satisfaction, he burped as well and grinned back at Bruno. "So, what brought on all this sudden socialization?"

Bruno looked at him and scratched his shoulder thoughtfully. "The boys jumped the fence and came over while I was fishing. We were just standing around talking and she swooped out of the house like a mother hen."

Rory rolled his eyes. "Oh god. She thinks we're child molesters. I get so sick of that bullshit. Well, I hope you didn't invite them over for sensitivity training."

Bruno just gave him a look in reply.

"You did, didn't you?" Rory asked incredulously.

Bruno nodded and held up his hands.

"Damn it, Bruno! You know what happened the last time you did that when we moved to that place in Plantation. The neighbors turned out to be fundamentalists. The whole time we lived there they kept trying to get me to go to their church. You blew them off, but I still had to deal with it. These people are Baptists! Do you have any idea what those people are like? Smile in your face and spit at you behind your back. Why couldn't you just let them be? It's not my job to make the world comfortable with gay people."

Bruno reached across the counter and lifted Rory's beer high over his head. "You're going to need a cold drink after you stop spitting all that fire, pretty boy."

Disgustedly, Rory turned his back and stepped toward the refrigerator. He opened it and began loading his hands and the crook of his arm with sandwich makings. When he had all he could carry, he returned to the counter and began to place them in front of Bruno without saying a word.

"Don't pout, Rory. People will say you're spoiled," Bruno said.

Rory gave him a deadly look and returned to the cabinet for paper towels, bread, and utensils.

"Look, Rory. I don't want to feel this simmering around me all the time. If they come over for dinner, they'll have a chance to get to know us and not think we're going to fuck with their children every time they set foot outside."

Rory gave him another cutting look.

"I know. I get sick of it too. But it's not a bad idea, okay?" Bruno lowered Rory's beer and sat it back on the counter next to him.

Rory went around the bar and sat next to Bruno. Grudgingly, he smoothed a paper towel on the counter in front of Bruno, then put a knife on top of it. "I suppose I have to cook for them, too," he said.

"You'll make something wonderful, I bet. C'mon Rory . . ." Bruno cajoled.

"Exactly when is this love feast supposed to be?" Rory asked as he drew two slices of bread from the bag and laid them on his own paper towel.

"Two weeks from tonight," Bruno said gently.

Rory took a slug of his beer, and looked a Bruno with a forgiving half smile. "Okay, I'll feed 'em. They seem like nice enough people. But I don't want to give you the wrong idea, I don't intend to get all close to them. They can stay on their side of the fence as far as I'm concerned."

Bruno gave him a gentle shove with his shoulder. "You aren't very social, are you?"

Rory opened the mayonnaise jar and sighed. "Nope. Not with people I have nothing in common with."

Bruno dipped his knife into the mayonnaise jar and snickered. "You don't have anything in common with anyone these days, do you?"

Rory didn't answer. While he had never been very social to begin with, his opportunities had peeled away the further his moves with Bruno had taken him from Fort Lauderdale itself and their orbit had shifted to the western confines of the county. Now, apart from Bruno, the only people he ever saw were his occasional clients and the people in the shops he still frequented. There were people in his church he recognized each week, but a nod and a smile were all the interaction they required of him and vice versa. What friends he did have had moved on or deeper into their own tightly knit circles.

The fact was, Bruno was jealous. Though he didn't own up to it, he made it clear time and again that he preferred their friends to be held jointly and seen in common. While Rory felt secure in Bruno's possessiveness, he realized that because Bruno worked in the world while he worked from home, Bruno's range of social contacts far exceeded his own, and Bruno didn't mind keeping him at a disadvantage. There were times Rory wondered if Bruno cheated on him. He was oversexed and often away from home. At the selective rate at which he displayed Rory, Rory wondered if he had things to hide. All of these nagging thoughts he chalked up to living in an isolated, if satisfied way. While it made Rory wonder, it also made him less than happy to report the fresh news he had to tell Bruno.

Rory took a piece of sliced chicken and laid it on a slice of bread lightly covered with mayonnaise. "Guess who I ran into this morning?" he said carefully.

Bruno, busily completing his own sandwich, only gave him an encouraging glance.

"Dazz Coleman," Rory said speaking of a friend he did recall from their college days, and one who'd managed to appear and reappear in all the ensuing years since. Dazz was a go-getter, a black kid with a Rolodex full of contacts in a fledgling music scene who had gone on to become a producer. He'd surfaced in Charlotte when Bruno and Rory lived there after school, and he had gotten Rory a few gigs doing voice-overs and commercials. Eventually he'd moved to South Florida about the same time Bruno and Rory did to take advantage of the Miami hip-hop scene in its infancy. These days, Dazz rather grandly called himself a hip-hop impresario, but he was a good guy, and he never forgot a name or a talent.

"Where in the hell did you run into that slimeball?" Bruno said warily.

"At the Galleria," Rory replied openly.

"What the hell were you doing way downtown at the Galleria?" Bruno demanded.

"I wanted to go to Banana Republic. I have a meeting with a new client this week, and I want to look sharp," Rory said simply.

"I don't like you traipsing around the Gay-leria by yourself. Who knows what you might get into," Bruno said and took a surprisingly considered bite of his sandwich.

"For fuck's sake, Bruno. I'm forty years old. No one at the Galleria is going to cruise me. Buy a clue," Rory snorted.

Bruno chewed and swallowed determinedly. "Well, Dazz Coleman found you, didn't he? My guess is he's got some bullshit deal he thinks you'd be perfect for. What is it this time, radio spots for steam-cleaning carpet?"

Rory took a deep breath and tried to answer in a way that wouldn't betray his interest. "He's producing a new group, some black guys who are doing some interesting work."

"What's this new group got to do with you?" Bruno demanded.

Rory picked up his sandwich and held it thoughtfully in front of him. "They need a strong voice to sing backgrounds for these old songs by the Isley Brothers. They're doing this really acid jazz kinda funked-out mix of rap and singing for the new arrangements. Dazz thinks I'd be great. Right now there's no club dates or anything. It's just studio work," Rory said hopefully.

Bruno thought for a minute and took a bite of his sandwich. Around his mouthful of food, he mumbled, "So what did you tell him?"

Rory put his sandwich back down and half turned toward Bruno. "I told him to get me a CD to listen to and I'd think it over."

Bruno dropped the remains of his sandwich on his paper towel and picked up another to wipe his hands and mouth. "No way," he said decisively.

"Aw c'mon Bruno. It sounds like it could be fun. It's been a long time since I've done any singing. They may hate me, but I'd like to give it a shot," Rory pleaded.

"No fucking way. Dazz Coleman's been trying to separate you from me since college for some bullshit group. Why are you always so damn eager to jump into one of his crappy little deals? And rap? What the hell do you know about acid jazz or rap and funk? Besides, I need you here when I'm here, not out all night in some nigger studio in the goddamn 'hood. Tell him you thought about it and you decided no. End of story," Bruno said with finality.

"Bruno . . ."

"Ba-da-bing, Ba-da-boom," Bruno said, wiping his hands against each other sharply and then holding them out. "End of story."

Rory took a disappointed bite of his sandwich, then slipped the rest to Bridget who was waiting on the floor by his stool. He chewed the tasteless bit and took a draft of his beer wordlessly. The demo CD was in his car with Dazz Coleman's card. It could wait until Monday, he decided. Inside, he rebelled against Bruno's typical high-handedness. On Monday, with Bruno safely at work, he'd listen to the demo CD and make up his own mind. It wasn't worth fighting about at this point.

"Hey, you didn't eat your sandwich," Bruno said. "Bridget got it."

Rory gave him a half smile. "It wasn't what I expected," he said.

Bruno nodded and looked down to watch Bridget hungrily finish Rory's sandwich. "You should have given it to me," Bruno said. "I still want more."

## 5160 ST. MARK'S COURT

MEG TOOK A rare glass of white wine out onto the pool deck and settled herself on a chaise lounge facing the view across the canal. The view was phenomenal. In the sky overhead large billowing clouds floated as fleet and stately as schooners. The blue of the sky was deepened by the enormous pool enclosure's screen, and it looked like a fairy tale picture of a sky. Meg took a sip of her cold wine and sighed. It wouldn't be long now before Austin and the boys returned from Home Depot, but it would be long enough for her to have a cherished minute to herself, free from chores, free from files, and free from the ungainly male animals who seemed to collide with her every intention to keep them organized and reigned in. It was like living with a bunch of big dogs, Meg thought, big unruly dogs.

Meg had a friend named Sabrina whom she saw regularly at Noah and Josh's soccer practices. Sabrina had four boys, and while she handled them with an easy, rough affection that seemed to make them calm magically under her hand, Meg thought she'd rather taken an "if you can't beat 'em, join 'em" attitude. Sabrina was always comfortably dressed in a T-shirt and shorts that bore testament to other's sticky hands and bloodied cuts and scrapes. Her hair was styled for ease, not effect, and her hands always seemed to scream in painful need of a manicure. Meg shuddered inwardly at the thought.

While she had to live in a world of boys, she had no intention of letting herself go to the extent Sabrina had. Though Sabrina's boys seemed to adore her, their adoration of their mother came at a price to Sabrina's femininity that Meg wasn't willing to pay.

Then, too, Sabrina's boys were a profane, rough-mouthed, scrappy bunch of brutes as far as Meg was concerned. They swore. They rough-housed. And they always seemed dirty to Meg. While she conceded that boys weren't meant to be delicate flowers, she had no intention of letting her boys grow up to be so uncouth. It was part of her self-identity that she could raise masculine little men who didn't scratch at themselves as if they had fleas or collapse into laughter at the thought of passing gas. And they watched their mouths around her as well. Thinking of these things, she nodded to herself and took a sip of her wine. Tiredly, she dropped her head to rest on the chaise lounge's back and sighed.

Distracted by her train of thought, Meg found Austin's unwitting form in the clouds over her head. Fondly, she thought of him much the same as she did her boys. He had their effortless enthusiasm and curiosity, or at least he once did. These days he seemed diminished by circumstance. She knew he was discouraged and disheartened by his new job. Somehow, she wished he could see through the current moment and resource his imagination. She knew he wasn't doing what made him happy, but she believed he was responsible for getting over that. She believed in him; she only wished he believed more in himself.

Meg took another drink from her cool glass. The ease the wine promised was stealing over her. She felt herself relax and became aware of how pleasant the rough texture of the lounge chair's weave felt under her feet. She drew them up with a bend of her knees and shivered slightly as the movement sent a wave of pleasure up her legs to settle near her groin. For now, this moment, that was satisfying enough. And that discrete knowledge brought to mind another nagging concern about Austin. It had to do with sex.

She wished Austin could understand that he wasn't attractive as he turned to her out of dissatisfaction with his life right now. His near-constant hovering with his hang-dog expression was certainly not sexy. In fact, it put her right off the idea. To her, his physical neediness reminded her of the boys when they demanded a closeness out of their own insecurity and unexamined hunger for her attention and care. She needed Austin to be masterful and assured, not pawing at her like an ignored dog.

Meg allowed her feet to slide back down the length of the lounge chair's surface. Their return to the end of its reach was no longer satisfying in its friction. Meg sighed once more. She realized she hadn't really been in the mood for sex in any event, all of Austin's problems aside. Her work was, quite simply, a bitch. Every day, in every way, she felt as if she was constantly under scrutiny and subjected to a microscopic examination of her every potential oversight and possible flaw. She was a professional. She knew the level of insight, detail, and discernment she brought to her caseload. She knew she could perform, but she also knew she'd risen very quickly to the position she'd attained, and she knew how many people would like to see her fail and fall. That was one thing she would not allow to happen. She would not, she absolutely would not, let her attention or control flag for one moment. She wouldn't at work, and she wouldn't at home.

Meg drained her glass of the remainder of her wine and stretched her arms up over her head. The sudden weight of tension drained down her arms to puddle in her shoulders. She dropped her arms and rolled her head from the neck to ease the stress. From the corner of her eye, she caught sight of the Griffin-Fallon's backyard and stretch of canal, empty now of Bruno's broad back, long legs, and handsome face watching the water for the tug on his fishing line. *Now that one,* Meg thought, *ain't nothing but a man.*

She allowed herself a moment to categorize Bruno's best features, from his hard jaw to his slim, flat waist improbably supporting those shoulders and deep chest covered with just the right amount of comforting black hair. He was something to look, at she grudgingly admitted. He was also somewhat winning when he wanted to be. She recalled his bashfulness when she remarked on his looks. It seemed too genuine to fake, but then again, the man was probably used to being assessed frankly and admiringly. Still, it was fun to flirt, especially when there was no real threat of it becoming anything more than it was. Meg decided he was a handsome idiot. Not bad to look at, probably pleasant to know, but ultimately a lightweight. His being gay obviated everything about him that could be so appealing.

She heard a sliding glass door move along its track across the way and turned her head to see who would appear. She was rewarded with a glimpse of the other one and the sight of their absurdly huge dog lumbering out onto their pool deck. Quietly, the sliding glass door closed against the heat and the dog settled itself with a thud near the lip of their pool.

Meg turned her head guiltily. She didn't want the other one to think she was overly concerned with their comings and goings. She searched for his name briefly until it appeared to her. *Rory*, she thought, *His name is Rory*. Try as she might, she could place neither of them from their college days, though Austin claimed they went to the same school. She pictured the man in her mind. What she recalled was a form lean and somewhat fey until his face appeared from her memory. Sleepy-eyed and slightly freckled, was her impression of Rory. He didn't strike her as a man who would put himself forward in any way. In fact, he seemed diminished by his boyfriend's obvious presence. She dismissed him out of hand.

Carefully, she placed her wine glass on the brick pavers of the pool deck, then let the back of the lounge chair down a couple of notches. She leaned back, gratefully surrendering herself to the wine's pull toward drowsiness. She recalled how quickly Bruno had responded to her concerns about the boys being next door. While she knew not every gay man was a child molester, she decided it would be better if he and his partner felt she did. It put them on the defensive in a way she could work with. One way or another, it was just a matter of handling men, and that was something she'd learned to do well. Gay or straight, they all were the same as far as she was concerned. The only difference was where they put their peckers. In that, they all were preoccupied and dimwitted in their single-minded focus.

Curiously, she thought of Bruno Griffin and Rory Fallon together. As far as she could recall, Rory was the slick and pretty one. It wasn't hard to imagine him in the passive role. She tried to picture him naked and only came up with a feminine blur. Rejecting the image dismissively, she turned her imagination to Bruno. His naked form was easier to imagine after seeing him shirtless and shorts-clad earlier in the day. Idly, she tried to imagine his penis and giggled to herself.

Closing her eyes against the brightness of the afternoon, she pictured Bruno hunched in concentration. His penis stood out as veined, gnarled, and knobbed as the shillelagh her father kept in the umbrella stand in the foyer back home. In response to the impressive notion, she drew her feet up against the lounge chair's fabric once more, enjoying the texture on the soles of her feet. She parted her legs and gripped the sides of the chair's frame with her toes. Bruno approached her as he tugged his ungainly penis, urging it downward as he moved between her legs. A heedless shiver of anticipation ran up her spine as she imagined the thought his weight sinking on top of her.

The sliding glass door slid open abruptly and Josh stepped from the family room onto the pool deck. "Mom?"

Meg jerked her knees together and raised her head and shoulders in abrupt and shame-faced alarm. "What?" She demanded sharply.

Josh's happy face fell. He stepped back into the family room as if she'd slapped him. "We're back," he said quietly.

Meg swung her legs over the side of the lounge chair and sat up guiltily. "I'm sorry sweetheart. You startled me. I didn't mean to snap at you," she said.

Josh nodded and backed further into the family room. "Dad wants you to come see. He bought you a present," he said warily.

Meg opened her arms and said softly, "Come here Joshie and give your mean ol' mama a hug."

The little fellow brightened and hurried toward her with arms outstretched. When he was close enough for her to grasp, his sneaker kicked her wine glass and sent it crashing across the pavers to the wall behind her lounge chair, where it stopped in tiny sharp shards of breakage. Guiltily, the little boy jerked back from his mother's grasp and looked at her with alarm. "I'm sorry! I didn't mean to do it," he cried.

Meg stole a look at the broken glass and then found the little fellow's face. Her mind registered the fact that the glass was one of a set of four, now diminished to an odd group of three. At the same time, she noted the panic in Josh's eyes. Her heart broke a little at his display of fear of her reaction. He was as thoughtless as a lumbering puppy, but he was her puppy, it seemed, and she had made him afraid of her. Quietly she said, "Don't worry about it, Josh. It's only a glass."

Josh looked at her dubiously. "I can clean it up," he offered.

She pictured him running with the broom and dustpan, stumbling, and falling face first into the sharp mess. "No," she said firmly. "You might cut yourself. I'll take care of it."

"I'm sorry, Mom," Josh offered once more.

Meg sighed and stood. "Don't worry about it, Josh. It's just a glass."

"You want to come see your present?" He asked tentatively. "Dad had to take us to Home Expo to get it. They didn't have one at Home Depot."

Meg smiled at him as she walked to the door. If she didn't follow him right away, any surprise would be forfeited by his eagerness to make her feel better. "Well, let's go see what I got, okay?"

Josh rewarded her by taking her hand and tugging her into the family room. "Dad says you've been wanting one," he urged.

Meg laughed. "Well, don't tell me what it is. That'll spoil the surprise."

Josh let go of her hand and nodded gravely. Without another word, he turned and headed past the kitchen toward the living room. Meg watched him go, feeling the absence of his warm little hand in her own as she followed.

When she arrived in the living room a few steps behind Josh, Noah and Austin were pushing the sofa that sat under a large painting away from the wall. "What's going on?" She demanded gently.

Austin looked at her and smiled. "Look in the bag," he said motioning toward her antique writing desk that stood on slim, elegant legs against the narrow wall by the foyer.

Josh scampered around the sofa ahead of her and tugged the bag from the writing table's top, pulling the leather blotter that it sat on along with it. She managed to reach the table before the blotter fell along with the silver pen stand, inkwell, and sand shaker crowded under the bag. She shoved the leather blotter and accessories back just in time. Josh gave her a worried look as he handed her the bag, but she only stroked the fair hair off his forehead before sitting on the sofa now askew in the middle of the area rug.

Austin walked around to sit beside her. Noah perched on the sofa's back and Josh settled by her feet. "This is like Christmas," she said happily.

"Open it," Austin urged.

Meg reached inside the bag and pulled out a long, narrow box with a picture of a painting light gleaming over an impressively framed old master work." She looked at Austin with a delighted smile. She'd been hankering for a light over her living room painting for years. While it was no old master, it was a large painting she and Austin had circled back to after three circuits around the Coconut Grove Arts Festival when Noah was only a baby in a stroller. It was impossibly expensive and set back their goal to pay off Mastercard for nearly a year, but Meg loved it all the more for the effort to make it their own.

Eagerly, Austin took the box from her. "It is the largest one they make. And, I remembered to get the antique brass finish you wanted," he said proudly.

Meg kissed him in reply, delighted with her present.

"Open it, Dad" Noah urged.

"Why don't you boys run go get me my tool box from the garage," Austin laughed. "And we'll get it put up right away."

Noah swung his legs over the back of the sofa and bounded off a cushion, leaving shoe prints on the pale blue fabric. Josh took off after him. Meg smiled and brushed at the marks and dirt Noah's sneakers had left beside her. She was too happy to make a big deal out of it. Every night, when she walked in the front door, she imagined the luminous glow of a light over her painting welcoming her home. It would be a meaningful testament to her own hard work and bespoke a kind of graciousness in her life and tastes, she thought. Impulsively, she put her arm over Austin's shoulder and gave his neck a playful squeeze.

Intent on getting the box open, Austin shrugged off her embrace, but tossed her a happy grin to show he appreciated the gesture. She watched as he freed the light fixture from its cardboard packing and plastic sheath. He tilted the box and was rewarded with another plastic bag containing a face plate, screws, and wire twists. He looked in the empty box again, gritted his teeth, and said, "Shit!"

"What's wrong?" Meg asked with an indulgent patience won from Austin's typical ineptitude around things requiring a certain type of handiness.

Austin turned the painting light over in his hands and slumped. "It doesn't have a plug. It has to be hardwired to a switch. Oh for fuck's sake."

The boys reappeared excitedly with a plastic tool box that rattled promisingly. Hearing their father's frustration, they stilled and looked at him anxiously.

"It's no big deal, Austin," Meg said calmly.

He looked at her with sheer disbelief. "It is a big deal. It means pulling a wire. It means using tools I don't have. It means I'll have to pay a damn electrician to get it working," he said furiously. "You know Meg, sometimes it seems like I can't get a damn thing right around here."

Josh sat the tool box on the floor within his father's reach and backed away, sensing a sudden parental storm he hadn't expected.

Meg patted his shoulder and gave the boys a conspiratorial look. Smiling, she said, "Look, isn't Rory next door an electrician? Maybe he can give you a hand."

Austin dropped the lamp on the cushion next to him and caught Noah smirking back at his mother. "Great idea, Meg," he said as he stood. "Why don't I go get a gay guy to show me how to wire a lamp. Why not?" Disregarding Meg, he shoved his end of the sofa back into place against the wall with two serious pushes.

Speechless, Meg and the boys simply looked at him. In sheer frustration he glared at the boys and said, "Worthless. This is just fucking worthless."

"Dad, maybe we could just . . . " Noah offered.

"Just what? Just what, Noah? Jury-rig it? No, it has to be done right, and your old man can't do this right, okay?"

Noah hung his head.

"Austin . . . " Meg began.

He shook his head and shoulders like an enraged lion and then became stock still, with another sudden mood shift taking him from angry frustration to simple defeat. Wearily, Austin said, "Josh, please put the tool box back where you found it. I wish we could get this up today, but we can't. Noah, help your mother get the sofa back against the wall." With that he looked shamefacedly at Meg. "I'm going for a walk."

"Sweetheart . . . " Meg began again.

Austin simply held up his hand, turned on his heel, and walked out the front door. Meg and the boys watched as he closed it gently behind him.

Meg sighed, her mind turning to what she could make better. "Josh, on your way back from the garage, please bring me the broom and dustpan so I can sweep up the mess by the pool."

Josh nodded, picked up the tool box, and backed away.

Meg stood and looked at Noah calmly. "Give me a hand with the sofa, okay?"

Noah stepped around her and shoved his end of the sofa back into place before she could turn to help him. Done, he looked at her proudly. Meg nodded and gave him a small smile.

"Mom, why was Dad so pissed off? It's just a stupid lamp."

Meg looked at him tenderly, but only said, "Don't say *pissed off*, Noah."

# CHAPTER FIVE

# What a lovely home

RORY WIPED HIS hands with a dish towel and looked around the kitchen and family room. Everything looked okay on final inspection, but Bruno had a way of growing clutter in his path like Mother Nature strew spring flowers as she passed. Harmlessly enough, Bruno was kneeling by the rack of audio equipment under the flat-screen TV, feeding CDs into their player. The empty cases were neatly stacked back on top.

"What did you choose?" Rory asked.

Absently, Bruno replied, "The Essential Luther Vandross, the new Jack Johnson, Wayman Tisdale, Grover Washington's Winelight, and, to spike things up some, some old Dire Straits, and that acid jazz rap thing you got from Dazz Coleman when I told you not to."

"What do you think of it?" Rory asked cautiously.

Bruno got to his feet and shrugged. "It's not really my kind of deal, but it's not bad. So, what did you tell Dazz?"

"It's only a few days of studio work, Will."

Bruno walked to the bar and picked up his glass of wine. "So it's Will now, is it? How much is he going to pay you?"

Rory carefully folded the dishcloth in his hands and placed it next to the sink before he met Bruno's eyes. "Not much point in talking about money until they decide if they want me, is there?"

Bruno took a sip of his wine and gave Rory an appraising look before sitting his glass back on the bar. "So how does this fit in with your clients?"

Rory stood in the glare of the overhead lights and stared at him. "I'm slack right now. The new client has me on hold until they get the lease signed for their space. They said they'd call by the middle of next month."

"When do you try out?" Bruno said.

"They're waiting for their keyboardist to get in from D.C. They want me to try out with the entire group. It should be some time next week, maybe as much as ten days."

Bruno nodded and said, "And just when did you plan to tell me you were going ahead with this? When they'd made their decision?"

Rory laughed and moved closer to him. "I figured there was no need to get you all freaked out unless there was something to be freaked out about."

Bruno nodded once more, then picked up his wine glass and drained it. "Sneaky little fuck, aren't you?"

"Aw c'mon, Will. It's not like that and you know it. It's just something I want to do. How long has it been since I had the chance to sing? They may hate me, but what's the harm in trying?"

The doorbell rang and Bridget started awake and let out a deep long baying. Bruno's eyes followed the sound back to the foyer. "This discussion isn't over," he said as he headed to the door.

Rory caught Bridget by the collar as she trotted after Bruno and steered her into the bedroom. Once she had found her place on the foot of the bed, he ran his fingers through his hair to get it out of his eyes, closed the door, and tiredly walked to the foyer. Secretly he hoped the Hardens hadn't brought flowers. He hated it when guests brought flowers. It meant hunting for a vase, trimming the stems, and finding a place for them when all he wanted to do by the time guests arrived was have a glass of wine and relax a bit before he had to start serving dinner.

Bruno opened the door and warmly welcomed the Hardens inside.

He shook hands with Meg, then Austin, and steered them toward Rory waiting behind him. Shyly, Meg extended a bottle of wine instead of a bouquet of flowers hastily bought at Publix. Rory smiled as he took it and welcomed her by taking her hand in his. Austin was waiting behind her with his hand extended. Bruno stepped between them and, taking Meg's elbow, offered the couple a tour of the house.

Austin glanced at his hand extended awkwardly and gave Rory a shy smile. Rory switched the bottle of wine he was holding and clumsily offered his own to shake. As they both laughed, Austin gripped his hand warmly and thanked him for having them over.

Rory squeezed his hand in return and waited for Austin to let his hand go. Austin held on just a beat too long and looked past Rory to where his wife and Bruno stood in the living room. Gently, Rory took his hand back. At once, Austin looked back at him and laughed again nervously.

"A little overwhelmed?" Rory asked with a smile, nodding toward Bruno.

Austin smiled. "I'm a little out of practice with social things," he said.

"It gets easier, I promise," Rory replied. "You're missing the tour."

"Coming along?" Austin asked hopefully.

Rory nodded and lead him into the living room where Bruno and Meg were examining the paintings that lined the walls. As Austin and Rory joined them, Bruno was pointing out a near-nude figure draped in dark wings, prominently featured at the side of the center painting. "That's me," he said proudly.

Meg leaned in for a better look, as did Austin. "My god, it is you," Meg said, her voice betraying both admiration and a hint of hesitation. She leaned back from the painting and gave Bruno an admiring once-over. "You haven't changed a bit."

Bruno laughed. "I've had my wings clipped, though."

Austin's eyes flared with recognition. "These are from your senior show, aren't they Rory?"

Rory nodded and smiled.

"You did these in college? Were you copying Raphael or Michelangelo? Someone like that?" Meg asked earnestly.

"Tiepolo, actually," Rory said and laughed. "Do you recognize the school library in this one," he said, pointing, "and the front of the art building in that one?"

Austin and Meg both leaned closer for a better look. "I need my glasses," Meg apologized.

"Yes, that is the library and the art school both," Austin announced, pleased.

"That one's Rory," Bruno said, pointing to another nearly nude angel, this time with white wings.

Meg and Austin stepped to the right to get a better view of the figure. Meg gasped. "It is you!" Her eyes swept Rory and generously she said, "And you haven't changed a bit either."

Austin turned to Rory and said, "A few weeks ago you said your senior show almost made you flunk out. Was it the paintings or your band playing?"

"They loved the band. They said it was the most original part of the exhibit," Rory snorted. "It was these paintings they hated."

"Why?" Meg asked. "These paintings are very good."

Bruno looked at Rory and grinned. "The art faculty didn't enjoy having their leg pulled. They had no sense of humor." Meg and Austin looked confused. "Show them Rory," he prodded.

Rory gestured at the characters inhabiting the paintings. "All of these characters are real people. Classmates. Teachers. What I did was take some of Tiepolo's paintings that showed these historical visits or whatever, and painted the people from the art school as the characters. This fawning cardinal? He's the head of the Art Department. The person he's welcoming is supposed to be the king of France. I gave him the the face of the vice-chancellor for academic affairs. Everything is contemporary but the costumes and poses. That's why the buildings are from campus and not from Venice."

"But that's a really interesting idea. Why did they have a problem with it?" Meg asked.

"They said it wasn't very imaginative," Rory explained. "All of my classmates in the painting program were showing these tedious, neurotic, nonrepresentational things. I like representational art . . . ,"

"Beside the fact he can actually draw," Bruno interjected.

Rory gave him a pleasant nod of the head and then looked at Meg once more. "Anyway, the senior show committee said it wasn't painting, it was illustration. They gave me a D for the semester's work."

"That's not fair," Meg said indignantly.

Rory gave her a smile. "It was all a long time ago. No big deal."

"So what are you painting now?" Meg asked.

Bruno gave him a pointed look. Rory ignored it. "I don't really paint anymore," he said. "I'm really just an electrician these days."

"Why aren't you still painting?" Austin asked. "These are very good."

"That's what I keep telling him," Bruno agreed. "I encourage him all the time, but he doesn't listen to me. He'd rather sing with some bullshit . . . "

"Not now, Bruno." Rory said firmly.

"You're singing again? That's great! You were fantastic the one time I saw you. It was this show," Austin said gesturing at the paintings.

"Tell them, star child," Bruno said and laughed snidely.

Rory cut him a sharp glance and shook his head. "Look, it's nothing really," he said to Austin. "I don't want to get into it."

"Rory has an audition in a week or so with some whacked out jazz funk rap fusion bullshit group that won't pay him squat. But you want to do it for creative reasons, don't you Rory? Stretch your boundaries or something, that right?" Bruno asked tauntingly.

"Maybe," Rory said. "We'll see."

Meg and Austin looked distinctly confused and uncomfortable with their exchange. They glanced from Rory to Bruno with pleasant smiles glued to their faces. Finally, Austin said, "I never got why you played at the senior show. I mean the band was great, but I wasn't sure why . . . you know?"

Rory shifted the bottle of wine from one hand to the other and looked to Bruno for help. Bruno only looked back at him, waiting along with Meg and Austin for an answer. He took a deep breath, looked at Austin, and said, "It was for a couple of reasons. Both of them personal."

Obviously, all three were eager to hear more. Rory wished they could just let it go, but their rapt attention demanded he continue. He straightened his shoulders and went on, "For one thing, the whole art school thing was so artificial. The most real thing in my life back then was the band. The other thing was Bruno. For the show, I dressed us up in the same wings we had on in the painting. It was like the words from the song "Best of Both Worlds" by Van Halen. In a gravelly voice, he half sang, half spoke:

*There's a picture in a gallery*
*of a fallen angel*
*Looked a lot like you*

Rory stopped singing and looked at each of them briefly before pointedly examining the picture of the black-winged angel. "I was so in love with Bruno. I really . . . I wanted the whole world to know it. I know that sounds stupid, but that's what you do when you're young, you go for the big statement." Half laughing, he stepped away from them and said to no one in particular, "And, I guess you don't mind making a fool out of yourself in the process."

For a moment, no one said anything, then Meg said, "That's probably one of the most touching things I've ever heard."

Bruno, who'd shut up for once, only offered him a quiet smile.

Austin focused his attention on the self-portrait Rory had painted at twenty-two, his neck and cheeks flushed.

"Well, enough of that," Rory said. "Can I get you some wine?"

There were murmurs of assent all around. "Let me show you my office," Bruno said. Rory left the room without another word as Bruno shepherded the Hardens toward his lair adjoining the living room.

In the kitchen, Rory opened another bottle of wine and poured it out into four fresh glasses. He emptied the dirty ones he and Bruno had abandoned to answer the door and loaded them into the dishwasher. Then he took the cling wrap off a platter of cheese and fruit and walked it over to the coffee table. Already he wished the evening were over, and dinner hadn't even been served. He made sure there were small plates within reach for the cheese and fruit on the coffee table before making his way back to check on the roast chicken resting in its pan on the stove. Before he could think about slicing it, Bruno and the Hardens made their way into the family room. Smiling graciously, he waited for Bruno to seat them on the leather sectional and then served them their wine.

The evening proceeded smoothly from that point through dinner, eased by a great deal of wine and a remarkably well-received chicken with an orzo and roasted vegetable dish that Rory had cribbed from the Barefoot Contessa. Bruno and the Hardens ate appreciatively and the conversation progressed from the merely polite to the sincerely genial.

Over dessert, Meg gestured toward the paintings in the living room and said, "I love the lights over your paintings, Rory. Tell me, is that something you can put up?"

Rory smiled indulgently and said, "Yes, I did those, as a matter of fact."

"Meg," Austin said anxiously.

She laughed and continued, "I'd hoped you did. You see, we just bought one, thinking the cord just ran down the back behind this painting we have in our living room, but it turned out to be one that has to be wired through the wall. Austin is hopeless with things like that; could you possibly give him a hand getting ours up?"

Austin turned beet red in embarrassment.

Noting Austin's discomfort and Meg's obliviousness to it, Rory directed his answer to him. "I'll be happy to give you a hand, Austin."

"I apologize for my wife," Austin said. "She has no idea when she's imposing."

Bruno noted Meg's own flush at Austin's reply. Before she could retort, he said, "It's no imposition, is it, Rory? It'll take no time at all to pull a wire and get it hooked up."

Rory nodded and smiled.

"It's not that Austin probably couldn't do it, he's just not used to doing it, that's all," Meg offered quietly. "And he doesn't have the proper tools, do you sweetheart?"

Austin looked at his dessert, forlorn and half-eaten on his plate. "No, I'm afraid I'm all thumbs with stuff like that, I admit it."

"Nothing to be ashamed of, big guy," Bruno said, "I can't screw in a light bulb without Rory. Hell, I thought the ceiling fans only blew one way until Rory showed me this little switch on the motor that you flick up or down depending on the season."

"You do what?" Meg asked.

"The blades push warm air down from the ceiling in wintertime. You flick it and they pull the cold air up in summer. Who knew?" Bruno said with a laugh.

"I didn't know that," Meg said. "I thought they just blew one way all the time."

"You could just wire the lamp with a cord and plug; couldn't you Rory?" Austin suggested hopefully. "I don't want to take your time pulling wires to a switch. There's a plug on the wall straight down from where the lamp is supposed to go. We could just plug it in there."

Meg looked at Rory appealingly. Rory knew she didn't want an ugly cord snaking down her living room wall. He winked at Austin and said, "Take it easy. We'll do it right. If the lamp has a switch on the fixture, we could wire it into the outlet below and you could turn it off and on from the fixture itself. That'll be a lot easier than pulling a wire behind more drywall, through studs to a switch. It won't take long."

"You can do that?" Meg asked happily.

"It's just magic," Bruno said and laughed.

"Is it dangerous to wire it into the plug?" Meg asked.

Rory smiled. "No. The lamp doesn't pull that much load. I promise not to do anything that will burn your house down."

"I'll check the lamp, if you're sure you don't mind, Rory," Austin said and glared at is wife.

"It's okay, Austin." Rory said reassuringly. "Eat your cake and don't worry about it. We'll git 'er done," he growled.

"Git 'er done," Bruno growled in return.

Meg and Austin looked at them, dumbfounded.

"Larry the Cable Guy, from *Blue Collar TV* . . . you know, *git 'er done*," Rory said. Noting their polite blank looks, he said: "The Comedy Channel?"

"We don't get a chance to watch much TV," Austin said apologetically. "You guys much watch a lot."

"No wonder you get our boys' jokes," Meg said appreciatively. "Half the time what they say goes straight over my head. I watched South Park with them that one time and I thought it would curl my hair."

Bruno lifted his brows and nodded at Meg with a neutral expression in reply.

"We like to watch TV later in the evenings, but we're not addicts or anything," Rory explained evenly. "We don't even have any premium channels, but Bruno likes to watch and unwind before bed."

"Must be nice," Austin snorted. "Meg settles into her evening with her legal files strewn all over the bed. She falls asleep with them in her hand. Sometimes it takes me fifteen minutes to put them away, *neatly*, before I can get into bed."

"I have to bring work home," Meg said, obviously hurt. "There are just not enough hours in the day."

Austin simply rolled his eyes in response.

Bruno noted the exchange and intercepted the ball. "I'm sure it's tough, Meg. You don't get to be a partner without putting in some long hours."

"No, you don't get to be a partner without letting everything else slide," Austin said nastily.

"You don't get a better job sitting on your ass playing computer poker either do you, sweetheart," Meg said icily.

Rory glanced at Bruno and stood. "I think I'll get these dessert things cleared. Austin, are you finished?"

Meg stood a little unsteadily and picked up the plate holding the rest of Austin's half-eaten cake before he could answer. "Let me give you a hand, Rory. It is so nice to have someone else cook for a change. The least I can do is help you clear the table."

Bruno stood as well. "Austin, why don't you come with me. We'll leave the wives to it."

"Gee, thanks," Rory said and laughed as he made his way into the kitchen.

Austin stood and made his way around the table. Bruno waited for him, and once he got within reach Bruno threw a heavy arm over his shoulders to lead him to the pool deck through the living room doors, avoiding the kitchen with sure determination.

In the kitchen, Rory left Meg to place Austin's dessert plate in the sink while he stepped through the family room to let Bridget out of the bedroom. When he returned, Bridget trudged along beside him until she caught sight of Meg. Promptly, she walked over and gave the woman a good sniff.

Meg froze and stood looking down at the huge dog as if it might suddenly tear her leg off. "My goodness, aren't you a big girl? Do you bite?" She asked nervously.

Rory glanced at Meg standing pinned against the counter and fought a smile. Deftly, he took Bridget's bowl from the floor and lifted it to the counter. "She's a love pig. Don't let her intimidate you."

Bridget caught his movement and promptly rushed to Rory's side in anticipation of being fed an unusual late-night snack. Meg watched as Rory slid the remains of the orzo and roasted vegetables into the dog's bowl. She made a little moue of distaste and said, "Does she eat people food all the time?"

Rory stooped and put the bowl on the floor, where Bridget immediately began slurping it with relish. Rory patted her big head and gave Meg a smile. "No, she usually eats dog food, but she was so well-behaved tonight I thought she deserved a treat. You guys don't have pets, do you?"

Meg watched Bridget as she untidily licked the inside of her bowl spraying small pieces of orzo on the floor. Barely disguising her repugnance, she said, "No. I've never been a big fan of animals in the house. The boys are bad enough."

Rory leaned against the counter and watched as Bridget nosed her now empty bowl out of the way and began to lick the stray remains off the floor. "We've always had mastiffs. Bridget is our third. Bruno got me the first one when he walked out on me to get married. He gave me a mastiff puppy because he said it would remind me of him and keep me company. The idiot."

Meg glanced toward the pool deck outside the sliding glass door. She could just make out Bruno's back blocking Austin from sight. She glanced back to Rory and, studiedly hiding her interest, said, "Oh? Bruno was married?"

Rory sighed and said, "C'mon Bridget. Let's go see Daddy Bruno." The big dog trotted happily toward the door and Rory followed along behind to obligingly let her out. Once she had made it outside, he closed the door against the lingering heat and smiled at Meg. When he'd made his way back to the counter, he said, "He was married for just over a year after he got his MBA. We lived in Charlotte then."

Meg nodded uncomfortably. "Whatever happened to his wife?"

Rory stepped around her to the sink and began rinsing the dessert dishes. "She's remarried. The last he heard from her, she's happy. Has a couple of kids now, I believe."

"That must have been difficult," Meg said evenly.

Rory opened the door of the dishwasher and placed the plates inside. "It just about killed me. Bruno left, but he wouldn't stay gone. He couldn't deal with committing himself to either me or her. It was a pretty rough time."

Meg shifted her weight to her other foot and watched him load the flatware into its basket. "What about his wife?"

Rory glanced around the counter, looking for stray dirty dishes. Satisfied the counter was clear, he closed the dishwasher door and gave Meg a direct look. "I really don't know. It was hard for me to be empathetic. You see, as far as I was concerned, she was the interloper. Bruno and I had been together for four years before he met her. She was just an easy answer for him."

"What do you mean?" Meg asked carefully.

"Well, it's sort of the path of least resistance when you're in a world like Bruno's. Everyone else has a pretty wife and two-point-three kids. It automatically makes you a member of the old boy's club, hail fellow well met, all of that crap. It takes a lot of guts to make it in that world when you buck the system and want to create a life with another guy."

Meg gave him a direct look. "Well, I suppose your circumstances aren't very typical in the real world."

Rory responded with a raised eyebrow. He knocked on the counter beside him, then folded his arms across his chest. "I don't know . . . our world seems pretty real to me. We have a real mortgage and a light bill that wants to be paid in real money."

Meg flushed with embarrassment. "I'm sorry. I didn't mean to imply . . .

Rory nodded. "Would you like another glass of wine? I'd love to finish up the bottle."

Meg knew he was letting her out of that particular conversational dead end. "Yes. I'd be happy to help you finish off the bottle if there's enough to share."

"I believe there is." Rory turned and reached into the cabinet behind him and took out a pair of clean glasses. He placed them on the counter within Meg's reach and said, "I'll be right back. I think we left the rest of the wine on the dining room table."

Gratefully, Meg watched him go. Her eyes fled around the large, neat kitchen looking for anything to comment upon to change the course of the conversation. At the opposite end of the bar, she saw a framed eight-by-ten picture sitting on a small easel. It was part of a small tableau that included a figurine and a white candle burning in a tall glass jar. She walked toward it to get a better look.

The picture looked to be quite old. It was a picture of Jesus Christ from the waist up, regarding her with infinite patience and a languid hand pointing to his breast where a heart rested, blood red, laced by thorns and topped by a gold crown. It looked almost kitschy, but it was far too reverent an image, rendered far too romantically, to be anything less than sincere. Next to the picture, opposite the candle, was a small statue of the Holy Family. Joseph led a donkey on which the Virgin Mary rode, holding the baby Jesus in her arms. Like the picture, the figurine looked to be very antiquated.

"It's a picture of the Sacred Heart," Rory said, startling her. "It was my grandmother's."

Meg stood back as if she'd been caught prying. "It's lovely," she said quietly.

Rory smiled. "Catholics believe Christ promised special blessings for a home that displays a picture of his Sacred Heart. I know it's old-fashioned to believe such things, but . . . "

"No, not at all." Meg interrupted. "I respect the fact you don't mind putting what you believe on display."

Rory nodded and stepped past her to the glasses he'd left behind. He poured the wine carefully and said, "My grandmother kept that picture hanging in her kitchen. She said that was the heart of the home. I'd hang it up, but in this open, big-ego kitchen, there's no clear wall space, really. And, there's nowhere to put the vigil candle."

Meg looked back at the face of Christ with something near guilt. As Rory handed her a glass of wine, she asked, "Why do you burn the candle next to it?"

Rory took a sip of wine and said, "The flame represents the Holy Spirit's presence in our home. Every morning, I say a prayer and light the candle. You're supposed to let it burn all the time, but Bruno doesn't like me leaving it lit when we're in bed asleep. He's terrified it will catch something on fire. Come sit," he urged and turned toward the sofa in the family room.

Meg looked again at the picture and saw something cold and mean in herself that she recognized with a dawning sense of shame. She followed Rory into the family room and perched across from him on the sofa. "We Christians believe that once you let Christ inside your heart, you have no need for pictures and statues and things. One of the Ten Commandments is 'Thou shalt make no graven images.' While

I'd be uncomfortable worshiping a picture, I do wish we had some kind of tradition, like you do, to keep God's image around to remind me that I can be a better person."

Rory felt a headache begin to grow where his head joined his neck. He realized it was pointless to try to explain to the woman that Catholics are Christians and that he didn't worship the picture of the Sacred Heart. He simply smiled and nodded politely.

Meg laughed nervously and took another sip of wine, fighting the urge to take a deeper drink. "Things have been so tense around the house lately, it'd do me good to have a picture of Jesus around to remind me to be a little more charitable."

"I'm sure it's been tough, Meg." Rory said gently. "Moving, working, raising two boys—it sounds like a lot of work to me."

Meg laughed a little. The wine she'd had all evening was kicked into another level of ease in her bloodstream by the new glass in her hands. "Oh, that's all manageable. It's Austin that's getting on my nerves. Ever since he was laid off and started this new little job, he's been so needy . . . "

Rory looked at her politely, but with some reserve, alarmed at what she might come up with.

"I'm sure you know how they get . . . guys, I mean." Meg said and raised her eyebrows knowingly. "You know they want sex more often when they're threatened," she said as she scooted back in her seat to lean against the cushions behind her. She crossed her legs and took another sip of wine. "Since I made partner, you'd think Austin was back to being seventeen, the way he pouts about needing me that way."

Rory sighed inwardly and leaned back against the sofa cushions himself. If there was no way to escape the girl chat that was coming, all he could do was make himself comfortable and pray the guys would come back in soon.

## 5160 ST. MARK'S COURT

AFTER SO LONG, it was accomplished quite simply, really. In the short trip across the front yards from the Fallon-Griffin's to their own porch, Meg had placed her arm around Austin's waist and drawn close to his side. He responded by bending to kiss the top of her head. They disengaged only to pass through the front door. Once inside, he took her hand and led her upstairs. Together, they checked on the boys, asleep on the floor in front of the TV. While Austin turned off the television, Meg spread a large comforter over them. They turned out the light and moved to their bedroom in the dark.

A little drunk from the unaccustomed amount of wine she'd had throughout the evening, Meg flicked on their bedside lamp, then stood there to undress, simply allowing her clothes to drop and puddle on the floor in a heap. Shyly, she looked at Austin as he undressed across from her on his side of the bed, until he looked back. His eyes betrayed surprise when he caught sight of her bare breasts. She smiled at him, and took off her panties. "Lock the door," she whispered and gave him a smile.

A little high from a visit with Bruno's bong on the pool deck, and clumsy from his share of the evening's wine, Austin hesitated as he watched Meg turn back the bed covers and laid down. He felt his understanding dawn in his groin before he did in his head. Stepping out of his slacks, he moved to lock the door against the boy's bad dreams or morning enthusiasm. When he returned to the bed, he unsteadily stood on one foot, then the other, to remove his socks. Meg turned on her side and propped her head in her hand, watching him. Long used to confusing her signals, he paused for a moment, stripped to his jockey shorts, until Meg lifted her eyebrows at him questioningly. He shucked them quickly and crawled into bed beside her.

"Don't turn off the light," Meg said quietly as he reached over her, but it was not a shy whisper, it was unapologetic and hungry. From that point there was no need for words. The signposts of touch and murmur were all along a well-traveled road for both of them. The sex was not inventive, but it was the comfortable and kind trip old lovers take together. And, so long in coming, it was mutually enjoyed.

Done, they lay beside each other, touching at the hip and shoulders, exposed by the kicked-away covers, cooling under the slow breeze from the ceiling fan. They spoke only in out-of-synch breaths until Austin whispered, "Welcome back."

In reply, Meg moved her arm off her midriff and awkwardly patted the top of his thigh, letting it rest there for a moment before bringing it back to cover her belly.

Austin stared at the ceiling, electrically aware of the tiny platinum hairs stirring on his forearms, stomach, and legs in the breeze from the fan above. "Why tonight?" he asked gently.

Meg sighed, drew one leg up, and pushed the hair off her sweaty forehead with her free hand. In helpless relaxation she allowed that hand to fall above her head and rest. Quietly she replied, "I think I got drunk enough to realize how sick I was of myself."

From the side away from her, Austin crooked his own arm and let it fall behind his head. His fingers found and held hers. "We were pretty nasty to each other tonight."

"I don't want to be that way," Meg said clearly.

"I don't either," Austin said.

What remained to be spoken went unsaid. They lay quietly next to each other, both turning long furrows in their own thoughts for quite some time. Finally, Meg moved away and turned on her side to face him. "What do you think of our neighbors?" She asked with every intention of changing the subject. In her sudden sleeplessness, she wanted Austin's company in his role as her best friend.

Austin moved the hand closest to her to his groin, shifted himself, and brought his hand to rest on his belly. "Rory's a good cook, I'll say that," he said and yawned.

"There are things going on there," Meg said assertively.

"What do you mean?"

Meg lifted her head to rest it in her hand and said, "Rory's a queer in a gilded cage. I think Bruno controls everything."

"Forget about it," Austin said dismissively. "They were the same way the first time I ever met them. Nothing's changed."

"Did you know Bruno was married at one time? He was with Rory before and after the poor woman. I can't imagine going through that."

Austin didn't respond.

"Really . . . , why would Bruno do that? It must have killed his wife."

Austin looked at her without turning his head. "I don't know, Meg. C'mon. Chalk it up to true love. Or, most likely, he got married in the first place because he thought it'd help his career."

"That's pretty much what Rory said, and I think it's pretty coldhearted," Meg replied with some heat. "I mean, you grow up expecting things. You grow up dreaming about the wedding, the kids, the living life together. Then all of a sudden, it's not anything like you always believed it would be. All because . . . "

"All because why?" Austin asked quietly.

Meg didn't respond at first, then she said, "all because your husband has the hots for another guy. It would be bad enough if it was another woman. It just doesn't fit in with anything you'd think of."

"You grew up believing those things, didn't you? The happy ever after," Austin asked gently.

"Yes I did," Meg said. "No little girl ever grows up thinking she's got to be worried about losing her husband to his best friend."

Austin let go of her fingers and brought his hand down to rest under his head. "Did you ever think your life would be all this? Is it what you thought it would be, or is it different?"

"What's that supposed to mean, Austin?"

"I'm just saying, my life isn't at all what I thought it would be,"

Austin said dreamily. "I never imagined us in a house like this, for one thing. Then there's the kids. You always think about kids, but it's just an idea. You never think about how they stink sometimes, or how they make your heart break sometimes. You never see any of that bullshit for the way it's going to be. I always just had these ideas about being an adult. I never thought I'd just wake up one day and be in the middle of it. To tell you the truth, I don't have a clue how I got here. Sometimes shit just happens." Austin spoke in a rush, as if she had opened a dam in his psyche.

"Are you happy?" Meg asked in a still, small voice.

"I don't sit around asking myself things like that, Meg." he said and raised himself on his elbow to kiss her. He patted her hip and kissed her again. "Right now I'm happy. This minute I am. How's that?"

"Thanks for that. I'm glad," she said and watched him give her a smile, then turn on his side away from her. He bunched his pillow under his head and drew his legs up into a comfortably fetal position.

"Get some sleep, sweetheart," he said.

Meg reached across the bed and ran her hand from his shoulder to his hip once, and then again, as if she were stroking a large dog that had found its way into her bed. She sighed and turned to face away from him. As she settled, she couldn't shake the feeling he was no one she had ever known at all.

At last, alone and untouched on his side of the bed, Austin's mind drifted with the current of his buzz through the backwaters of the evening. He found the picture of a nude white-winged angel and stared. When the angel looked back with a sleepy-eyed look and an amused smile, he felt his dick stretch lazily and lie along his thigh in its interested ease. Austin moved his hand from his side and freed a crease in his scrotum from between his legs. *I don't know how I got here,* he thought, unalarmed and bemused, and unquestioningly drifted on toward sleep.

## 5150 ST. MARK'S COURT

RORY REAPPEARED IN the kitchen shucked down to his boxers and a guinea-T. "Well, that was excruciating," he said to Bruno as he walked to the cabinet to get a clean glass.

Bruno looked up from the pot he was washing and grinned. "Aww, c'mon. They weren't that bad. They just had a little too much wine. *In vino veritas.*"

Absently, he tossed Bridget a dog cookie and watched as she caught it deftly and trotted into the family room. As the old dog turned before sinking to the floor, Rory opened the refrigerator and loaded his glass with ice. "I don't particularly care about their *veritas.* You should have heard Meg with the girl chat while you guys were outside. I sort of felt sorry for Austin." He walked back to the cabinet by the sink and searched for a moment. At last, he took out a bottle of aspirin, opened it, and tipped the bottle to his lips before he recapped it and put it away. Dry swallowing the tablets, he walked to the bar and poured what was left of a bottle of water into his glass. "That wife of his is a piece of work."

Bruno rinsed out the pot, slopping water onto the bar. "I bet he ain't seen no pussy for a right good little while."

Rory walked over and picked up a dish towel. Absently, he mopped up the water Bruno had sloshed and took the dripping pot from him. "You got that too, right?"

Bruno walked from the kitchen into the family room and pulled his shirt over his head. "He almost shit when Meg asked you to come over and put up that picture lamp." Bruno tossed his shirt and managed to fling it precisely on top of a bar stool. That done, he took off his pants and tossed them in the same direction. The heavier pants landed on top of the shirt, and pulled them both off the stool into a heap on the floor. Bruno ignored the heap and sat on the edge of the sofa in front of the TV in his boxer shorts.

"She showed him up. It embarrassed me, and I know how to do it." Rory said as he finished drying the pot and put it away.

"So are you going to do it?" Bruno asked as he settled into the corner of the sectional, put his feet up, and picked up the remote control. Idly, he began flicking through the channels.

"I said I would. I'll wait until the guy calls me though. I'm not going to strap on my tool belt and show up at his door like Joe Electrician. Sheesh, poor guy." Rory gave the kitchen a last glance and satisfied, turned off the light. He walked into the family room and pointedly looked at the pile of Bruno's clothes on the floor.

Bruno caught the look. "I'll pick it up in the morning," he said as Rory moved between him and the coffee table. He spread his legs and patted his chest. "Right here, star child," he said and grinned.

Rory settled on the sofa between his legs and laid his head back on Bruno's chest. "*Mad TV* is on seven until *Saturday Night Live* comes on," he said tiredly.

Bruno grunted. "*Saturday Night Live* is already on. It's one we've seen."

"I can't believe it's that late already," Rory said and closed his eyes.

"*Modern Marvels* is on the History Channel," Bruno said and punched in the number.

"Which one is it?"

Bruno watched for a moment. "Hydraulics!"

"Cool," Rory replied without opening his eyes. "Leave it there if you want to."

Bruno tossed the remote onto the coffee table, where it slid out of reach. Bruno put his free hand under Rory's T-shirt and slid his palm just under the elastic of his boxers. "Are you going to go to sleep on top of me?"

"Probably," Rory said and sighed happily.

Bruno reached his little finger out and tugged at the top line of

Rory's pubic hair. He studied the screen where a huge dump truck lumbered over an excavation site.

"Look!" he said, "Big twucks!"

"I wike twucks," Rory said and grinned. "Bruno? Do you think those two are as good together as we are?"

"I don't know, maybe." Bruno considered the screen a while longer, then said, "It's probably different for them with kids and shit. They probably have their kind of fun. Straight people stuff. I've never thought about it."

"For a minute there, they were at each other's throats." Rory said thoughtfully.

Bruno grunted in reply.

"I mean, we don't do that, though I could have punched you for bringing up the whole deal with the new band."

Bruno looked at the top of his head and grimaced. "I still don't want you to do it. I don't understand what the big deal is."

His face out of Bruno's line of sight, Rory rolled his eyes. "The big deal is the point that it's something I want to do. It's not going to affect you, it has nothing to do with you. It's about me doing something for myself."

Bruno moved his hand off Rory's belly and rested his arm over the back of the sofa. "Why can't you just be satisfied with how things are? What's this rush to go out and embarrass yourself with a group that has nothing to do with the kind of singing you know anything about? Besides, face it, you're forty years old. Your singing days are over."

Rory decided to let that dig go by. He was too tired to get into it with Bruno and there was no way he could explain his drive to be something more than what he was these days to someone who was happily in thrall to his own career. He stirred and sat up. "Whatever, Bruno. Whatever." He twisted neatly and got his feet on the floor under Bruno's leg. "I've got to go to bed or I will fall asleep on top of you," he said and yawned.

"I don't care," Bruno said sincerely.

"I know. But you will in the morning when you wake up with a backache," Rory said. "Do you think they had a nice time?"

Bruno turned his attention from the screen and looked at him levelly. "Changing the subject is a little juvenile. Besides, I thought you didn't really care." He turned his attention back to the trucks on the screen. "They acted like they did."

Rory thought about Austin for a moment. He really did seem whipped and a little lost. Meg had confided far too much personal information while she helped him after dinner. Rory leaned toward Bruno's feet and retrieved a sofa pillow. He stood and Bruno obligingly shifted his foot to the coffee table to let him stand. Instead of going to bed, he simply walked around the coffee table and curled up on the sofa at the right angle to Bruno's. He lay there for a moment before he felt Bruno's hand smooth his hair and then pass down to rub his side a couple of times. When he was done, Bruno lifted his arm and let it rest on the back of the cushions over his head.

Satisfied that the ultimate showdown about the new band had been deflected, Rory closed his eyes and turned his thoughts to the Hardens. *In their own way, they probably are each other's best friends, like we are when Bruno's not being an asshole. They probably have to be; neither one of them mentioned having any other friends. Meg's a little nuts, but Austin seems like a pretty nice guy.* He mumbled as he thought.

"What's that, Rory?" Bruno said. "We'll talk about this band thing later, okay?"

Sleepily, Rory nodded while his thoughts flowed past responding. Soon his thoughts merged with the narration from the television. The marvel of hydraulics soothed him toward sleep. Bruno stirred and grumbled softly. In no time at all, Rory slept.

# CHAPTER SIX

## *It's no big deal*

AUSTIN AND RORY sat next to each other on a pair of chairs flanking a low table across from the sofa in the Harden's living room. The focus of their rapt attention was the picture lamp's satisfying glow. All in all, it taken a little over an hour from the time Rory knocked on the front door until the lamp was wired successfully, the painting rehung, and the sofa shoved back into place under it. As Rory had promised, it was no big deal. For Austin, however, it represented a success that was worth more than the time it took to get the lamp up and turned on.

"I thought that outlet might be wired to the switch in the foyer," Rory said pleasantly. He stood and looked at Austin kindly. "Builders do that a lot so you can turn on the living room lamps when you first come in."

"I never would have imagined," Austin said truthfully as he stood as well. "I really appreciate you taking the time to do this."

Rory smiled and shook his head. "Well, I'd better be getting back next door."

Austin looked hurt. "What's your rush? The least I can do is offer you a beer or lunch or something . . . "

Rory smiled and looked at his watch. It wasn't quite eleven a.m., but he could sense Austin didn't really want him to go. He had eagerly opened the door on his arrival and hadn't managed to stay three feet from him the entire time he'd done the work. At one point,

Rory had taken him by the shoulders and moved him out of his way politely, but firmly. From that, and the amount of chatter Austin produced while he was working, Rory understood that Austin was both bored and lonely. Rory was used to people who hovered while he went about whatever job called him into someone's home—that was why he'd long since stopped doing handyman work. Now Austin stood looking at him with a look that would have embarrassed him if he could have seen his own face. Rory shrugged and said, "I have some time before I have to be somewhere, but it's a little early for that beer. Could I please have a glass of water with a lot of ice?"

Austin grinned and said, "Sure, sure. Let me get it for you. Have a seat."

Rory sat down once more as Austin hurried past him to the kitchen. The chair, one of a pair of cheap matching fauteuils, complemented the sofa across from it. The whole living room made Rory sad. It appeared to have been furnished with a living room suite purchased in early marriage that strove to imply the owners had taste and a sense of the good things. The upholstery was mauve, peach, and sea green, telling of its age and a style long since passed. Even the large painting which the hapless picture lamp now illumined was expressionistically slathered in the same tones, as if it too had been purchased and financed along with the furniture.

Rory imagined the room as a place roped off and only used at Thanksgiving and Christmas. It appeared to be that place where the ladies of the house eased off their pinching shoes and chatted while the men watched football in the other, more personable, rooms of the house. For a moment, he felt a particular type of panic he hadn't felt in a long time rise in his throat. The room seemed to close in on him with a threat that he'd be locked in there forever, living a life in which he couldn't breathe. When Austin loped back into the room and offered him his glass of water, he took it gratefully and nearly drained the glass in an effort to choke down his fear.

"Jeez, you were thirsty," Austin observed. "You should have said something."

Rory wiped his top lip with the back of his hand and shook his head. "No problem."

Austin looked around the living room and said, "So what do you think? Meg did this room herself."

Rory smiled. "That's an interesting painting."

"We got it at the Coconut Grove Arts Festival," Austin said proudly.

"Nice," Rory said and glanced toward the door.

"Why don't you paint anymore, Rory?" Austin asked genuinely. "I think you're great. I'd hang one of your paintings in my home in a minute."

The thought of one of his intellectually freighted paintings hung in a room awash in a sea of mauve and green was enough to startle Rory. He fought the urge to laugh, but he knew Austin was being sincere. It was a question no one had asked him in a long time. He briefly considered the harmlessness of Austin's rather peripheral interest, and for once felt obliged to answer as honestly as he could. Fighting the urge for a cigarette, he leaned forward and sat his glass on the carpet in front of him. He held his hands together between his widespread knees and looked across at Austin under his lashes. "This probably sounds stupid, but I don't paint anymore because I don't have anything to say."

Austin was seduced by Rory's suddenly serious tone into adopting the same earnest pose before he said, "I'm not sure I understand what you mean. Please explain."

Rory sighed. "For me, I paint because I have some problem I'm working out. I'm looking for a way to say something. Usually, I painted in series . . . a body of paintings that worked out some intellectual, technical, or representational idea . . . like the ones from my senior show. All those works used Tiepolo as a jumping-off point, and then

I made that imagery mine to say something about my life and the world I found myself in. Do you understand?"

Austin nodded. "I think I do. Go on."

Rory gave him a rueful smile. "That's pretty much it. I haven't really had much to say since Bruno and I got back together all those years ago. My emotions were too raw and undisciplined then to make much sense of them in paint. Since then, the art world has left me behind. There's not really any interest in my kind of painting, if there ever was. I didn't establish myself as a name in New York back when I had the opportunity, which I didn't take advantage of because of Bruno. That chance has long gone."

Austin straightened and leaned into the chair's cushioned back. "What do you mean because of Bruno?"

Rory picked up his glass and stood. He looked around the living room nervously, feeling all the more claustrophobic for having said far too much. "Could we go sit outside so I can smoke? I'm dying for a cigarette."

"Sure," Austin said as he got to his feet. "I'm sorry, I didn't know you smoked."

"I don't smoke unless . . ." Rory moved past Austin toward the sliding glass door to the pool deck, already reaching in his back pocket for his cigarettes. "I just don't smoke that much anymore."

"Am I making you nervous?" Austin asked, watching Rory as he opened the door and moved outside. He was aware of the mild flirtatiousness in his question and decided he would enjoy hearing Rory's answer.

Rory only acknowledged the flirt with a grin and lit a cigarette. He looked around until he spotted a deck chair and sat down. Settled, he drank the last of his water and rattled the ice in his glass absently.

"Better?" Austin said as he sat on the deck chair closest to Rory.

"I get a little claustrophobic sometimes," Rory explained. "I didn't mean to be rude. I just don't usually talk about things like this."

Austin tugged a bedraggled potted hibiscus toward Rory's foot and indicated he should use it as an ashtray. "I didn't mean to pry. I was just interested, that's all. I mean, it's so obvious you have all this talent. I wondered why you just walked away from it. It's like your singing. I guess Bruno doesn't approve of that, from what he said at your house the other night."

Rory gave him a sharp look and thumped his ash into the potted plant. "I had this offer to be an assistant to a rather well-know painter in Manhattan when I graduated from college. He was someone who was doing some very interesting work and I admired him a lot. Bruno was going on for his MBA and he pitched a fit about me moving to New York. So . . . "

"So you chose Bruno. I understand," Austin said gently.

Rory took another drag off his cigarette and examined the glowing coal at its tip. "One of us had to work. I'd taken all these electrician courses at the community college because my folks said I had to have a way to earn a living besides art. Bruno went to school, and I got a job wiring houses for a construction company. It was good money, but there wasn't any room left in my life for painting after coming home dead tired and being there for Bruno." Rory snorted. "If you back the queer part out of it, it's a fairly typical story."

"But now Bruno is doing well, and it seems like you have all kinds of time. You should get back to painting," Austin said.

Rory cut him a sharp look, "That's what Bruno says. But it's not like this switch you can just turn off and on." Rory looked out over the canal behind the house and studied the clouds laying fat and marbled over it. "I just don't have anything to say."

"So what's his problem with you singing?" Austin prompted. "If he doesn't mind you painting . . . "

Rory took the last drag on his cigarette and stubbed it out thoughtfully into the soil around the plant before he looked up at Austin with a wan smile. "Two things. Singing requires me to be outside of the house with people he doesn't know. And, being in a band again is something he considers me to be too old for. It's a dream he's given up and he doesn't see why I shouldn't do the same."

"I don't think you're too old to be in a band," Austin offered. "Hell, Sammy Hagar had to be fifty when he joined Van Halen. Wasn't he?"

Rory shrugged eloquently in reply, then said, "Sammy Hagar already had a reputation of his own when he joined the group. That's something I never stuck with long enough to have . . . for anything, really."

Austin sat back in his chair and spread his legs wide before moving into a prolonged stretch with his arms overhead. His feigned indifference didn't fool Rory, who watched him as he returned to a less showy ease opposite him. He tensed as Austin looked at him with a gently probing smile once more. The stagy stretch was only a bid for time until he could come up with another small liberty.

"I think you should go for it," he encouraged. "The hell with Bruno."

Rory laughed. "I've come to the same conclusion. I feel like I've got to do something or bust. You want to know what I'm going to do this afternoon?"

"Sure," Austin said casually as he tried to hide his growing interest. He suddenly found the whole idea of Rory intriguing. "What's up?"

Rory reached into his back pocket once more and pulled out another cigarette. He got it lit and looked out over the canal, stalling a bit out of fear he'd sound ridiculous. "My producer friend, Dazz Coleman—he's the guy who's hooking me up with the band—he's made an appointment for me at this trendy hair salon. I'm going to get my hair buzzed and blonded up some. He says if it's good enough for Brad Pitt, it's good enough for me."

Austin looked at Rory's full head of reddish blonde hair and tried to imagine him without it. It was shorter than it had been all those years ago in college, but essentially it was much the same. On Rory it looked careless and comfortable. It suited him. "Wow," was all he said.

"Old school . . . that's what he said I looked like. Can you fucking believe it? Anyway, he thinks if I'm going to fit in with this group of cutting-edge musicians I've got to look . . . well, stylish at least. He even told me what to wear for my audition," Rory said.

Austin ran his fingers through his own thinning hair. Once blonde, it had gone ash and darkened to only a memory of what it had looked like back in college. He couldn't imagine a change so radical for himself. "So you're going to do it? It sounds kind of severe."

Rory snickered and took a long hit off his cigarette. He blew a long stream of smoke jauntily toward the canal. "At least it will be a change. Nothing ever changes out here. Even the damn weather stays the same day after day." He looked at Austin and grinned, "Who knows, a whole new look might do me some good."

Austin shook his head. "I never believed a new haircut could change my life."

"But you're not gay, are you?" Rory said and laughed. "Don't you ever watch *Queer Eye For the Straight Guy*? I thought straight people loved that show."

"I've never seen it," Austin admitted. "I've heard of it, but I've never watched it."

"No big deal," Rory said breezily. "I don't watch it myself. There's one gay guy on it that makes me want to puke, he's such a queer Step'n Fetchit. But the whole point of it is this group of gay guys come in and do over some straight schlep, and suddenly he's a whole new man, still straight, but suddenly kewl. It would lead you to believe that a decent haircut, some personal grooming, a great recipe, and chic furniture can change your life."

Austin thought about it. He wondered if Rory thought he was a straight shlep, and it bothered him that he cared. "So when's your audition?" He asked, wanting very much to change the subject.

Rory visibly tensed. He feigned a casualness he didn't feel by idly flicking his cigarette into the pot next to him. "In four days. If you hear something that sounds like a cat in heat being cut up with a hack saw next door, it's me practicing."

Austin laughed. "I promise not to call 911."

Rory nodded and gave him an unexpected conspiratorial look. "I haven't told Bruno, yet."

"Are you nervous?" Austin asked solicitously.

Rory regarded the tip of his cigarette and stalled for as long as he could. "Yes," he admitted. "I'm going to be singing things that are not exactly out of my range, but they are nothing you'd associate with me by looking at me. It's R-and-B inflected jazz rap. I don't look the part, for real." He glanced at Austin, then shyly looked away. "I'll be trying out with this group of incredibly talented black musicians. I know they wonder what they ever did to deserve this white boy trying to invade them. The only thing I've got to prove myself with is my ability to sing like they need the songs to be sung. I'm scared I'll look like this gigantic poseur. Rory Fallon trying to be Eminem."

"Who's Eminem?" Austin asked sincerely.

Rory gave him a disbelieving look. "Austin, baby. I've got to get you out more. Where the hell have you been?"

Austin felt an electric shock both at being called *baby* and at the faint promise of being *got out more*. Then, he resented the implication that he was somehow out of it, somehow unhip, uncool. His world wasn't bound by bizarre new television shows and au courant music. His world was limited by trying to keep two small sons from jumping headfirst into that very world that seemed so loose, so threatening, and yet shining with the vivid, digitally enhanced color of everything new, forbidden, and promising. He suddenly felt old and distinctly schleplike and he resented it. He resented being reminded of it a great deal. "I've been busy," he answered with great dignity that betrayed his hurt. "I've been busy with other things."

Rory knew he'd overstepped his bounds. He looked at the suddenly middle-aged boy sitting beside him and felt ashamed of his own unconscious condescension. Guiltily, he felt as bad as the guy he detested on *Queer Eye*. He felt like an ass. "Pretty amazing things, Austin," he said. "Things I don't do, like raise kids and keep a family going. I'm sorry if I sounded like an asshole."

Austin sighed and then offered Rory a small smile. "I feel really dull next to you. I'm just stuck out here, with nothing interesting going on but trying to push medical equipment. I'm pretty boring."

"No you're not," Rory said quickly. "I don't think you're boring at all. And don't take it like I'm some big fascinating person. I'm just as stuck out here in this suburban Disneyland as you are. Hell, if I hadn't run into Dazz Coleman a couple of weeks ago, you and I would be talking about how slow work is right now. I never meant to give you the impression I was some big deal."

"No, you didn't," Austin offered quickly. "I never got that from you at all."

"Tell me about you, Austin," Rory encouraged. "I've been going on and on about my stupid little life and I know nothing about you, really."

"There's not much to tell," Austin demurred.

"Sure there is, you're not giving yourself any credit. You said something about getting laid off when you mentioned you'd met me and Bruno back in college, but I don't really remember. Pretend I knew you well. Fill me in on what's been going on."

Austin turned his gaze out over the still canal. "I got married. I got an MBA. I moved to Florida, started a family and a career. Did well," Austin replied in a sing-song voice. He sighed, then his face hardened. "About a year and a half ago, I was an assistant CFO with this software development company up in Boca. We managed to hold it together after the big Internet stock fall in 2001. Everything seemed like it was going well. Then, I discovered my boss, the CFO, was cooking the books. With all the Enron crap going on, I tried to be a good soldier and clue in the CEO. He didn't want to hear it. My boss got wind of what I was doing and I got fired for not being a team player. I got a severance package and a hearty encouragement to seek excellence elsewhere. Only there was no elsewhere to go to. So, I ended up selling medical equipment," Austin concluded bitterly. He looked at Rory with a hard smile. "I'm not very good at it. No. I suck. That's my happy story. No big deal, that's just the way it is, you know?"

Rory only nodded when Austin finished his unvarnished recitation of facts. He felt sorry for him in a way he hadn't before.

"Do you have any idea what it's like being stuck out here when you're used to going in to an office every day of your life? When all your friends and all your social interaction is based on being this big, semi-important go-to guy?" Austin asked calmly.

"But you get out, right? Rory asked gently. "You make sales calls."

Austin snorted. "That's all bullshit. You walk in to see someone who really doesn't give a shit. They pretend to be interested, but you know the minute you leave they've put you out of their mind like you never even showed up. Or, if they are interested, they're covered by so many layers of bureaucracy that you may never see anything come of their interest. Then there are the ones who have the most stupid-assed problems and make some big federal case out of it if you can't give them immediate satisfaction." Austin paused for breath and gave Rory a genuinely pleading look. "I hate it. Goddamn, I hate it."

Rory fought the urge to reach out and touch him in some way. There was no gesture in his cache of encouragement that seemed appropriate to soothe such naked unhappiness. "I'm sorry," he said simply.

Austin shook his head as if tossing off a bad dream. "I appreciate that, Rory. I really do. I just wish you could have met me when I was at my best. I am better than where I find myself right now, and I'm not really happy." He sighed and gave Rory a half smile. "I'm sorry I unloaded on you like that."

Rory shook his head and gave him an encouraging smile. "S'okay. Good neighbors and all that."

"No one really wants to hear it. My wife certainly doesn't anymore. I hate it that you had to," Austin said tiredly.

"Hey, I'll ask for paybacks if I don't get this deal with the band. I'll come over and cry on your shoulder. Bruno will just be happy I didn't get it. You'll make me feel better, how's that?" Rory said and stuck out his hand.

"Deal," Austin grinned and took his hand in a tight grasp. For just a moment, he felt the returning clasp hesitate and then grip his own hand back firmly. He wanted to be surprised that he didn't want to let go, but he wasn't. He looked at Rory to read what he might be thinking.

Rory looked back, then dropped his eyes and let go of his hand. "Right," he said hastily. "I guess I'd better be going," he said as he stood.

"Right," Austin said and smiled as he stood. "You have a whole new you to meet this afternoon."

Rory looked at him questioningly.

"New haircut," Austin explained. "If that can change your life, I wish I could go with you."

Rory laughed and reached over to rub Austin's unstylish layered hair brusquely. When Austin ducked under his stroking hand, he said, "Tell you what, I'll go first. If it works, I'll let you know."

"You do that," Austin said shyly and looked like he meant it.

### 5150 ST. MARK'S COURT

BRUNO CLOSED AND locked the front door behind him. He called out into the silent house and set his briefcase by the door. His greeting was welcomed only by the sound of Bridget's over-long claws scrabbling over the hardwood floors. Loosening his tie, he knelt to absorb her great weight as she greeted him. "Where's Rory?" He asked her. "Did you eat Rory? Where's Rory, girl?"

The big dog responded by circling under his stroking hands and taking off for the family room. He followed along behind, stripping off his tie and yanking his shirttail free of his trousers. Stopping at the bar in the family room, he watched as Bridget looked back at him over her shoulder before she disappeared out the sliding glass door to the pool deck. Bruno pulled his belt free from the loops around his waist and laid it, along with his tie, over the back of a barstool. "Rory?" he called once more. "I'm home."

Answered once more by silence, he strode across the room to the door and looked out. Rory stood under the roof's sweltering overhang in an area cleared of deck furniture facing out toward the canal. Dressed only in a pair of loose cargo shorts, his feet were planted at shoulder width apart and his hips moved to a beat only he could hear, rhythmically pulsing through the headphones of his iPod. His shorn head moved sinuously on his neck with his eyes fixed somewhere out in the middle distance. In a smoky voice pitched at some level Bruno had not heard before, he sang:

My mind drifts now and then,
looking down dark corridors,
and wondering what might have been

Bruno knew the tune. It was one of Rory's favorites. It was from "Footsteps in the Dark," an Isley Brothers song Rory had played unceasingly years ago, back during a time Bruno didn't want to recall. After he'd gotten married, he'd often show up at Rory's apartment without warning, only to find him listening to that song with a full ashtray and a half-empty vodka bottle on the kitchen table before him.

Now, he growled the song with an abandon unsoothed by an audible melody. With his hair cut nearly to the scalp and lightened as though he'd been in a summer's worth of sun, he looked as if he'd stepped back in time to the early fall Bruno had met him. There was not a spare ounce of flesh around his waist. His slim hips betrayed the elastic of his boxers shorts above the top of the baggy shorts. The pants had slipped low as he moved his hips to the song playing in his head. He looked assured of his seductiveness, yet as vulnerable as a stripling boy. It was the voice that betrayed his years. Rough-edged and tinged with a weariness that ran as a stream of torn silver through the song, it made Bruno want to take him and hold him against any darkness he saw out where his eyes had fled.

Then he realized Rory was rehearsing. Anger flooded him with a sudden ferocity that made the cords on his neck stand out. He wanted to snatch the earphones from his ears and bitch slap Rory, then shake him until his neck snapped. This, this shapely form with a voice that could make sinners and angels cry didn't belong to anyone but him. He did not belong out in some dark, hot club with writhing niggers nasty-dancing in a sea of sweat and funk at his feet. He had no right to shake his ass and moan to any half-drunk horny straight college boys with dirty dreams and hard-ons they couldn't explain. Rory had no right to tease the single bitches who heard a promise in those hungry cries, panties wet with an anticipation of communication and shared pain. Those things belonged to him and him alone.

Bruno's anger and jealousy made him tremble. He folded his arms across his chest and slumped against the door frame and watched Rory move under a sheen of sweat from his concentration and surrender to a beat even Bruno could feel in the silence rent only by his plaintive, pleading voice. As the anger simmered to slowness, a larger hurt replaced it. It throbbed in his chest. Why, he asked himself, couldn't Rory just be satisfied with things the way they were? Why did he feel he had to put all this, all he was, out there for strangers?

Bruno understood him. He understood even where he stood. The roof's generous overhang was nothing more than an imagined proscenium. The great open distance he faced across the canal was nothing more than an unreceptive audience he faced alone and nearly naked. Rory was opening himself out to the neighbors across the canal in the same way he would have to open himself to a derisive and doubting reception from a group, a roomful of strangers, and a dubious world. And he didn't have to, Bruno decided. He didn't have to at all.

Some intuitive signal cut through Rory's concentration. He glanced toward the door and saw Bruno watching him. He smiled at him with a happiness that at once made Bruno want to hurt him and also pull into an embrace that would crush him with pure love. Bruno was torn. Bruno was hurt and he was utterly disarmed.

Rory took the earphones from his ears and said, "What do you think?"

Bruno shrugged. "Your hair looks like a little baby chick."

Rory's smile dimmed. "Is that good or bad?"

"Depends," Bruno drawled. "Did you just do it or did you do it for your audition?"

"It was just time for a change, Will." Rory replied evenly.

Bruno nodded and stepped from the doorway onto the pool deck. He made his way slowly to his favorite chair and sank into it heavily. His stash box with its small bong sat on the table next to his chair. He busied himself by pinching off a small part of a bud and loading it into his bong as Rory sank down on the pavers in front of him. Bridget joined him happily. Each sat before Bruno, both awaiting his judgment and his approval.

Bruno tossed the baggie on the tabletop and reached in his box for his lighter. He looked down at Rory and said, "I wish I was enough, Rory. I wish you didn't feel the need to do this when I try to give you everything."

Rory watched as Bruno lit the bong and drew a long hit deep into his lungs. He waited until Bruno exhaled the stinking smoke and settled back into his chair before he said gently, "Will, didn't you ever hear the story about the little boy and his baby duck?"

Bruno shook his head and coughed deeply.

"There was this little boy who had a baby duck," Rory said. "He loved the little duck and wanted it to stay small so he could hold it in his hands. Every day, he would squeeze the duck to keep it from growing. One day, he squeezed too hard and the little duck died."

Bruno spread his legs and shifted his balls through his pants. "So now I'm squeezing you to death, right? I'm keeping you from growing, is that it?"

Rory looked up into his eyes for a long time. Bruno refused to break the stare or give anything away. Finally, Rory hung his head and said, "I won't go through with it if you tell me not to."

Bruno looked down at Rory's shorn head lowered in submission. He wanted to take it between his hands and crush it like an egg. He wanted to kiss its crown like a father would a baby's. Instead, he simply leaned forward and smoothed the bristly thatch under his palms, enjoying the feel of it. Rory lifted his head and looked pleadingly into his eyes. Bruno stood up and started to the door. "Do what you want to," he said.

### 5160 ST. MARK'S COURT

MEG NOTICED THE picture lamp as soon as she locked the door behind her and set the alarm. For a moment, she simply stared at the living room lit by its warm solitary glow. It made her want to cry. It was such a simple thing to be greeted by, but the room looked elegant to her, it looked like everything she was working so hard for. The lamp was more than a lamp. It was an aspirational accomplishment.

When Meg was a little girl, she had a friend named Mary Katherine Ellis who lived in a large, lovely home many long blocks from the small house where Meg grew up. Mary Katherine's father was an attorney, and Meg remembered being there when he got home one evening. Mary Katherine had skipped across the Oriental rug in the foyer to hug her father. Meg watched, unnoticed, as the large, prosperous man dropped his briefcase and knelt to hug his little girl. Meg could see into the dining room and living room that flanked that foyer. In each space, a tasteful painting hung on a cream-colored wall, lit by a picture lamp. The tableau was engraved on her mind, the image of accomplishment, of home, of everything poor little Meg wanted to grow up to have and to be.

Meg moved from the foyer into the living room and sat her briefcase by one of her proud fauteuils. In her mind, she surveyed the room and jumped to the next goal, the room needed an Oriental rug, one that complemented the furniture but retained its own presence. The image embraced her, and made her own sixteen-hour day worthwhile.

"Oh. It's just you Mom," a relieved small voice said behind her.

Meg turned to find Josh brandishing a baseball bat. She inwardly jumped at the image of his small form, feet planted wide, bat readied to club her unsuspecting back. "Who did you think it was, sweetheart?" She knelt and opened her arms.

"Home-invasion robbers," Josh said anxiously. He lowered the bat and stepped toward her gratefully. As she hugged him, he said, "They followed this lady home in Sunset Lakes. They made her go in the house and they taped her with duct tape. They stole her Rolex and shot her, execution-style."

Meg took the baseball bat from him and laid it gently next to her briefcase. "Where did you hear about this?" She asked cautiously.

"Channel 7 Live at Ten," Josh said matter-of-factly.

Meg glanced at her watch. It was ten twenty-three. Rising to her feet, she took Josh by the hand and led him to the sofa under the peaceful picture lamp and sat down. "Why aren't you in bed?"

Josh shrugged off her hand and backed away slightly. "I don't

know. I wanted to stay up awhile. Dad told me I could stay up until
*Animal Planet* went off."

"*Animal Planet* goes off at nine," Meg said gently. "It's waaay after
ten now. Where's your dad?"

Josh moved to her side and looked at her patiently. "Dad is asleep
in his chair in the loft. He's had a bitch of a day."

"Ah," Meg said understandingly.

"Mr. Fallon came over this morning and put up your picture lamp,
then Mrs. Torres-Aristobal got sick so Dad had to carpool. He was on
a conference call almost the whole time, so we had to be very quiet.
Then we went to Target and bought boxer shorts, see?"

Josh took a step back and held his arms out. The elastic hugged his
small waist, and the underwear bloomed to fullness below. Shirtless,
his tiny nipples were the same color as his skin, and his belly still
held the slight swell of toddlerhood. Meg reached out and nearly
encircled his tiny waist with her hands to draw him to her. "Fancy,"
she said. "But I just bought you guys underwear."

Josh struggled from her grasp. "You bought the wrong kind, Mom.
The guys made fun of Noah for wearing tighty-whities."

"Why did they do that?" Meg asked, concerned.

"You need room for your unit," Josh explained patiently. "The baby
kind you bought keep you all squashed up down there."

"I see," Meg said. Inside, she felt a leap of time that disoriented her.
It was a dizzying sensation and she slumped back against the sofa.

"Dad got some too," Josh told her. "He said it was a guy thing you
wouldn't know about."

Meg nodded. "I see. What did you have for dinner?"

"Dad said you'd kill him if we went to Taco Bell. He bought a
whole roasted chicken and some salad in a bag at Publix. He let us
pick out our own dressing. Me and Dad ate Ranch and Noah ate the
Green Goddess," Josh said and snickered.

"Did you take a bath?" Meg asked tiredly.

"A shower, Mom. Damn. Only very small children take baths," Josh said with some exasperation.

Meg reluctantly decided to let the curse word slide. "Did you brush your teeth?"

"Uh-huh. I brushed them in the shower. It saves time."

"That's disgusting, Josh. Does your father let you brush your teeth in the shower? Germs can get all over your toothbrush."

"It doesn't matter, Mom. Roaches crawl all over our toothbrushes to eat leftover toothpaste when we're asleep. I saw it on my insect show."

Meg shuddered at the thought. She tiredly closed her eyes and rubbed them with her fingers feeling once again she might cry. *Only very small children take baths,* she thought and wondered when Josh, her little Austin, stopped being a very small child in his own mind. She felt him settle in next to her on the sofa. He took her free hand and squeezed it gently.

"Was your day a bitch, too, Mommy?" he asked solicitously.

Meg opened her eyes and gave him a tired smile, ignoring the tears that welled in her eyes. She never noticed when Josh had stopped calling her *mommy.* It seemed like ages since she'd heard it. "It was a very long day, Josh. But it got much better when I saw you."

"Poor Mommy," Josh said sweetly. He gave her a gently manful look and said, "Let's get you upstairs." With that, he stood and tugged her hand until she rose with him. He steered her toward the stairs and only let go of her hand long enough to pick up his baseball bat and glance carefully at the alarm by the front door.

Meg noted his glance as she paused and considered turning off the light over the painting. "Do you think we ought to check the alarm before we go upstairs, Joshie?"

He looked from his mother's face to the alarm panel by the door and then back again. "Are you absolutely sure you set it?" He asked gently.

"You know, I think I better check to make sure," Meg replied with feigned seriousness. She stepped to the panel and saw that she had indeed set it as a matter of habit. The alarm set indicator light was glowing bright red.

"It's all good?" Josh asked anxiously.

Meg smiled and glanced toward her picture light once more. "All good," she said. "But just to let the bad guys think we're still up, I think we should leave that light on over the painting. What do you think?"

Josh nodded gratefully.

Meg stepped to him and took his hand once more. "I'm beat, let's head on upstairs, me and you. Nobody's going to invade our home now."

# CHAPTER SEVEN

# The most amazing color . . .

THE LATE-WINTER SUN felt good on Rory's back as he tamped the geraniums from their plastic containers and transferred them to a terra cotta pot. It was late in the winter to be planting geraniums, but Rory loved the bold bursts of red that continued throughout the spring, almost through June, when the sun grew so brutal that very few flowers could live. The selection of remaining red geraniums was picked over at Home Depot, but he was able to get enough to brighten up the area around the pool deck. He sang to himself as he sifted the rich, black potting soil around their tender green stalks. Within a week, with some watchful tending, they'd be fully in bloom and he'd be rewarded with rich red flowers standing among the deep green leaves.

With another pot finished, Rory grabbed it by its lip and lifted with the muscles in his legs. After a few awkward steps, he arrived at a likely spot and looked over his shoulder to gauge the pot's angle from the family room doors. Satisfied he'd have a terrific view of the foliage, he gently sat it to rest on the pavers and wiped the sweat off his forehead with the back of his hand. From the grit he felt, he had no doubt he'd streaked his forehead with dirt, again. His chest and ankles were covered with it. The breeze blew the dirt over him as he worked, and it caught in the tiny white hairs that grew there. He knew before he could go back in the house he'd have to shuck down to his underwear and dive into the pool or face making a mud bath in the shower.

The sun was strong and hot overhead despite the morning's cool breeze. While the pool would be cool, it would certainly be nice enough for a quick swim. Rory looked forward to his swim and to some time spent in the sun drying off afterwards. He glanced up into the clear blue sky and grinned for the simple amiableness of the day. From behind him and overhead he heard the whisper of a window opening along an aluminum track. He turned to look in time to hear his neighbor call a loud greeting.

"Hey Austin," he called and waved. "Why don't you come over?"

"Give me a minute," Austin replied. "I'll take a break."

Rory waved again in reply and turned to look around for the last half-dozen geraniums left to be potted. The six plants were destined for only two more large pots and he'd be finished. All in all, he figured he could bullshit with Austin for awhile. He hadn't seen him for a few days, and he was interested to hear how Meg had liked her picture light.

While he was waiting for Austin to appear, he looked again around him. The sun shone so generously and warmly, it was one of those days that made him glad he'd moved to South Florida all those years ago. Freed from the long gray winters up home, he had truly become a different person. Since he was a child, he'd succumbed to a type of depression that deepened through January until it became almost crippling by the dark long weeks of February's thankfully short calendar. Down south, in the aptly named Sunshine State, his winter depression had disappeared and, after so many years, despite the weariness that arrived with middle age, he felt good as his life and moods contentedly spread out under the subtropical sky. Now, with his pot gardening near done, he allowed himself to feel that it was a really good day.

The screen door that led from his side yard opened with a sigh, and Austin appeared grinning on the pool deck. "Look at you. Are you having a good time playing in the dirt?"

Rory glanced down at himself and looked back at Austin with a grin. "It's big fun," he replied. "You should try it sometime."

Austin looked around and nodded. "The flowers look good out here. I need to learn from you. My pool deck looks like nobody lives there."

Rory perched on the edge of the chair nearest him and motioned for Austin to sit as well. When he chose a seat next to Rory's, he warned him off, "Don't get too close. I stink."

Austin waved it off. "Honest sweat doesn't stink."

Rory laughed again. "Then I must be a liar, because I can smell myself."

"You sure are in a good mood today," Austin observed. "Did the haircut change your life?"

Rory looked at him blankly for a second before he recalled their conversation earlier. "So far, so good," he replied with an amused optimism.

"Did you tell Bruno your audition is tomorrow?" Austin asked.

Rory looked around the pool deck, stalling for time until he could think of a way to neutrally answer the question. He decided the straightforward answer was best. "He wasn't pleased, but he told me to do what I want. I took it as a yes."

Austin nodded and said, "I hope he liked the haircut."

"He said I looked like a baby chick. What do you think?" Rory asked with a mock preening seriousness.

Austin leaned back in his chair and took an unhurried look. "What camp are you going to, little boy?"

Rory kicked at his leg with feigned anger, making Austin's legs dance a bit. "That wasn't the look I was going for. I was thinking maybe 'hot recruit'?"

"Okay," Austin said and laughed. "I'll call you jarhead if it'll make you happy. But that isn't how you look at all."

"Fine. Fuck you," Rory said good-naturedly. "See if I get you an appointment to get your hair *did* and change your fucking life, then."

Austin laughed. "Oh man, I was hoping I could get an appointment for next week."

Rory smiled and the conversation suddenly stilled. The momentum of their bonhomie suddenly becalmed despite the morning's amiable breeze and bright sailing skies. Rory looked to Austin for help, but they were left simply looking at each other for a long moment. Rory began, "How did Meg . . . "

"You did change my life . . . " Austin said on top of him. The two starts of sentences collided and bounced off each other disorienting both of them.

"Go ahead," Rory said. "What were you going to say?"

Austin grinned nervously at first, then said, "There's been an underwear rebellion by the Harden boys. Oldest to youngest."

"Oh yeah?" Rory said.

"Yeah. When you're married, your wife ends up buying you three-packs of Fruit-of-the-Loom briefs," Austin explained. "But I've seen you strutting around down here in some really cool boxers. You looked so comfortable, I took the boys to Target and outfitted us in some nice roomy ones. My genitals thank you. My boys thank you."

"Well, what are neighbors for?" Rory said, a little taken aback by Austin's forthright admission that he watched him and noted his clothing.

"Seriously, where do you get yours? Target didn't have anything like them," Austin pressed.

"Umm, the Gap, Hollister, Abercrombie . . . just wherever I see them," Rory said uncomfortably.

Oblivious to Rory's embarrassment, Austin nodded as if he were making a mental note of Rory's shopping resources. "I'm a lot more comfortable, let me tell you."

Rory snorted and shook his head, "Well, anything I can do for your 'nads, man. Whatever. Just let me know."

Austin, whose fair complexion left no emotion unexpressed, flushed.

Noting his neighbor's sudden change in color, Rory tried not to smile. "Umm, how did Meg like her picture lamp?" He asked quickly.

"Great . . . I mean she *really* liked it. She has these very set ideas about how things are supposed to look. Thanks to you, I'm off the hook for a while until she needs to fill in another piece of the decorating puzzle in her head. She's already talking about another picture lamp for the dining room."

"Oh yeah?" Rory said.

"Oh hell yeah. It's something about creating a welcoming glow when people enter the house. I think gracious good living was mentioned as well,' Austin replied sarcastically.

"Aw give her a break, Austin." Rory said breezily. "I think she's doing what comes naturally. Let her have some fun."

"I like your and Bruno's style better." Austin admitted. "It doesn't look so forced."

"Well you would," Rory said. "There's no fussy lady stuff over here."

"No, it's different," Austin insisted. "Everything is the right size, the right color."

"Austin, if you start talking about fabric I'm going to have to stop seeing you," Rory said firmly.

"Why?"

"It's just a little gay, that's all," Rory said and laughed.

Austin colored once more and looked genuinely flustered. "Okay. Keep your gay decorating secrets to yourself, then. Don't share."

"There's no secret to it, Austin," Rory said gently. "Pick out a room or place in your house and tell Meg you want to help her put it together. You have a big house. Tell her you want the loft, maybe."

"Whatever," Austin said dubiously, "I don't think she'd let me."
Then, steering the conversation once more to other shoals, he said,
"Are you nervous about the audition tomorrow?"

Rory shrugged, but didn't say anything. He looked at Austin and
raised his eyebrows as if to say it didn't really matter whether he
was nervous or not.

"C'mon, man. You can't be that cool about it," Austin said firmly.

"It is what it is, Austin. Either they'll like me or they won't. Best
I can do is give it a shot," Rory said firmly. "I'm a little concerned
about being this white boy trying out with a black group that's tack
sharp and talented as hell. But, if I embarrass myself, well . . . two
tears in a bucket, mother fuck it."

Austin nodded, then leaned forward with his elbows on his knees.
"I heard you singing last night," he said huskily. He cleared his throat
and went on, "I couldn't see you, but I could hear you. You sounded
good, considering there were long spaces in between the parts you
sang."

Rory looked away and took in the finished pots of geraniums
already sitting with pride of place on the pool deck. He was suddenly
embarrassed, and he knew that wasn't necessarily conducive to his
upcoming performance. "I was only singing my part," he explained.
"I'm just a vocalist. Like background coloring. The music and the
rapping are out in front."

"Can I hear you with the music and everything?" Austin asked
sincerely.

"Aww man," Rory sighed. "Don't make me do all that."

"C'mon, Rory. It'll be good practice. If you can't sing in front
of me now, how are you going to sing with a bunch of strangers
tomorrow?"

"No way," Rory said. "There's no music out here."

Austin looked pointedly over his head at the Bose outdoor speakers mounted under the roof's overhang off the living room. "Liar. Bruno was really proud of how good the stereo sounded out here the other night."

Rory rolled his eyes and snorted. "Leave it to Bruno." He eyed the speakers himself and for a moment seemed to consider it. Then he said, "Naw, Austin. It's the middle of the morning. I don't want to be playing music and shaking my ass all out here in the middle of the neighborhood. It'll be too . . . "

"Too what?" Austin asked. "Your only neighbor nearer than a quarter mile across the canal is sitting right here. You can't use that bullshit excuse."

"I have to move when I sing," Rory explained. "I'll feel like I'm giving you a lap dance or something with just you sitting here."

Austin laughed as he leaned back in his chair and spread his legs, "C'mon, baby, don't be afraid give me what you got."

Rory looked at him and something close to anger crossed his face. "Okay, asshole. Turn your big ass around and face the living room doors. If I'm going to do this, I want to be under the speakers."

Austin raised out of the chair enough to reposition it facing the small stagelike space below the roof's overhang and then sat back down. He folded his arms across his chest and said, "Okay. Tear it up."

Rory stood and walked across the pavers into the house. Austin shortly heard amplified white noise come from the speakers, followed by a taut bass line merged with a fast drum syncopation that thumped along like jerking electricity. He recognized the song as Rory reappeared and took his place in front of him. It was a faster arrangement of the Isley Brothers' "Take Me to the Next Phase." Austin and Meg had danced to the original version as junior high–schoolers. Rory found his groove in the rapid beat and began to move from the balls of his feet. After an elegant rap intro, Rory came in on the beat with a husky falsetto sparkling with ground glass. According to the lyrics, he called on volunteers, enticing the people who party here. But he sang with his back arched, his hips moving with an authentic push. Austin couldn't tell if he was being unselfconsciously suggestive, but his movement seemed a kind of surrender to an urging force as steady and sure as an act of sex.

Austin felt himself grow hard.

When the song finished, Rory stood stock-still for a moment and locked eyes with Austin. Casually, he reached into to his back pocket and took out a pack of cigarettes. He managed to extract one and get it lit with his eyes never leaving his audience's. It was a look that was self-assured and nonchalantly challenging.

Austin shifted uncomfortably in his seat and said, "Damn."

Rory nodded and stepped away to return inside. After a moment, Austin heard the stereo's volume reduce to a background level. He glanced at the family room door before he tugged at his crotch and leaned forward once more with his elbows on his knees as Rory walked back onto the pool deck.

"Think I'll do alright?" He asked quietly.

"Where did you learn to move like that?" Austin asked.

Rory laughed. "It's a soul move, not a rock-and-roll one. Soul moves are about fucking. Rock-and-roll moves are about strutting to get some. You see the difference?"

"I never thought about it until now," Austin admitted.

"So I can move, so what? How did I sound?" Rory demanded.

"I wish I could hear you sing something slower," Austin said, suddenly all business.

"You would have if you hadn't pissed me off," Rory replied evenly.

"Fair enough," Austin said and wondered what he could say next. "Are all the songs Isley Brothers ones?"

Rory bent and took another deep hit off his cigarette before laying it on the pavers and grinding it out with the heel of his sneaker. "Not all the songs the group does are, but the only ones they're interested in me for are," he said and exhaled an impressive stream of smoke.

Austin nodded. "They're classics, anyway."

With nothing really to add, Rory felt the conversation lapsing once more. His earlier embarrassment over Austin's noting his attire on his own pool deck returned to needle him. Rightly, he felt the need to tackle the subject. As the moment of silence between them lengthened and threatened to drag, he cleared his throat and said, "Austin, there's something I've been meaning to ask you."

"Shoot," Austin replied gratefully.

"For a pretty long while, well, until you guys moved in really, we never had any neighbors," Rory began. "Well, Bruno and I got used to a lot of privacy, and don't get me wrong, we're not exhibitionists or anything, but neither one of us is particularly modest. And I . . . well, I noticed you said you'd seen my down here in my drawers . . ."

Pale Austin felt the telling flush rise from his neck to spread over his face once more. Quickly he said, "Well, it's not like I'm spying or anything."

"No, no. I didn't mean anything like that," Rory retorted. "It's just Bruno and I have been known to get carried away, and I didn't want you to think we were trying to put on some kind of show. I mean, I know you have little kids . . ."

Guiltily, Austin recalled the long moments he had spent looking, watching for Rory to appear on his pool deck. At first, he'd attributed his interest to simple boredom, but he'd done it so many times, it had grown into a near pastime. Then, too, there was the time when his vigil at his office window had provided him with a view of Bruno and Rory's lovemaking that had rooted in his imagination and had since grown in significance out of any proportion to mild curiosity. That was something he couldn't admit. "Don't worry about it," he said gruffly. He looked over his shoulder toward his own house, and was relieved to see the only window with a view onto Rory's pool deck was the one he'd always thought was. "The only room that really has a view of down here is my office, and no one's ever in there but me."

Rory mistook his reddening and gruffness for a different kind of embarrassment. "Austin, please. If you ever see anything down here that offends you or anything, please just let me know, okay?"

Austin felt the urge to get away from the conversation so strongly that he stood up and looked down at Rory, who continued to sit, looking up at him earnestly. "Rory, look. What you guys do down here is your business. I'm a big guy and I'm not a prude, okay? I just want you to know I respect you guys' privacy."

"So we're good?" Rory asked.

Austin forced a smile and held out his hand to shake. "We're good."

Rory took his hand and stood. "That's a relief," he shook Austin's hand and let it go. "To tell you the truth, not ten minutes ago I was thinking of shucking down to my shorts and getting in the pool to get the worst of this dirt off before I go in the house. I'm glad you're not going to think I'm doing it to fuck with you."

"Don't worry, Rory. It's *kewl*," he said, trying to imitate his sons' ironic inflection of the word as nearly as possible.

### 5150 ST. MARK'S COURT

BRUNO PLACED HIS suitcase on the bed with a sense of haste that told of his annoyance with Rory's task and the late hour he'd put it off until. "Damn it, Rory. When do you think my underwear and T-shirts will be dry?"

Unperturbed, Rory sat on the side of the bed opposite the suitcase and watched as Bruno unzipped the top and allowed it to fall, nearly brushing his knees. "I'm expecting the dryer to buzz any minute. If I'd known you were leaving, I'd have done laundry this afternoon."

"I should have done this a long time ago," Bruno said. "I can't believe I let it go this long."

"What time is the car service picking you up?" Rory asked as he watched Bruno pull suits still sheathed in the dry cleaner's plastic from the closet and toss them over the suitcase.

"My flight's at ten thirty. Between the goddamn crosstown traffic on 595 and the line at security, I've got to be on the road by seven forty-five, eight o'clock at the latest." Bruno said as he flung a half-dozen shirts, still on their hangers, toward the bed.

"Calm down, you're making a mess," Rory said. "Why don't you let me pack this stuff for you?"

"Don't worry about it. I have a system," Bruno said irritably as he threw a handful of ties toward the bed as well.

Rory watched as they hit the plastic-covered shirts and slid in silken sibilance onto the floor. "They didn't give you much notice for this trip, did they?"

"No, but they don't usually. They're New York. As far as they're concerned, all my office is good for is just sitting around waiting for their beck and call," Bruno said as he turned and regarded the pile of clothes on the bed. He looked at Rory and smiled. "But, in a way, I'm flattered. If they want me in Manhattan, it at least means they haven't forgotten who I am."

"It is kind of a compliment, isn't it?" Rory asked.

"In this case, it is," Bruno said as he shoved the clothes to one side and began to fold a suit into the bag. "This is a good-sized project. I did all the preliminary research. If they want me on the team, it means they think I have something significant to offer."

"You're moving up to the show, then."

Bruno nodded absently and continued to pack. Rory watched him with growing alarm as he more or less crammed his pressed, clean clothes into the suitcase. Somewhat satisfied with his packing thus far, Bruno turned and stepped into the master bath. As he left, he said casually, "Rory? What would you think of moving to Manhattan?"

Rory listened as he yanked open drawers and drawers and shifted their contents hurriedly. "My god, how long do you think you'll be gone?" He called toward the bathroom.

Bruno reemerged with his dop kit, its contents crammed in sloppily. "This trip shouldn't be longer than a week, maybe ten days. But I'm interested in what you think about moving," he said as he placed the open dop kit on top of the clothes in the suitcase and sat down next to Rory at the head of the bed. In a move that was unusual for him, he sought Rory's hand and took it between both his own before looking him in the eye.

Rory noted the abrupt shift in energy and the searching look. "Will, are you trying to tell me something? What is it you aren't saying here?"

"I've been talking to Shimon Saperstein. He thinks he might have a place for me in the New York office," Bruno said and squeezed Rory's hand before letting it go. "I think this command appearance up there might be like some kind of audition."

"No way," Rory said.

"You mean you won't even consider it," Bruno said earnestly. "Damn, Rory. This could mean so much for . . . "

"Whoa, whoa," Rory said and held up his hands. "I never said I wouldn't consider it. I didn't mean that at all."

"Well, what did you mean?"

"What I meant was, how cool is that?" Rory said patiently. "I know how much moving up to the New York office means to you. It's a big deal, baby."

Bruno put both hands behind his head and leaned back against the headboard. "Yeah. It's a big damn deal, for both of us."

Rory sighed. He was not at all as excited about the prospect of moving to Manhattan as his partner was. "Will, you know I'll follow you wherever you end up taking us. Haven't I proved that over and over?"

Bruno looked for his eyes without turning his head or breaking his pose. "I know, and yes you have. But, I want you to be excited about it too."

Rory laughed and turned to lay his head on Bruno's lap. When he was comfortably situated there, he looked up into Bruno's eyes and smiled. "I will be excited about it when the time comes. But right now, I'm not going to get all freaked out because Shimon Saperstein might, maybe, *perhaps* wants you up there."

Bruno dropped a hand and smoothed back the bristly hair on the top of Rory's head. "So what am I gonna say if he does ask me?"

Rory took a deep breath and closed his eyes. He didn't want to move to New York. He didn't want the long winters. He didn't want to live in a tiny apartment and hand out money in tips every time someone stuck out their hand. He didn't want to live in the biggest terrorist target in the world. He didn't want to move in the social circles Bruno would be called into. He didn't want to live in a city that offered Bruno sexual opportunities as casually as other places offered Starbucks coffee on every corner. He sighed as this ran through his mind with frightening speed. Despite all his fears and misgivings, he opened his eyes and found Bruno's. The longing and excitement was written large across his face. "Tell him yes," was all he said.

Bruno grinned. "I love you," he said.

The dryer buzzed urgently in reply. Rory eased off Bruno's lap and stood. As he turned to leave for the laundry room, Bruno leaned across the bed and caught his arm. "I said I love you," he insisted.

Rory gave him a smile that hid his ambiguity over the possible move with an indulgent look of love in return. He had known and loved Bruno a long time. If Bruno told him he loved him without prompting, it often meant he'd gotten his way in some way or another. Where a different man would have found this trait obnoxious, Rory still found it appealing despite his seeing it for what it was. "And I love you back, you big crazy ox."

Bruno laughed and let go of his hand. "I'm going to my office to go online and print out my boarding pass. That'll be one less thing I have to do tomorrow morning," he said as he bounded off the bed and followed Rory from the room.

"Will it let you do that this early?" Rory asked as they walked through the family room.

"I think so," Bruno said. "Anyway, I have a report I brought home to print out that I need to go over on the plane. I hate fucking with my laptop while we're in the air."

Bruno left him in the kitchen as Rory made his way to the laundry room. Bruno's underclothes were dry, and Rory gathered them from the dryer into a pile in his arms to take back to the bedroom to fold.

As he made his way back, Bridget woke and followed him eagerly. Happily she wove back and forth in front of him until he nearly tripped on her broad form just as he got to the bed. In an effort to keep his balance, Rory tossed the mound of clothes onto the suitcase. Once he patted Bridget and got her settled down, he slid the tangled underwear and T-shirts off Bruno's suitcase and the dop kit came off along with it. From its unzipped top, the contents spilled onto the bed. Among the items that lay mixed in with the clothes were several condoms and a partially emptied tube of KY Jelly.

For a moment, Rory ignored them as he placed Bruno's razor, toothbrush, toothpaste, dental floss, and bottle of aspirin back into the black leather bag. When he was down to the finality of the condoms and the KY, he froze with a partially opened roll of antacids in his hand and registered the feel of its coil of paper and foil where it looped and touched his fingers. In his state of heightened perception and awareness, the touch of the simple wrapping felt as if it had scrapped his fingers raw.

Bruno had been on five trips since they'd last gone away together, all five of them to New York. Rory marveled at his need for condoms and KY when they never used them, and beside that point, Rory himself had never accompanied him to Manhattan even once. It wasn't really a marvel. It seemed to be a planned for and expected need. Rory dropped the antacids into the leather bag and gathered the condoms in his fist. At first he wanted to throw them into the trash until the thought registered that Bruno's intended partner could be a woman who might get pregnant, or a man who might propose a different kind of serious risk to Rory's own well-being.

With a suddenly sure hand, the condoms promptly followed the antacids into the dop kit. Then, he picked up the tube of lubricant and felt its sticky surface with a revulsion so intense it made him instantly nauseous. Fighting back the urge to vomit, he checked to make sure all Bruno's toiletries had made their way back into the dop kit before he laid it back on the clothes in the suitcase in as close an approximation to it's original location as he could muster.

Only then did he walk to the bathroom. Once inside, he turned the hot water tap on the sink to hot, full blast. He couldn't look at himself in the mirror. He didn't want to see his own face in a state of such bewilderment and pain as he was feeling. When he was sure the water was hot, he rinsed his hands in the scald and lathered them with soap. He rinsed them for a long time, wondering at how much he could really hurt; wondering if Bruno's lovers were men or women; wondering if they were different each time or long-standing, ongoing affairs.

After he dried his aching hands, he returned to the bedroom and folded Bruno's underwear imagining unknown hands slipping inside them to cup his scrotum, to squeeze his ass. He folded Bruno's T-shirts, imagining unknown hands tugging the hems free from his pants, running under the material and up Bruno's back, urging the bottom hem up his sides. After he'd completed the task and left them in neat stacks by the suitcase, he walked out the bedroom's sliding glass door onto the pool deck.

The moon was near full. It reflected in a thousand silver refractions on the canal's surface. Each ripple seemed sharp and cutting to Rory's eye. Everything hurt, everything gave pain with the evidence of Bruno's infidelity placed so simply, scattered so casually, in front of his face. Rory turned away from the hurtful view of the water and found his way to a chair by the table where Bruno kept his stash box and Rory left his cigarettes. He found the pack and lit one, drawing the burning smoke deep into his lungs and holding it until his eyes watered. But no other tears came. So he sat, and watched the clouds, pinkish in the suburban darkness, that drifted over the water, and wondered why it took him so long to be sure of something he'd imagined for so long.

## 5160 ST. MARK'S COURT

MEG FOUND AUSTIN sprawled in his worn-out recliner in the loft. Looking around the nearly bare space, she wondered why Austin and the boys chose to spend all their time there. The space was nothing more than two slightly offset rectangles that provided the transition space between the boys' bedrooms, the guest room, Austin's office, and the large master suite. The windows let in light, but very little view, as they were mostly an awkward assortment of small openings never intended to be more than architectural accents to balance the windows on the outside of the house. The spaces were furnished with a hodgepodge of furniture. The boys did their homework in one rectangle, each claiming a side of a worn, heavy folding table of the type often seen in church basements or cheaply furnished offices. They sat there for their lessons, in cast-off kitchen chairs from a dinette set Meg and Austin had scavenged from a condo yard sale when they first moved to Florida.

In the rectangle off the master bedroom, Austin had pride of place in front of the elderly television with his beat-up recliner. The boys contented themselves with beanbag chairs picked up on the cheap at

Wal-Mart. The beanbag chairs wept tiny, pearly balls of Styrofoam. Austin's chair bled stuffing from the torn seams under the rolled arms. The television, VCR, and DVD player each sat on an improvised system of mismatched plastic milk crates Austin had stolen from behind a supermarket back in his college days.

The boys had attempted to cheer up the walls with soccer and movie posters. Their efforts were more successful in enthusiasm than in lining up the images on the square. The brightly colored pictures tilted with astigmatism. The push tacks barely held against their curling corners. To Meg, the space seemed unwelcoming and askew. She hated coming up the stairs and making her way through the loft to go to bed, or picking her way through its clutter, dressed for work as she was, so well put together, in a space that seemed chaotic and defeating to her morning's firm resolve.

Yet, her men seemed to love the space. They never spent any time downstairs in the generous family room. Even though it was furnished with the best of the things from the house they'd lived in before, it remained abandoned most of the time. Austin, Noah, and Josh used it only as a through-way to the pool deck and the backyard beyond. Meg had put some serious thought into the room she'd furnished and financed from Ethan Allen. For everyone in the family but her, it had lost its appeal long before it was paid off.

Meg liked to imagine her family relaxing in the tasteful family room as she prepared meals in the kitchen. She saw the boys happily doing their homework, grouped around the generous coffee table. She saw Austin watching the news in his stocking feet, settled into the deep comfort of the expensive wingback and matching ottoman she'd chosen for him. Instead, she spent most evenings alone with her laptop at the farmhouse kitchen table, with its chairs upholstered to coordinate with the springlike lavenders, yellows, and pale green stripes of the family room. While upstairs, Austin and the boys lounged around in their new boxer shorts on ugly furniture in a room that made her feel unwelcome and unsuccessful.

Austin looked up at her from his spavined old chair and smiled. "Are you ready for bed?" he asked.

"I'm exhausted," Meg admitted. "And, just looking at this loft makes me more tired."

"I made the boys pick up before they went to bed," Austin said defensively.

"Well, it is neat," Meg said in an effort to placate him. "But that's about all you can say for it. Where are the boys?"

"Josh was in bed reading *Harry Potter* and Noah was asleep when I checked about an hour ago."

Meg nodded tiredly. "I should check in on Josh, but he's probably given in to sleep by now. He's better off in his room than out here."

"Meg, I've been thinking . . . " Austin began.

"Why do you guys stay up here?" Meg interrupted. "There's a perfectly nice family room downstairs."

"We like it up here," Austin said simply.

"Why?" Meg retorted. "It's about as gracious and welcoming as something furnished by the Florida Department of Corrections."

"The boys like doing their homework together so they can share the computer," Austin said gesturing toward the boys' computer on the top of the sway-backed folding table. "I like being near them when they're working and watching TV."

"But I don't understand why you all can't do that downstairs," Meg insisted.

"It isn't comfortable," Austin said quietly. "Besides, it was you who designated this part of the house as the boys' domain."

"Yes, I did. But I never intended for it to become a boys' club." She looked around the loft and shook her head with disgust. "I've just not had the time to think about designing this area."

"Would you consider letting me and the boys do it?" Austin asked.

Meg snorted in reply.

"No, seriously, Meg. I've been putting a lot of thought into it today. Tonight, I looked through this catalogue and asked the boys' opinion about some of the stuff . . . desks and things. We have some ideas."

"Well, this should be interesting," Meg sighed. "Where do you intend to install the Coke machine?"

"You know, Meg. You're not the only one who lives here," Austin replied, hurt.

"Well, I don't intend to live in a house that looks like a bunch of guys went wild at Rooms To Go," Meg countered firmly, ignoring the hurt tone in Austin's voice.

"Can't I even show you?" Austin pleaded. "You're not being fair."

"Okay. Show me," Meg demanded.

Austin leaned over the edge of his chair and searched through a pile of magazines and old newspapers stacked at its side. When he found what he was looking for, he stood and walked to the clean end of the folding table and placed a catalogue on it. "It's Pottery Barn, not Rooms To Go, he said with great dignity.

"Their stuff is way too expensive for what you get," Meg insisted. "And the shipping charges will eat us alive."

"Will you at least look at it to see what we're thinking about?" Austin replied.

Meg walked sulkily to the table to look and listen as Austin showed her a pair of hutchlike desks for either side of the boy's rectangle and a small dining table with matching chairs that would sit between the desks. Then, he turned the pages to a large sectional sofa with a huge square ottoman and an entertainment center to go in the loft's rectangle off the master bedroom. Austin's voice grew excited as he explained that he'd measured to see if it could all fit, and the loft's area could comfortably accommodate all the pieces. Meg had to admit to herself that the dark wood tones and cheery rust color of the upholstery went well together. The furniture Austin and the boys had selected looked good, and though it hurt her to admit it, it was what they wanted, without her input. "Well, you certainly did put a lot of thought into this," she grudgingly admitted. "But, where do you intend to get the money to pay for it?"

Austin's enthusiasm visibly drained from his face. "Meg, we can swing it," he said miserably. "We paid off all our consumer debt in order to get into this house. We could use the emergency Mastercard. It's clean and it has more than enough in its credit line to buy this stuff."

"At 23 percent interest?" Meg asked incredulously. "Have you gone crazy? You know how long it took us to get that card paid off."

"I get offers in the mail every day for cards with 6.9 percent or even less," Austin pleaded. "Couldn't we get one of those and use it just for this?"

Meg looked at him. He looked like a little boy pleading for a toy. Harsh things came to mind to counter that pleading look, not the least among them how long it had been since he'd earned a commission on a sale of any sizeable amount. But she didn't say those harsh things. Something in her warned that her reaction had more to do with her own taste and self-designated place as their home's interior designer than it did with the money. She couldn't argue with Austin's logic. She couldn't really even argue with the necessity of the expense. Instead she simply saw herself sitting alone downstairs with her laptop and a cold mug of tea, her dreams of family togetherness supplanted by Pottery Barn furniture and a clubbiness from which she'd always be excluded. "Just do whatever you want," she said and turned toward the master bedroom door.

"I want you to like it too, Meg," Austin said with a naked need for approval.

She stopped and turned around. "You're a grown man, Austin. You've done your homework. What can I say? If you want that catalogue crap, go for it." With that, she turned back and went into the bedroom closing the door behind her.

Austin stood stunned for a moment. He felt Meg's dismissal as sharply as a slap. Then there was only anger. He felt his back pocket and reassured himself his wallet was in place. Satisfied it was, he picked up the catalogue and stomped into his office. Once inside, he resolutely closed and locked the door behind him. He removed his wallet and searched through its many plastic offerings until he found the card he was looking for. Then he sat down in front of his computer.

With an economy of clicks, he found himself at the Pottery Barn Web site. It was amazingly easy to navigate and use, and he clicked his way through ordering all the furniture he'd pointed out to Meg, also clicking through several thousand dollars in the process. Every click gave him back a piece of his role as head of the house. Every item he added to his shopping cart reinforced his notion that he'd pay it all back with his own money, and Meg could kiss his ass. By the time he clicked on the efficient *place order* button, he felt clearer and stronger than he had in many months.

The panic didn't set in until the order confirmation e-mail arrived in his in-box. He leaned back in his office chair and looked out over the canal. He checked his panic over the money he'd spent with the fact that he could apply for a new credit card in his own name and take advantage of the low-rate interest for balance transfers any of them proffered. By the time both his anger and his elation subsided, he simply felt tired and sad. Austin knew, but didn't want to admit, that his own vision of family togetherness increasingly accommodated the reality of Meg's absence in her late nights at the office or her need to do work once she was home. Still, his thoughts insisted, that was Meg's choice. If she wanted to sit downstairs at the kitchen table with her laptop for company, it was fine with him. It was her idea, he reminded himself, to move them all to this ridiculously large house when everything had been fine at the old one.

Still, he'd won. And there was a small victory in that. He'd put together a pretty cool space he and the boys would be comfortable in. He couldn't wait to tell Rory. He'd picked out the sectional sofa for his loft because he liked the one at Rory's so much. As far as he was concerned, Meg could keep her prissy striped furniture and her goddamn picture lamps downstairs.

With Rory on his mind, he swiveled in his chair to look down on the pool deck next door. Surprisingly enough, he found Rory sitting there, smoking and deep in thought. It amazed him how someone so self-assured could manage to look so lonely and abandoned out in the moonlight. Austin felt a flash of concern. Rory was smoking, and he'd admitted he only smoked these days when he felt nervous or claustrophobic.

Austin watched him below and wondered what was going on next door that would force Rory to sit outside and smoke. He wondered if Bruno had said or done something to hurt him, or if he was simply nervous about the audition he would be going to the next day. He wondered why he cared, then grudgingly admitted he did care, he cared a great deal.

Austin watched as the bedroom door slid open and Bruno stepped out onto the pool deck. Rory didn't turn or acknowledge his presence. Bruno stepped toward Rory, but suddenly looked up into Austin's window. The moonlight outside caught Bruno's face with enough illumination for Austin to tell he was looking straight at him. The look turned into a challenging stare. Austin watched as Bruno finally broke off his stare long enough to walk over to Rory's still form. He bent over Rory and kissed him gently on the top of his head, then, placing his hands under Rory's arms, he lifted him to a standing position. Without looking back, Bruno put his arm over Rory's shoulders and steered him into the bedroom. The only indication he gave Austin that he knew he was watching was a raised hand, the middle finger well-extended.

Guiltily, Austin turned off his desk lamp. Somehow, in the past hour, he had managed to piss off two people he'd really rather not piss off at all. But, when he'd had a chance to think about it, he decided he didn't care. He didn't really care about Meg or Bruno one bit. To his mind in that moment, they might as well be the same person. He hoped Rory was okay. As for himself, he was just fine with everything, thank you very much.

Smug in his defiance, he watched the rectangle of light that shone from Rory's bedroom. For many minutes, it betrayed nothing, not even a shadow. Then, he caught a glimpse of Rory as he moved to his side of the bed and sat down. Before he could get the T-shirt over his head, the light went off abruptly and Austin was left staring hopefully at a rectangle of deeper darkness than the moonlit pool deck.

Austin was disappointed. After he'd seen Rory and Bruno making love, he kept vigil at his window on the nights he found himself alone in his office late at night. He was remarkably honest with himself about his curiosity. He justified it by thinking that if Rory and Bruno made love with their light on in a room without drapes or blinds, they must not care if anyone looked.

Rory had explained and apologized for their activities that afternoon. While Austin was uncomfortable with the conversation at the time, that was one thing. His harmless voyeurism, he felt, was quite another. He even took some pleasure in the fact that Rory might be wondering if Austin was there, like a silent witness at the window, watching as they did the things men did to each other. Austin could admit to himself without shame that the sight of it turned him on in a deeply male kind of way. Their activities didn't disgust him. They were personal, just as his interest was personal. It was something that was his alone, and he was coming to like the freedom and assertion he felt when he had something that was his alone.

Tonight, he was disappointed by the blackness at Rory's door. But his curiosity grew. His dick, warm against his leg in his boxer shorts, had priorities of its own. When the light never returned to Rory's door after many minutes, Austin swiveled his chair back to face his computer. He pulled down the menu of Web sites he'd recently visited and smiled to himself when Pottery Barn was listed at the top. A little further down was his favorite search engine. He highlighted it and was rewarded with its home page nearly immediately. He clicked the cursor into the search box and typed "g-a-y x-x-x," then clicked search. Within an instant, he saw a map to a million places his curiosity could take him.

## CHAPTER EIGHT

# *It's all about give and take*

THE EXODUS OF any morning traffic out of St. Mark's Court had finished by the time Bruno stepped out of his house and walked to the end of his drive promptly at seven thirty. Bruno noted the winter's sunlight hadn't even made it over the tops of the houses on his side of the canal yet. So he stood beside his still street, glad of his suit coat in the chill, with his briefcase and suitcase waiting by his feet. The car service was behind schedule, but not yet late enough to give any cause for alarm. Still, he unclipped his cell phone from his belt and looked at its digital screen to make sure he hadn't missed any calls saying the driver had been delayed. Bruno hated this in-between time of travel, this waiting to get going, this stasis before leaving home and Rory behind to join the world of work and larger concerns.

He was not one to look behind him with longing at any time, never less so than when he was leaving on a trip. Long last looks were for losers and pessimists. Bruno had no doubt he'd soon be back in this drive with a successful week in New York under his belt. He gave no thought to towers that might collapse and fall in on themselves. He wasted no time wondering what horror could suddenly come from a madman's urge to snuff him out as a by-blow in a larger condemnation of his world. Bruno didn't move but in one direction, and that direction had no exits for fear or unanswerable questions about the nature of things beyond his control.

Still, something about leaving Rory this time niggled at the back of his mind. It was nothing he could put his finger on. They had not fought. They hadn't exchanged any cross words. But there was an underlying sense of something not quite right, not quite said, not quite usual in Rory's goodbye. It was as if Rory was holding something back. There were hints of storm clouds in the atmosphere that Bruno couldn't see, but made the hair on the back of his neck stand up just the same.

Bruno glanced over his shoulder toward the front of the house, half expecting Rory to be watching him from behind a window or a crack in the door. The house betrayed nothing but its usual grand façade. It was the home of a successful man, and Bruno relished its stolid presence at his back for just that reason. But this morning, it was as if the house had turned its back on him, wearily. It called to mind the same look and feeling his mother used to give him and his brothers when their antics had pushed her beyond all patience and endurance. She'd turned her back on them as if to say she really didn't care anymore about anything they did. Her turned back seemed to say her disappointment with them was too great to waste time on recrimination, correction, or tears.

There was something of that in Rory this morning. Usually, he followed Bruno to the door and, along with Bridget, gave him the fondest of farewells. They both managed to communicate a goodbye filled with a genuine sense that he would be sorely missed until he reappeared, as if by magic, and they could live in the sunshine once more. Today, he'd left Rory with a cup of coffee out on the pool deck. Bridget couldn't be bothered to get up from her postbreakfast nap, much less walk him to the door. It didn't occur to Bruno that something was off-kilter with this until he found himself waiting for the car service on the chilly, sunless side of the house.

Bruno turned once more and glanced up to the second story of the Hardens' house. There was the window he'd caught Austin watching them through the night before. He hoped the bastard got the message when he'd given him the finger and lead Rory to bed. He made a mental note to say something about it casually to Austin, maybe suggest he get blinds installed. If he couldn't keep his eyes to himself, the least he could do was put up some shutters or curtains. While Bruno didn't really give a damn what Austin might see, the thought of him watching Rory from his upstairs perch gave him the creeps. It was a territorial thing as far as Bruno was concerned. Rory wasn't Austin's to watch. To Bruno's way of thinking, Austin needed to mind his own damn business and keep his eyes off Bruno's property.

Just then he heard the Hardens' front door open and close abruptly. Bruno spun around, happy for the opportunity to get his irritation off his mind. But it was Meg he found at the front door, busily searching her pocketbook for her keys, her thick lawyer's briefcase sitting squatly at her feet. She looked all business, dressed in a winter white suit, her legs sheathed in the smooth sheen of stockings, her feet perched becomingly in café au lait colored high heels.

Bruno grinned, admitting to himself that she was a fine-looking woman, but imagining she wielded a set of balls as heavy and clunky as his own. The thought made him mischievous. He gave her an appreciative wolf whistle that startled her attention away from her purse to look his way. "You're certainly looking professional this morning, Mrs. Harden," he called out.

Meg spared him a smile when she'd located her keys and stepped down her drive toward him, leaving her briefcase and purse by the driver's side of her Rover. "Good morning to you, Bru . . . Will," she corrected. "You're not looking too bad yourself."

"Thank you, ma'am," Bruno said with a slight bow.

Meg arrived within arm's reach of him on the sidewalk and sighed. "Are you having car trouble? Do you need a ride downtown?"

Bruno could tell her offer was extended with a projection of how much time it might cost her. He glanced at his watch quickly and noted she would be at least twenty minutes late if she meant to be at work at eight. "No, thank you," he said sweetly. "I'm waiting on a town car to take me to the airport. They have exactly two minutes to get here before I call and give their dispatcher an ass chew . . . umm . . . a new perspective," Bruno corrected himself, "on their service."

"A town car?" Meg said wryly. "Aren't you grand."

"Not really," Bruno replied airily. "It's an expense account item. It actually costs less than keeping your car parked for a week, when you think about it. And there's a lot less hassle to it if the fricking car service shows up on time," he added with an irritable glance down the street.

"Oh my," Meg said worriedly. "I hope you don't have an early flight."

"It's later," Bruno said, "But my comfort window is narrowing. How about you? Are you running late this morning?"

Meg raised her eyebrows and nodded without smiling. "I'm afraid I had a bit of personal housekeeping to take care of with my husband this morning. He spent some time on the computer ordering new furniture last night, he informed me this morning. Let's just say I'd rather have started my day differently. Where are you heading out to?"

"I've been called to our office in New York for a week or so's worth of work," Bruno said evenly.

"It must be nice," was Meg's brisk reply. "I could use a week in a lovely Manhattan hotel far away from Austin and the boys. In fact, it sounds like bliss," she added with something that sounded like wistfulness.

"It is good to get away," Bruno said. "I enjoy being my own man from time to time myself."

Meg nodded but said, "I think when you're a wife you never really get to be your own person again until you've seen your children married and your husband snug in a cemetery somewhere."

Bruno gave a low whistle and said, "You have had a challenging morning, I take it."

Meg gave him a falsely bright smile. "It's all about give and take, I suppose."

Bruno laughed. "You got that right. You can't live with them and you can't kill them."

Meg laughed in turn and gave him a smile that was less forced. "Does it ever strike you as a bit unfair that we're out here in suits when they're inside lounging around in their underwear, scratching and being difficult?"

"Oh, I got the moody, silent treatment this morning," Bruno said.

"Lucky you," Meg replied. "At least you were spared being told in so many words that you are an emasculating bitch."

"Uh," Bruno said and looked at the bags at his feet. "Harsh."

"I get enough of that at the office," Meg said. "I certainly don't need it at home. Do you work with many women at your level, Will?"

"A fair few," Bruno said carefully.

"Be extra nice to them when you get to New York," Meg said. "Take it from me, they've earned it."

Bruno looked up the quiet street at the sound of an approaching vehicle. With a great deal of relief, he saw it was a long, black Lincoln. He waved it down, and looked at Meg with a gentle smile. "I hope your day gets better, Meg."

"Thanks," Meg said and turned toward her car, "Have a nice trip."

"Meg?" Bruno said as the car stopped at the end of his drive.

"Yes?" Meg replied and turned back to face him.

The driver got out of the town car and opened the door to the back seat for Bruno. As he picked up Bruno's suitcase, Bruno looked at Meg and said, "I have one of those desk calendars, 'a saying a day' things. A few days ago it said, 'if you eat a live frog every morning, the rest of your day will be excellent because nothing could be worse.'"

Meg looked at him with bewildered consternation clear on her face.

Bruno stepped behind the door to the backseat and rested his arm on the top of the town car. "I'd bet you've eaten your frog for today."

Meg laughed. "Maybe you're right," she said.

"Count on it," Bruno said and gave her a dazzling smile. With that, he got into the town car and the driver closed the door behind him.

Meg turned once more and walked toward her car, deciding on the way that she would have a good day. For the time being, she was done with frogs and annoying husbands both.

### 5150 ST. MARK'S COURT

RORY TOOK OFF his headphones and looked calmly through the glass into the engineering booth. The assorted musicians inside were laughing and exchanging mysterious handshakes. Dazz Coleman opened the mic to the sound studio and said, "Okay, slick. Good job. I'll see you in the parking lot." With that, he turned off the mic and pushed his chair back to stand.

The large black man sitting as inscrutably as a Buddha at his side nodded at Rory. He leaned forward and switched on the mic once more. "You keepin' it crunk, white boy. Real down home. Ronald Isley need to shut up. Dazz'll let you know."

"Thanks," Rory said into the mic suspended in front of him.

"Don't be thanking me," the man replied. "You the one brought it." With that, he switched off the mic and turned to speak to the group of musicians behind him. Rory noted that Dazz sat back down in deference to the man and swiveled to turn his back to Rory.

There was nothing more for Rory to do. He straightened his shoulders. Now distinctly ignored after having been under such impassive scrutiny for the past hour, he swallowed his dismissal and made his way outside to the parking lot.

Once he made it to his car, he stripped off the shirt he'd bought new at Banana Republic for this audition. He stood in his guinea-T in the bright sunshine and shook for a minute as the pent-up adrenaline from his performance drained from his body. When the shaking stopped, he opened his car door and leaned into the cool, shady interior to extract his cigarettes and lighter from under the sun visor. He tossed his shirt onto the passenger seat, backed out of the car, and stood in the sunshine once more. He welcomed the warmth and glare after the studio's dim air-conditioned chill. The cigarette pack, so smooth and sure in his hand, promised an immediate reward and relief from all the anxiety that had built up in his subconscious leading to this telling moment. He opened the pack and, extracting a cigarette, promised himself he wasn't going to start chain-smoking again. He'd managed to quit that once. But for right now, he wanted a cigarette more than he'd ever wanted one in his life.

Once he lit up, Rory shoved the pack and lighter in his back pocket and closed the door of his car. Dazz had told him he'd meet him in the parking lot, and he resigned himself to waiting. For all he knew, Dazz could keep him waiting for five minutes or for an hour. Rory took another hit off his cigarette and walked to the front of his car. He sat on the hood with his feet resting on the front bumper so he could watch the door of the studio and also be in plain sight from the lobby.

Through one cigarette, then another, he analyzed his performance. The points where he felt he was flat stabbed at him. The parts where he felt he'd pulled off a particularly smooth note buttressed his eroding confidence. By the beginning of his third cigarette, he had a hung jury in his own mind. There was nothing left to do but wait for Dazz to tell him what was most important, and that would be the result of the reckoning going on inside the engineering booth.

By the time Dazz opened the door and stepped out to meet him, Rory's shoulders were turning red and his mouth and throat were parched. Rory didn't move from the hood of his car. He simply looked up and waited for the verdict.

Dazz laughed. "You look like you lost your mama, sitting out here like that," he said by way of a greeting.

"Uh-huh," Rory replied. "I'm just keeping it crunk."

Dazz gave him a sober look, "You said that right, my nigga. To' it up."

Rory rubbed his blond head and looked toward the door to the studio. "I'm way too light to be your nigga. I'm just a white boy trying to make it in a black man's world."

Dazz laughed at the reversal of the age-old complaint. The irony of the situation rested well beneath his neatly dreadlocked skull. "You a nigga whether you like it or not," he said.

Rory snorted and shook his head. "You know I can't say that word and not get shot, whether I tore it up or not." Rory slid off the hood of his car and reached in his back pocket for still another cigarette. He put it in his mouth and looked at Dazz as he got it lit, then said, "So, cut the bullshit. What's the deal?"

Dazz nodded. "It's like that, huh? Okay, all business, homes. We can use you for two, maybe three cuts. "Footsteps in the Dark," for *sho'*. You brought the flavor on that, know what I'm saying?"

Rory grinned. "What else?"

Dazz looked over his shoulder toward the street. "All studio, no dates. Pay you scale. No promises for anything but a liner note credit."

Rory took another drag off his cigarette and flicked an ash into the wind. "That's typical. I got no problem with it." He waited for Dazz to acknowledge his presence once more. "Why no dates?"

Dazz looked at him and shook his head. "You know why, baby."

Rory nodded. "Too light, too bright."

"Look, Rory, you gots to understand. These guys are straight up ghetto. That's their positioning. It's all about marketing. You living in the black man's world, right?"

Rory shrugged. "I thought they were more than that. I thought it was all about breaking into LOVE 94 and shit."

"LOVE 94 come way after being on 99 JAMZ, then Hot 105, player," Dazz said. "The marketing ain't up to me. It is what it is, baby. Take it or leave it."

Rory took another hit off his cigarette and, reaching past Dazz, flicked the butt out into the parking lot. "I'm hungry, Dazz. You know that. I just want to get back into the studio. Fuck live dates, then. At this point in my life, I don't need the travel. You tell them I'll bring the flavor. Just let me know when to be back here."

Dazz nodded and gave him a hug that threatened to lift his feet off the pavement. "You'll be back here next week. Maybe three day's work at most. From what you did today, I can get you in here in the daytime to lay down your tracks. We're burning the music right now."

Rory stepped away from his old friend's embrace and walked to his car door. "Thanks for the shot, Dazz. I'm happy it worked out."

Dazz stepped away from the front of Rory's car back toward the studio door. "I'll call you tomorrow, maybe the day after. You got any questions before then, text me."

Rory nodded and opened his car door. "Take me to the next phase," he sang.

Dazz laughed and went back into the studio.

Rory got into his car and cranked it up. It was, he thought, not an unqualified success, but he'd settle for the studio gig and a chance to hear himself on the CD. He was not a little bit disappointed about being cut out of any live performances, but he'd settle. He threw the car in reverse and smoothly cut his back end into the parking lot. Settling was something he was used to. He thought about the condoms in Bruno's dop kit. At least he had succeeded at something himself today. He still had his voice, and that was all his. He put the car into drive and headed out toward home.

The recording studio was in the warehouse district of Sunrise between 44th and Commercial Boulevard. The neighborhood where he and Bruno had bought their first house in South Florida, after moving from their East Fort Lauderdale condo, lay between where he was and where they called home these days. He decided to swing by the old neighborhood and visit memory lane.

Within five minutes, he found himself on the familiar street. Raw and new when they'd bought their first house there, the area had matured and mellowed into the kind of lower middle-class haven it had promised to become all those years ago. To Rory's eyes now, all the houses seemed small. It was like going back to the school where you attended first grade. The place that harbored such big dreams, and so many new experiences, appeared little and worn when you returned to it years later. Everything on the old street seemed narrow and closer together. Even the eternally blue winter sky arching overhead seemed to have a lower threshold to heaven. It was the same, but everything had changed. Rory knew he'd grown along with the trees that had been mere striplings when they'd moved in and now reached high. In a very real way, Rory longed for the way it had been back then. Even if it had been constricted and small, he'd been so happy then.

So he eased on the brake as he passed their old house. He could smell the air and feel the same late afternoon sun on his shoulders that he had when he used to pull in that drive, walk up that walk, and let himself into that small house.

With a stab as sure as a knife's thrust, what he did miss came to him with a poignancy undimmed by all the years left behind. He missed who he was back then. He missed the Bruno who was Bruno back then. Those days when he'd lived in that house were so full of love and open-ended promise. His expectations were unlimited and there was solid proof they were being fulfilled. Bruno was back, and only his, and that seemed like everything he wanted. Back then Rory's life had a second act that was just beginning. Sadly, he took his foot off the brake and glided on down the street. Somehow, he couldn't shake the feeling that the second act was coming to a close.

In the end, he'd never told Bruno that his audition was today. After the night when Bruno had told him to do what he wanted, he'd never brought the subject up again. If Bruno had either forgotten or declined to express any further interest, the result was the same. Rory had something that was his and his alone. In giving everything he was to a dream of marriage and living with someone else, there was still an echoing emptiness in the space that was left. This one chance, this gig in the studio, was only a small rebellion in the hope of filling the void.

Bitterly, he thought how Bruno filled his own empty spaces. But there was no question he still loved Bruno, maybe even because of his bad behavior. He loved him more than he had in the days shaded by the trees on that street, if that was possible. There was no question that he'd stay with him. To leave him was unimaginable, even if his disappointment with him tested his patience over and over again.

The only way Rory knew to distance himself from Bruno's shortcomings was to retreat into himself. He knew he'd only just begun to find ways to keep a part of himself from being swallowed by Bruno's oblivious self-centeredness. He thought about Bruno the night before, talking about how he needed Rory to be excited about a potential move to New York. Yet Bruno couldn't even manage to get excited about Rory's audition. Rory knew things would never really change. He'd signed on to be Bruno's property a long time ago. It was just the way things were.

Rory heaved a sigh that was far more appropriate than any tears. He pushed the gas pedal to slowly build the speed he needed to leave memory lane behind, again. With half a life spent loving Bruno in his rearview mirror, he accelerated toward home, knowing he'd settle. Living, he knew, was full of compromise. Living with yourself was just another kind.

## 5160 ST. MARK'S COURT

AUSTIN SAT IN his car, in the shade of the black olive and live oak branches, just to savor the moment. He never dreamed a simple email would bring him such satisfaction. He hadn't recognized the name of the sender, but he did recognize the Web address it came from. It was a site he visited often and with a longing he was ashamed to acknowledge, even to himself. So when Dave Handley invited him to go to lunch, he'd at first wanted to decline. Finally, simple curiosity led him to accept the invitation. After all, he'd thought, it was really sort of harmless, just two guys getting together for lunch. Dave Handley had a come-on that couldn't fail. He simply said he wanted to know Austin better, considering what they had in common.

So Austin agreed to meet him for lunch at the Cheesecake Factory on Glades Road in Boca. It was a place Austin knew well from back in the days when he worked at the hi-tech firm. At first, he was nervous about meeting Dave there. He didn't particularly want to run into anyone he knew, but finally he decided the hell with it. Lunch didn't mean anything. Austin told himself it would be crazy to believe it could lead to anything more.

At first it had been very pleasant and all general bullshit. But, by the time the food arrived, Austin got the distinct impression he was being subtly courted. It grew increasingly obvious that Dave found him a real possibility. By the time lunch ended, Austin was utterly seduced. He found the possibilities Dave Handley hinted at to be something he'd wanted for a long time, but had been too proud to own up to. By the time the check came and Dave suavely handed the waiter his corporate card, Austin found himself liking Dave very much. They agreed to meet again, though no date was set. Dave said he'd call him next week, and Austin found himself fantasizing about getting that call now.

It turned out Dave Handley was the new CEO at the hi-tech firm Austin had worked for. It seemed that, in the bizarre corporate permutations and power plays since Austin had been asked to leave, the true extent of the old CFO's perfidy and the old CEO's blind complicity in it had come to light in a very harsh way. When Dave had come onboard, he'd heard the real story about Austin's honesty, and he was a man who valued honesty among his department heads. Austin's name and reputation had stuck in his mind. Once Dave had successfully moved people and situations to his advantage, he'd known precisely the right moment to give Austin a call.

It seemed to Austin that Dave liked him a great deal. He offered to bring him onboard as the new CFO, with all the benefits and perks associated with the job. After all, even after his extended absence, to Dave's mind, Austin's learning curve would be considerably shortened by the length of time he had been with the firm before. He'd made certain overtures and Austin had responded in the appropriate ways— at least he had to his own way of thinking. Corporate courtship dances were as complex and orchestrated as minuets at the Czarist court. In plain Texas talk, Dave had asked Austin if he wanted to dance. Austin had said hell, yeah. There was little more to do now than wait for Dave to signal the band and get the music playing.

After lunch, Austin walked slowly to his car and waited a decent interval to make sure Dave had put some road between them before he cranked his own car and followed him to the office. Now, he sat in his car in a visitor's space far from the front door and savored the feeling of returning to the place not only vindicated, but victorious. It was a very good feeling. The last time he'd walked under these trees he'd been carrying a photocopy paper box stuffed with an assortment of personal things that had collected in his office over the years. That box had sat undisturbed in his old garage for the many months since he'd come home angry and defeated. The box waited while Austin moved unhappily into a job where he had no real office. It sat undisturbed until it was moved and placed unopened in Austin's new garage. Now, Austin idly enjoyed the sunshine and the breeze in the office parking lot and thought about the pleasure he'd take in finding the box, opening it, and getting out the old frame that once sat on his desk. He had new pictures of Meg and the boys to put in it. Pictures he'd had copies of and left sitting in a drawer because he couldn't face opening the box that contained his old office life.

Austin looked fondly at the building in front of him sprawling strong, solid, and squat. Inside it, there were people busy making things happen. They sat hunched before keyboards, or leaned back in their ergonomic chairs on conference calls with headsets in their ears. People were in the break room, going for that fresh three o'clock cup of coffee. They were alive, they were vital, and they were going to see him back happily among them after an exile of far too long. He missed it; god, how he missed it so.

To his mind, that office was what held the life of a man. To be fully alive with his mind humming like a calculator offering up facts and figures, even entire spreadsheets on command; that was what he wanted to do. He didn't want to sit at home anymore trying to peddle diagnostic equipment to poorly funded hospitals. He didn't want to be cut off and apart from the brilliant activity happening in that building, in that world, and in that life. More than anything, he wanted not to fill his time thinking about new furniture for the loft. He didn't want to worry how he would pay for it.

He didn't want to worry about picking the boys up from school or ferrying them to and from soccer practice. He didn't want to be beholden to Meg's hours and schedules and whims and paycheck.

And that was at the core of it. Quite simply put, he didn't give a fuck about those things, not when he could stride back into the working world of men and big decisions.

He glanced at his watch and realized the day of his redemption hadn't yet come. He had no more than a clear understanding with Dave Handley and a vague idea of when this next act of his life would begin. Austin looked around the parking lot he'd made his way through over seasons before. He saw himself at Christmas, on the day before the Memorial Day weekend, on Good Friday, as he made his way into and out of the office that lay across the parking lot. He longed to stride across it with self-assurance and pride again. He wanted to come home.

For now, it was his secret. When it came down to it, he knew he wouldn't tell Meg. Not yet. For a time, this new opportunity was private and beautiful and his alone. Out of the emptiness he'd felt after he'd been forced out, this dream always somehow survived. Until it was a fact, he didn't want to jinx all the possibilities that were so close at hand. He knew he'd had to settle for doing less than his best for a time, but that time was over. No more compromises.

Unsurprisingly, he knew there was one person he could tell. Rory. Today had been Austin's own audition of sorts. Rory would know how he felt. Austin cranked his car and backed carefully into the parking lot. He pictured swapping success stories with Rory. He had no doubt he'd aced his audition. With an expansive spirit that was fueled by his own new victory, he wanted to hear all about Rory's. He'd wasted enough time asking him about furniture, he wanted to talk to him about guy stuff. And, for Austin, guy stuff was about motion. It was about moving forward into wonderful, exciting change. Rory would understand he wasn't just a schlep now. Austin was going back to being large and in charge.

*Oh man*, he thought. *This is going to be big fun.* With that, he put the car in drive and headed home.

## CHAPTER NINE

# *Two grown men, playing hooky . . .*

IT WAS A NEAR-PERFECT day on the beach. The highs for the day had been predicted near eighty, and the winds were near calm. There was just enough breeze off the ocean to blow away any notion of burning skin, and the late winter sun was more inclined to caress than sear in any event. Austin sighed happily and slipped a fresh Bud Light can into his neoprene holder. As he contentedly sipped his beer, he noted that it was the precise moment when you realize the morning had turned to afternoon. He still had plenty of time before he had to pick up the boys from school. For the moment, he was becalmed in the sea of the day, and he was very happy.

The beach lark was all Rory's idea. He'd been out watering his geraniums that morning when Austin got the good news. Feeling the need to shout, Austin flung open his office window and called down,: "I just got off the phone with Dave Handley! I start back in two weeks!"

"Wanna celebrate?" Rory yelled back.

"Celebrate? Hell, I want to get drunk," Austin said and laughed particularly long and well.

"Let's take the day off and go to the beach and get drunk together," Rory said. "I got finished in the studio last night and I feel like celebrating myself!"

Austin didn't need much persuading. Within a half hour, he found himself in Rory's car with the music blasting, the windows rolled down, and after a quick pit stop for beer, the road to the beach rolling along under him. He hadn't felt so good since he'd had beach hooky days back in college. Rory was easy company, as most listeners are. He'd patiently sat in thrall through Austin's first rush of beer buzz ramblings. He didn't make too big of a deal of his own studio achievements from the past few days; he simply let Austin's excited expansiveness fill the time between when they'd arrived on the beach and when he'd run out of steam a couple of hours later.

Having talked himself out, Austin realized how he'd dominated the conversation and felt chagrin at the way he'd played to Rory's audience of one. He'd apologized, but Rory just smiled and told him he was used to it. Thinking about it now, with a fresh beer in his hand and his happiness undiluted in the fine day, Austin considered that Rory was probably right. "I bet you'd make a good wife," he teased.

Rory chuckled and turned from his back to his stomach on his beach towel. "I've had a lot of practice," he said dryly as he pillowed his head on his arms and looked up at Austin sitting next to him.

Austin sipped his beer and leaned back on his elbows. "Is that how it is with you and Bruno? Are you the wife?"

Rory snickered. "It always comes down to that question doesn't it?"

"Well, he treats you like one," Austin said. "I've noticed it."

"We fascinate you, don't we?" Rory asked without being condescending. "I've seen you watching us. What did you think you'd see?"

Austin colored under his sun-exposed skin. He took another sip of beer and tried to think of how to reply.

Rory laughed. "Austin, you're the only person I've ever seen who could blush under a morning's worth of sun. You're busted. It's no big deal, I just figured you were either totally bored, or mildly curious. There's nothing wrong with that."

"Okay, I'll cop to being curious. That's why I'm asking," Austin said. "Are you the wife?"

Rory closed his eyes and sighed. "It's not like that. I mean, I can see how you'd think that way. Bruno is this big-assed businessman. I'm marginally employed. Bruno is all man. I'm just an aging pretty boy. Bruno is always pulling me around. I'm always taking it. I'm sure that's what you see."

"Yeah, pretty much," Austin admitted.

"Well, that's just what you see. Most of the time, it's more like this, like me and you hanging out right now. Only more," Rory tried to explain. "At least that's the way it feels to me. We talk. We get each other, we're best friends, but we've been best friends for so long, sometimes it's like we're the same person," Rory said carefully. He opened his eyes and looked at Austin. "I'm not blind to the way Bruno comes off, like he owns me and shit. He's just protective and territorial. He's always been that way. I put up with it because I know him and I love him for how he is."

"But," Austin began and faltered. He took a longer drink from his beer bottle.

Rory rose up on one elbow and rested his cheek in his hand. "But that's not what you're curious about is it?"

Austin looked at him uneasily, but Rory's open face and slight smile disarmed him. "No. I guess it isn't."

"You want to know about the sex. You want to know if Bruno is always the pitcher and I'm always the catcher," Rory said and laughed.

"Well, yeah," Austin admitted. "I mean, you have to wonder."

Rory shook his head. "Boy, anatomy really is destiny for you breeders isn't it?"

"I don't get it," Austin said, somehow offended, but not knowing why. "I mean, I don't get your point . . . about what you just said." Rory always made him feel slightly stupid for no reason at all.

"I'm just saying that I don't see sex as about who's putting it to who. You both are fucking, right? It's like you both are *there*," Rory explained.

"Okay . . . And?" Austin urged.

"So do you fuck thinking about 'my man dick is all up in this pussy so I'm a man,' or are you thinking; 'boy, this feels good.' When I'm having sex, I'm busy thinking about what I'm feeling, not who I am." Rory snickered and said dismissively, "I don't have any psychological identity crises while I'm in the middle of a right proper pounding."

"Must be nice," Austin said sarcastically. "I'm always thinking, "'Am I crushing her?' or 'I hope I make her come this time.' Or the old standby, 'I hope to hell she doesn't get pregnant.' You got it easy, buddy, if all you're thinking about is how good it feels."

"I'm sorry, dude," Rory said. "I'm glad I'm queer. I enjoy fucking too much for all that shit." With that, he settled back down with his head on his arms and closed his armseyes.

Austin had nothing to add to that. He simply finished his beer and closed his eyes. In his early afternoon stupor, he wondered what it would be like to have sex with someone who was just in it for the fun. It had been years since he and Meg had anything approaching fun in the bedroom. In fact, it usually seemed like it was a chore in her eyes, or a hasty opportunity to be seized upon in his.

As it did with increasing frequency in the past few weeks, his mind turned to having sex with Rory. In those weeks, ever since he'd moved in next door, in fact, Rory became the object of a kind of curiosity he'd not indulged in since he was a kid. The idea had grown from a distraction to an ever-increasing itch. Austin wasn't introspective enough to think about why he found himself so attracted to Rory. He wasn't having any sort of "psychological identity crisis," as Rory put it. He was only interested in the possibilities of an abstract kind of sexual availability Rory presented.

He stole a glance at the slender form stretched out next to him.

With his narrow shoulders and slim build, Rory could almost be mistaken for either a boy or a young woman from behind, if you didn't look further up than the neck. His crew cut was too blunt an affirmation of his maleness to allow the comparison to proceed any further. As Austin allowed his eyes to wander, he noted Rory had a trim ass that curved suggestively under his swimsuit, and it wasn't until Austin's eyes ran down to his calves that he encountered any suggestion of hairiness. The rest of him was as slick as a baby's butt.

Austin wondered at that form engaged in nothing but feeling good. He mused on the abstraction of what it would be like merely to freely fuck that body and have it respond so willingly, so eagerly to his touch and command. It didn't really disturb him that those simple thoughts had progressed to more concrete, personal imaginings. He wondered at Rory's capacity for shivers and hard panting. He wondered how it would feel to run his hands over that back and grasp that narrow waist. Up until now, that imagining had been enough. It was an enjoyable personal fantasy, but he intuitively understood he wanted to take it further than fantasy. Increasingly of late, he wondered if Rory might be thinking the same thing. In so many ways, it would be so easy and uncomplicated. Austin thought about how it might be an act so separated from any of the baggage he was used to packing in with the notion of sex, that it could be like being young, a teenager, once more.

For once, he was glad of the bagginess of his trunks. His dick took his musings further than where his courage, so far, had allowed him to go. He was glad Rory had apparently drifted off to sleep. Still, he bent his leg closest to Rory to cover his rampant curiosity and rested the hand holding his beer on that hip. His eyes were smarting from the salt breeze and the frank appraisal of another guy's body. The sun and his growing insistent ease with his thoughts made closing them a welcome idea. Alone in the dark behind his eyes, he allowed his curiosity to move even further.

Austin almost had drifted off to sleep when he heard the laughter. The sound was bright and derisive, cutting sharply over the susurrant sound of the waves. He opened his eyes and through the sudden glare caught sight of two teenaged boys walking by. When they were even with where he sat, one shoved the other toward him. "Here, faggot. This guy's looking for a *special friend.*"

The boy who'd been shoved looked at Austin and lisped, "I like guys too."

"Fuck, you kid," Austin said irritably.

The boys stopped and took a threatening step forward. "I bet you'd like that, faggot," the shover said.

Austin clenched his beer and angrily retorted, "Ask my wife, punk."

"Wife?" The lisper said and laughed. "Does she know you're here with your pussy-boy?"

Austin got to his feet, damning the sharp creak in his forty- year-old knees. "Watch your mouth, asshole. I'll beat your head in."

The shover moved forward as lithely as a powerful cat and once more shoved his friend out of the way, "Oh yeah? Well bring it, fudgepacker," he challenged.

"C'mon, man," the lisper urged and grabbed his shoulder. "It ain't worth it."

Shrugging off his friend's grasp, the kid took another step toward Austin and said, "Bring it, bitch. I'll fuck you up."

Wearily, Rory got neatly to his feet, a beer bottle already in his hand. He locked eyes with the shover and pulled the bottle out of its cozy. He just dismissively glanced at the lisper and transferred the bottle to his other hand, gripping it by the neck.

"C'mon, man," the lisper urged once more. "You made your fucking point. Quit fooling around."

The shover lunged once more, pulling a punch. When neither

Austin nor Rory flinched, he hesitated, then spat. "I want to kill you gay motherfuckers," he hissed.

"And I want to see you eat this beer bottle, dickwad." Rory said casually. "I wonder what those big cocksucker lips of yours would look like wrapped around it."

The boy hesitated at the unscripted reference to his own appearance, and for an instant a flicker of hurt crossed his unsure face before he went back to trying to look murderous.

The lisper simply looked from Rory to Austin, and then, apparently deciding the two older men were capable of taking him and his friend, turned and walked away. As he moved into the other boy's peripheral vision, the shover glanced his way and turned to follow him. "You're lucky this time, faggots."

Rory laughed. "Yeah, yeah. You suck my dick, you little bitch."

The boy trotted backwards for a moment and yelled, "You better not be here when I come back, pussy." With that, he turned and trotted away toward his friend's receding back.

Unimpressed, Rory sat back down on his blanket and casually opened the cooler and dropped the empty beer bottle in.

Austin stood looking down at him. "You really handled that well."

Rory shrugged and smiled. "Believe it or not, when Bruno's being an asshole, he's also being a good teacher. I can talk shit right up there with the best of them."

"Yeah," Austin countered, "But when it comes down to business, how are you?"

Rory looked up at him and gave him a frankly appraising look. "I would have done my best to break that beer bottle across his front teeth."

"Doesn't shit like that ever get to you?" Austin asked incredulously.

Rory smiled. "It wasn't meant to get to me. It was meant to get to you. And I think they pretty much succeeded. You're shaking."

Austin looked down at the beer bottle still clutched in his hand. It was trembling violently. He hadn't come this close to an actual fight since he was a freshman in high school. Adrenaline, sparked by a long-dormant fight-or-flight reaction, pumped from the recesses of the most primitive part of his brain, had flooded his body.

"Never let 'em smell fear, Austin." Rory said solemnly. "Oh, and if you're going to use a beer bottle as a weapon, you need to remember to take the cozy off first. If you don't, it just bounces off their heads."

Austin felt the adrenaline-triggered trembling reach his legs. Embarrassed by it, he hid the reaction by sitting on his own beach towel. "You seem to know a lot about getting in fights for a gay guy," he said to Rory sarcastically.

"I played in a lot of rough clubs back in the Bad Halen days," Rory laughed and shoved Austin's shoulder. That physical contact initiated by Rory shot across his skin like electricity. Austin couldn't tell if it was because he'd gotten too much sun, or if he welcomed the touch. "Are you ready to head back to the 'burbs, or do you want to hang around and wait for the tough guy to come back?" Rory asked.

"I want to watch you kick his ass," Austin said tiredly.

Rory snorted. "There's a big difference between talking shit and stepping in it, big guy. It's getting late. We need to head home." With that Rory stood and bent to gather his beach towel.

Austin watched him as he raised the fabric into the wind and let the sand that clung to its damp surface fly free. A mild scent of sun and flesh and some deeper calling note blew toward Austin, and he found himself inhaling it deeply. He knew it was Rory he smelled, and somehow it stirred a yearning to breathe it in more deeply. Austin stood and simply gathered his own towel into a wad while Rory folded his carefully. Austin picked up the beer cooler with his free hand and looked at Rory with a sense that what his face said was too telling. "Rory, what would you say if . . . "

Rory looked at the riot passing across Austin's face and waited for him to finish. Finally, he prompted, "If what?"

Austin looked away and said, "Nothing." He looked at Rory once more, searchingly, but only said, "Are you okay? Are you good to drive?"

Rory caught the look on his face and visibly seemed taken aback. "I'm good," he replied confusedly and waited for Austin to say more. Instead Austin nodded curtly and headed to the parking lot. Rory waited for a moment and thought about calling Austin back. Instead he watched his tall, broad- shouldered form stride away with a measured dignity and reserve.

Austin felt Rory's eyes on his back, and couldn't bear the scrutiny. He stopped and turned asking, "You coming or what?"

Rory nodded and offered him a smile before he followed along behind.

Their ride back was subdued for the first few miles. Rory adjusted the volume and tunes to something right for the end of a time playing hooky than leaving for its beginning. They rode through Dania and took in the last of the decrepit buildings left from a time when Federal Highway in the town was a beach road and not merely a thoroughfare along a forgotten place between Hollywood and the airport. At the traffic lights, Austin either stared straight ahead or pretended to be interested in the traffic outside his window. It wasn't until they hit the on-ramp for I-595 that he felt compelled to speak.

"Rory, I can confide in you, right? I mean, I can tell you something as a friend . . . " he began tentatively.

Rory was distracted by traffic leaving Port Everglades. He looked in his rearview mirror and also behind him before gunning the Volvo into the right lane. Once he had made it inside, he gave Austin a quick look and an encouraging smile. "Sure, Austin. Your secret's safe with me."

"I hope you're telling the truth," Austin said seriously. "Because, this is private, personal stuff."

Rory reached toward the dash and turned the radio's volume low. "It's alright, Austin, I'm a good listener, and I don't make it a practice to tell everything I hear, okay?"

"I'm counting on that," Austin said gravely. Then he cleared his throat and shifted uncomfortably in his seat. "Well, when I was a kid, fifteen, just turning sixteen really . . ."

"You had a buddy," Rory encouraged him gently.

"You act like you've heard this before," Austin said stiffly.

"I have," Rory replied and gave him a smile. "It's nothing to be ashamed of. More guys than you think have had a buddy at some time or another. It's okay."

"Am I that obvious?" Austin asked miserably.

"Not at all, Austin. You're just freaked by hanging out with me and having those dickheads call you a faggot. Let it roll off your back. They were assholes, that's all. You remember being that age."

Austin stared out the windshield for a mile or more. When he decided to speak, he chose his words carefully. "I do remember being that age. And I've been thinking I want to do it again. With you."

Rory nodded and reached up to the sun visor and pulled out the pack of cigarettes and lighter he had stashed there. Expertly, he managed to extract a cigarette and light it using only one hand. "Austin, I . . ."

"I hope I haven't offended you or pissed you off," Austin interrupted. "It's just that I feel like I had to say it, you know?"

Rory put the cigarette between his lips, then reached across with his free hand and patted Austin's knee reassuringly. Austin flinched at his touch as if he'd threatened to burn him with the cigarette. Rory drew back his hand and took the cigarette from his lips. Grinning, he said, "Settle down, Austin. I wasn't going to grab your dick or anything." Then he laughed until Austin found himself smiling.

"So it's okay?" Austin asked tentatively. 'I mean me telling you that . . . I'm not out of line, am I?"

Rory transferred his cigarette to his other hand to steer the car with his right. He took a hit off the cigarette and flicked its ash into the wind rushing outside his window. "I'm actually flattered," he said and gave Austin a warm smile.

"Is it something you'd think about?" Austin asked miserably.

"Well, I do like tall guys," Rory teased.

"So you're saying, maybe, right?"

Rory didn't answer right away. He took his time, smoking thoughtfully. At last, he flicked his butt out the window and sighed. "I found a handful of condoms and a half-used tube of KY with Bruno's stuff last week when he was packing to leave."

Austin nodded and looked at him intently without saying anything for awhile. It wasn't the direction he'd intended for the conversation to go. Rory's aside threw him off balance. Finally, he said, "Did you say anything to him about it?"

"No," Rory said. "I didn't." He glanced at Austin and then focused on the road in front of him. "Right now, I'm angry. Your timing is perfect. I could take you home and satisfy your curiosity with all the trimmings. I'd wear you out."

"Sounds good," Austin said. "But . . . "

"But that would be too easy, Austin. I have more respect for myself and for you than that."

Austin wanted to tell him to respect him a little less, but he satisfied himself with keeping quiet and letting Rory come to that conclusion himself.

"I've never cheated on Bruno, Austin."

"And I've never cheated on Meg, but this is different," Austin retorted.

"Is it? How?" Rory asked quietly. "Is it different because I'm a guy or because you're not mad at Meg?"

"Well, I don't know . . . maybe it's that since now you're mad at Bruno, you're scared you'd do it just because of that." Austin said quickly, avoideding answering Rory's question altogether. "I understand that. You see, if we ever did this together, I'd want you to get off on it, not end up being all ashamed and never talking to me again."

Rory nodded, but didn't say anything for awhile. "Is that what you did to your buddy all those years ago?" Rory asked quietly at last. Then he snorted and said, "That's usually how it goes. What did he do? Did he slip up and tell you he loved you?"

Austin looked out the window and mumbled, "Something like that." He leaned forward and fiddled with the stereo controls on the dash. "What makes you think you know so much about it?"

"Because, let me tell you something, I *was* your buddy a long time ago. I had an Austin when I was fifteen, got it?" He looked across the seat with a sudden rage that made Austin shrink. "I had more than one Austin. And it was Bruno who never acted like he was ashamed of me. He may act like he owns me, but he's never turned his back on me because he was scared of what people might think, or because he'd satisfied his fucking curiosity." And this, Rory knew, was at the heart of what he felt most privately for his partner. He told Bruno he loved him constantly because that was what Bruno wanted and needed to hear. He had no real way to tell Austin that, for himself, his real love for Bruno had become a fierce loyalty over their many years together. It was a sudden and sobering realization.

"I didn't know, Rory. I'm sorry," Austin said quickly, truly chastened.

Rory shook his head and stared out the windshield, stagily concentrating on his driving. After a few awkward minutes, he sighed. "No, I'm sorry Austin. I didn't mean to dump all that on you."

For a while, they rode without saying anything. The tension in the car's close air dissipated somewhat, and the radio played companionably as they each found their way through their own thoughts.

As they neared the gated entrance to Venetian Vistas, Rory glanced over at Austin and once again reached to touch his knee. This time Austin didn't flinch; in fact, he found himself spreading his legs to accommodate Rory's touch. "This conversation isn't over, okay?" Rory asked quietly.

"I'm glad," Austin replied. "I didn't want it to be."

Rory squeezed his knee and unexpectedly ran his hand quickly up Austin's thigh toward his crotch. Austin jerked and shifted away quickly. "Jesus, Rory!"

Rory laughed until he braked for the security gate. When it swung away before them, he looked at Austin and said, "I'm curious. Why me? Why now?"

Austin waited nervously as the gate opened automatically and Rory had driven past the guard in the gatehouse before he said, "I think you're very attractive, and I haven't thought about another guy that way since I was a kid. I don't know . . . ," he faltered. He looked out the window at the repetitive manicured landscaping that flowed along the street like a well-groomed stage set. "I just thought it would be kind of sexy and fun . . . you know, if we could just get together every once in a while and . . . you know, no big deal."

Rory fought the urge to both laugh and punch Austin on the side of his head. Instead, he settled for a wry smile. "What's a little blowjob between friends, right?"

Austin turned a deeper shade of red under his sun-flushed face. "Well, maybe just not that. I mean, I'm willing to try different things. I'd really like you to be my . . . to be the guy I could try them with."

"Sorta like a sexual Disney World, right Austin?" Rory said sarcastically. "You want to visit Queer-Land and have me be your tour guide. Kinda lead you around by your dick, is that it?"

Austin covered his discomfort with a sickly grin. Again, Rory was making him feel small and uncool when he was being real. At a loss for words, he simply blurted out the first thing that came to mind. "Actually, I just want to kiss you, really long and really hard for as long as I want. I want you to touch me like you really want to and don't have to . . . " Austin broke off and considered how lame he sounded. "It would be so nice to have someone want to . . . to just be about me again." Ashamed, he said "Aw, just forget it, man. It's not just . . . well, it's not just what you think." Austin watched as the turn onto St. Mark's Court loomed ahead.

Rory was taken completely off-guard by what Austin had said with such a lack of calculation. He did sound like a sincere kid, not a horny middle-aged man looking to break off a piece without any complications. Rory was undone, having suddenly come to understand much of what Austin couldn't adequately articulate. He took his foot off the gas and slowed the car to a crawl. Just before he had to make athe turn onto their street, he stopped the car on the deserted street and looked at Austin sitting large and surprisingly vulnerable beside him. When Austin looked at him, questioning their lack of movement, Rory said, "I didn't know, Austin. I didn't understand it was like that."

Austin nodded. "Well, now you do," he said with gruff dignity.

Rory took his foot off the brake and eased the car into the left-hand turn onto St. Mark's Court. Looking to the left toward their waiting houses, he said, "I don't know what to say. Maybe . . . maybe when it feels right, we'll . . . okay?"

Austin nodded and reached across the seat to lightly lay his palm over Rory's bare knee. "Thanks," he said quietly.

## 5160 ST. MARK'S COURT

AUSTIN HAD LITTLE time to think as he picked up the boys and their carpool mates from school and drove his appointed rounds toward home. The mini-van full of boys and a single girl was loud as they became increasingly competitive in asserting minute points of opinion, arcane degrees of kewl, and inflated X-Box prowess. The lone girl, one of the Diaz clan, held her own. But it was effortless, with a knowing detachment,. She was sure in her nascent sense of her own femininity that the amount of posturing from her carpool mates was for her benefit. Between the clamour of their out-sized personalities and 99 JAMZ, the hip-hop radio station they insisted on as a soundtrack, Austin couldn't keep a coherent line of thought in his head.

With each child that exited his mini-van, his excitement over the two small victories he'd won that day was calibrated up by a notch. When at last he'd gotten his own boys home and settled with snacks in front of their computer in the loft, he escaped to the master bath for a much- needed shower and some time alone.

Josh and Noah expressed little interest in their father's slightly sun burned skin, or the events of his day for that matter. They were perfectly preoccupied with the stations of their own daily wind-down. Austin was able to shower in peace, and as he did, he enjoyed planning a surprise dinner for Meg. He wanted to take her someplace special, just the two of them, to celebrate the news of his triumphant return to work. He pictured her coming home tired, as she usually did, but for once there'd be no bickering about what to have for dinner. He'd order the boys Chinese delivery so they'd be happy, and he'd take Meg for a wonderful Italian dinner in Plantation, at the place they'd always loved. He sighed with pleasure at the thought as he toweled himself dry.

With those plans set in his head, he stepped from the shower to treat himself to a shave with a razor, no electric razor shortcuts for him tonight. He wanted to be as smooth and suave as a guy on a shaving cream commercial. He lathered his face and selected a new double-blade from the pack. With these simple ablutions, thoughts of Rory rose in his mind. They skittered from his appreciative assessment of Rory's beach-lounging form, slick with sweat and glowing in the sun, to their close conversation in the car on the way home.

Austin had never thought, no, even his best imagining of seducing Rory had never taken the direction it did in real life. His mental scenario of presenting the topic of the two of them having sex was lit by a dull illumination of the request and enthusiastic acquiescence. The reality of his actual words and Rory's response amazed him. Austin had no idea something he'd actually say would come out so right. He felt like he'd successfully managed to call an unknown girl he'd long admired and scored a date. It made him laugh out loud. He wasn't sure when the sex would actually happen, he only knew it would for sure.

The sex itself was still only vaguely imagined. He wasn't lying when he'd told Rory the simple gist of it. He did want to kiss him. He did want to feel Rory's touch, sincere and searching, it was a type of touch he longed for without seeming to know about it until he said it. The thought of it made him half-hard even now. As he'd told Rory, the dull mechanics of gay sex weren't out of his realm of experience, but that wasn't what he really craved. What he truly wanted was a ripening connection, as warm and intimate as his first thrilling time spent actually exploring someone else's body after all the time spent imagining it. Austin wanted to be awakened to the forbidden once more.

Looking at himself in the master bath's generous mirrors, he noted how red he was from his long morning in the sun. He glanced at the bathroom door to make sure it was shut. Satisfied it was, he squatted and searched for some skin lotion he knew he'd seen behind a door under the sink. It was waiting, close at hand, an intensive skin care lotion in a pump-top bottle. He grabbed it and straightened to put it on the counter.

At first, he slathered it over his shoulders and neck until the sensations of the ministrations of his hands invited their attentions elsewhere. He watched as his hands rubbed the chilly lotion over the still-firm swell and declivities of his chest. He felt the responsive rise of his nipples with some surprise. Those long-ignored small bumps of flesh firmed and stiffened under his palms, drawing his fingertips to explore and marvel at their individuality on the smooth plane of his flesh. He wondered how they'd feel to Rory. Would their smallness make some sort of difference? The flood of electric pulse they sent said they were more than sufficient to make the more southern regions of his groin respond with an insistence that intrigued him. Likewise, he renewed his palms with lotion and explored the reddened surface of his belly. He tracked its slight hill and fingered the rim of the pool of his navel wondering what it would feel like as Rory discovered that geography on his own.

Only then did he pump a generous amount of lotion on his hand and smear it across his palms and reach for the exclamation point of his physical being. He slid it in his fist and marveled at how hard it had become. There was nothing half-hearted in its wondering at another man's touch. There was nothing tentative about its desire for an unknown hand. Austin grabbed his scrotum and tugged at its generous contents. That loose dropping bag had a yearning of its own. Austin stroked it gently wondering, half-dreaming, while his other hand found an insistent rhythm on his shaft. His knees buckled involuntarily as the center of his being was paid attention to. He was close, so close, when he felt a rush and gathering coolness in the steamy room around him that hadn't been there a moment ago. It distracted him. He opened his eyes.

Noah stood just inside the master bath's door, his mouth and eyes wide with wonder and, Austin was shocked to see, a certain frank interest.

"Noah! Goddamn it!" Austin said as he let go of himself and spun around, his feet catching awkwardly in the chenille mat on the bathroom floor.

"Sorry, Dad," Noah said quickly. I didn't mean . . . "

"You didn't mean to barge in without knocking?" Austin shouted over his shoulder.

"I'm sorry, Daddy!" Noah said with alarm. "I won't do it again."

Austin reached for his towel and took two awkward, crab-like steps sideways to retrieve it from where he'd slung it over the shower door. He quickly wrapped it around his waist and turned to find Noah half-retreated behind the cover of the door. "Come in here, son," he said firmly. "And close the door behind you."

Miserably, Noah stepped back into the bathroom and did as he was told without looking any further than the tops of his feet.

"Noah, don't you know some things are private?" He demanded.

"Yes sir," Noah said quietly.

"Do you know what you just saw?" Austin said lowering his voice and half-believing the inspiration for his wanking could be read as easily as his gleaming greased hands.

Noah nodded his head.

"What?" Austin asked.

Noah took a deep breath and looked up defiantly into his father's eyes. "You were beating off," he said in a near whisper. His bravado didn't reach below his eyes.

Austin was taken aback by his son's simple assertion of fact and his familiarity with the act itself. "Have you started beating off?" Austin said gently.

"Aw Dad, don't make me tell you that," the boy moaned.

"Fine then," Austin said, he had his answer in the boy's reluctance to answer. "You know what I mean by private. I wouldn't watch you do something like that. The thought of it makes me sick. You understand me?"

His feet and eyes fidgeting with the need for flight, he nodded.

"Were you curious about me? About what I look like?" His father asked calmly.

In response, Noah just rolled his eyes and looked away. "I wasn't trying to be gay or anything," he managed.

"It's okay, son," he said wearily, then quickly amended the statement with, "It's okay to be curious about adults. There's going to be a lot of adult things you're going to want to ask me, but you have to trust me enough to ask and keep it between you and me and not sneak around, okay?"

Noah nodded gratefully.

"Do you have any questions now?" Austin asked calmly.

The boy shifted on his feet and looked everywhere but his father's eyes. "Why did you use lotion?" Noah asked with down cast eyes and in a near whisper.

Austin fought the urge to smile. Noah was not quite fourteen. He debated exactly how much to tell him about the parallels between a firm greased grip and the reality of anatomy it tried to duplicate. He considered carefully what to say. Finally he settled on, "Because it feels better. It's smoother."

Noah grinned. "Better than spit?"

Austin grinned back, "Ten times better. Do you have any lotion in your bathroom?"

Noah screwed up his dark brows in consideration. "I don't think so," he said.

"Well then," Austin said. "I'll buy you some to hide in your room. But let's not say anything about this to your mom . . . ."

"*Hell* no," Noah said and looked over his shoulder. "She's *home*," he said conspiratorially.

"Is that what you came in here to tell me," Austin asked incredulously.

Noah nodded.

"Oh man, do I feel stupid," Austin said and smacked his forehead.

"Aw Dad. No way," Noah put in quickly. "You were just . . . you had to just do your dad thing. It's okay."

Austin grinned at his kid. "So you're not psychologically scarred or anything?"

"What?" Noah asked blankly.

Austin felt a dull ache in his groin from his unexpected interruption of a very personal act. "Nothing, son. Just go downstairs and tell your mom I'll be down as soon as I get dressed, before she barges in here wondering what we're doing in the bathroom," he said.

Noah's eyes grew wide again, in horror this time, at the thought of his mother joining the discussion. "Gotcha," he said and ducked gratefully out the door.

Austin watched the door close behind him and pulled off the towel. He made short work of wiping his hands and genitals before searching the counter for his boxer shorts and slipping them on. For just a little while he'd managed to feel frisky and free as a bird, just buck naked and having a good time. Now, he looked in the mirror and noted how diminished he felt. *Kids*, he thought, *have a way of making you old way before you want to be.* Still, he straightened his shoulders and shifted his mental gears effortlessly as he left to get dressed. He was very much looking forward to taking his wife on an unexpected date.

### TRIBECA GRAND HOTEL, CANAL STREET, MANHATTAN

BRUNO ALWAYS SPLURGED on expensive trendy hotel rooms when he was in New York. He knew how much his travel allowance would allow, and it was usually generous enough for him to indulge himself, as long as he stayed not too far out of range from the firm's offices in the financial district. Since 9/11, the hotel where the firm had kept a corporate account had been at first unavailable, then haunted. Bruno never faced any disapproval for the small idiosyncrasy of staying where he chose. The design, services, and personal pampering that came with these pricey rooms were significant parts of the things he looked forward to when he came to Manhattan. In much the same ways, so was Nan Bradfield.

Nan held a position that was parallel to Bruno's, with the exception that she earned her reputation in the New York office, while his was tilled, hardscrabble, in a field location. Nonetheless, Nan admired him, and Bruno held an equal amount of respect for her. She was something to look forward to when he came up. He enjoyed her company, her mind, and her professional insights. Of course, the sight of her was more than welcome as well. In fact, Bruno appreciated the design of her total package as much as he did the particular services they rendered for each other.

They were well-matched and complementary. Nan had the blunt-cut blondeness and leggy poise of a certain type of Manhattanite. Soignée and vastly intelligent, she was also feral in a business world that idealized a kind of corporate ravening in the women it allowed to play on a level playing field. She was as strikingly attractive as Bruno was aggressively masculine. In another kind of circumstance, they would have made a perfect New York couple. As it was, they were simply perfect New York lovers. Well-matched in hunger, well-suited for fucking with no strings attached. Neither wanted it any other way.

It was from Nan's sleek SoHo co-op that Bruno arrived back at the Tribeca Grand at 6:10 A.M. Unshaven, rumpled, and tired, Bruno was nonetheless very satisfied with himself. The women he still fucked were few and far between, but the sweaty, groaning orgasms like those Nan had abandoned herself to the night before were a point of pride for him. In the vain and proud part of himself he kept for himself away from Rory and his fuller life, he was stroked and very affirmed by his night's activities as he let himself into his room.

Bruno didn't even bother turning on the lights or striding into the larger room itself. He simply walked into the bathroom and began shucking his clothes, so recently put back on, and kicked them out into the room's small foyer before running himself a hot shower and stepping gratefully into it. Efficiently, he bathed himself, conscious of the fact that he had very little time to clean up, order something quick from room service, and make his way back downtown for the meeting that would be the culmination of so much hard work over the past week.

It wasn't until after he'd shaved and carefully examined himself in the mirror for bite marks or fingernail tracks that he was awake enough to find his way to the phone on the desk to order a large pot of coffee and some breakfast. It was then that he saw the red blinking light on the phone alerting him to the fact that he had messages. He ignored its insistence until after he'd placed his morning order with room service. Then, still naked and warm from his shower, he dialed in to see who had called the night before. He couldn't really imagine who it might be. He'd slipped into Nan's bathroom to check in with Rory at nine-thirty. He'd gracefully told him he'd had his dinner and planned on falling asleep like the dead, snug in his hotel room bed.

At 10:30, Rory had called. Brightly, he'd said, "Wake up beast. Pick up. This is urgent."

At 11:10, Rory had called again. Concern tightened his voice as he'd said, "Bruno, I called your cell phone a minute ago in case you'd changed your mind and gone out for a drink. There was no answer. Please . . . this is urgent and I don't want to go over it on the voice mail. Call back as soon as you get in."

At 11:56, Rory had called once more. "Bruno, where the hell are you? Call me as soon as you get in. It's very important. Call home, please."

At 1:09: "Will? It's bad news. I need you to call me, what ever time you get in. Call me!"

At 2:04, a resigned sigh, then, "Oh Bruno. You poor, dumb

bastard. I wondered why you needed condoms and lube in your dop kit." Rory gave a small, thin laugh remarkably free of any bitterness and said, "Whoever you're with, I hope it was worth this." And Rory hung up.

The last message came in about the time Bruno would have been getting out of the cab in front of the hotel. For a moment there was a humming silence of white noise, then what could only be Bridget barking for her breakfast. He heard Rory say, "Will, call your mother on her cell as soon as you can." He gave him a number, repeated it, and then Rory simply disconnected.

Bruno placed the receiver back in its extremely well-designed cradle and slumped into the bespoke chair at the desk. He was still trying to think of what to tell Rory when he called him back when room service tentatively knocked at his door and he realized how utterly naked he was.

# CHAPTER TEN

## It's not about you

**ST. MARK'S COURT**

AFTER BRUNO'S CALL, Rory made himself a plain piece of toast and a glass of milk. It wasn't that he was particularly hungry, quite the opposite in fact. He ate mechanically, without any sense of pleasure in the toast despite the fact that it was sunflower bread from the Publix bakery, a particular favorite of his. Likewise, the cold glass of two-percent milk didn't satisfy him the way it normally did. His spare breakfast was simply a means to an end. He tidied up the bread crumbs and rinsed the glass before putting it in the dishwasher. Those little chores accomplished, he looked around the kitchen. It was as pristine as a show home. Pleased, he turned to his last morning chore.

The picture of the Sacred Heart sat along with its vigil candle and the small statue of the Holy Family where it always had, on the counter at the end of the bar. As was his habit, he lit the candle and contemplated the gentle face of Christ before saying the prayer he'd been taught as a little boy. This morning, however, he tacked on an unscripted plea for forgiveness for a sin he hadn't committed, but knew he would. If, as he believed deep in his heart, a sin was simply a poor choice that you made, a choice that was sometimes the wrong thing for the justifiable reasons, then he had already sinned in making the choice. If sin was more than a choice, if it was an act, a choice made concrete, then the sin was to come. However, he'd made his decision. In either event, he was a sinner today. And he repented then and there in the bright morning light before he moved away from his small altar and found his way into the bedroom.

Tucked away, at the very back of the drawer that held his underwear, there was a small prescription bottle. There was really nothing remarkable about it other than the fact that he'd kept what it held squirreled away against the time he felt like he'd really need it. Inside the brown plastic bottle was a half-handful of Oxycontin that Rory had hoarded from a nasty episode with an abscessed molar the year before. Rory's dentist was never generous with such painkillers, but the script was a testament to the duration of the pain and treatment of the infection that had spread from an abscessed root into his sinuses and the small bundle of nerves at the jaw joint.

Rory kept the Oxycontin like a small hoard of gold, and he spent each pill grudgingly for a couple of reasons. The first reason was the fact that he hated being high. The second reason was he loved being high. He simply loved the drug too much. But, today was a day when he wanted to feel its lush ease, when he wanted to be free of the tug of gravity. For just a little while, eight hours perhaps, if he ate only enough to keep him from feeling nauseous, Rory would feel simply wonderful. Tomorrow would take care of itself.

So Rory took out a treasured pill and dry-swallowed it. He felt it go down his throat like a small rock, but he was definitely sure it went down. Then, without another thought, he went into the bathroom for a shave and shower. He wanted to feel smooth and clean in his coming druggy ascent to the touch of the day.

Once he was sleekly towel buffed and smelled of the coconut-scented shampoo and conditioner he loved, he dressed as he did on most days. He pulled on a generously cut pair of boxer shorts, patterned brightly with orange hibiscus blossoms on a yellow background, and then slipped a gleaming tight white tank T-shirt over his head. He glanced at himself in the mirror and roughly ruffled the shiny bristles of his crew cut. He could tell by the shiver than ran through to his shoulders that his pill was kicking in. He glanced at his watch on the vanity where he left it each night. It was no more than quarter of nine. There was nothing left to do but go out on the pool deck and wait.

The morning sun was warm again, as it had been on the beach the day before. With the pill's gift of a supersensory awareness of his own skin, Rory enjoyed feeling the morning in a tactile kind of way. Bridget obligingly lay at his feet and stretched against the searching massage his toes gave the fur on her back. Rory found his stashed pack of cigarettes in Bruno's buzz box and lit one to enjoy while he waited. He thought it was the best tasting cigarette he'd had in a long time. It wasn't half-gone when Austin called down from his office window.

"Hey, Rory! What'cha doing?"

Rory looked up and smiled. "Just hanging out. I'm slack until my new client calls the first of next week."

Rory couldn't mistake the look of happiness on Austin's face. "Feel like some company?"

"Sure," Rory said. "But how about I come over to your place? I'm so sick of looking around here I could scream."

Austin hesitated a moment. Rory imagined he swallowed hard as he considered it. Finally, he said, "Sure. Why not? I'll meet you down front."

"No. I'll jump the fence and come in through the pool deck," Rory said and then added, "I don't feel like getting dressed enough to wander across the front yards." He didn't wait for an answer or look up for the reaction on Austin's face. He only flicked his cigarette into the pool and was out the screened door of his pool enclosure before Austin had a chance to respond. The grass felt extraordinary on the soles of his bare feet as he walked the few steps to the low fence between his house and Austin's. He easily vaulted it and found himself waiting on Austin's pool deck before Austin had even made it downstairs.

For a moment, he looked around and registered the slight shift in perspective of the view out over the canal to the houses and sky beyond. While it was much the same scene as the one only fifty feet away, there was a difference that was marked and noted in his mind. As Austin opened the sliding glass door, Rory caught and held the thought that his world had changed in such a short space and time. He turned and gave Austin a smile.

"You look sleepy," Austin said. "At least more than you usually do," and laughed.

"It was a long night," Rory admitted.

Austin didn't move from the open door. Taking in the slender form standing before him, he felt poised between steps. He had a sense of transition in his hesitancy and it confused and unsettled him. "Is everything alright?" he asked at last.

Rory gave him tight shrug. "Bruno's oldest brother, Brian, had a massive coronary yesterday afternoon. I was on and off the phone a lot last night with Bruno's mom."

"I'm so sorry," Austin said and stepped toward Rory with concern. "Will he be alright?"

Rory pursed his lips and nodded. "He's going to have bypass surgery. He's only fifty. But there's always the real risk of . . ."

"How's Bruno taking it," Austin asked. "Were they close?"

Rory turned away and looked out over the canal. "Bruno and Brian are close in their way. Bruno's going to fly in from New York for the surgery."

Austin tentatively stepped toward Rory's turned back. "How about you? Are you okay?"

"I'm fine," Rory said as he turned around and gave Austin a sleepy-eyed smile. "I'm sure Brian will be okay. He's another ox like Bruno. They have a way of bullying their way through things."

"Can I get you something? There's some coffee left," Austin offered. He felt a strong protective surge and was unaware he had reached out to lay a hand on Rory's shoulder. "I could make some fresh."

"How about some water? With ice?" Rory said with a direct warm look into Austin's eyes.

"Sure, sure," Austin said and gave his shoulder a squeeze before he dropped his hand. "Make yourself at home, sit down out here where you can smoke if you want."

"I won't be smoking while I'm here," Rory said.

"You mean I'm not making you nervous anymore?" Austin teased.

Rory shook his head and felt the coolness on the bony knob of his shoulder where Austin's warm hand had rested. "Actually, I'm scared I might make *you* nervous today." He took a half step closer to Austin as though to herd him toward the door. Austin swallowed and Rory watched his Adam's apple bob in his throat. "How about that water?"

Austin gave Rory a quick nod and turned. Together they walked into the house. Austin hesitated after they passed through the door and waited for Rory to walk ahead before shutting the sliding glass door behind them and locking it. Rory waited for him and gave him a shy smile. Austin felt an unexpected jitteriness in his legs that propelled him along into the kitchen, with Rory following close behind. As Austin busied himself with ice and water for Rory's drink, Rory looked around the kitchen and family room without comment. "It's all Meg's design," Austin said nervously. "She's pretty proud of it."

"It's nice," Rory said noncommittally as Austin handed him the glass of ice water. He took a sip against his suddenly dry throat, then said, "I've always been curious about what your office looked like."

Austin looked at him with some dismay. Somehow, he felt as

nervous as if Rory had said he wanted to see his bedroom. "It's not much," he countered. "There's just my desk and an old couch left from our first place. Meg calls it my nap couch."

"I'd like to see it," Rory said.

"Really?" Austin asked incredulously.

"Sure," Rory said. "Why don't we go up there and sit and talk for awhile?"

"Well, if you want," Austin said in a constricted voice.

Rory nodded and gave him a smile that broadened into a grin.

"I don't know . . . ," Austin said. "What do you want to talk about?"

Rory turned and stepped toward the staircase. "I wanted to ask you about your friend, your buddy from back in high school."

Austin followed him and overtook him at the foot of the stairs. "I should have never said anything about that," Austin said as he moved past Rory and began to take the steps two at a time. "I was a kid, just experimenting."

Rory took the steps singly. "No," he said. "I'm glad you told me. It makes me feel like a friend."

Austin reached the top of the stairs and waited for Rory as he made his way up. "Considering what you told me yesterday, I was afraid it just reminded you of bad memories, of someone that hurt you."

Rory reached the last step at the top of the stairs and hesitated. He looked up at Austin and said quietly, "No matter how it ended, it was still my first time. I don't think I'd do things any differently looking back on it. Would you?"

Austin looked down at Rory and shook his head. "No," he said gruffly. "I don't think I would either." He gave a dry laugh. "I had a girlfriend who kept saying no, no, no. He said yes. I thought I'd die if I didn't, if I couldn't just . . . well, you know." With that he turned and walked toward his office door. Rory followed him across the sparsely furnished loft's space. "The new stuff from Pottery Barn should be delivered in about a month," he said as he stopped at his office door and gestured back at the loft. "I'm glad I did what you suggested."

"I look forward to seeing it," Rory said obligingly as he stepped past Austin into the office. He walked straight to the window overlooking his pool deck and peered down. As Austin came into the room and stood awkwardly beside him, he looked up at him and smiled. "You have a pretty good view from up here."

Austin blushed and swallowed.

Rory looked out once more. "It's a little strange imagining seeing yourself from someone else's perspective like this," he said casually.

"I watch for you," Austin admitted. "I'm always happy when you come out."

"Why?" Rory asked softly. "Why is that?"

"I told you," Austin said a bit unwillingly. "I think you're attractive. I like watching you. It's not meant to be weird; it's just something that's mine. Aren't your fantasies something that belong only to you?"

Rory took a sip of his water and said, "Not if you share them." With that, he placed his glass of water on the desk top, turned and slowly walked the short three steps to the old sofa across the room. "I've decided I want to share your fantasies," he said simply.

With everything he'd coveted, with every possibility he'd encouraged himself to consider and daydream about now so near at hand, Austin hesitated. He quickly searched for an out. "What about Bruno," Austin asked nervously.

Rory looked Austin in the eye. "Bruno has his own fantasies and things that are only his, as he's made perfectly clear to me." He shook his head as if to ward off thoughts as stinging as biting flies. "I don't want to talk about Bruno with you," he said. "I want to talk about me and you. Why shouldn't I share your fantasy and make it mine too?"

Austin felt himself trembling. He looked over Rory's lightly muscled form standing across from him. On his face he read no derision or condescension. There was only an open and honest questioning on Rory's face. Austin could feel the pulse in the hollow of the base of his throat. He could smell him in the room. This wasn't some daydream; this wasn't anything other than honestly real. Austin looked away, and asked only, "Are you sure you want to?"

"Yes," Rory said clearly, then offered Austin his out. "But I won't make the first move. I can leave if it's not what you really want."

Austin heard the wind push at the screen of the open window rattling it in its frame. He glanced at the clock and noted the time. He looked at the stars whizzing past on the screen of his computer. He heard the song playing low on the radio by his desk. He looked up at Rory with many unsettled questions blurring his eyes.

Rory nodded slowly, resigned, and started for the door.

In one stride, Austin caught him by the upper arm and swung him around to face him. "Don't," he said and searched Rory's eyes for permission.

"Okay," Rory said and smiled. "Okay."

"Wow," Austin said and laughed nervously. He released his grip on Rory's arm and noticed the redness on the skin where his tight grasp had caught and held. "Okay, then." He looked quickly into Rory's eyes and gently reached up once more and touched the redness on his upper arm. Rory instinctively flexed the muscle below Austin's fingertips. The sudden flicker of firmness surprised Austin; the strength it bespoke was alien. This was not soft, yielding flesh under his touch. It held some other promise altogether. He met Rory's questioning gaze and dropped his fingers. "I don't know how to get started," he said hoarsely. "It's too strange."

Rory's eyes answered with genuine caring. In reply, he reached and took Austin's upper arms in his grasp and kneaded the muscle there firmly. Then he drew Austin to him and laid his face at the side of his neck and with his lips barely brushing the smooth skin there he whispered, "There's no way to get it wrong, buddy."

Resolutely, Austin placed his hands on Rory's waist, amazed at the shallowness of the space and narrowness of the flesh between his hands, it was so different from Meg's body. He drew Rory's body to his own hips and his groin registered a yearning sigh at the contact. He felt Rory's erection give against his thigh and paused. The insistent firm stretch of flesh was as familiar as his own body's terrain, yet shockingly alien. He almost felt as if he was feeling his own body as someone else would. It disconcerted him, but it did not stop his need to feel more.

Austin's hands left Rory's waist as he shifted his leg behind Rory's to hold him still closer to his hips. He found the top of Rory's T-shirt and urged it upward while Rory obediently lifted his arms to allow him to strip it away. Once the barrier of the material was off Rory's torso, he placed an arm over his shoulders and ran his palm over the stretch and reach of him, marveling at the tautness of the smooth skin and the tightness of the muscle underneath. He lingered his fingertips over Rory's small nipples, amazed at the economy of their aroused expression, so different from when his fingers normally found and teased another's superfluity of flesh. Austin teased the rim of Rory's slightly protuberant navel, so unlike the shallow pool of his own. The hard, bald whorl of flesh was something else new and forbidden. He found it hard not to bend and attempt to map its topography with his tongue. Instead, he placed his palm flat on Rory's belly and forced his fingers below the elastic of his short's waist until he encountered the sudden surprise of hair and the rounded root of his penis. Shocked, he drew his hand away quickly. It was too much, too soon.

Rory stepped away from his enclosing embrace and smiled at him shyly. Then, he turned and sat on the sofa. "Take off your shirt," he whispered.

The words snagged and caught on a memory. As a kid, Austin had been embarrassed by the long lankiness of his torso, its flatness and lack of definition. But by the time he was sixteen, his shoulders had grown almost freakishly broad and his chest had expanded and swelled with the promise of the larger man he would become. He recalled the boy so long ago who had hungrily requested the same nakedness. That was the first time someone had craved a view of his form and made it known. Meg rarely seemed to feel the need to see his body. He thought she merely took his nudity as inevitable. The boy back then had articulated his desire in a whisper, and now Rory huskily commanded him to offer himself once more. Austin grinned now where once he had been so shy. He grasped the bottom of his shirt and pulled it over his head, enjoying the flex and stretch of his torso as he did so. Once he'd tossed the shirt aside, he proudly looked for Rory's reaction and wasn't disappointed by the look he found.

Enjoying his height, Austin took a step toward Rory and undid the button to his khaki shorts. As he reached for the zipper, Rory said, "No." Austin looked down on his upturned face and Rory plainly said, "I want to do it."

Austin almost laughed, he was so surprised and happy, as Rory undertook an attention that his wife had early on made well known she preferred never to do. As Rory's bright head nuzzled and suckled him where he stood, Austin stroked his head enjoying the rough bristles he found under his hands. The novelty of the act was heightened by his long subsumed desire for it. It was as if a song was being coaxed from him with a deep vibrato that made his knees weak. At last, fearful that it might lead too quickly to the end of the touching, the end of the thing itself, he pulled away.

Rather than offering him a put-off grudging expression of duty, Rory actually wiped his mouth on his shoulder and rewarded him with a grin of complicity. Austin knelt in front of him and took his face between his palms and kissed him deeply. He searched the inside of Rory's mouth with his tongue and traced the texture of the teeth he found there, marveling at their small sharpness and their skillful restraint from causing him any pain.

Amazingly, Rory began to laugh. Austin broke off his kiss and sank back on his heels to see Rory's face. He was almost hurt by the merriment, not knowing its cause. "What?" He said, "What did I do?"

Rory looked in his eyes and laughed once more. Suddenly, Austin understood he wasn't laughing at him, he was laughing with him. "Nothing. You didn't do anything but suck my breath away," Rory said. "Are you having a good time?"

"Hell yes," Austin whispered fervently. "Are you?"

"Can't you tell," Rory teased.

"I didn't know," Austin admitted. "I wasn't sure."

"You're a hell of a good kisser," Rory said. He held up his middle three fingers and grasped his pinky with his thumb. "Scout's honor."

Austin reared up on his knees and wrapped his arms around him. Rory responded by licking his throat. Austin moaned despite himself.

"Can I have my water?" Rory said, his hot breath against Austin's throat.

Wordlessly, Austin let him go and negotiated the small space to the edge of his desk on his knees. He took the glass and handed it to Rory, who drank deeply and sighed before handing the glass back to Austin. He simply set it on the floor out of reach and knelt before Rory once more. "What do you want to do now?" he asked eagerly.

Rory gave him a sweet smile and shrugged. "It's your fantasy."

Austin was momentarily at a loss. Once outside of the moment, his limited range of experience faltered and stalled. In the highly scripted scenarios of the intimate acts of his marriage, there wasn't much variation. Improvisation wasn't encouraged by Meg, who held very definite opinions of what was permissible or distasteful. However, there was a demanding physical reality between his legs that refused to be daunted by his lack of creativity. He glanced down at himself and then looked at Rory proudly. "I bet I haven't been this hard since I was eighteen," he said.

Rory nodded and stood. Unashamedly, he stretched the waistband of his boxers to clear his own erection and let them drop to the floor. Austin looked at him with unhidden fascination. Rory was beautifully built, not imposingly, but proportionately. Without a second spent in hesitation, Austin reached out and took Rory in his grip. He teased, stroked and tugged the stretch of flesh, wondering how it could feel so unremarkably familiar yet be so utterly free of corresponding sensation in his own body.

In response to Austin's touch, Rory shuddered. He looked at Austin hungrily. Austin continued his rhythmic pull and considered tasting Rory. It was a favor he could return. But even as the idea was considered, he rejected it. Something in him rebelled at the thought. It wasn't that he was put off by the thought of taking Rory into his mouth. The act itself did not repel him, but what it represented did. It was every epithet he'd heard hurled like so many sharp blows against men he considered himself above. Central to Austin's notions of his self, there was no room to be a cocksucker. It was too passive an act in concept to allow him to perform. He tugged at Rory once or twice more and then let him go. He reached for his hand and urged him down on his knees in front of him and leaned forward to kiss his mouth once more.

Rory, for his part, had had a marvelous morning so far. With his inhibitions and guilt obscured by the drug, he'd concentrated on the experience of the touch and taste of another man. He loved the fact that Austin was slick, like he was. There was no friction from Bruno's friendly fur against his skin. Austin's skin was simply cool and naked to his touch. He liked the feel of the man. He liked the generosity and angularity of his body. He had none of Bruno's bulk; instead he was all angular and flat planes. Rory liked his genitals, as innocent and smooth yet hard as a statue's. He liked Austin's simple, direct hunger for him. He even liked the abrupt dead ends of Austin's erotic experience.

All of these things had made sex with Austin appealing so far for Rory, but it wasn't enough. Rory had long stretches of road that needed to be covered, which Austin had no idea even how to map. Rory looked at him so close to his eyes, his smooth cheek betraying not a shade of darker beard. For a forty-year-old man, Austin was an innocent. Rory knew it was time he took over to show Austin where they needed to go.

And so, for an hour more, Rory led and Austin followed. Yet, despite Rory's repeated attempts to make himself accessible, Austin could not make himself go to the ultimate joining that gay sex approximated with his own straight experience. Finally, their groins aching with the unfulfilled need for thrust and reception, Rory and Austin sweatily slid apart. As they lay panting in the morning's heat that flowed into the small office from the open windows, Austin threw his arm over his eyes, and Rory leaned back on elbows. "I've got to come soon," Rory said plainly.

Austin nodded in reply. "Me too," he admitted.

Rory looked down at him. Austin was flushed all over with the effort of his exertions and their lack of resolution. "Don't you want to fuck me," Rory asked directly.

Again, Austin nodded from under his covered eyes. He lay hiding himself for long moments more before he dropped his arm away from his face and turned on his side toward Rory. "I want to," he said, "But I'm not ready . . . "

Rory was tempted to ask what he was ready for, but Austin continued before he could respond.

"When I was a kid, I tried it. I liked it a lot. It's really tight and everything . . . , but I got this infection. It was so embarrassing. I had to sneak to the public health center. I rode my bike over because I couldn't explain to my father why I needed the car. I was so scared

I had VD. It really freaked me out. They made me answer all these questions. I had to admit . . . , I had to say I'd been with this other boy. It turned out to be just this simple infection in my urethra. But now . . . now I don't, I can't go through that again."

Rory nodded and smiled at him gently. "I bet you don't even have any condoms, do you?"

Austin gave him an incredulous look. "I've been married for nearly twenty years. Why would I need condoms?"

Rory answered by placing his warm palm on the inside of Austin's thigh and stroked him gently, his thumb just barely caressing the underside of Austin's scrotum. "It's okay. No problem," he said softly.

Austin allowed himself to be petted, but growled in frustration. "I never thought you'd say yes," he said resentfully.

In response, Rory simply urged him up and into another position where he could at once administer to Austin and still take himself in an experienced grip. Within a scant few minutes, they were both sated. Austin was stunned and grateful at Rory's refusal to turn his head away, even as he climaxed, and Rory was simply interested in the man's reactions to the end. As for himself, Rory's hand was an old partner in accompanying his own fantasies. Now he had a willing new partner to indulge along the way. He climaxed happily despite the obstruction of the drug that he'd allowed himself to help him come as far as he did.

Finished, there was little left for either one to say. They both dressed quickly, avoiding the other's eyes. As Austin was doing up his pants, Rory saw the clock on his desk. He noted the time and thought of the long hours of the day ahead to think about what he'd just done. There was much time left to either brood over the simple facts or to relish the memory of it. He thought of the brown bottle waiting at the back of his dresser drawer. Quickly he weighed how much he might need to stave off any guilt against taking too much. He decided a half of a pill would be enough, and he yearned to be out of this room, this house, and as far away from Austin as he could get.

"I still want to kiss you," Austin said and laughed nervously.

Rory smiled. "It would be a little stupid to just shake hands right now," Rory said and allowed Austin a rueful chuckle of his own.

Austin stepped to him and at first merely brushed his lips. Then he looked at Rory's upturned face and kissed him fully. The kiss intimated more than he could articulate and betrayed a renewed hunger for more. Rory responded by hugging him close, but only briefly. Austin let him go and took a step toward the door. "Next time, I'll be ready," he said awkwardly.

Inwardly, Rory rebelled at the notion that there would be a next time, but he knew there would be. He had awakened his own curiosity in the most convenient way possible. "I . . . I'll be looking forward to it," he admitted.

Austin smiled and led the way out of his office and down the stairs to the sliding door in the family room. Before he unlocked and opened the door, he looked searchingly into Rory's eyes. Finding them open, frank, and unashamed, he stiffly said, "Thanks," ultimately unable to say anything more.

Rory fought the urge to touch him in reply. Instead, he lowered his eyes and nodded, and waited for Austin to open the door.

### 5150 ST. MARK'S COURT

WHEN RORY LET himself back into his house, he walked straight into the bedroom and got the bottle of Oxycontin from his dresser drawer. Bridget snuffled along behind him curiously and sniffed at him with unfettered enthusiasm. As he took the bottle back to the kitchen, she happily followed along with him, unable to contain her interest in his strange new scents. It made Rory shudder. Bridget's frank animal interest was too close to his own feelings and reactions as he'd initiated and consummated his morning's activities. He'd only fulfilled an animal need, divorced from any real caring or deeper connection. He felt like a dog.

With this in mind, he quickly cut a pill in two with his sharpest kitchen knife and returned half to the bottle before dry swallowing his bump. He made himself swallow twice more, tracking the sharp edges of the pill as it traveled down his throat. Once he was satisfied it was well down, he swatted at Bridget's nose and made his way to her cookie jar.

"Cookie for you?" he teased. Bridget bobbed her big head agreeably. "Rory got a cookie. Cookie for me," he said and selected a Milkbone from the jar. "Cookie for you," he said as Bridget snapped at the treat and caught it in midair. Rory laughed. The big dog considered him gravely as she chewed. He imagined her look as accusing, having scented another man on his skin. Suddenly, he felt nauseous.

In all the years he'd been with Bruno, he'd never once cheated on him. It wasn't as if he'd lacked opportunity. He'd had his share of chances. Not taking advantage of them was the one way he held the moral upper hand over his partner. It had been Bruno, after all, who had abandoned him unceremoniously when they were so much younger. Once Bruno was back, Rory had decided that was what he wanted more than anything else in the world, and he would pay for it with his fidelity. In all the years since they'd been back together, Rory had held himself firm in his commitment. He was nearly superstitious about it. Now, within the space of two hours, he had thrown all that away. Despite his anger with Bruno, he realized he was no longer any better. He gagged.

Fighting the urge to throw up, he got a glass from the cabinet and the milk from the refrigerator, and poured himself a fair amount. He stood at the counter and took small sips of the cold milk until the revolt in his stomach was soothed. Now he wished for a cigarette with an addict's pure need. His open pack and lighter were outside where he left them, but he couldn't stand the idea of walking outside under Austin's seemingly ever-present gaze. He couldn't imagine walking casually to Bruno's stash box and, finding his face looking down at him, simply offering Austin a friendly wave before retrieving his cigarettes and returning inside. He could still feel him on his skin. He could smell him still.

Instead of going outside for his cigarettes, Rory turned and searched the kitchen drawer where he kept his spare packs. Luckily, there was one pack left and one of many lighters that found their way into the drawer as well. He tamped the top of the pack against the counter and opened the box hungrily. Then, taking his milk, cigarettes, and an ashtray retrieved from under the kitchen sink, he sat at the small kitchen table by the window that provided a sunny view of the pool deck. Luckily, the angle of the window's view also gave a look out over the canal, but cropped any glimpse of Austin's house. Rory sighed and lit his needed cigarette.

He smoked in silence. But for Bridget knocking around under the table and her deep sigh as she settled at his feet, the only sound was the hum of the air-conditioner and refrigerator. Rory welcomed the company of the white noise, but didn't want any other distractions. He sat wandering his way back through the maze of his morning so far. The minutes ticked away until the bump of the drug eased him back into a place without recrimination. There he found that the edges of the fresh memory of having sex with Austin had softened and were tinted with a kind of pinkish-gold glow. For what it was, it wasn't bad, he decided, as the time lengthened unnoticed and cigarette butts collected in the ashtray. And for the first time since he'd climaxed, he smiled. And, he nearly purred at the thought of his own performance on the sofa and on the floor. If Austin had found him attractive before, he concluded, he would have nothing but an increased appetite for him now. Unalloyed by guilt or any deep mental vivisection, it was a tremendously satisfying feeling.

The sudden, sharp ring of the phone made Rory jump. With the second ring, he considered letting the voice mail pick it up. Then, it occurred to him it might be news of Bruno's brother. Quickly, he stood and picked up the phone from its place on the counter. "Hello," he said tentatively.

"It's me," Bruno said.

"Hey," Rory replied, unwilling to say more.

"I'm at LaGuardia waiting on a standby to Raleigh-Durham," Bruno said.

"Okay," Rory replied automatically. "You sure were able to get away quickly. How did the team take it? Didn't you have a presentation this morning?"

"I talked to Shimon. He wasn't really pleased. You know what he told me? He said, 'We all have families, Will. But we need to be mindful of our *priorities*.' The bastard." Bruno said.

"So, I guess you weren't there for the presentation," Rory replied evenly.

"Oh no, I was there. It just took less time than I thought it would. I stayed mindful of my fucking priorities. I sat through the whole goddamn thing and then took the firm's car service directly to the airport. I got here thirty minutes ago."

Rory looked at the digital clock on the microwave. He was astounded to see it was after one o'clock.

"Rory, I need you to look in the lockbox on my closet shelf. You know, the fireproof one?" Bruno said urgently.

"I know what you mean," Rory abruptly assured him.

His tone gave Bruno some pause. "There's an envelope in it that's got Brian's name on it. It's the documents giving me his power of attorney and his living will," he explained patiently. "I need you call his surgeon's office and fax all the pages to them. Here's the number . . ."

"Wait a sec, let me get something to write with," Rory said and scrambled to find a pen and a scrap of paper from the drawer under the phone. "Okay, shoot," he said agreeably. He listened and wrote as Bruno recited the number and repeated it.

"And I need you to FedEx the originals to Mom's house. Overnight it, for delivery by ten a.m., okay? Brian's stabilized enough that they're going to do the surgery tomorrow," Bruno said anxiously.

"He never revoked that after he and Helen got back together after the separation?" Rory asked.

"No," Bruno said firmly. "He still doesn't trust that crazy bitch. That's why Mom was so fierce about getting me down there."

"Okay, Bruno. I'll take care of it right away," Rory said. "Anything else?"

"Only I love you," Bruno breathed into his cell phone.

Rory didn't answer.

"Rory? Rory are you still there? Goddamn it! Rory?" Bruno nearly shouted into the phone.

"I'm still here, I'm just trying to think of what to say," Rory said carefully.

"Look, please say you love me. I'm about to get on a plane for chrissakes," Bruno pleaded.

Rory sighed. "I do still love you, and that makes you the luckiest bastard on earth."

"Baby, you know last night wasn't about you . . . " Bruno said.

Rory laughed. "For once, Bruno, I really believe you."

"Really, Rory? Because it was about work." Bruno pleaded once more. "I work with her, I told you."

"Oh, yeah. That's right, it's about work," Rory said calmly. "It was about work the last time you left me. I believe that's what you said."

Bruno, stung, didn't answer. "I've cleared standby, Rory. I got to go. Please tell me everything's going to be okay. Please," he said finally.

At just that moment Rory felt no more than pity for Bruno's

neediness despite his lack of concern in kind. "It's okay, beast. Get on your plane. Give me a call later and let me know you got there safe and sound," Rory said gently.

"Will you be there?" Bruno demanded.

"I love you, stupid. Where else would I be?" Rory said and hung up the phone.

## 5160 ST. MARK'S COURT

MEG HUNG UP the phone and sighed. For such a complicated chore, it had really gone rather smoothly after all. After the initial excitement of Austin's announcement that he was returning to a normal, lucrative job had worn off, her mind went into overdrive. There was little time to waste. Once more, it had been her chore to collect the shards of details his announcement had scattered and to put their lives back into some semblance of order.

She stood up from her seat at the kitchen table and looked out the window to the pool deck. She saw the boys' heads bobbing in the water as sleek as seals. They had no sense of the many threats that trailed them, from their wet chill in the late winter's evening to the care of strangers. Likewise unconcerned, Austin sat in a lounge chair staring out over the canal's moonlit surface without an apparent thought for the boys in the cold water of the pool. She felt as if she would have to look after them all forever.

Meg moved to the counter and refreshed her glass of wine. She absolutely refused to consider her parents' many prohibitions, especially the one against alcohol. Her parents lived in simpler times; their choices and consequences were so unlike her own. With all she had on her, a second or even third glass of wine this evening was her due. She took a sip and then a deeper swallow from her glass and sighed. Once more she refreshed her glass and walked to the sliding glass door that led to the pool. Of course, it was open, as was the screen. A bright jolt of irritation shot through her as she made her way outside, deliberately closing the door behind her with perhaps more force than necessary.

The noise of the sliding glass door's angry hiss made Austin turn from his contemplation of the canal and stilled the boys' splashing. Satisfied that she had their attention, Meg sat on the edge of the lounge chair closest to the door and announced, "Family conference, okay guys?"

The boys paddled to the edge of the pool and clutched its rim to steady themselves in the water. She heard Austin sigh pointedly, and then she watched as he rose from his chair enough to angle its orientation to face her. She waited for him to say something, but he only offered his resigned attention, as did the boys in the pool.

"Okay," Meg said and took a sip of her wine. She chose to address herself to the boys, as her news most directly affected them. Austin she would deal with privately. "Josh? Noah? You know your dad is going back to work in Boca, right?"

"That's cool," Noah said agreeably. Josh only glanced at his dad and then looked back to Meg and nodded.

"Well, that means some changes around here," Meg said firmly. "You remember Mrs. Guiterrez?"

The boys nodded. Meg glanced at Austin, but found him staring off toward the house next door. "Well, Mrs. Guiterrez is coming back to work for us. She's going to be picking you up from school and taking you to soccer and making us dinner. On Thursdays, she's going to be here all day doing housework. I want you to be respectful and helpful to her, because she's doing us a tremendous favor. Is that understood?"

Josh looked at Noah, waiting for his response.

"Okay," Noah said, "Whatever."

"Whatever," Josh echoed.

Meg was surprised by their equanimity. "Does that sound okay with you guys?"

"Sure," Noah said and shrugged. "Somebody has to pick us up from school."

"Mrs. Guiterrez is nice, she teaches us Spanish," Josh said. "She cooks good too, *las comidas latinas*," he explained.

And she listens to *la musica latina*," Noah elaborated. "*Yo quiero la salsa y meringue!*"

"*Yo soy Joshilito, tambien?*" Josh said and splashed backwards into the water. Noah followed him and ducked underwater. In a moment there was a shriek from Josh as Noah tugged down his bathing suit. Struggling to keep his head above water, the little fellow kicked himself free of the bathing suit and waited for his brother's head to pop up. Once Noah had emerged he roundly punched him on the side of the head. "*No me moleste!* he shouted.

Noah lunged for him and he screamed "*No me jodas!*"

"*No me jodas!*" Noah mimicked in a high-pitched voice. "*No me jodas!*"

Austin laughed out loud and merely watched their antics with obvious enjoyment.

"Austin? Say something!" Meg demanded.

Austin shot her an annoyed glance, but he said, "Boys! That's enough. Apologize to your mother." He looked at Meg and said, "I'm sorry, but it really was funny."

The boys stopped their roughhousing and said in unison, "Sorry, Mom."

Meg looked to each of her males blankly. "What are they apologizing for?"

The boys snickered.

"Alright, you two." Austin said. "I think it's time for you to get out of the pool and go get showered. Bedtime's coming up."

Aw, man," Noah said and snatched Josh's bathing suit from where it was floating at hand.

"Give me that," Josh said and snatched at his suit.

Noah responded by flinging his brother's bathing suit out of the pool, where it sailed just past their mother.

"*Maricon!*" Josh screamed.

Noah laughed and pulled himself out of the pool. "You're the *maricon*. With your little pecker hanging out."

"Dad!" Josh whined plaintively.

Austin strode toward Noah and stopped just shy of him but certainly close enough to make him flinch. "Enough!" he said. "You're not funny anymore. Get upstairs."

Josh shot him a dirty look, but did as he said.

Meg drained her wineglass and watched as Austin picked up a towel and walked to the pool's steps. "What on earth are they saying?"

Austin looked at her and shook his head. He opened the towel and said encouragingly to Josh, "Come here, buddy,"

Josh gratefully slogged through the water to the steps and, giving his mother a bashful glance, turned his back to her as he stepped into the waiting towel his father wrapped around him.

Austin let him step onto the pool deck, then he knelt on one knee before him and gave him a brisk hug. Then, taking him by the shoulders, he said gently, "I want you to promise me you won't use that kind of Spanish around Mrs. Guiterrez, okay? You know it's not nice and it would hurt Mrs. Guiterrez's feelings."

Shivering now, Josh shamefacedly nodded his head.

"Okay, Joshilito. Go get ready for bed," Austin said.

Again, Josh nodded and walked quickly inside.

Austin watched him go, then turned to Meg with a smile. "Would you like some more wine?"

"Maybe," Meg said. "Just tell me what they were saying.

"You're going to want some more if I tell you," Austin warned and grinned.

Meg wearily held out her glass, "So tell me," she said.

"*No me jodas* roughly means 'Don't fuck with me,' and *maricon* means 'faggot,'" Austin said and laughed.

"Why do they only pick up the worst things?" Meg asked wearily. "Why not 'I love you' or 'Dinner was delicious.'"

"They're kids, Meg," Austin replied.

"That's no excuse," Meg countered irritably.

"I'll get you that wine now, ma'am," Austin said and turned.

"You're as bad as they are," Meg called after him. She watched as Austin paused momentarily. He just shook his head and made his way on toward the kitchen. A wave of frustration and resentment threatened to overturn the hard-won relaxation her previous glasses of wine had brought her. Austin was too preoccupied with the boys' antics to even ask about Mrs. Guiterrez or how much it was going to cost the household budget. The woman wanted four hundred a week. Meg shuddered at the thought. Luckily, she wanted cash. Meg couldn't even imagine the hassle of the paperwork if she didn't.

It was then that she noticed the pot of hibiscus sitting oddly by a chair across the pool deck. It was definitely out of place. Unsteadily, she stood and walked over to move it to its proper place. When she leaned over to grasp its lip to tug it back, she saw two cigarette butts laying crushed out in the soil.

"What are you doing, Meg?" Austin asked from behind her.

Meg picked the cigarette butts out of the pot and stood holding them out in her palm. "Who's been smoking here?" She demanded.

"Oh," Austin said evenly. "Rory was over. He wanted to smoke so we came out here."

Meg dropped the cigarette butts back into the pot and brushed her hands together with distaste. "Well, at least you didn't let him smoke in the house." She walked over and took her glass of wine from Austin. "Exactly how much time does he spend over here anyway?"

Austin walked past her and said, "I don't know. He drops by sometimes. Why?"

Meg stood looking at his back. "If you're spending your days hanging out with him, I'm glad you're going back to work."

Austin took the seat he'd been sitting in earlier and turned it back toward the canal. "I don't see what the problem is," he replied.

Meg sighed. "He's the problem. I have no idea when he actually works, and it seems like he's getting you into some bad habits."

"Exactly what is that suppose to mean?" Austin said defensively.

"Running off in the middle of the week to go to the beach, for one," Meg stated baldly. "What was that about? It's not as if you don't have a semblance of a job right now, for all you're leaving it soon. I don't know what's gotten into you."

Austin looked at her and started to say something, but thinking better of it, he simply sat in his chair with his back to her.

"Well. I can tell this conversation is finished," Meg said. "I get the hint."

"Good night, Meg," Austin said.

"Don't you even want to discuss Mrs. Guiterrez's wages? It's got to come from the house account. We need to discuss it," Meg said petulantly.

"It's a cost of doing business, my dear. You don't want to cut back on your hours," Austin said and turned to look at her. "And I'm sick of being a stay-at-home dad. It is what it is. Two tears in a bucket, mother fuck it."

"I'm going to bed," Meg said angrily.

"Good night," Austin said evenly. Across the lawns, Rory came out on his pool deck following a trotting Bridget. He opened the screen door and let his dog out into the backyard. Austin watched as Rory, hugging his bare chest against the night's chill, stood in the dull moonlight while Bridget snuffled around in the grass.

Meg turned and went inside, her resentment once more articulated by the brusque sound of the sliding glass door traveling along its track to the door jamb.

Rory whistled once, then twice again in short succession. Bridget squatted tiredly and then trotted happily back to the door where Rory waited. As she stepped back into the screen enclosure, she caught either the scent or sight of Austin sitting across the way. The dog bayed deeply and Rory looked across the yards. When he saw Austin, he paused and stared at him intently through the darkness.

Austin stood and stared back, hoping their exchanged dark gaze communicated something, some part of the connection they'd shared. Finally, Austin lifted his chin in greeting. Rory nodded and then turned and went back into his house with his dog.

Austin sat back down in the dark and wondered for a long while how he'd gotten to this uncharted place.

# CHAPTER ELEVEN

# A cheap hotel

AS IT HAPPENED, Austin made the only big score of his sales career a week before he was to quit the job and return to work in Boca. It all came together so suddenly, he was amazed and thrilled. The commission would be enough to pay off the furniture he'd impulsively ordered and still leave plenty left to salt away. When the time came to drive across Alligator Alley to Fort Myers to finalize the paperwork, he asked Rory to come along. They were on the road by eight fifteen, and he had all the signatures and a purchase order from the hospital in hand by ten thirty. When he returned to the car where Rory had waited patiently in a shady spot, he tossed his briefcase inside and gave Rory a frankly sexual leer.

"Would you consider celebrating with me?" Austin said mischievously.

"Not right here in the parking lot, I hope," Rory said and laughed.

"Oh no," Austin said as he climbed in to the driver's seat of the minivan. "I've been thinking about this for days," Austin said. "I'm ready for you now."

"Oh boy," Rory laughed. "One time didn't cut it for you?"

"Hell no," Austin said as he cranked the engine and carefully looked behind him before backing out of the parking space. "That wouldn't really be fair to you, would it?"

Rory smiled and shook his head.

The place Austin chose for the event announced its single and double room rates on a pole eighty feet high. It loomed like a beckoning promise of inexpensive haven above the exit where I-75 west merged with I-75 north. Rory wondered, as Austin paid for the room, how he could let himself be had so cheaply. It was almost laughable. But, he told himself, sometimes cheap and dirty felt good. He was enjoying the adolescent excitement and very adult tackiness of it all. When Austin returned to the car and drove around to the back of the motel, he sang a few quick lines from a song that had been popular when they were children, "Third-rate romance, low-rent rendezvous . . . "

"Stop it," Austin said seriously as he parked the car and turned off the engine. "It's not like that."

"Isn't it?" Rory asked.

"Look, I've dreamed of doing this for days," Austin said with genuine hurt. "I want to be with you. I really want to do this," he added emphatically.

Rory wiped the smile off his face and said, "I didn't realize how important this was for you."

Austin reached past him and picked his briefcase off the floor in the backseat. He opened his car door and said, "It is. Don't make fun of me."

"I'm sorry Austin," Rory said, chastened.

"I don't think you know how much I . . . " Austin began.

Rory answered by opening his car door and stepping out into the parking lot. The walls of concrete and glass were unremarkable and forbidding. It was a barren, lonely place. There was not another car parked along the side of the building. "What room are we in?" he asked soberly.

Austin got out and gave him a hungry look over the blunt hood of the car. He gestured with his chin toward the door waiting little more than three feet from the front bumper. "We don't have to do this," he said impatiently.

Rory closed his car door, stepped the few feet to the door, and waited.

Austin looked at him searchingly, then smiled. He closed his door and pressed the button on the key to automatically lock the car against every intruder, including both their consciences. Then he put the car keys in his pocket and drew the room key from the pocket of his suit coat. Resolutely, he stepped to the steel door, with its rust patches blooming from under the red paint, and let them in.

Rory stepped inside with Austin on his heels. He walked into the room and breathed in the scent of cheap hotel deeply. It was a combination of commercial soap, spray air freshener, and stale smoke lying like fog over commercially washed linens. Under the low hum of the air-conditioner, silence waited interestedly for the sounds of their occupation. It seemed to anticipate with jaded curiosity the echoes they would certainly leave with the other aural ghosts of the room. Rory shivered in the drawn-curtain darkness.

Austin placed a hand on his shoulder and steered him toward the bed closest to the chipped Formica vanity in the dressing area off the bathroom. Once their journey of steps had arrived at Austin's intended destination, he moved past Rory and sat his briefcase on the bed next to the one he intended for them to share. Rory watched as he opened the briefcase and fished in the pocket of its lid. He took something in his grasp and lifted it out, proudly extending his hand for Rory's inspection. On his palm lay two condoms and two small pillow-shaped plastic containers of personal lubricant.

Rory looked up and met Austin's grin. He swallowed hard and, avoiding Austin's eyes, pulled his shirt over his head and tossed it across the room. When he looked back, Austin had his fingers knotted in his tie. Gently he pushed Austin's fingers aside, looked him in the eye, and said quietly, "Let me do it."

## WAKE MEMORIAL HOSPITAL, RALEIGH, NORTH CAROLINA

AFTER BRUNO PAID the check, he stood and waited for his mother to pick as cheerful a spot as could be had in the sprawling hospital's cafeteria. When she finally found a place that suited her, she turned back to find him and smiled. He returned her smile brightly, but inside he felt his heart tear a little at the familiar sight of his mama. Tall and zaftig, always impeccably dressed, she nonetheless had always been a woman for sons. She had heard every story her boys could come up with, and could either bawdily share their laughter or handily call them on their bravado. For the first time he could remember, Bruno found himself wanting to hug and comfort her, rather than turn to her for the same. Standing by the cafeteria table, she had somehow aged, shrunk in on herself.

The last few days had not been kind to his mother. It seemed as if the many years' cares of rearing boys to men had depleted her swagger and stature. She was no stranger to Wake Memorial's cardiac care unit; she was there first with her husband, now with her eldest son. For all her bluff self-assurance, the hospital and its routine had obviously diminished her. The gentle smile she returned to Bruno with a questioning nod toward the table was only a shadow, not the comforting bright beam that had guided her sons home over a lifetime.

Bruno nodded in answer to her unspoken question and negotiated the few late-morning staff and visitors who populated the cafeteria. It was too late to be having breakfast, but the hospital's cafeteria was more than a place to eat, it was a haven from the horrors and tedium attendant on patients and loved ones warehoused in the warrens and halls above. By the time he reached her, she'd already sat down and relieved her tray of its few items of food and drink. Bruno emptied his tray as well, picked up his mother's, and strode away in search of a place to put them down.

Task accomplished, he reached in his jacket pocket and retrieved his cell phone. The slit of its window showed no light alerting him to missed calls. He'd left Rory several messages over the past couple of days, the most recent one at eight thirty that morning, only to be faced with a chilling silence from Venetian Vistas that spoke louder than any cold conversation. Swallowing his increasing disappointment and fear, he slipped his cell phone back into his jacket pocket and took the seat opposite his mother.

"You're not eating much," his mother commented. "Dry wheat toast, a banana, and a glass of *skim* milk? What the hell happened to your appetite? You were my best eater."

Bruno picked up a slice of toast and regarded it skeptically. "Rory's got me on a diet. He's trying to keep me from ending up upstairs with Brian."

Bruno's mother nodded, looked at her plate of bacon and eggs, and slid it away from her. "Good for Rory, even though he just killed my appetite as well." She watched as Bruno took a generous bite of his toast and then began to peel his banana. "Why the diet? You look healthy as a horse."

"I am healthy, Mama. I just have to think about things I didn't used to," Bruno replied easily.

"For god's sake, don't tell me you've got your father's cholesterol as well. I don't know how many more times I can go through this cardiac routine."

Bruno swallowed his toast and laughed. "Sorry, Mama, I'm a daddy's boy. Mine got up to over 300, but it's coming down, I promise."

She snorted and asked, "How much of that is thanks to you and how much is Rory's pushing you to do it? He's a tough little knot."

"Hey, no fair, Vivian," Bruno said, calling his mother by name. "I'm running five miles a day, and my doctor's got me on Vytorin. Rory's just making sure I eat halfway decent."

Vivian sighed. "Brian's on Vytorin and Plavix, and look where he is. Of course, he'd have been better off with someone like Rory than with that crazy heifer he's supposedly still married to."

Bruno took a bite of his banana and tried not to laugh imagining his bellicose and very outspokenly macho oldest brother being married to another guy.

"You laugh," his mother said. "But it amazes me that out of four boys I managed to raise, my gay kid has the best marriage. Timmy's on his third wife, Jamie and Janine had to find Jesus right on the doorstep of their lawyer's offices to get it together, and Brian . . . well, enough said."

Bruno nodded, swallowed, and reached for his milk. "I'm a lucky guy," he admitted with an inward pang.

His mother rubbed her eyes tiredly, then generously creamed her coffee. "Have you talked to Rory since you've been up here?" she demanded.

Bruno put down his milk and picked up his piece of toast, avoiding his mother's eyes. "He's busy. I think he was doing some studio work for this new group. He's fine."

His mother waited, studying him over the rim of her coffee mug. She expertly paused until he had a mouthful of toast before she asked, "So you haven't actually spoken with him, is what you're saying."

Bruno looked up at her slowly, but with still not enough time to mask his eyes.

"That's what I thought," she said smugly. "There haven't been any messages from him on my phones either. And," she added, "I noticed it took you a right long time to get back to me when I called him to tell you about Brian's heart attack. Rory didn't have a clue where you were or what you were doing."

"I was in New York, remember?" Bruno said calmly as he put down his toast and picked up his banana. "Look Mama, it's not anything you should be worried about, okay?"

Vivian took a sip from her mug and leveled her eyes once more on another of her predictably loutish sons. "You can't bullshit me, Will. I've wiped your ass. What happened, you couldn't keep your pecker in your pants?"

"I hate you sometimes, you know that Vivian?" Bruno, defeated by her predictably knowing checkmate, responded without any real heat.

"You are a daddy's boy, aren't you?" his mother said tiredly.

Bruno put his banana back down on his plate and pushed it away angrily.

Calmly, Vivian drank the rest of her coffee and sat the mug back on the table between them. "Go home, Will," she said evenly. "There's nothing more you can do here. Brian's going to pull through and I can take care of myself. Your daddy taught me that. If that's what you're teaching Rory, take it from me, you need to get your big ass home and make it right." With that she stood and glared at her son.

"Mama . . . ," Bruno began.

"Don't *mama* me," she said dismissively as she picked up her purse and began rummaging through it. "Get on your cell phone and see if you can't get on a flight out of here today," she said as she pulled an ever-present pack of Virginia Slims and a lighter from her purse.

"You should really quit that nasty habit," Bruno said. "Your voice is deeper than mine."

Vivian laughed. "Don't you worry about me; it's you guys with the heart problems." She sighed and gave him a loving look. "Look son, I'm only butting in because I've seen how people screw up over and over. Your daddy made my life miserable because he had the same problem keeping it zipped. That's something else you boys inherited." She sighed tiredly. "I stayed with him because I had to. I had four boys to raise and I couldn't do it by myself. I owed you guys a home."

"I know, Mama," Bruno said gently.

"Rory doesn't owe you, Will," she said firmly. "Don't fuck it up." And she turned her back on him and walked away.

Bruno watched her leave, feeling both angered and choked with love for her. She was a pragmatist and a survivor, but she was also a mother whose plain-spoken advice, tendered with well-worn affection, had guided him and directed him all of his life. That didn't mean Bruno didn't resent it. As he watched her disappear from the cafeteria, he could easily imagine her standing in the cold at the entrance to the hospital, puffing away on a Virginia Slim, mentally getting him to the airport and on his way back home to Rory, where he belonged.

Chastened, Bruno did as he was told. He took his cell phone from his pocket and speed-dialed Delta Airlines. To add insult to injury, the only seat he could get was in first class for a punishing up-charge. He surrendered his credit card number to someone at the call center in Bangalore and found himself confirmed for a late evening flight. Even so, he already knew he'd get to Raleigh-Durham early and wait for a standby seat. Suddenly, all he wanted to be was home.

With that bit of business accomplished, he placed his cell phone on the table and picked up what was left of his banana. He bit it and chewed slowly, stalling to make time before he called Rory to let him know he was on his way home. Glancing at his watch, he saw it was after eleven. Even if Rory had been out walking Bridget when he'd called earlier, he was sure to be home by now. Still holding his banana in one hand, he picked up his cell phone with the other and nimbly dialed the familiar number with his thumb. The line rang four times before he heard his own cocksure voice. "You have reached the home of Rory Fallon and Will Griffin. We're not available to take your call . . . if you want, you know what to do."

## ST. MARK'S COURT

THE SEX ITSELF had been more remarkable for its novelty than for performance. While Rory put his best encouraging lies into it, and Austin attacked him greedily, it was no more than a disjointed dream for Rory and a personal proof of prowess for Austin. If they had been total strangers, it would have been no less intimate or disconnected. Afterwards, they had little to say to each other. The room didn't invite depth of feelings; it was merely the locus of sex. It wasn't a place for deepening friendship; it was a place for shameful coupling and rough touch. It wasn't until they had showered separately and got back on the road that any real connection, other than physical, returned between them.

Austin cleared his throat nervously. "Was I any good?" he asked.

Rory reached across the small space between them and touched Austin lightly on the arm. "You were there with me. I hope you could tell, dude."

Austin nodded and gave him a grateful smile. "It was pretty damn good," he said.

Rory stretched. "You should be pleased with yourself," he said and laughed.

Austin laughed as well and drummed nervously on the steering wheel. "I just didn't want you to feel like you'd made some kind of mistake or anything," he said, suddenly sober.

"I don't feel that way at all, Austin."

"Good," Austin said confidently. "I just want you to know I don't feel like I've made any mistake." He stole a glance at Rory. "I really had a good time."

Rory nodded. "I'm glad, Austin. I didn't want you to blame me if you had any regrets later."

"No way," Austin said, then added sincerely, "I'm just scared a little that it might get out of hand. My feelings about you are getting pretty strong."

Rory sighed. "We can't make this bigger than it is, Austin. Please be careful."

Austin hesitated, then said, "Still, I *fucked* you. I'm not some jerk who goes around trying to get laid whenever he can. I want you to understand that. You're pretty special to me. I'm not just doing this because I'm curious, you know," he looked at Rory for emphasis.

To Rory it was obvious that Austin cared what he thought. He searched for something reassuring to say in return, but he was scared of saying too much. What Rory was afraid of was his lack of feelings for Austin, not any excessive emotion. "You're a good friend, Austin," he said finally, hoping that would be everything Austin needed to hear.

"That's what I'm talking about," Austin replied quickly. "Since I met you, I realized I don't really have any friends, no guys anyway. When I was working in an office, I had a lot of people I knew and liked, but work friends aren't really close, are they?"

"No. I don't suppose they are," Rory said quietly.

"All these months I've been working at home, I realized I didn't have a single friend I could just bullshit with, or talk to about something other than my wife and kids. It's like nobody knows me."

To Rory, Austin sounded more vulnerable and lonely than he could have ever imagined. It dawned on him exactly what his first sexual experience with another guy far in his past had really meant to him. Rory thought of what Austin must have felt back then. Carefully, he said, "I think I understand what you mean. I don't mean to harp on this, okay? It's just that when I was a kid, like you were, I met this guy named Scott. I felt this really close connection to another person for the first time in my life. It was like he really knew me, and he fascinated me as well. You know how it is when you're a young guy. You have all these things that you're figuring out on your own about yourself . . . about the world. It's very lonely because you don't really feel like you can share them, or you just haven't learned how, and then along comes somebody who wants to hear what you have to say . . . and who wants to fuck you too . . . "

"Exactly!" Austin said excitedly. "That's just the same way it was for me." Austin looked at Rory and grinned. "I knew you got it. I knew it."

"But life never stops making you lonely, does it?" Rory said and looked away out the window. The road ran in a straight line along canals lined with cypress and live oak. In all its grandeur, the Everglades looked as solitary as he felt inside, despite the fact that he understood so much about Austin. "I mean, even if you're married or have been with someone a long time. You still keep learning things about yourself that you can't share . . ."

Austin nodded sagely. "Sometimes I think marriage can be the loneliest place in the world." He glanced at Rory only to find him looking out his window, withdrawn deeply inside himself, even in the small confines of the car. Austin felt a deep tenderness for his neighbor settle over him. He couldn't help it; he felt the need to say, "I don't feel so lonely with you."

Rory was still for a moment and then rubbed his eyes tiredly. "Don't make me love you, Austin."

"Don't friends love each other, Rory?" Austin asked defensively to hide his sudden hurt.

"Yes, I guess straight friends do, in a different kind of way," Rory said. "But you straight guys come with brakes. The problem is, I'm gay. I don't have the brakes you do. That's how I've gotten hurt before."

"But can't you keep it casual?" Austin asked anxiously. "I know you love Bruno. And I love Meg. This thing . . . this thing between you and me. It doesn't have to get in the way of that. It can't."

Rory gave him a sad smile and nodded. "I know, Austin. I know."

"I don't see why we can't just be best friends, close buddies," Austin offered pleadingly.

"Because we're not sixteen anymore, that's why," Rory said irritably. "We're adults. We've mixed sex with love and friendship and had it work in a mature way. We can't go back to buddies messing around and sharing dirty secrets."

"But you like me fucking you," Austin said smugly. "I made you come twice today. We already are sharing some pretty dirty secrets."

Unexpectedly, Rory laughed. "I guess we do, Austin. You're right, buddy. We do."

Austin was confused by his laughter. He stole a glance at him to make sure he wasn't making fun of him. He found Rory looking at him with what he took for affection. "Look, Rory. I'm just saying this doesn't have to be some psychodrama. I like it when we do it. I know you do too. Can't we just keep it simple and have a good time? Give me a chance to be your friend, man."

"Butt-buddies," Rory said with a smile.

"If you want to put it that way," Austin said stiffly.

"I don't know if I'm any good at being friends with another guy," Rory admitted honestly. "It's pretty hard for me to spit your come out of my mouth and then just act like you're some guy who lives next door."

"What about me?" Austin said angrily. "Do you think I can just have sex with you and not care anything about you? Give me a little credit for being a decent guy . . . for having some respect, for chrissakes."

Rory shifted uncomfortably in his seat and said, "I do give you credit for that. You've been one of the most decent guys I've ever met."

"Well that's fucking good news, Rory," Austin replied petulantly, "because your opinion of most men is pretty damn low. I wish I knew the guys you'd slept with before Bruno, because I'd beat the shit out of them for making you so scared to have any friends."

Rory said nothing in reply.

Austin took his quiet for hurt and immediately felt ashamed to have hit so below the belt. "Will you just trust me to be your fiend, Rory?"

"You sure make me want to," Rory answered quietly.

"Good," Austin said firmly. "Because a friend doesn't fuck up your life or make things difficult for you. For once in your life, I'm going to prove that to you."

Rory watched out his window and caught sight of the many alligators sunning themselves on the dry banks of the canal that ran alongside the road. Each lay out of range of threat or contact with any others, despite how close to each other they appeared. They were dark sketches of danger and solitude, frightening in their stillness for the knowledge of how quickly they could lunge and kill. It was hard for Rory to forget that.

*We're moving toward the center of things now*, he thought. He knew that soon the open grasslands of the Everglades would spread out around the road and the sun would lie open and honest over the river of grass. Before long, they would be back at Venetian Vistas, and he had little choice other than to believe the man who was driving them back home.

Fundamentally, he knew Austin meant what he said. It wasn't Austin's boundaries he feared, it was his own. For so long he'd kept his distance to ensure he wouldn't be caught in the teeth of caring too much about anyone else. Bruno was a different case altogether. Bruno made it easy for Rory to withdraw and feel safe. Nothing would ever come before his gratefulness for that. Not even Austin. Safe with Bruno at the gate, Rory would never let anyone in to gain any real knowledge of who he was.

Rory sighed inwardly. With complete understanding he realized he'd taken advantage of Austin the way he'd been taken advantage of himself. He'd slept with him and was more than ready now to simply walk away. With his curiosity satisfied, Austin was now no more than a burdensome responsibility. Rory looked across the car and watched the man as he drove. He was in many ways no more than an emotional sixteen-year-old. He was searching in Rory to relive an uncomplicated genuine emotional attachment he'd had when he was just learning to connect with another human being.

Austin felt him looking at him and turned his head and smiled. With unabashed tenderness, he reached across the seats and took Rory's hand. For a moment, he ran his thumb over Rory's fingers and then squeezed his hand before letting it go and returning his attention to his driving.

"I'm going to try and be a good friend, Austin," Rory said knowing all the while that being the best friend he could be would involve letting this lonely, kind man go as gently as he could.

"I'm glad," Austin said happily, "because I like you a lot."

### 5160 ST. MARK'S COURT

WHEN HE TURNED onto their street, Austin saw Meg's Range Rover in the drive. For a moment, he panicked. It was still early afternoon; it should have been hours before she got home. Rory looked carefully at his own drive and said nothing. Deciding he had nothing to be ashamed of, Austin clenched his jaw and drove straight into his own drive and tried his best to give Rory a more significant goodbye with his eyes than he could manage to articulate. Rory gave him a kind smile in return and let himself quietly out of the car. Austin stole a look at him as he crossed the sidewalk to his own front door and let himself in. Once he had, Austin removed his briefcase from the backseat, got out and closed his door. Resolutely, he made his way into the house only to be greeted by an accusing silent emptiness.

"Meg?" he called. "Meg?" When his only response was more silence and quiet, he set his briefcase by the closest chair in the living room and looked around. He caught sight of her lying on a lounge chair by the pool. By all appearances, she looked sound asleep. He sighed with relief and made his way to the family room. Gently, he opened the sliding glass door to the pool deck and said softly once more, "Meg?"

She smiled before she stretched and opened her eyes. "Hello, sweetheart. What time is it?"

"Just after two," Austin said and stepped outside.

Meg yawned and gave him a smile. "No kiss for your wife?"

Austin walked to her and bent over to kiss her quickly before stepping away and sitting down in a chair a few feet away. "What on earth are you doing home so early?" *I smell like hotel soap,* he thought guiltily. *How in the hell can I explain that?*

"I had a particularly successful morning," she said with a smirk of satisfaction. "I managed to get an apology from the IRS, in writing, on that case that's been driving me crazy. So I decided to take a partner's prerogative and give myself the afternoon off."

Austin whistled appreciatively. "That's a big fat deal, darling. I'm proud of you."

"Thanks!" Meg said proudly. "Do you have to pick the kids up today?"

Austin nodded and glanced at his watch. "Yes, and I need to grab a quick shower. The air-conditioner quit on the way over this morning," he lied neatly. "I smell like a pig."

"Did everything go well with your big order?" Meg asked solicitously.

Austin stood and grinned nervously. "Yes ma'am. And for once I'll get paid for all the bullshit, and very well, I might add."

"Excellent!" Meg said happily. "Look, I thought I'd go with you to pick up the kids. After we drop the other ones off, I was thinking maybe we could grab an early dinner and take them to the movies or something."

"On a school night?" Austin asked incredulously. "Where is my wife and what have you done with her?"

Meg laughed. "Oh, I'm only the bitch some of the time. Today I'm trying to be one of the guys."

Impulsively, Austin wanted to hug her, but he checked himself, fearful of his guilty scent. "Can you be ready in ten minutes?" he said tenderly instead.

"All I have to do is put on my shoes," Meg answered with a smile.

"Damn," Austin said. "Are you sure you're my wife and not a pod person?"

"Austin, sit down for a minute," Meg said seriously.

"Look hon, I really want to get a shower," Austin insisted.

"Fine, go," Meg said. "But I just want you to understand something. I know I've been preoccupied with work and I know I haven't really been fair or maybe acted like I just wasn't very excited about you going back to work in Boca, but I love you. You know that, right?"

"I know," he said. "But I want you to understand that I know I've been really disconnected ever since . . . well, since they let me go. Now that I'm going back, not only vindicated but in a better position, well . . . I just feel more like . . . "

"More like the head of the house?" Meg asked gently.

"Yeah, I guess that's part of it," Austin admitted.

"Austin, I'm really sorry for making you doubt that you are the man of the house." Meg said with genuine regret. "It's just that I want so much for us as a family. I know I push and push and push, but I . . . I just can't help it sometimes, you know?"

"I know Meg, but you've got to look how far we've come." Austin responded quickly. "Look at our kids, this house. I know we wouldn't be here or have what we have if it had been up to me, but . . . " he said and faltered.

"But?" Meg said quietly.

"But it's not worth any fucking thing if we lose each other in the process," Austin concluded.

"I know," Meg said sadly. "I want us to be friends again. I'm tired of all the sniping. I'm tired of feeling like I'm way over there," she said, pointing behind her to the inside of the house, "and you're way over there," she said pointing toward Rory's house.

Her gesture gave Austin a jolt. He stood silently for a moment looking at her before he said, "I'm right here, Meg. And I'm not going anywhere."

"Promise?" Meg asked.

Her unfeigned hopefulness stung him. Austin nodded. "Promise," he replied with conviction.

Meg rewarded him with a happy smile. "Well, go get your long, tall butt in the shower then, boy. We got places to go."

Austin grinned and made his way from the pool deck into the house. He was happy that Meg was trying to get back to where they always been before. He also felt as if he'd been shot at and missed.

## 5150 ST. MARK'S COURT

BRUNO STOOD IN the darkness of his drive and gave the driver a tip. For a moment after the man closed his door and drove away, Bruno stood looking at the dark hulk of his house. There wasn't a single light on to greet him. It was only a little past seven, and Rory didn't expect him until after ten. He dreaded going in to find a cold welcome. The black weight of his home loomed over him as heavy as a promise of punishment. Where he had left as a confident man of the world, he'd returned as a shamefaced boy. With a bowed head, he grasped the handle of his carry-on bag and made his way up the drive, dragging it behind him.

Once he'd found his house key in the tomblike darkness of his porch, he let himself into the darker air-conditioned chill inside. Rory was nowhere to be seen; not even Bridget ran to greet him. He was immediately flooded with panic. He left his bag and briefcase by the door and headed to the family room. Unable to bear the still, black silence, he turned on every familiar light along the way. He saw a glow through the sliding glass door that turned out to be a candle lit on the table that held his stash box. Rory sat like an angel in a nativity scene within its shallow yellow pool. He could just make out the calm outline of his dog at his lover's feet. His already rapidly beating heart broke a little at the tableau, and he wanted more than anything to be already there, a part of it.

Bruno slid the door aside as quietly as he could so as not to startle them; still, Bridget got quickly to her feet and growled threateningly. Rory only turned his face toward the sound and sat tensed, waiting to see what unexpected threat was poised in the doorway. Bruno had taught him long ago never to show fear, it only escalated the threat. Now, Rory sat waiting for whatever would be undeservedly thrown at him next. "It's me," Bruno said, his voice cracking, "I'm home."

Bridget barked happily and rushed for the door. Rory stood in the near darkness and waited for the dog to welcome Bruno first. Bruno quickly knelt and rubbed her big head before he and the dog both walked toward Rory. Surprisingly, he simply opened his arms and lifted them, welcoming Bruno into his embrace, welcoming him home.

Bruno stepped into his arms gratefully and hugged him close. He nuzzled the top of Rory's head and breathed in his deep, clean smell as if it was the best scent in the world. He held Rory so long that he finally took Bruno's upper arms in his hands and gently pushed him away. "I caught an earlier flight," Bruno said. "I just wanted to come home."

Rory nodded and said, "Poor beast, can I get you something to drink?"

Bruno sank into the wicker sofa's generous cushions and pulled Rory down to sit beside him. "I was scared you wouldn't be here when I got back," he said. "Then the house was all dark. Jesus, Rory, I'm so sorry I fucked up."

Rory laughed gently and reached to undo Bruno's tie. "No you're not. You're sorry you got caught. You've been fucking around on me for years." He swiftly loosened the knot and pulled the tie free from Bruno's collar. Efficiently he lifted Bruno's hung head by the chin and undid the top button of his shirt, then the next one down. "C'mon, give," he said and pulled back the lapels of Bruno's suit coat.

Obediently, Bruno moved his large shoulders in the small space and shucked the jacket. Rory took it from him and draped it over his arm as he stood. "Don't bother to apologize. You've already explained, and I really don't want to hear any more. I got your phone messages and I think you've punished yourself enough."

Bruno raised his head and tried not to smile. "Will you forgive me?"

"Goddamn you, you're like a six-year-old who's been caught in a lie," Rory said disgustedly. "You know every way in the world to get around me, why would this time be any different?"

Bruno looked genuinely hurt, even in the near darkness.

Rory decided that was enough. "Will, you stupid, stupid man. You know I'm stuck with you. Of course I forgive you. I'd forgive you murder, though God knows I've wanted to fucking kill you on more than one occasion."

"I guess I'd deserve it," Bruno said miserably.

"Yeah, yeah, you do this time, and probably all the times to come, but right now you're home and that's all that matters."

Bruno leaned forward and, resting his forearms on his thighs, hung his head once more.

"How's Brian?" Rory asked gently.

Bruno looked up at him and shook his head. "They slit him open like a hog, Rory. You should have seen him laying there in ICU zippered up from his throat to his navel. They shaved him slick as a baby. That's what he looks like, a big cut-up baby."

"But he's going to be okay, right?" Rory asked with real concern.

"Yeah, now it's all diet and exercise. I couldn't believe how much he'd let himself go. I mean, he was always my big mean-assed brother.

He had a body that was built like a brick shithouse. Now he's got these man tits. It scared me, Rory," Bruno admitted hopelessly.

"Why, Will?" Rory said gently.

"Because without you, if I had a bitch of a wife like his, I'd end up being the same way. Butchered like a fat hog on a hook," Bruno said fearfully. "I don't want to end up that way."

"You won't as long as I'm looking after you," Rory said softly and stroked his big head as fondly as Bruno had stroked Bridget's not moments before.

Bruno's shoulders trembled and he sniffled. "Please don't leave me," he said bleakly. "I know I'm an asshole sometimes, but . . . " with that he sniffled once more and awkwardly wiped at his eyes with the heel of his hand.

"Hush," Rory whispered. "I'm not going anywhere. Got it?"

Bruno nodded and sat up. The wetness on his cheeks gleamed tellingly in the candle's glow.

"Good. Now dry up and tell me what you want to drink," Rory said with earned authority.

"Can I have something to eat? I'm starved," Bruno said hopefully.

"Jesus, you're just like a dog. You at least had enough sense to come back home where you belong," Rory said and laughed. "And that's all I want."

"I'm glad," Bruno said honestly, "because I love you a lot."

"Whatever," Rory said breezily and turned to go.

"Wait," Bruno said anxiously. "What have you been up to? I mean, were you just ignoring my calls altogether or have you been out having fun?"

Rory paused, almost imperceptibly and then continued toward the door. "I'm here now," he said over his shoulder.

"Yeah," Bruno said as Rory stepped into the house. "Right where *you* belong," Bruno teased.

Though Bruno waited, Rory didn't respond.

# CHAPTER TWELVE

## Tender loving care

### ST. MARK'S COURT

AT FIRST, JOSH only complained of a headache coming home from church on Sunday. By suppertime he had chills and fever. Noah's head began to ache in sympathy. By Monday morning the Harden household was in the unforgiving grip of the flu. Austin's last week at home before returning to work in Boca became focused on providing the boys with all the tender loving care they needed to mend as rapidly as possible in order to return to school. Any thoughts of Rory were subsumed to temperature takings and medication dispensary, until his own headache grew crippling and Meg tiredly pronounced it was time for him to get into bed himself.

While the boys' resistance triumphed over the virus enough to have them back in school on Thursday, Austin's flu raged into a ragged deep cough that necessitated a trip to the doctor's office early Friday morning. By eleven a.m., he pulled back into his drive with a diagnosis of bronchitis, and a bag holding three bottles of drugs and another of Vicks VapoRub. Aching and tired, he had long since left behind any thoughts of Rory as he got out of the minivan and heard him say, "Where have you been all week, stranger?"

Austin looked across the yards to see Rory standing by his car with a thick roll of blueprints in his hand. "It's been a rough week,"

Austin said hoarsely. "We've had the flu."

"You sound like you're still sick," Rory said with real concern.

"Bronchitis," Austin explained and held up the drugstore bag. "I feel like shit."

Rory laid the roll of plans on the hood of his car and walked quickly across the yards. "I'm sorry," he said as he came to stand close to Austin's tall form. "I wondered why I hadn't seen you. I was wondering if, well . . . you know how we left it after we got back from Fort Myers. I had no idea you were sick. You should have called."

Austin tried to smile, but instead glanced at his front door longingly. "I was busy taking care of the kids at first," he said and looked back to Rory. "Then I came down with the stupid shit. I'm sorry, Rory. I feel like hell, I better get back inside," with that he turned toward the door.

"Wait," Rory said and took his arm. "Is there anything I can do? I've got to drop off those plans with a contractor for a job I'm doing, but I'll be right back."

Austin looked at Rory's hand on his arm, then looked around nervously. "I'm okay, seriously."

Rory let go of his arm quickly and took a step back. "How about I bring you some lunch, some soup maybe?"

Austin looked at him gratefully. "That would really be nice of you, if it's no trouble."

Rory glanced at his watch and then firmly said, "You get inside and take it easy. I'll be back within an hour."

Austin smiled at him. "Thanks," he said and looked around, "buddy," he added tenderly.

Rory rewarded him with a grin and took off back across the yards.

Austin watched him until he backed his car out of the drive. Rory waved at him as he pulled off down St. Mark's Court, and Austin returned his farewell with an upraised arm. Once he'd turned off their street, Austin sighed and let himself into the house. He quickly went upstairs and changed into a ratty but clean pair of sweat pants and T-shirt before returning downstairs to wash his first dose of medicine down with a cold Coke straight from the can. Absently, he lined the bottles of pills and the Vicks on the bar before a coughing fit overtook him. Suddenly he felt like he either needed to lie down or fall down.

Austin really wanted to find his way to a lounge chair outside in the sun. The promise of warmth to soothe his aching chest had a great deal of appeal, but he also realized how much he wanted to see Rory. The thought occurred to him that if he was outside he wouldn't be able to hear him knocking when he came back. Believing Rory would simply think he was sleeping and go away wrenched at him, he looked into the family room and considered Meg's prim sofa as an alternative. Sighing in resignation, he made his way to it and stretched out. It didn't accommodate his tall frame, so he turned on his side and drew his legs up. It was only grudgingly comfortable, but he thought it would do until Rory came back, and then he was sure everything would be much better.

So Austin lay on the sofa while his fevered imagination conjured thoughts of Rory. Today's visit would in no way match how he'd dreamed of spending his last day off, enjoying Rory all to himself. Austin had some pretty big plans for the two of them going into the past week. All of them involved putting Rory through some inventive paces. Instinctively Austin understood that something special was coming to a close. He had no doubts that he and Rory would manage to *do it* after he went back to work, but Austin's creativity didn't extend to imagining situations convenient enough and lasting long enough for the kind of sex the past few weeks had provided.

So Austin lay and drowsed, tumescent with desire and regret. Pictures flitted in his mind as rapidly as gay triple-X galleries on a computer screen. Mentally he could select any one and be rewarded with jpegs of specific acts. All Austin could do was allow them to cross his mind until he'd satisfied himself with the earnestness of the images and begun to call on his own recent reels of actual experience. He played his scenes with Rory over and over in his mind, lingering on some and skipping over others to replay and repeat his favorites. Finally, he groaned from the new ache in his groin that had arrived to add to the catalogue of flu-induced aches. Austin was fervid for some touch, and he finally slept, lightly and haunted by his need.

Startled by the doorbell, he sprang to his feet and was rewarded with a dizzying, blistering cough for his effort. He had to stop and hold on to the edge of the bar to steady himself along the way to the front door. At the doorbell's second chime, he managed to croak that he was on the way, damning himself for his weakness and need.

Rory greeted him with a clear plastic bag holding a quart container of soup. "Jewish penicillin," he said and stepped past Austin into the house.

"What the hell is that?" Austin said tiredly.

"Matzoh ball soup," Rory explained around a grin.

Austin smiled. "I've never eaten that in my life," he admitted.

"Then this is the best time to try it," Rory said and waited for him to lead the way into the kitchen. "What else have you eaten today?"

"Nothing," Austin said miserably.

Once they arrived at the bar, Austin stepped around it to retrieve a spoon and napkin as Rory sat and took the container from the plastic bag. Once he had the items in hand, Austin joined Rory on the opposite side of the bar and sat next to him. Peering inside the container he regarded the matzoh balls skeptically. "What are they made of?"

"A kind of cracker-type meal," Rory replied. "Don't think about it, just eat it."

"I guess some work came in for you, huh?" Austin asked as he cautiously cut a small section of a matzoh ball with the edge of his spoon.

"Yeah," Rory said. "And I just picked up two small jobs from the same client when I dropped the big job off. They're not any big deal, just nice simple money-makers."

Austin ate the grainy-looking stuff in his spoon and chewed thoughtfully. "It's sorta like chicken and dumplings," he said with relief. "But not as corny tasting."

"Exactly," Rory said. "Now eat."

Austin obliged him with a whetted appetite that surprised him. "This is pretty good," he admitted.

Rory watched him eat and chattered along easily about his work, while Austin consumed all of the matzoh balls and most of the soup before putting his spoon down and pushing the container away. Unapologetically, he burped and gave Rory a grin. "Thanks, I really needed that."

"I thought you might. Feel better?"

Austin nodded.

"Works every time," Rory said and started to stand.

"When are you going to hear from that record producer guy?" Austin asked suddenly. He wasn't ready or willing for Rory to leave yet. Already disappointed by his flu, he didn't want to abandon all hopes for intimacy now that, with some lunch in him, he was feeling better.

Rory relaxed back into his seat. "I have no idea. It could be weeks or months yet. The tracks have to be tweaked and sweetened, then the CD has to be burned," Rory sighed and gave him a rueful smile, "The group could run out of production money or split up. Anyway, I got paid and the check was good. That's about all I can count on really."

Austin nodded. "Sounds like a lot of bullshit to put up with."

Rory mistook his terse answer for forgivable irritation. He said, "Well, I better scoot and let you get back to work on feeling better."

"Don't go," Austin said quickly and put his hand on Rory's wrist. "Keep me company a little while, please?"

Rory searched his face, and then said casually, "Do you feel like sitting outside? I could use a cigarette."

Austin looked a little disappointed, but he thought once more of sitting in the sun and feeling it warm his aching chest. He stood and said, "Just for a cigarette, okay?"

Rory nodded and followed him out through the sliding glass door. Once Austin had settled into a sunny spot, Rory sat nearby, but far enough away to keep the cigarette's smoke from getting anywhere near Austin.

"I wish you didn't have to sit way over there," Austin said irritably.

Rory lit his cigarette and grinned. "You don't need the smoke, and I don't need your germs."

Austin gave him a hurt look. "I'm not contagious now," he said stiffly. "But I can imagine you are scared of bronchitis, the way you have to smoke all the time."

"Actually, I've gone back to smoking only three a day," Rory said calmly. "It's only when I'm around you that I seem to want to smoke so much."

"Do I still make you nervous?" Austin said and grinned.

"Yeah," Rory admitted. "You have this sexy way of looking at me and making me want to do things I shouldn't."

"Yeah, right." Austin said with an irony that freshened his grin. "I know I'm such a stud. It's you that's got this sexy thing going . . ." At that, he launched into a series of coughs than grew to deep dry hacks.

Rory took a deep hit off his cigarette and stepped out of the pool enclosure to flick the thing in the yard. While he was outside and well away, he exhaled and stood for a moment, waiting until he heard Austin's cough subside before returning inside. "You need to get back in the house," he said firmly, "and I need to go."

Austin motioned him back into his seat. "I'm not dying, yet," he said.

"You sure do sound like it," Rory said.

"Sit," Austin said with authority. "I'm not ready for you to leave."

Rory hesitated, but sat, perched only on the edge of his seat.

"How are things since Bruno came back," Austin asked.

Rory looked at him and shrugged. "They're good. Nothing's changed between us, if that's what you mean."

Austin gave him a searching look. "So nothing's weird between you then, because of . . . "

"No way," Rory interrupted him. "Bruno understands how he fucked up and I understand why I did what I did. There's no need to drag him into that." Rory hesitated a moment, then continued, "What we've done . . . that's just for you and me. It's separate and apart from who I . . . from my life," he concluded awkwardly.

"Okay," Austin said quietly, "I just wanted to know."

"How about you?" Rory asked softly. "Are you good with it?"

"Other than still wanting you very much, I'm fine," Austin admitted. "This isn't how I planned to spend time with you today, before I go back to work. I want you to know that," he added sadly.

"I'm not saying it'll never happen again," Rory offered, "But we're closer now . . . good friends. Maybe we should accept that and move forward. My conscience won't let me . . . "

"But, you're good for me," Austin began before launching into a coughing fit once more.

Rory stood and walked across the pavers to him. Firmly, but gently, he tugged on his arm and got Austin to stand. "Enough of this for now, Austin; you need to get back inside and lie down."

Austin allowed himself to be led back into the house. Sullenly he watched as Rory replaced the lid on the container of leftover soup and placed it in the refrigerator. Then, wordlessly, Rory crumpled his napkin, deposited it in the trash, and put his spoon in the dishwasher before washing his hands methodically with the soap he found on the sink's back rim. Finished, he looked around for something to dry his hands on. Seeing nothing, he simply dried his hands on his shirt. He gave Austin a smile and said, "I'd better go."

Austin looked away regretfully. Out of the corner of his eye, he caught sight of the jar of Vicks VapoRub on the counter. He reached for it and held it out to Rory. "Would you rub some of this on me before you go," he asked pitifully. "Please?"

Rory looked at the jar in his hand and then into Austin's pleading eyes. He sighed and shook his head. "Austin, I don't . . . "

"My chest and back hurt so bad," Austin pleaded. "Could you please just be a buddy and do this for me? Then you can go home. I swear."

Reluctantly, Rory took the jar from his hand.

"C'mon," Austin said with an air of gruff urgency and headed toward the stairs.

"Wait a minute . . . " Rory began.

"We're just going to my office," Austin said over his shoulder. "I want to take a nap up there. Besides, Meg would kill me if I got any of that stuff on her furniture in the family room."

Rory had no choice but to see the logic in what he said. Wordlessly, he followed him up the stairs and into his office. He watched as Austin pulled his T-shirt over his head and lay down on his stomach with an anticipatory sigh.

Rory shook his head against the sigh. He quickly walked to the edge of the sofa and knelt opposite Austin's broad back. As he uncapped the jar and spread the cold, unyielding unguent on his back, a flood of other, older memories came back to him. It was as if he was back in high school. Back rubs were the earliest methods of seduction in his long repertoire. He suddenly felt guilty and aroused simultaneously. As his slick hands heated the cold stuff and kneaded it into the depths of Austin's muscled back, he thought of other times, other bodies, and other places far from that still, bright room, which was now deepening in tone as the sun made its way overhead.

"Do my chest," Austin said and turned onto his back. He laid an arm over his eyes with feigned helplessness and said, "It feels so good."

Rory's nurselike intentions turned slower and instinctively attuned to elicit other responses. It could have been a completely different time, a completely different boy, but the touch of another's smooth flesh traced the same dangerous route in him. He knew this territory of touch and aching need well. He had been there before. And he had returned unwillingly and compulsively to what he thought he had left behind. It was child's play, and he knew he was no longer that skinny, hungry boy he had been. Even as he touched Austin, he wanted to just get up and leave, but he was held to the spot and to the act by an old need. Filled with both disgust and longing, he wanted to cry.

Austin moved his arm from his eyes and looked at Rory hungrily. It was a familiar place for Austin as well, but his place held none of the fear and shame of Rory's memories. For him, it was the return of an explorer to a long-abandoned landscape he had once traveled and moved on from. His return to this touch was a fond and guarded secret. He had found the place again, and he wanted all it offered with the simple eagerness he'd forgotten he owned. Gently, he took hold of Rory's wrist and guided his hand to the tented arch in his sweat pants. "Help me out, buddy," he whispered gruffly. "I really want you to."

Rory rested his palm over Austin's hard demand. His eyes traveled up over the long length of Austin's offered body until he found his pleading eyes. Rory saw the superior glint there lurking under the mocking plea. He was humiliated by his own hunger to respond, yet the proof of his own power and Austin's desire for him throbbed hot under his hand. So, sad but resigned, Rory turned and bent to the unchangingly familiar task, knowing all the while he never wanted to return there again.

## 5150 ST. MARK'S COURT

WHEN HE GOT home, Bruno found Rory sitting and dreaming in his chair by the kitchen window. The house stank of cigarette smoke, and a full ashtray sat in front of Rory along with a half-finished glass of orange juice. "Oh boy," Bruno said, "here's a cat who's been in the cream. You've gotten into your stash of pills, haven't you?"

Rory nodded and tipped his head up to receive a kiss from his partner.

"Any particular reason, or did you just decide to take the afternoon off?" Bruno asked as he loosened his tie and pulled it free from his collar.

Rory grinned and found the well-considered lie slid easily from his mouth. "I dropped off that big job today and picked up two small ones. I had them finished by four, so I decided to celebrate the return of being a legitimate income earner." In truth, he had returned from Austin's house on a wave of self-hatred and regret. When he found he couldn't scrub off the sense of shame he felt in the shower, he found his bottle of painkillers waiting and measured out half a precious dose to lift him up and over his funk. By the time Bruno had returned home, he'd firmly resolved never to sleep with Austin again and had forgiven himself his sin in the process. He'd decided never to waste another pill on thoughts of Austin. Gratefully, he stood and walked over to Bruno and nestled his head against his chest.

Bruno put his arms around him and laughed. "You're pill horny."

"No I'm not," Rory said and hugged him tightly once more. "I'm just really, really aware of how lucky I am."

Bruno returned his hug, then pushed him gently away. "I hope you still feel that way after I tell you what I have to tell you."

For a moment, blind panic swept through Rory with the certainty of divine retribution. With a kind of Catholic certitude, he was profoundly aware that God's punishment was swift and sure. Considering how he had behaved of late, he was utterly convinced that his time had come. Involuntarily he flinched as though Bruno had made a move to hit him.

Bruno saw the stark fear in his face and said gently, "It's nothing like what you're thinking, baby. Please don't think that, okay?"

Rory took a defensive step backwards. "What do you have to tell me?" he demanded.

"I'm not leaving you, Rory. Settle down," Bruno said and stripped off his shirt. "Goddamn, I'm never going to stop paying for that, am I?" He laid it over his tie on the barstool closest to him and stepped out of his shoes. "I know I have no excuse lately to make you believe I'm not going anywhere, but you don't have to act like I've got my bags at the door every time I make an offhand remark. Jesus, Rory."

Rory made his way back to his seat and nervously lit a cigarette. He watched Bruno tiredly shuck down to his boxer shorts before he said, "I had a long talk with Shimon Saperstein today," he began. "Aw fuck it, let's go outside. I need a buzz myself."

Somewhat relieved, Rory gathered his drink and cigarettes and followed Bruno outside. From the bend of Bruno's heavy shoulders and exhausted, resigned looks, Rory could tell something was wrong with him. As Bruno carefully loaded his bong and took a deep hit, Rory hesitated at the door, watching him. When Bruno let go of a deep lungful of smoke and stared out over the canal, Rory said, "Something's wrong at work, isn't it? I've never seen you looking so . . ."

"Disappointed?" Bruno asked as he turned his head to look at him.

"I guess. I can't really tell," Rory admitted cautiously.

Bruno shook his head and stretched his legs out in front of him. "Come sit down and I'll give you the whole story."

Rory made his way to the wicker sofa along with Bridget, who had wandered out to share the evening with them. As Rory sat next to Bruno, he leaned forward and petted his dog until she clumsily allowed herself to sink on the pavers at their feet with a sigh of simple satisfaction. Bruno nudged her gently with his toes and let go of a sigh almost as deeply articulate as the dog's. "Dumb dog," Bruno said with a small smile.

Rory stubbed his cigarette out in the ashtray on the table by the sofa's arm and settled his orange juice nearby. "What's going on, Bruno? You didn't get fired did you?"

Bruno leaned into the sofa and stretched an arm over its back behind Rory. "Not hardly. I've been promoted."

"To the New York office?" Rory asked evenly.

Bruno shook his head. "No. The consensus of opinion between Shimon and my new boss, Nan Bradfield, is that I'm better suited to fieldwork in the southern region. They want me down here, essentially reporting directly to them."

"I know you're disappointed Bruno," Rory offered quietly. "I know how much you wanted to move up to the big show."

"You don't know the half, Rory. A person I thought was my friend pushed ahead of me into the place Shimon was creating for me. Now I have to answer to her as well as Shimon," Bruno said bitterly.

"So, it's personal then?"

Bruno looked at him searchingly for a moment, then turned to stare once more out over the canal. "It's never personal, Rory. It's just about recognizing your main chance and screwing who you have to in order to take it. I got screwed, no hard feelings."

"But you said you got a promotion. What does that mean? More money?"

Bruno snorted. "Yeah, there's that. I look at it as a stud fee."

Rory felt himself draw inward, retracting from the inference. He put the pieces together in his mind and came up with the right conclusion. He looked at Bruno, who answered with a noncommittal shrug and a small nod. "It doesn't mean anything in the grand scheme, Will," Rory offered gently.

"Right, but . . . " Bruno said grudgingly. "It also means another move, Rory," Bruno said and drew Rory close under the shelter of his arm. "That's where they turned the knife."

Rory looked up at him with a careful smile and reached up to take his hand. "So. Where are we off to next?"

"We have a choice. Either Charleston, South Carolina, or Lexington, Kentucky," Bruno said grimly.

"Those are odd choices," Rory remarked honestly.

"They want me untainted by the politics of the big offices in Charlotte and Houston. I'll be independently auditing and reviewing their research before making a final recommendation to New York. In a sense, I'll be close enough to them to fly there when necessary for meetings before moving on to present findings to New York. I'll be on the road a little bit more, so I'm leaving the choice up to you. You have to be happy wherever we end up. At this point, I don't really give a fuck. Nan's made my place very clear. They think I'm good, just not good enough to play in their goddamn New York world."

With that, Bruno stood and stalked around the pool. "If I didn't have a southern accent, or if I had gotten my MBA from Harvard, or hell, if I was Jewish, I would have been in the New York office for years now. They draw ranks and close the doors no matter how fucking good you might be." Bruno stopped and stood staring out at the night sky. "I've jumped through every flaming hoop they've put up for me, and I've landed on my feet and took off running every goddamn time, Rory. But every time I open my mouth, I'm still a dumb-ass hick as far as they're concerned, and that ain't never . . . excuse me, that is never . . . gonna change." Bruno turned and looked at him defeatedly, "I get so tired of it, Rory. Sometimes I just want to tell them to go fuck themselves . . . but I just keep on . . . "

Rory had learned long ago when to talk and when to keep silent. This was not a time for him to either soothe or cajole. It was better to let Bruno talk himself through this funk alone. He simply lit a cigarette and briefly considered his options. He ruled out Lexington immediately. That was a city he couldn't consider, being anything but hostile to the intimate life he and Bruno shared. Having never been to the place, he saw it only as a deeply religious fundamentalist stronghold with nothing but mint juleps and bluegrass to offer.

Charleston, South Carolina, on the other hand, held a lot of appeal to him. It was a bright, warm southern city, close to the ocean, and it offered a certain tacit live-and-let-live ambience underneath its usual regional drawbacks. Also, there was a wealth of artsy activities that he'd frankly come to miss since their days in cities other than Fort Lauderdale and the Miami-Metro area. He hated driving down to Miami and neglected to attend any cultural activities there in the face of the hassles particular to the city itself.

Bruno moved hesitantly around the pool and returned to a spot at its edge directly in front of Rory and Bridget. He smoothly sat on the pool coping and allowed his legs to hang over the side and sway in the cool water. "What do you think, Rory? Where would you like to go for awhile? I mean it could be for awhile or it could be forever. I never know."

Rory stubbed out his cigarette in the ashtray and moved to Bruno's side. He positioned himself close next to him and let his legs dangle in the pool as well. He braced one arm against Bruno's back and nudged his shoulder. "Do we have enough money to live out on the Isle of Palms or Sullivan Island?"

Bruno looked over at him and nudged his shoulder in return before he grinned. "We have enough money to buy a place in the Charleston historic district, if that's what you want. We're going to make a killing on this place."

"I want to live at the beach," Rory said firmly.

"Remember how we used to dream about buying one of those shitty condos up in Kitty Hawk?" Bruno said sweetly.

"Yeah," Rory said. "We had so many big plans back then. Everything was so simple twenty years ago, before our world got so big."

"You mean before my head got so big," Bruno snorted.

"Well, there is that," Rory said and laughed until Bruno snickered as well. "You've shared every big scheme with me, Will," Rory replied tenderly. "And look at where we are. We're pretty lucky, don't you think?"

Bruno put his arm around Rory's shoulder and hugged him against his side. "I knew you would choose Charleston," he teased.

"Oh yeah," Rory grinned. "Why's that?"

"Something you said a long time ago, don't you remember?"

Rory shook his head and gave him a quizzical look.

"You said you were like Flipper; you'd die if you got too far away from the sea," Bruno said and grinned. "Frankly, I've wondered how long I could keep you all the way out here in the damn Everglades for as long as I have."

Rory looked out over the canal and to the great sky hanging above it. The large clouds sailing on the forward horizon were streaked with Tiepolo hues from the remnants of the sun as it set far across the flat Everglades into the welcoming Gulf of Mexico. "I've felt stranded here, Will," Rory said honestly. "I'm ready to leave as soon as you can get us out of here."

"You won't miss Venetian Vistas at all?" Bruno said gently.

Rory snuck a glance up to Austin's office window. Already there was a lamp lit inside and the place glowed like the memory of spent sin. Rory turned his head and met Bruno's eyes. "How soon can we leave?"

Bruno laughed and stood. "I'll call Shimon and Nan tomorrow and give them the good word that the decision is Charleston. Meanwhile . . . " he reached down and took Rory's hand to help him to his feet. " . . . let's go get on Realtor.com and see what's available on the beaches outside Charleston. I don't think Shimon or Nan would have a problem with me taking a few days off to fly us up there to go house hunting."

Once Rory was on his feet, he once more wrapped his arms around Bruno's waist and hugged him close.

Bruno could smell his hair and he leaned down to kiss the top of Rory's head. "Thanks for being so cool about this, Rory," he whispered.

Rory looked up and found his eyes. He tried to communicate in a long look how much he loved Bruno and was filled with an unexplainable joy when he found the same look returned to him without hesitation or reserve.

### 5160 ST. MARK'S COURT

AS SHE SETTLED into Austin's chair in the loft, Meg was determined to keep up her defense against the boys' flu, even though the worst of it appeared to be over. Though their return to school the day before was a decisive victory, she had no plans to lose any ground to a relapse, or worse, letting any lapse in vigilance result in a case of bronchitis as severe as Austin's. She encountered no resistance from Josh when it came time to slather the newly purchased Vicks on his chest and back before bedtime, but Noah was resentful and sullen when his turn came.

"Mom, I can do it myself," he said in a new tone of boredom and contempt for her care that had started appearing out of nowhere.

"Noah, how can you rub this on your own back?" She countered reasonably.

Her eldest son sighed as if she was demanding he submit to a mustard plaster rather than something as simple as a daub of Vicks applied with tender loving care. He pulled his T-shirt over his head and flung it across the room.

Before he turned his back to her, Meg glimpsed a curl of sparse hairs around his navel and a suspiciously dark area on his chest. Gently, but firmly she grasped his arm and pivoted him back around to face her. Sure enough, there were perhaps ten dark strong hairs sprouted between the immature cut of his pectoral muscles and a few more brave shoots around his small nipples. Impulsively, she reached as though to tug at his bit of thatch and said, "You're becoming a young man!"

Noah batted her hand away and took a quick couple of steps back from her. "Mom," he whined miserably. "That's totally private. Don't look at me that way."

Meg reached for his hand and pulled him against his will into a hug. "It's nothing to be ashamed of, sweetheart. I'm proud of you. You're taking after the men in my family."

Noah squirmed away, blushing from his face to his newly hirsute chest. "Mom, it's so not cool to talk about my body. It's embarrassing, god . . ."

"You're maturing, son," Meg said tenderly. "It's a little earlier than I expected, but pretty soon you're going to . . ."

"Mom, please! I don't want to talk about it," Noah howled, "Dad's already told me all that stuff. Will you just leave me alone!"

Stung and a little hurt, Meg said, "Okay, Noah. I'm sorry. Here," she said and held out the jar of Vicks. "Help yourself." Rebuffed and shamed for reasons she couldn't name, she felt her eyes tear up at the thought that she was now entering a totally new and alien expanse of the landscape of motherhood. It was territory she had arrived in unexpectedly, and its unwelcoming terrain was disorienting and painful in a way she hadn't anticipated. A tear made its way down her cheeks and she wiped one away with her free hand.

"Aw Mom," a thoroughly miserable Noah pleaded. "Please don't cry. I didn't mean to make you cry, okay?"

Meg couldn't fight it off. Noah was her first boy, now she realized he was becoming her first man in a way no other man would ever become again. She choked back a sob and started to get up.

Instantly, Noah stepped up and eased her back into Austin's chair. Awkwardly, he gave her a hug and whispered near her ear, "I still need you to do my back. Will you do that for me? I really want you to."

Meg hugged Noah back fiercely and then pushed him away with complete gentleness. At birth he had separated himself from her for the first time. Then, he was no longer a part of her, but she could still hold him and stroke him and admire every part of him with wonder for what she had made. Now, he was wrenching away from her touch in a terrifying new way. Soon she would have almost no intimate contact with the flesh of her flesh. She would be deprived of his touch, and she experienced a visceral ache as though he had physically wrenched himself from her once more.

Yet Noah obligingly turned and offered the suddenly long expanse of his back to her, and she bent to the unchanging tasks of nurture and tenderness, all the while knowing she might never get to return there again.

# CHAPTER THIRTEEN

# Asking for a favor

## ST. MARK'S COURT

AUSTIN'S FIRST FEW days at work were deeply satisfying, more so, in fact, than he had expected. Even his time-consuming commute offered him a chance to first anticipate his day, then analyze it in a way he'd had no chance of doing when he was stuck working at home. As Austin joined the river of traffic on the turnpike, he felt himself a part of the great roar of commerce of the day. Even the radio stations he flicked between seemed like welcoming old friends who invited him back into the world of the working man.

At the office he was welcomed back as well, but with a kind of deference and an undertone of respect that followed both from his new position and from his reputation as someone who stood up for what was right and not only paid the price for his principles, but was ultimately rewarded for it. Austin was pleased to respond with humility and effortless bonhomie.

At home as well, Austin felt that things had shifted seismically in harmony and in his favor. Mrs. Guiterrez seemed to be genuinely delighted to be back looking after the boys, and Noah and Josh slipped easily into the routine of being under her capable hand. Meg, too, seemed to subtly shift in her attitude toward him. Where there had been what he perceived as condescension, she now exuded camaraderie. Where she had been smug and put upon about the demands of working in the world, she now referred to them as a kind of presumed shared experience. And, somehow sensing an element of enhanced manliness in his enhanced status, she seemed to become more deferential to his judgment, authority, and opinion. Austin, in turn, became quicker to solicit her opinion and offered less resistance to the keener points of insight she proffered.

When the phone rang on Friday night, they were sharing one such moment. Meg was patiently explaining the qualities of the paint color for the loft, and Austin was genuinely being persuaded. Having come to see the inherent good sense and good taste in Austin's impulsive furniture selection, Meg winningly wanted to contribute to the loft's new look by selecting a paint color for the walls, and she was wisely urging that they get the painting done in the few weeks remaining before the new furniture pieces were delivered. "It's between papaya and mango," she explained, ignoring the phone.

"Well, it's fine by me," Austin agreed as he loped toward the phone in his office. "As long as you don't think it'll be too dark." Even after managing to locate the phone under the last of his sales paperwork, Austin caught the phone on its third ring. "Hello," he offered pleasantly.

"Austin? It's Bruno. Rory and I were wondering if we could come over for a minute. We have something to discuss with you and Meg."

Austin reflexively gripped the receiver in his hand so hard it hurt the joints in his fingers. Bruno had never called his house before, and Austin could see only one clear reason why he would do so now. His eyes darted nervously around his office as if it leered with evidence of every sexual act he and Rory had performed within its walls. For an entire week, Rory had not crossed his mind once, not in a sexual context or in any other. Now Rory filled his mind with the enormity of a small explosion between his temples.

"Austin? Are you there?" Bruno prompted.

Austin glanced at his watch. It wasn't even seven thirty; he knew there was no way he could plead the lateness of the hour to forestall the visit. "I'm sorry," he said. "I got distracted for a minute."

"So can we step over? We won't be long," Bruno insisted firmly.

Austin fought the urge to sigh with resignation. Instead he managed to summon some manly bravado. "Sure," he said confidently. "Come on, I'll meet you at the door."

"Excellent," Bruno replied confidently. "We're on our way."

"Excellent," Austin seconded, trying his best to sound as casual as he could manage. Once he'd clicked off the phone, he growled, "Shit," between clenched teeth and walked from his office back into the loft, needlessly closing his office door behind him as if its unwelcome ghosts could follow him to meet Bruno downstairs.

"Who was that," Meg asked, with her eyes still fixed on a glossy magazine page featuring her preferred paint color as she held it at arm's length against a wall.

"It's the guys from next door," Austin replied noncommittally.

"What on earth do they want?" Meg said and shifted her magazine page to an area by a window.

"They're coming over for a minute, Bruno said they have something they want to discuss with us," Austin told her as he walked past her turned back to the head of the stairs.

Behind him, he heard Meg say "Shit, I was just about to get a clear picture in my mind of what this paint color could do for this room, now it's gone."

Austin noted that Meg had become less careful in her language of late, and also less quick to discipline the boys for the same laxity. He didn't know if it reflected an overall slackening of her attempts to keep every detail of their lives under her authority, or if she was finally giving in to a more congenial "if you can't beat 'em, join 'em" attitude. In either case, it made Austin smile. She had certainly become easier to live with. With a visceral twisting sensation, he walked down the stairs toward Bruno's anticipated knock and news, wondering at the damage it would do to his wife's love and trust. In the time it took to get to the front door, he cursed himself for his foolishness with Rory and prayed he wouldn't be called to account for it.

The doorbell rang as Meg's soft footfalls stopped behind his shoulder. He turned impulsively and gave her a quick kiss which took her totally off guard. For a moment, she looked almost as if she wanted to wipe at her mouth with the back of her hand, but the look faded as quickly as it bloomed and she took his hand and squeezed it instead. Austin took an audible deep breath and opened the door.

Bruno responded by quickly raising a bottle of champagne. Austin ducked before he could see Bruno's smile, so sure he was that Bruno was about to break the bottle over his head. "Jesus, Austin!" Bruno laughed, "Chill out. We've come to celebrate, not brawl, dude!" With that he laughed deeply and pushed his way past Austin to quickly peck Meg on the cheek.

Rory gave Austin a brief glance and only nodded his head calmly as he followed Bruno's explosive entrance into the Harden's foyer. "Hello, Meg," he said warmly and stepped shyly to Bruno's side.

"Will, have you gone crazy?" Meg exclaimed as she recovered from Bruno's impetuous peck on the cheek. "What are you up to?"

"Bruno is about to burst to celebrate," Rory spoke to Austin's eyes. "He insisted we come to see you to share some good news. I hope we're not intruding."

Austin felt as if he'd stumbled into a fight only to find it was a circus parade. Unexpectedly, he was calmed by Rory's riveting gaze and only nodded at him gratefully.

"Let's get this bottle open and poured, and I'll fill you guys in," Bruno said as the boys tumbled downstairs to check out the hoopla.

"Hello, guys," Noah said calmly.

"You guys sound like home invasion robbers," Josh accused.

Bruno responded with a laugh and playfully lunged at him. "We've come to steal *you*! You wanna come live at my house?"

"You can have him," Noah smirked.

Josh looked from Bruno to his parents and then back again. "Can I have my own computer and an iPod Nano?"

"Whatever you want," Bruno teased.

"Watch out, Will," Meg cautioned, "He'll be packed and waiting at the door when you're ready to leave."

"I'll help him pack," Noah said.

Josh swallowed uneasily and moved toward his father.

Austin put his arm around him and pulled him to his side. "Sorry, guys. Joshie's mine. I can't let you take him. Right, son?"

Relieved, Josh nodded and leveled a long look at Bruno. "Not even for nothing, but you can still give me an iPod if you want to and I'll come over sometimes."

"Awww, man," Bruno groaned.

Meg nodded and smiled. "Okay, boys, you've said hello. You should head back upstairs, now. Tell Mr. Griffin and Mr. Fallon goodnight."

Both boys obliged quickly and trotted back upstairs.

"Okay, Bruno," Rory urged calmly, "can we tell Meg and Austin what this is all about?"

"Can we still have the champagne, *mother*?" Bruno teased.

"Let's go into the family room and get comfortable, guys," Meg said happily as she shooed everyone inside. "I'll see if I can find some champagne glasses."

Austin shot Rory a quick questioning look and was answered only with a pained smile. Once they were in the family room, he steered Bruno into the leather wingback Meg had always intended as Austin's own domain and sat next to Rory on the sofa. Despite Bruno's ebullience, Austin preferred to be near Rory if any unpleasant revelations were to surface. Like a child, he wanted to be closest to his partner in crime if there were to be any fingers pointed.

"Champagne?" He asked Bruno as he settled in next to Rory.

"Well, we needed to toast your new job at last, didn't we," Bruno said diffidently. "How's that working out for you?"

Despite his barely concealed nervousness, Austin felt an entirely justified smile tightening his lips. "Very well, thanks. I don't know if Rory told you, but I returned to my old job, promoted to CFO."

"He did indeed," Bruno said as he stretched his hand across the coffee table separating them and took Austin's in a firm handshake. "All the more reason for champagne, now that you're a big dog, son."

Austin returned Bruno's hard grip with a quick shake and looked up as Meg came into the family room bearing three stemmed wine glasses and a simple tumbler. "I'm afraid we don't have any champagne glasses," she said apologetically. "I hope these will do."

"No problem," Bruno said placatingly as he tore at the foil over the bottle's cork. "It's what's in the glasses that counts." With that, he stripped away the foil, crumpled it, and laid it on the coffee table where Meg was arranging the glasses.

"Do I need to get you a dish towel just in case?" Meg said as Bruno twisted the wire that held the cork's cage in place.

Bruno removed the wire and placed it next to the foil as he gave Meg a confident smile. "No ma'am," he said. "You don't need one if you know what you're doing." With that, he grasped the bottle by its neck and gently coaxed the cork out until it released with an understated pop. Bruno grinned at Meg and gave her a wink.

"You must have had some practice doing that," Meg said admiringly.

"Not as much as I'd like," Bruno said cheerfully as he poured the champagne into the four glasses. When he was finished, he set the bottle on the coffee table and gracefully took the awkward tumbler for himself. He waited until the others had a glass in hand before he raised his own. "To new jobs!"

Every one echoed his toast and clinked glasses all around before sipping at the surprisingly good champagne.

Meg sighed with pleasure and remarked casually, "This is awfully good stuff for a typical Friday night at home, Will. Tell us what's going on, the suspense is killing me."

"You said new jobs . . . plural," Austin said eagerly.

"That I did," Bruno said and took another sip at his champagne. "I've gotten a promotion. It's a different set of responsibilities in some ways, but it's basically doing what I do now, only with a different direction in focus."

"That's the good news," Rory said and sat his glass down on the coffee table.

"There's bad news?" Austin said anxiously.

"Well, we hope it's bad news for you guys," Bruno said cheerfully. "My new base of operations will be Charleston, South Carolina."

"Oh no," Meg exclaimed sincerely. "You're moving?"

"I'm afraid so," Bruno said seriously. "But I'm happy to see you guys aren't jumping for joy."

Austin looked at Rory first, then turned his attention quickly to Meg who came to perch on the sofa's arm next to him.

"You can't be serious, Will. We're very happy you're moving up, but we're genuinely sorry to be losing you as neighbors. With the tiniest pause of hesitation, she glanced at Rory and added, "You guys are wonderful."

"Thanks for that, Meg." Rory said quietly. Then he said to Bruno, "You better give them the rest of the news."

Bruno picked up the bottle of champagne and offered it around with a questioning glance at everyone before he freshened their glasses. Only Rory declined. Bruno took another quick sip from his tumbler, then followed it with a deeper swallow. "We've sold the house," he said quickly. "I'm almost scared I'm going to jinx it even talking about it so soon."

"But you haven't even put it on the market," Meg exclaimed.

"How long have you known this?" Austin asked Rory quietly.

Rory looked from Austin to Bruno, who had cleared his throat in preparation for the longer speech now that the preamble was over. Rory couldn't believe the look of pure grief Austin had shot him with his question. It was discomfiting and too telling to be faked and disingenuous.

"Do you guys remember getting a flyer letter in your mailbox from a guy in Venetian Vistas looking to buy a place in the neighborhood for his parents?"

"I remember it vaguely, I didn't pay too much attention to it," Meg admitted.

Austin shrugged. Now that the reason for this unexpected visit had been revealed, and he realized it had nothing to do with his relationship with Rory, he realized it had everything to do with his relationship with Rory, and he felt suddenly drawn to even the simple body heat Rory radiated just by sitting so close to his side. Where he had been panicked only minutes before at the threat of being found out, he now felt a keener sense of having something he wanted taken away from him. Nervously, he drained the champagne from his glass in a deep draft. The stuff made him lightheaded and deeply sad at the same time.

Rory, for his part, kept his gaze trained on Bruno. After being raked by the rawness of Austin's emotional glance, he felt hyperaware of the situation between them. It was all he could do not to stand and walk to another chair in the room.

"Well, I'd kept the letter because I felt some change in the wind at work. I gave the guy a call about it after our move became set. It turns out his parents are pretty well off and had already sold their place on Long Island to move down here. Right now, they're renting a small condo in Boca from some friends of theirs, but they're anxious to get out here," Bruno explained happily.

"When?" Austin managed.

"That's the beauty of it, Austin. They can do a cash deal right away. No realtors, so I was able to give them a little bit off of what I was going to list the place for, but Rory and I need to be out of here by the end of the month."

"That's only a couple of weeks," Austin said blankly.

"My god," Meg said sympathetically. "Have you even found a place to move to?"

"Not yet," Bruno said optimistically. "That's why we need a favor. Rory and I are flying up to Charleston tomorrow to go house hunting. We're going to be up there until we find a place. We're wondering if you guys would get in our mail while we're gone."

"Certainly," Meg said firmly. "But what about your dog?"

"Bridget's boarding at her vet's," Rory explained. "I took her in this afternoon."

"That's a relief," Meg laughed. "I have to admit I'm scared to death of her."

Rory smiled and stood. "We wouldn't ask you to look after her. She's old, but she can still be a handful."

"Where are you going?" Bruno asked him.

"Actually, I'm going outside to smoke," Rory said defiantly.

"I'll go out with you and keep you company," Austin said quickly and stood as well.

Bruno glanced sharply at Austin, then imperiously waved Rory away, and said, "Go on then and have your cigarette."

"Austin, if you don't mind, you guys go out on the lawn," Meg said dismissively. "No more butts in my hibiscus pots, okay?"

Rory walked toward the door to the pool deck, already drawing his pack of cigarettes from his back pocket. Austin moved along at his heels.

"Rory," Bruno said quickly. "Don't forget to give Austin the key to the front door while you're out there."

In reply, Rory jammed his hand in his front pants pocket and drew out a lone key on a key ring. He held it aloft for Bruno to see as he walked out the door. Once Austin had followed him out and closed the door behind them, Rory gave him a rueful smile and handed him the key.

Austin took the key and shoved it into his pants pocket without looking at it. He looked at Rory instead until Rory turned away and led them from the pool deck and deep into the backyard. Once they reached the edge of the canal, Rory stopped and lit his cigarette. Austin watched the flame flare in his eyes, and Rory looked at him as he drew the small glow into the cigarette's tip. Even when Rory allowed the lighter to click off, the image of his bright eyes stayed in Austin's mind. "How long have you known about this?" he asked Rory gruffly to mask his confusion and hurt.

Rory turned away from him and faced the canal. A breeze off its choppy surface caught and ruffled his shirt until it hugged against his chest tightly. "We've known about Bruno's transfer for about a week now," he said precisely. "The house sold today. Bruno called you as soon as the buyers left."

"When did you plan on telling me Bruno had been transferred," Austin demanded.

"There never seemed to be a good time this week," Rory said quietly. "You were busy getting started at your new job . . . "

"You could have called any evening, Rory," Austin said impatiently.

"It wasn't something I wanted to go into over the phone," Rory countered calmly, "for this very reason. I had a feeling you wouldn't take the news very well, and it seemed like it would be unfeeling to just give you a quick call and say, "guess what? I'm moving.' I was hoping to have a chance to talk with you this weekend. Then everything started moving so fast."

Austin put his hands in his pockets and bobbed up and down on the balls of his feet a couple of times before he said, "I was scared Bruno was dragging you over to confront me about us. It freaked me out," he admitted.

Rory sighed and took a deep hit off his cigarette. He glanced at Austin and then looked back out over the canal. "That's one reason why this all is probably for the best," he said thoughtfully.

"Yeah," Austin said bitterly. "Don't *you* get off easy."

"I don't know what you mean," Rory said stiffly.

"I mean, you get to just walk off, scot-free. It would have been a whole lot harder for you to stay here and be my friend," Austin said with the hurt palpable in his voice. "Now you can forget I ever happened."

Rory flicked his cigarette off into the wind from the canal. Both men watched it as it fell into the water in a rush of sparks that died as quickly as they flared. "You can't believe that's what I feel," Rory said, hurt tone striking against hurt.

"I don't know what you feel," Austin said tonelessly. "I never did, and I guess I never will." With that, he turned and started to walk away.

"Wait a minute," Rory said quickly. When Austin turned and stepped back, he said, "Don't walk away from this like that." He glanced nervously at the house and tugged his cigarettes out of his back pocket. "I guess they won't miss us if they know I'm chain-smoking out here, right?"

Austin smiled, but said "Why don't you just say what you have to say?"

Rory lit his second cigarette and gave it a look of distaste. "Did you know I've gone three days without one of these damn things before the last ten minutes?"

Austin grinned in the dark. "So, you're saying I still make you nervous."

Rory stepped up the bank and bumped him gently on the shoulder.

"I'll always have lung cancer to remember you by—does that make you happy?"

Austin laughed. "Well, that's something, I guess."

Rory took a hit off his cigarette and turned once more to the canal, but looked at Austin nonetheless. "Let's don't leave this with you being hurt and angry."

"But I am hurt and I am angry," Austin said quickly. "I'm hurt because I find out now how much I care about you, and I'm angry because I do. Christ, what a mess."

"How did you see this going on, Austin?" Rory asked and turned to look for his answer.

"I don't know," Austin said miserably, "but I didn't see it ending like this."

Rory nodded and smoked on in silence for a moment. Finally he spoke, not looking at Austin but at the night sky lying over the wind-ruffled water. "You made me feel good, Austin. And I hope you feel the same way. That's not something two people who belong to somebody else get to say all that often."

"Well, that's not enough," Austin replied urgently.

"It's all I have to give you," Rory said honestly. "I'm sorry."

"Is that all you have to say?" Austin said incredulously.

Rory only nodded and stood silently against the stiff breeze off the water. Then he sighed and said, "I wish I could tell you what I think you want to hear me say, but I can't."

"Then you're no different from all the guys that used you and hurt you so bad when you were a kid," Austin whispered harshly. "Because I feel now what you must have felt like back then," Then, seeing Rory was unmoved, Austin said resignedly. "I hope you feel like you got your revenge."

Rory turned and flashed his eyes on Austin angrily but before he could speak, Austin looked at him pitifully and said, "I just hope you realize someday that I didn't deserve it."

Rory looked out over the canal and flicked his cigarette out over the water before he angrily responded. "No, you don't deserve that. And you also don't deserve what happened to me back then. You see, Austin, what really hurts and what really *kills* is the betrayal that comes along with that territory. I won't tell everybody you know that you're a faggot." He looked at Austin with sincere sympathy. "That's where *you* get off easy. And that's where you learn how much I really care about you."

Austin just looked at him, reeling from a return blow he hadn't expected, and then hung his head. "I guess we better be getting back inside," he said at last and, defeated, turned to lead the way.

## 5150 ST. MARK'S COURT

WHEN RORY FINISHED packing, he pulled his bag from the bedroom to the foyer to wait through the night alongside Bruno's roller bag. Once he satisfied himself that the front door was locked, he made the same swift circuit he did each night among the switches that turned off the lights in the front of the house. Even in the darkness, the silhouettes of the furniture in each of the rooms humped themselves comfortably together to sleep until the light of day crept in from the glassy rear of the house. For Rory, their shapes were as comforting and familiar as animals in a barn. He stood for a moment in the dark, looking out over the rooms and their contents that flowed into each other in the house's open floor plan. For two years, it had been his home. Now it would be time to herd these beloved things together and move them to a new house, yet unseen. The thought of it made him both a little sad and also tremendously excited. Rory couldn't count how many times he'd moved in his life. In ways that were both comforting and familiar, he felt an old kind of excitement growing. He was ready to move on.

After he made his way into the kitchen, he dumped the empty

bottle of champagne into the recycle bin and loaded the coffeepot for the coming early-morning rush. Satisfied he had done all he could do to ease the morning's tension, he came to stand before his small altar on the counter to murmur his evening's prayers. At the last minute, he offered a quick prayer for Austin's hurt, and an act of contrition for his part in it, then crossed himself quickly and blew out the vigil candle burning beside the portrait of the Sacred Heart. Comforted, he turned to join Bruno on the pool deck, waiting in the dark.

"Hey beast," he said from the door.

Bruno turned his big head sleepily and gave him a grin as he patted the empty cushion on the wicker sofa next to him. "You're all ready to take off in the morning?"

Rory walked over and sat next to him, fishing his cigarettes from his back pocket as he did. "Yep. Packed and waiting," he said as he lit a cigarette in the night.

"I thought you said you were down to three a day again," Bruno commented easily.

"I was, but we don't sell our house every day, either. Cut me some slack," Rory said and laughed.

Bruno stretched an arm over Rory's head and laid it across his shoulders before locking him in a tight hug," Everything's going to be all right, baby. Don't get all nervous. We're gonna get on that plane, go to Charleston, and rent us a car, and go find us a big-ass house. Ba-da-bing, ba-da-boom. If we're lucky, you'll be walking on the beach in two weeks."

"Seriously, Will, do you think we'll manage that before we have to be out of here?" Rory asked soberly.

"Have I ever let you down?" Bruno said with utter self-assurance.

Rory cut him a sideways glance that wasn't meant to be unkind, just skeptical, and took a hit off his cigarette.

Bruno chose to ignore the look. "So, you're sure you want a beach house?"

"Yes," Rory said firmly. "I am sure. All we really need is a kitchen, a bedroom with a bath, and a porch like this one, and I'll be happy."

"I'm going to buy you a better view than this one," Bruno said with certainty. "This is crap compared to where we're going."

"Well, I don't know, boss." Rory said, "Venetian Vistas doesn't exactly suck."

"Compared to where we're going, baby, this is pure-d ghetto," Bruno said and laughed.

"Your southern is falling all out your mouth," Rory said dryly.

"You know what, boy? I don't give a flying fuck. I ain't going to New York City, so New York City can kiss my rebel ass. If they want to keep me down home, I'm gonna keep my southern mouth and talk like I damn well please," Bruno said heartily.

"Sounds good to me," Rory said and added, *"Beau."*

Bruno stretched his legs out in front of him and sighed. "You never really wanted to move up there anyway, did you?"

"I wanted to if you wanted to," Rory said, then added honestly, "but I ain't crying into my pillow about not going."

"That's what I figured," Bruno said and sat thoughtfully for a moment. After a few peaceful minutes he said, "I'm really lucky that you've stuck with me for so long. I just want you to know I don't ever take you for granted, no matter how it might appear sometimes."

Rory put his cigarette out in the ashtray on the table next to him, then stretched his shorter legs out alongside Bruno's and nudged his leg with one of his own. "Will . . . "

In the dark, Rory saw Bruno wipe the side of his face quickly, then mask it by making an exaggerated show of scratching the side of his nose. However, his voice didn't lie. Choked by all he couldn't say, he simply managed, "I just don't want to risk messing things up anymore, you know?"

Rory reached up and patted the hand Bruno still had resting on his shoulder, then he laid his head back against his arm and watched the slow sailing clouds, blushing pink and gold on their undersides from the reflected lights of the great city that stretched away under the moon to the east. "You know, Bruno," he said softly, "I feel exactly the same way."

## 5160 ST. MARK'S COURT

AUSTIN PLED THE first quarter earnings report as his excuse to take refuge in his office. While it was true the heavy document filled with charts, graphs, and endless statements of figures needed to be gone over during the course of the weekend, it didn't really need to call him away from Meg and the boys on a Friday night. Still, Austin wanted and needed to be alone. He settled his family comfortably in front of a DVD featuring Harry Potter, Hermione Granger, and Ron Weasley battling wits with yet another incarnation of Lord Voldemort and hid himself away to brood.

For the most part, the earnings report lay open on his desk, and Austin watched out his window as Bruno and Rory moved noiselessly in the lamp's glow beyond their bedroom door. Austin sat riveted to the scene as Bruno finally came to sit on their pool deck and contented himself with a few bong hits. Austin stared at him with unbridled venom and hatred until Rory finally joined him and they sat close, talking their way intimately into the night.

A variety of emotions pulled at Austin, though he was mostly desolate and sore of heart in a way he couldn't remember being since he was a punk kid, just learning he had the capacity to hurt at all. He felt betrayed. He felt abandoned. He felt murderously jealous, and he just felt unassuagably sad. Even as he watched Rory, so definitely and unassailably possessed by Bruno, he tormented himself with thoughts of how unfair the situation was. Austin had moved past any shame for what he had done or how he was feeling. He only felt the weight of burdensome self-pity for a kind of love that had no possible shape in the reality of his life. There was no justifiable place for Rory in his life other than what his neighbor had sensibly shared with him to its limit. But Rory had shared too much still, and Austin now stung with the loss of something he had never really had.

After a long while, Rory and Bruno stood together and walked side by side into their room. With a crushing finality, the light through the door went dark and Austin was utterly shut out of everything but his own hurtful imaginings of what might be happening next. He stared for a long time at the black emptiness beyond Rory's bedroom door and willed himself not to cry.

"You're going to miss him, aren't you?" Meg said quietly from the door of his office. She had come upstairs in silence and caring concern, only to find him pitiably brooding in the near dark of his bolt hole.

Austin sat silently until he felt her hands on his shoulders and her lips brush the top of his head. "I didn't know it showed," he said when he could manage.

Meg sighed and moved her hands to gently rub the muscles where the column of his neck grew from his shoulders. "Poor Austin," she said. "Did you think I couldn't tell?"

Austin swiveled in his desk chair to look up at her, "Tell what?" He asked defensively. "That he was my friend?"

Meg smiled down at him and turned to walk the few steps to his sofa opposite the desk. She said coldly as she sat, "Austin, it's time you and I have a talk about you and Rory Fallon."

"I don't know what you're talking about," Austin told her miserably.

"Sure you do," Meg said encouragingly. "You're guilty as sin. You're just like the boys when they get into something they shouldn't." She laughed bitterly. "Austin, I'm your wife, give me some credit for knowing you better than anyone else. For weeks it's been 'Rory said,' or 'Rory told me,' or "Rory and I.' In all the years we've known each other, I've only seen you act like this one other time, and that was the summer my parents tried to separate us and you got close to that jerk Greg Norris."

Austin rubbed his eyes miserably.

"You slept with him, and I'm pretty sure you've had sex with Rory Fallon," Meg said firmly.

"What makes you so sure?" Austin asked defiantly.

Meg smirked. She knew what Greg Norris had told her long ago and she knew what Rory Fallon's studiedly cool eyes would not. "Let's just say two cats recognize each other in the dark, and leave it at that," she said, smug and sure in her own secrets.

"Meg, I'm not like that," Austin said and waved his hand brusquely in the direction of the house next door.

"Of course you're not. Do you think I'm an idiot?" Meg said calmly. "We have a wonderful life and two gorgeous children. You just were lonesome and bored." She drew a deep breath and then continued with steely determination, "But I seriously need you to tell me whether or not you fucked that man."

"He was my friend. He . . . "

"Whether or not he is your friend is immaterial," Meg interrupted. "Did you or did you not fuck him?"

Austin just looked at her and tried to stare into her eyes defiantly.

Meg finally nodded and stood. She walked the few steps to the door and closed it firmly. Turning back to Austin, she took two steps toward him and folded her arms over her chest, forcing him to look up at her. "For just a minute, let's leave how that makes me feel out of it. Let's just talk about how stupid you are."

Austin opened his mouth, but before he could respond, Meg locked him in a cold stare and said, "Don't you have any idea how *filthy* gay people are? Did you even stop to consider the chances you were taking with your health and with mine?"

"First of all, Rory told me he'd never cheated on Bruno, ever," Austin replied heatedly.

"And you believed him?" Meg asked incredulously. "Even if he wasn't lying, do you have any idea how many people Will Griffin's probably slept with? Even if your precious *friend* has been as faithful as he claims, his partner doesn't strike me as being anything but a total whorehound. He's flirted with me, for godsakes."

"We . . . I was careful," Austin said miserably. "I used condoms . . . "

"Well, that's fucking great news," Meg spat. "So you admit you did screw that man."

"Meg . . . "

"And let's look at your success rate with rubbers," Meg continued acidly. "It's not so stellar is it? You have a six-year-old son as living proof of how great condoms work for *you.*"

Austin drew a breath as if he'd been slapped, and hung his head.

"Have you had sex with me since you started exploring your bisexuality?" Meg demanded.

Austin looked up furiously and spat, "You should know that as well as I do."

Meg's arm flashed in the air, but before she slapped him, her entire body froze. Tiredly, she dropped her arm, turned, and made her way to the sofa, where she slumped and put her head in her hands.

Austin stared at her, feeling the anger drain from his own body only to be replaced by a bitter fatigue.

Without looking up, Meg said quietly, "You *will* have an AIDS test and VD tests before you touch me ever again. And I *will* be there to hear the results. All secrets stop now. Do you hear me, Austin?"

Austin felt a cold fog of shame and dread steal over his fatigue. There was the price to be paid for touching and loving another male. It was this same humiliation of his teen misstep come back again. The knowing nurse. The veneer of clinical concern over a doctor's repugnance. He swallowed hard and tried to control the tremble in his voice as he said, "Of course, Meg. I'll get it taken care of immediately."

Meg lifted her head and nodded. With a tremble in her own voice, she said simply, "What about me, Austin? Did you never think I would leave you? Did you never think you would hurt me doing what you've done? Didn't you even think of me?"

"It didn't really have anything to do with you, Meg," Austin choked out. "It was just mine." Tears of frustration stole into his eyes. "I know how selfish that sounds, but I swear to god," he snuffled, "I swear to almighty god, it didn't have anything to do with you."

Meg saw the tears that now fell from one eye, then the other. She nodded, but said, "Thanks for that, but I know it's not true."

Austin wiped his face and hung his head before he choked back a pitiable sob.

Meg looked at his humbled head and wanted to both slap him and hug him. When she was a girl, she had seen her mother break a long branch off a poplar tree that grew in their backyard and strip the leaves off the slender stinging branch with one clean downward swipe of her hand and a look of murder in her eyes. Her brothers would begin to walk backwards away from the whipping that was inevitable. Pitiless, her mother would make them stand stock still as she beat them with the branch until she broke down in sympathetic sobs. Her tears blended with those of her switch-chastened sons, until her anger was spent and her love stilled her arm. Meg pushed her own tears away in the sight of her husband's guilty hung head. This switching was done, her love had overcome her anger, and she was exhausted by the effort.

Meg stood and walked to his desk and switched off his lamp, willing him not to turn and look once more out that damnably haunted window. "C'mon, Austin," she said quietly and pushed his shoulders gently. "It's time we went to bed."

"I'll still need to say goodbye," he said miserably.

"Of course," Meg said. "He was your friend and he's leaving. But you'd better do it vertically," she said wearily.

Austin looked up at her and nodded with guilty seriousness.

Meg fought a smile at his endearing male artlessness. He was, and now always would be, no more than another unruly child in her eyes. The mother triumphed over the wife and she said threateningly, "I'm warning you, Austin, I'll know. And my understanding has its limits. I will divorce you."

Obediently, Austin stood and took her hand. Hopefully, he watched her as he stood. Meg gave him a small smile and he put his arm around her waist and held her as they took the first steps out of one door and into another place altogether.

# CHAPTER FOURTEEN

# The good neighbor . . .

## 5160 ST. MARK'S COURT

WHEN RORY TURNED onto St. Mark's Court, the truck in front of the Hardens's house was just pulling away. For a second, he felt a flash of panic. The movers weren't due to arrive and pack his household goods until the following day. He was scared somehow they'd come a day early, only to find him gone and the house locked tight. However, by the time he completed his turn as the unwieldy truck made its own turn in the cul-de-sac at the end of the street, he could see it wasn't the large moving van he was expecting. He breathed a sigh of relief until he saw Austin waiting at the end of his drive.

Rory hadn't seen or spoken to Austin since the night two weeks before when he and Bruno had gone over to tell him and Meg the news of their sudden departure. The weeks that followed were fully consumed by house hunting so far away and making all the arrangements to get the thing accomplished in such a short space of time. But, that was only part of his failure to see Austin. It was really the excuse. The reason lay in the fact that Rory simply couldn't deal with the emotions of saying goodbye to the man. Though it was a necessary detail, he knew, he couldn't find the way to do it.

Yet, here was Austin now, waving him into his driveway as though guiding an airliner into its berth at the gate. Rory met Austin's grin with a reluctant smile of his own as he shut off his car and reached for his backpack on the seat next to him. Before he could open his car door, Austin opened it for him and said, "I was wondering if you were coming home this morning."

"I had some errands to run," Rory explained. "We're getting down to the wire."

"When do you close on the house?" Austin asked as Rory got out of the car and he closed the door behind him.

"Done," Rory said. "We met at the attorney's office yesterday afternoon. Your new neighbors are being very kind and are letting us stay on a couple of more days to get packed and out."

"When are you actually leaving?" Austin asked sadly.

"Sunday morning," Rory said. "What are you doing home on a Thursday?"

"Our new stuff from Pottery Barn just got delivered," Austin explained. "I had to stay to take delivery. Meg has depositions this morning. I'm heading into the office in a little while, now that they've come and gone."

"Is it nice?" Rory said with a smile at Austin's obvious happiness.

"Come see," Austin said and took his hand.

"I don't know," Rory said reluctantly. "I've got a ton of things to do before the movers come and you need to be getting to work."

Austin took a step toward his house and pulled Rory along by the hand. "It won't take long, I promise."

Rory gently took back his hand from Austin's grasp. "Austin . . . I'm not sure . . . "

Austin stopped and looked at Rory for a moment before turning his gaze toward his house. "It's nothing like that, Rory." He looked back at Rory once more and said seriously, "I really want you to see the loft. In a big way, you're responsible for giving me the guts to put it together. This isn't some big ploy to . . . to get up to something. Okay?"

Rory nodded. "Okay. Anyway, this will give us a chance to talk. I've been putting off . . . "

"Saying goodbye?" Austin said gently. "I have noticed, you know."

"Fair enough," Rory said.

"Okay!" Austin said and turned to lead the way to his house and loft.

Rory followed along behind him silently. He had too much to say to make small talk, and any way he could imagine the conversation turning lead straight into minefields he was scared to negotiate.

For his part, Austin remained silent as well. He let them into the house and on up the stairs, remembering other occasions for this same trip of steps. Then, the destination was decidedly different, but in a growing way, increasingly Austin found himself wishing it was the same. Once he arrived at the top of the stairs, he felt a familiar ache swell in his heart and his groin. He stepped out of Rory's way, not merely to give him an unobscured view of the loft, but also hide his own unexpressed longing.

Rory stepped past Austin and on into the loft. He took in the view of the new furniture, in place against the carefully calculated color of the newly painted walls, with honest appreciation. "My god," he said. "It's wonderful."

"Do you really like it?" Austin asked bashfully. "I picked out all the furniture and measured and everything to make sure it would fit right."

Rory turned and gave him a huge grin. "You nailed it, Austin. Everything—the scale, the colors, the wood finishes—you just did a fantastic job."

"Meg chose the new paint," Austin admitted.

"Well, her choice was inspired," Rory said ungrudgingly. "You tell her I said that."

Austin looked at him and then away quickly. "That might not be the right thing to say."

"Why?" Rory said confused. "She did a great job."

"Could we sit down a minute?" Austin said pleadingly.

"Oh hell, don't tell me . . . " Rory said bleakly.

"Let's go into my office, okay?" Austin urged. "We need to talk. Just talk, okay?"

With resignation, Rory allowed his backpack to slide off his shoulder and caught it with his hand on the way down. Then, nearly dragging his feet, he turned and walked into Austin's office with the man close behind. Once inside, he walked straight to Austin's desk and stood with his back to the room, looking out the window and down onto his own pool deck.

Austin moved behind him and sat awkwardly on his sofa. "Come sit down, Rory," he said gently. "Isn't it time we did this, or did you just plan to leave without . . . "

"Without the painful goodbye?" Rory interrupted without turning around. "I thought about it Austin," he said truthfully.

"Me too," Austin admitted. "Come sit," he insisted.

Reluctantly, Rory moved to the sofa and sat down next to Austin with a closeness that surprised both of them. Rory placed his backpack between his feet and then swiveled until his knee was touching Austin's leg. "She knows, doesn't she?" He said quietly.

"She figured it out," Austin said. "Completely on her own."

"I'm so sorry, Austin," Rory said and touched him lightly on the thigh. "Please believe me when I tell you I never wanted that to happen."

"It's okay, Rory." Austin sighed. "She's been very mature about it and I . . . well, I have done a lot of thinking." Austin placed his palm over Rory's hand and tenderly asked, "Do you think Bruno knows?"

Rory turned his hand under Austin's palm and gave his hand a squeeze before taking his own back. "He hasn't said anything if he does. But I have to wonder. He got us the fuck out of here like a hurricane was on our tails."

Austin laughed. "Either that or he knew I was on your tail."

Rory snickered. "You're lucky he didn't break your jaw."

"He really loves you that much, doesn't he?" Austin asked suddenly sober.

"Yes," Rory said without hesitation. "For all he fucks up on occasion, he's never for one second made me feel I wasn't very much loved."

"I wanted you to love me, you know that don't you?" Austin said plainly.

"Yes, I know you did," Rory admitted. "But you know I couldn't, right?"

Austin sighed deeply and leaned against the soft sofa's soft back cushions. "Right."

"It's my conscience," Rory explained hopefully. "Maybe it's a Catholic thing, but I could give you my body, but I couldn't give you my heart. My love belongs to somebody else. You just needed my heart worse than you did my body. I wish we could have just been friends, without the sex."

"Those were your brakes," Austin said gently. "You had them this time, I didn't."

Rory looked at him questioningly. "I'm not sure I follow you."

"That time we were coming back from Fort Myers," Austin explained. "You were trying to explain why gay guys fell in love with straight guys. You said straight guys could fuck but couldn't love. You said those were their brakes."

Rory nodded. "That's what I always thought."

"Yeah, but this time you were wrong," Austin said and looked him in the eye. "I fell in love with you. But I don't regret it."

"I'm so sorry, Austin," Rory told him gently.

"Don't be," Austin demanded. "I can't take pity. I can take you saying you just fucked me because you felt like it, or to get back at Bruno, but for god's sake, don't tell me I was a pity fuck."

"That's not how I feel at all," Rory insisted.

"Then how do you feel, you stingy fucker?" Austin demanded. "Did you feel anything at all?"

Rory took a moment to consider what he must keep against giving away himself. "For the first time in forever, you made me feel wonderful and fascinating and sexy as hell. I can say I love you for that and not be lying. You want me to love you? Well, there you are. Don't act like I didn't feel anything." Rory finished his little tirade and then hung his head.

For a little while, they didn't say anything, they just sat together in a way more intimately than any act they had shared on that very sofa, in that sun-filled room. They both knew there would never have been any complete understanding between them. What they did share was the comfort of an animal warmth that resonated deeper than words could articulate. At last, Austin reached for Rory and pulled him against his chest. Rory didn't resist, but rather settled in against him, listening to him breathe, listening to his heartbeat. Austin stroked Rory's lightly muscled side and buried his lips in the freshly shorn bristles on his scalp. He breathed in Rory's scent of coconut shampoo and sighed contentedly. For just these few moments, they both found what they had blundered along looking for before.

Finally, Rory stretched away from Austin and gave him a smile. "I have something for you," he said and opened the flap of his backpack.

"Is it a going-away present?" Austin asked, concerned. "I didn't get you one."

"Don't worry about it," Rory said dismissively and handed Austin a CD.

Austin looked at the artwork featuring an African-American man moodily looking away from a saxophone.

"Two of my three studio songs made it on the CD," Rory said proudly.

Austin looked up at him incredulously. "This is it?"

Rory nodded and smiled. "The two I'm on are 'Groove with You' and 'Footsteps in the Dark.'"

"When did you get this?" Austin asked excitedly.

"This morning," Rory said, "when I went to get my haircut. Dazz Coleman, the producer, he's on the down-low with this twink hairdresser who cuts my hair."

"Have you heard it?" Austin asked as he started nicking the wrapper with his fingernail.

"Please," Rory said sardonically, "until I'm sick of it. They played it non-stop in the salon. They all love it. I got a free haircut out of it, anyway."

"I want to listen to it right now," Austin insisted.

Rory gently placed his hand over the CD. "Not while I'm here unless you want me to cry."

"Why?" Austin said incredulously.

Rory smiled. "Both of those songs have a lot of meaning for me. I guess that comes through in the way I sang them. I just want you to know, if you ever have any more questions about what I've felt for you, just listen to those two songs."

"No one's ever sung for me before," Austin said shyly.

"I have," Rory said. "And, I did."

"Thanks, Rory. I really mean it," Austin said and placed his palm on the side of Rory's face.

Rory gently reached up, and took his hand, and brought it to his lips. He kissed Austin's knuckles and then stood. "Goodbye, you wonderful man."

Austin stood and reached for him, but Rory stooped for his backpack and was in full retreat the moment its strap was grasped in his hand.

**VENETIAN VISTAS**

MEG COULD TELL spring was near. It was still light outside the breakfast nook's window when she shut down her laptop and made her way upstairs to the loft. Though she had seen the new furniture in place against the freshly painted coral-orange-ish shade of the walls when she got home, she found herself anticipating the loft's new look with some excitement. The space that really contained the heart of her home was a triumph of give and take between husband and wife, in her way of thinking. She freely admitted Austin had been inspired when he chose the U-shaped sectional sofa and the other pieces as well. Now the loft embraced instead of excluded her, though it still was primarily the domain of Austin and the boys.

When she got to the top of the stairs, Meg closed her eyes and opened them again slowly to take in the room and its contents. Austin sprawled comfortably in one corner of the sofa, watching CNN on the TV in its new entertainment center. Josh worked contentedly at the computer the boys shared, which was perched at its place at the end of the new table that ran between their matched pair of new hutch-like desks. The entire area was as serene and upscale as a spread from the Pottery Barn catalogue itself.

She paused and mentally placed new sconces and a hanging lamp or two that the room called for. The desks lacked adequate lighting, and Austin definitely needed some light to read by, just there, suspended over the sofa's spot on the sofa he'd claimed as his own. She smiled. Austin might have made the grand gesture embodied in the furniture, but she was the one who knew what details to place in order to make the room really come together. For a quick moment she regretted the fact that Rory Fallon was moving. He'd have come in handy when it came time to put up light fixtures, but Meg decided she'd gladly pay for an electrician herself if the little bastard would just get the hell away from her husband and her life.

Meg mentally deleted the disturbing thought of Rory Fallon and took her new loft in once more. Everything and everyone seemed to be in place, save one. "Where's Noah?" she asked as she stepped into the loft itself.

Austin looked away from the TV and glanced around the room before turning his attention once more to the news. "He's in his room, probably."

"He's in there masturbating," Josh said matter-of-factly.

Before Meg could form a response, Austin snickered and Josh said, "He masturbates a lot."

"I am not!" came Noah's muffled roar from behind his closed door. There was the sound of his feet hitting the floor and striding to his door. The knob turned violently in place but didn't give against the lock. "You little bitch!" Noah yelled as he unlocked the door.

Josh yelped and was struggling to get out of his new chair when Noah's door flew open and was immediately followed by the charge of his stocky body. Meg watched in shocked horror as Noah landed on Josh in the full force of flying fists. Josh laughed manically as he took a glancing blow to his chin and a more solid one in his solar plexus. He managed to get away with a hard wrench from Noah's grasp and took a vaulting leap over the low back of the new sofa.

"Austin!" Meg cried, pulling the two syllables of his name into three.

Austin simply reached out and grabbed Josh's arm as he landed feet first on the sofa cushion next to him, and then used the boy's momentum to swing him off the sofa and onto the ottoman, where he crashed neatly, butt-first.

Meg stepped toward Noah as he stood panting furiously, the milky skin of his bare chest and face flushed a deep shade of red in evidence as much of the truth of Josh's assertion as of his own private exertions. Meg got behind him and grabbed his hand, finding it surprisingly slick as Noah snatched it away from her.

From his perch on the ottoman, safe behind the sofa's buffering back, Josh extended the first two fingers of his left hand and tapped a furious tattoo on his right wrist as he said in a singsong voice, "Oooh Sarah, I *love* you . . . "

"Faggot!" Noah bellowed and launched himself across the sofa's back toward his laughing brother.

"Austin! Do something," Meg cried as Austin laughed and tried to place himself between his two sons while dodging to avoid the worst of Noah's blind fists. "They'll destroy the new furniture!" Meg wailed.

"Meg, go for a walk," Austin said firmly as he grabbed at the back hem of Noah's sagging britches and yanked him backwards away from his still-laughing brother. "I can deal with these two, but I can't deal with them and you too."

"Fine!" Meg shouted as she turned on her heel and stomped back down the stairs. The hand that she'd grabbed Noah's with slid on the banister. Confusedly, she lifted her hand to her face and caught the unmistakable scent of Vaseline Herbal Intensive Care Lotion over a raw note of man and musk. "Oh good God!" she wailed and marched straight into the kitchen. Finding no hand soap, she reached under the sink for something to wash her hands with and pulled out a bottle of Soft Scrub. Fighting back her dark discovery with the gritty harsh cleanser only made her angrier as she heard another great thud and Austin's angry bellow join the din from overhead.

Taking not even her keys, she nearly ran out the front door, slamming it behind her. Blindly she stalked the winding streets of Venetian Vistas. Had anyone happened to be out, they would have taken one look at her thunderous expression and turned away before her gaze lighted on them. As it was, the streets were falling into the dusk of the dinner hour. It was too late for people to be getting home and too early for the joggers and bypass-surgery convalescents to have begun their evening rounds.

For her part, Meg's strides slowed to a stroll as her anger and confusion cleared. She strove valiantly to push away any thoughts of her baby touching himself. Such self-knowledge was precocious at best and perverted at its worst. She didn't quite know where to put this new knowledge of her son and the harsh evidence of his sudden maturity. All his young life, it was Noah she identified with and cherished most as her own. He had her fair coloring and dark hair. He had her quick bright mind. He was hers, while Josh was of the totally alien and beloved temperament and likeness of his father.

But that disturbing revelation was only a part of her larger confusion. The grander unknowing was bound up in what was essentially male. Both boys had exhibited growing aggression and a fierce physicality that was impossible for her to control or temper. They were these little boy beasts, and they were suddenly oblivious to the very presence of her authority and female influence. More than ever before, she was alone in a camp of males, and the thought of it bewildered her and made her sad.

As she walked and fell deeper into thought, she felt hot tears come and fall. She considered Austin and the apparently unthinking way he'd followed his dick into a mess she couldn't really rail against or turn a blind eye to. He was as much a cipher as his sons, and she was only on the outside, wounded and alone. In her most private moments, she'd considered leaving him, or rather asking him to go. She had the grounds for vindication and vindictiveness, her professional lawyerly training informed her. But then she thought about the emptiness of his absence as opposed to his flawed presence. She thought about handling a situation like the one she'd just walked away from and left in his hands. She knew she could never handle Noah and Josh on her own. She also knew she couldn't bear to be without him in her life or in her bed. Austin was the love of her life. For better or worse, she'd promised. Meg just wasn't sure how much worse it could get.

When she finally had walked her way through both dusk and the conversation in her head, Meg looked around and realized she had no idea where she was. The streets of Venetian Vistas wound round on themselves. Every fourth house repeated itself in shape and size, from the one she'd just passed only to begin again with each new façade part of the repeating variation of home styles. Every house had a lone royal palm on one corner and a cluster of queen palms on the other. All the houses were skirted with a low hedge of ixora or ficus. Anxiously, she realized she had never walked so deeply into her own neighborhood before. There were no familiar landmarks in this world of planned variety to point her home.

Meg stopped and turned to look back in the direction she'd come. The street behind her mirrored the street ahead of her. She swallowed panic and decided the only way she'd find her way back home was to try and retrace her steps, as unpromising as that sounded considering her lack of attention to the turns taken in the deepening dusk. She walked a little way resolutely, but felt a stirring of fear when she heard a steady pounding of running feet behind her. The tread was heavy and determined. She made a concerted effort not to look behind her, but carefully made her way to the center of the street, intuitively understanding she'd have room to break and run if the heavy-footed stranger behind her intended her harm. Her heart beat faster as she kept a measured, confident pace. The pounding behind her came closer.

"Meg!" She heard a familiar deep voice say as the footfalls drew up beside her. Meg looked to her right and saw Bruno trot past her, and then turn to run backwards to break his momentum and slow to a sort of effortless jogging in place. "You sure are a long way from home."

Bruno was sleekly wet as a thoroughbred. He looked glossy and healthy even under the yellowish gleam of the streetlights. Meg almost expected him to snort and whinny like a horse, yet at that moment, he was the handsomest thing she'd ever seen. "Boy, am I glad to see you," she said gratefully. "I have no idea where I am."

"You'rve over near the clubhouse," Bruno panted as he walked back to stand next to her. "Did you walk all this way?"

Meg nodded. "I didn't plan to. I was just walking and thinking . . ."

"And crying, too, from the looks of it," Bruno said gently.

Meg wiped at the dry tracks of tears and telling drip of mascara. "Males," Meg said as she attempted a smile, "the grown one and the little ones."

Bruno nodded sagely and gently took her elbow to steer her down the street. "I have all brothers. My mom used to take a lot of long walks."

Meg allowed herself to be steered so gracefully, but was pleased when Bruno knew precisely when to let go of her elbow and merely walk beside her companionably. "Did she ever get lost?"

"My dad used to say she'd find her way home when she was ready," Bruno said. "I'm uniquely qualified to listen if you'd like to talk," he offered.

Meg shot him a wary glance, but saw he was only looking ahead. "I don't know what to say," she said guardedly.

Bruno nodded, but kept his gaze resolutely ahead. "I thought you'd want to talk about Rory and your husband."

Meg stopped so abruptly that Bruno got in two steps beyond her. When he stopped and looked back for her, she said, "You know?"

Bruno nodded sadly. "Yes. I have for a few weeks now."

"Does Rory know you . . ." Meg began.

"No way," Bruno said quickly. "You see, I can't throw stones. I've cheated on him, and he found out about the same time he and Austin . . ." his voice trailed off in his own hurt, and he only vaguely gestured to complete the thought.

Meg looked him in the eye and nodded grimly.

Bruno looked ahead and forged on, "In a way, I have to take responsibility for the whole mess. Rory has never cheated on me before. I guess I just pushed him past his limit."

Meg walked the two steps to him and then continued on, "Let's walk," she said. "Right now I can't stand still."

Bruno agreeably began to walk beside her, measuring his normally long strides to her smaller ones. "I haven't let him know I know, Meg. But since I started the whole thing, I decided to end it. That's why we're moving so suddenly."

"But I thought you got a promotion and they were relocating you," Meg said.

Bruno laughed. "That much is true, but I had a choice of working from where I work now, moving to Manhattan, or moving to Charleston."

"Moving to Manhattan would seem to be ideal for what you do and for your career, Will. Why on earth would you choose Charleston?" Meg asked gently.

"We turn here," Bruno said and gestured the way with his chin. When they had rounded the corner, he said, "Rory didn't really want to move to Manhattan, for several reasons. Not the least of which is the fact that the woman I'd been having the affair with became my new boss."

"I see," Meg said evenly.

"But Meg, he would have done it. He would have moved with me to Manhattan if that's what I wanted. He loves me that much." Bruno looked at her and gave a short, unhappy laugh. "I lied and told him my other option was in Kentucky, of all places."

"Did you tell him you had the choice of staying here?" Meg asked sincerely.

Bruno only looked at her and shook his head.

"And you didn't want to stay here?" Meg asked. "Why rearrange your whole life?"

Bruno looked down at her and simply said, "I don't want to lose him. I love *him* that much."

"Will, you don't think he and Austin would have . . . " Meg said incredulously. "Do you know something I don't?"

"No, Meg," Bruno said quickly, "nothing like that. Those two aren't in love with each other. Please," he snorted. "Austin is just a symptom, not a solution to what Rory's problem is."

"And just what is Rory's problem?" Meg asked, vaguely offended at the inference that her husband was only a symptom.

"Me. I'm his problem," Bruno admitted. "I destroyed his trust a long time ago, and I've made a lot of mistakes, Meg. I guess you've noticed I don't exactly find women to be unappealing."

"Hardly," Meg said dryly. "But that's something I just don't get, the whole bisexual thing. Why? Why Austin or you? I'm sorry. It just doesn't make any sense to me."

"That's because you're hardwired to equate sex with love. Most women are," Bruno responded gently. "For me, and for a lot of other guys, sex is one thing; love is something else all together." Bruno snorted, "Meg, most men would fuck a keyhole if they could get it wet enough."

"Thanks for that image, Will. I'll never forget that," Meg said, repelled.

"Look, I'm gay. I know that because I've screwed around a lot with women, but I've only ever really loved Rory," Bruno explained patiently. "That's why you don't really have anything to worry about with Austin. You're the one he loves."

I want to believe it's that simple," Meg said evenly. "You're awfully sure of yourself, in any event."

"Meg, haven't you noticed that neither Rory nor Austin really have any other friends? They met. They found themselves attracted to each other as friends. Then, being men, they took it a little too far. It's not too hard to see how it happened, considering . . . "

"Considering what?" Meg asked.

"Considering they both had a chance to be themselves," Bruno sighed. "They're both in a position where their whole lives revolve around us," Bruno pointed out sagely.

Meg thought about it briefly. "I see that, but isn't that the way it's supposed to be when you're married?"

Bruno laughed. "Well, that's part of the problem. The truth is, I know I'm selfish and self-centered. For nearly twenty years, I've treated Rory as part of the Will Griffin Show. I've made a good show of leaving him room for some life for of his own, something that's just his, but I . . . I made it impossible for him to be an artist. I discouraged him from his singing . . . " Bruno sighed deeply, but never broke his stride. "I'm a bastard. I realized that recently, and I want to make things different, better for him, for us."

"Did it take your partner screwing my husband to make you realize that?" Meg said tartly.

"No. It took my oldest brother almost dying to do it," Bruno said honestly. "Meg, he was my hero, he always has been. But not too long ago, he had a massive coronary, bypass surgery, the works. He's just like me, only worse. I had to fly in to see him, well, because his personal life is a total mess. I had the power of attorney to pull the plug, not his wife, if that gives you any idea of how badly he's fucked up his life."

"I see," Meg said quietly. "I think I understand."

"Do you, Meg?" Bruno asked. "Because you know, you're a lot like me."

"I don't see . . . " Meg began.

"Don't even try it, girl," Bruno interrupted. "You should have heard yourself at our house that night you came over for dinner. It was so obvious you considered Austin a bit player on your own big show . . . ."

"I've already come to understand and correct with my past attitudes toward Austin, Will," Meg said stiffly. "I don't see what that has to do with . . . "

"Don't you?" Bruno said impatiently. "Neither Austin nor Rory are the cheating kind. Admit it, Austin's never cheated on you before has he?"

"How would I know?" Meg said miserably.

"Oh, take it from me, you'd know."

"Yeah, I guess I would." Meg admitted. "I figured him out this time quickly enough."

"I'm just saying you and I both have some things to think about," Bruno said with conviction. "That's what I think, anyway."

"Maybe you're right, Will," Meg said grudgingly. "Maybe you're right."

After that, they only walked along comfortably together for a few more twists and turns until Bruno finally said, "We're home."

Meg looked up from where she'd been watching her feet rhythmically step once and again, over and over, as she'd considered everything Bruno had said. Looking up, she realized she knew the cars in the drive, and she caught a glimpse of Josh peering out the window before dashing toward the front door. The sight of her home, as imperfect as it was, still gave her a tremendous rush of happiness and relief. "Thank you, Will," she said sincerely. "For everything."

Bruno nodded. "I'd hug you, but I stink."

Meg stepped up to him and hugged him instead. He didn't smell bad at all to her. He smelled deeply masculine with strength enough to make a man's right decisions as well as acknowledging the wrong ones. Awkwardly, Bruno put his hand on the back of her head and cradled it against his chest for a moment before she stepped away. "I'm going to miss you, neighbor," Meg said.

Bruno smiled and nodded as Josh opened the front door and said, "Mom?"

"She's home safe and sound, big guy," Bruno said.

"We've been very worried," Josh said petulantly. Meg could hear her own voice and tone from his little mouth.

"That's the one who will need you to be understanding about gay stuff, sooner or later," Bruno whispered.

"Mom!" Josh said insistently and crossed his arms across his chest.

"You think so?" Meg said with real weariness, but no disbelief. The possibility had crossed her mind more than once.

Bruno laughed. "We have a way of knowing these things."

"After what I've had to deal with out of his father and brother lately, I'd almost be glad," Meg said breezily.

"I don't know, Meg. No matter what, boys will be boys," Bruno said with a grin.

"You know that's right," Meg said and laughed easily, then she turned to meet Josh and go inside, strangely ready again for whatever all her boys threw at her. When she got to the door, she turned once more to find Bruno watching her with kind encouragement on his face. Meg gave him a small wave and he acknowledged it with a self-assured lift of his chin before he turned toward home himself.

# CHAPTER FIFTEEN

## Sunday morning coming down

### ST. MARK'S COURT

RORY FOLLOWED ALONG behind an obviously tiring Bridget. For her size and weight, the vet had told him to give her 150 milligrams of acepromazine to keep her nice and sleepy for the long ride to Charleston's Sullivan Island and their new home. With each step, she determinedly led Rory back to her familiar drive, hopeful for a chance to lie down.

The walk just before the drive was as much for Rory's benefit as for Bridget's. Though he was not normally sentimental, Rory wanted an image of Venetian Vistas to carry with him. The other neighborhoods of his long residence in Florida were forever etched on his mind and fixed there. This subdivision, however, was still as hazy as a thoughtful watercolor in his memory. This long, last look around was his effort to capture the look of the place and to keep it.

This quiet Sunday morning was ideal for his purposes. The bright sunshine held a promise of a day lengthening into a shiny South Florida dream fulfilled. Rory marveled at the tall royal palms and their cousins, the slender queens. He heard the rustle of their fronds in the warming breeze, sounding like a shower of rain. He drew in the colors of ixora and bougainvillea and held them. It wasn't as if there were no palms in South Carolina, but the palms that were there were scrubby palmettos, not the coconut palms with their golden promise of sweetness hanging in great globes ripening in the sun. All of what he saw in Venetian Vistas was particular to South Florida, from the soft pink barrel tiles on the roofs to the carefully mandated variety of colors on the homes' stucco walls. It was a place like no other, and Rory suddenly found himself with something new to say.

In the weeks of his affair with Austin, Rory had found new visual ideas first teasing, then flooding, his brain. He found the broad stretches of sky reflected in the man-made canals and lakes to be a kind of simulacrum for his feelings. Without making a big deal of it, he had quietly taken his earnings from the studio and the electrical plans and had invested in a rather good digital camera. With it in hand, he had revisited the neighborhoods he had known and loved, furtively barging into backyards when the residents were at work and taking wide-angled pictures of the low run of houses poised on the small strip between the sky and the water.

Rory had also been consumed with other ideas. He had given much thought to materials and methods, researching the plausibility of making photo prints on stainless steel and immense sheets of watercolor paper. He had contacted screen printers and darkrooms in Charleston. He had mentally brushed thinned oils over the vastly different materials he was considering, calculating drying times and color-enhanced varnishes and finishes for the large-scaled works. In his long awaited epiphany of imagination, he had found he had much to say and he was ready to begin.

Of course, there was the immediacy of a long drive up I-95. As he took his last walk through Venetian Vistas, he ached for it. He knew that for every mile that rolled under Bruno's SUV, this place and his life in it would become more real in his imagination than it had ever been when he had lived in it. Rory found his step quickening to meet Bridget's. Now that the urge for going had brought him to the reality of actually leaving, he longed for the road.

As they neared the house, Bridget bayed and strained at her leash. She had caught sight of Austin waiting in his coat and tie on the sidewalk. Rory had forgotten that the time for the Hardens to be leaving for church had drawn near. He cursed Bruno's brother Brian for calling at the last minute and keeping them from leaving as planned. The phone was ringing as they entered the house to pick up Bridget. He had begged Bruno not to answer it, but that wasn't in Bruno's nature. So he'd given Bridget her pills and launched out on their walk. Now, Austin stood there, all good, solid Sunday handsomeness with his carefully combed hair, hands in pockets, and bashful grin.

"Who's a good girl?" Austin cooed and squatted down on his haunches. Bridget gave Rory a resentful look over her shoulder and pulled all the harder against her training collar. Rory smiled and simply let go of her leash. Doped and ungainly, Bridget merely trotted when she usually charged. She approached Austin happily and stood close enough to him to bathe his face with her broad tongue. "Goodbye, sweetheart," Austin said and rubbed her big head gently. "She's really a good dog, you know?" He said to Rory as he stood and wiped his face with the back of his hand.

"I'm glad you think so," Rory said as he opened the hatch of Bruno's Envoy. "You can help me get her in the truck. She's too old to jump up these days."

"No problem," Austin told him.

"C'mon girl," Rory said and patted the inside of the cargo bay. "Wanna go somewhere?"

Bridget gave him a skeptical look, then trotted to the back of the truck. She managed to jump and stretch enough to get her front paws up and onto the edge of the back, then she looked at Rory expectantly.

"Oh boy," Austin said. "What do you want me to do now?"

"Her hips are bad and I have to be careful not to torque her back when I pick her up to get her in," Rory explained. "If I do, she'll bite me. I want you to put your hands against the small of my back and steady me so I can lift her cleanly."

"Now I know why Meg won't let me have a dog," Austin said cheerfully as he came to stand behind Rory.

"On three," Rory said as he bent at the knees and wrapped his arms under Bridget's hindquarters. In seconds, it was done. Bridget's back feet made a purchase on the bumper and she stepped as easily and daintily into the truck as if she were a toy poodle. Then she turned and sank gratefully onto the pillows Rory had already put into the cargo bay to keep her comfortable.

As the big dog yawned, Rory turned and stepped away from Austin's lingering touch. "Thanks," he said awkwardly.

Austin nodded and backed away. "Where's Bruno?"

"Hopefully, he's wrapping up a phone call from his brother Brian," Rory said and glanced toward the front door.

"How's he doing?"

Rory shrugged. "It's a shame he couldn't have a personality bypass. His heart is getting better, but he's still an asshole."

Austin nodded and fought a smile. "Look," he said growing suddenly serious, "I've been listening to the CD. You're pretty amazing, you know that?"

Rory gave him a shy smile in reply.

"I think if that's how you remember me, you must have loved me some," Austin said quietly.

"I did," Rory said evenly. "And I always will."

From behind them, they heard Rory's front door open and close. For a second, there was no sound; then they heard Bruno pull repeatedly on the door, making sure it was both closed and locked tight. Austin flushed and took several steps away from Rory and the back of the SUV before Bruno himself appeared. He glanced quickly from Rory to Austin and his face clouded, but he must have resolved his anger because he only said, "So you got my big girl ready to go?"

"She's about to go to sleep," Rory said easily. "She ought to be knocked out until at least Jacksonville, then I imagine she'll need a pee break."

"Her and me both," Bruno said and smiled as he closed the Envoy's hatch. "Whazzup, Austin?" he said by way of a friendly greeting.

"Waiting for Meg and the boys," Austin said and smiled. "I don't think we've been on time to church since we moved out here."

"Say a little prayer for us, will ya? We've got a long drive ahead," Bruno said.

"Count on it," Austin assured him. "How long do you think it will take?"

"When I drove the Volvo up last week, it took about ten and a half hours, but that was the middle of the week." Bruno said. "On a Sunday? Hell, I can probably do it in nine."

"Not if a sharp-eyed Georgia highway patrolman gets a look at that joint behind your ear," Rory commented lazily.

"My bad," Bruno said and grinned. He plucked the joint from behind his ear and impulsively handed it to Austin. "Here, my treat," he said.

Austin looked over his shoulder, but took the joint anyway. "If you're sure."

Rory snorted. "Don't look a gift horse in the mouth."

Bruno gave Austin a threatening, long, hard look. "No, don't," he said.

Austin broke the challenge of his pugnacious gaze at last and nodded as he slipped the joint into his suit coat pocket.

"There are six more just like it in my pack of cigarettes," Rory said to break the tension of the moment. "I rolled them for you myself."

"That's my baby," Bruno said approvingly and put his arm around Rory's shoulders and pulled him close.

"Dad!" a voice from behind Austin called. "You left the coffeepot on again!"

"That's why I have you, Josh," Austin called back. "Just shut it off."

"I already did," Josh said wearily as he came to stand with his dad. "Are you guys really leaving now?"

"Yeah buddy, we have to hit the road," Bruno said and smiled. "But I think you'll like your new neighbors."

"But they're old people," Josh said. "They're not kewl like you are."

Unexpectedly, Bruno squatted down and said seriously, "No, you're *really* kewl. You're one of the kewlest kids I've ever met, seriously dude."

"What about Noah?" Josh asked skeptically.

"Oh, he's okay," Bruno said, "But he's kinda bossy."

Shyly, Josh stepped forward and reached out his arms. "Goodbye, Bruno."

Bruno hugged him stiffly for a moment, then he closed his eyes and hugged him without reservation. "You know, I'm sorry sometimes I don't have a really kewl little kid like you around."

Josh stepped back and regarded him seriously. "Maybe you could adopt," he said soberly. "A lot of gay people are doing that."

"Oh for god's sake, Josh!" Austin groaned and rubbed his temples.

Bruno only laughed and stood up.

"You should think about it, for real," Josh said encouragingly as the sound of their door closing and Meg rattling in her purse for her keys came across the narrow front yard. "Austin? Josh?" she called distractedly.

"Out here, Mom!" Noah said as he came to stand next to his father.

"Bruno, the keys," Rory reminded him suddenly.

"Oh yeah, right," Bruno said and reached into his pocket. He extended two sets of keys to Austin and said, "Could you please give these to the Coluccis for us? I had a set made for them, but I told them I'd leave ours with you."

"Sure thing," Austin said. "When are they moving in?"

"I believe they'll be bringing in some stuff by the time you get home from church," Bruno said as Meg joined her family on the sidewalk in front of the two yards. "They are really excited about moving here."

"The new neighbors?" Meg asked, "They'll be here that soon?"

"Bruno was just saying," Austin said and smiled.

"They're very nice people," Rory offered. "I think they'll be good neighbors."

"You two will be missed," Meg said quietly.

"Thanks, Meg," Rory answered gently.

"C'mere girl and give me a hug," Bruno said and opened his arms.

"He hugs good," Josh encouraged his mom.

"I bet you'd know," Noah murmured under his breath, but not quite low enough for Austin not to hear him. Austin shot him a look that made Noah quickly begin to examine the palm fronds overhead.

Meg stepped forward and into Bruno's arms. She lingered there just a beat too long and then pushed him away gently and gave him a private smile before she stepped back. "Well . . ." she said.

"Well, we better get in the wind," Bruno said.

"We're already late for church," Meg responded.

Austin nodded at Bruno and turned to face Rory with carefully veiled eyes as Meg took his hand and turned toward the car.

Rory felt Bruno's friendly grip on the back of his neck. He smiled at Austin and turned to look up at Bruno with a grin. "I'm ready," he said happily. "Let's go."

WITH THAT, THEY drifted apart more easily than they had come together. The best of neighbors, like the best lovers and friends, always know when to simply say goodbye and walk away.